URNABHIH

Sumedha Verma Ojha was born on the shores of the River Ganges in modern Patna; ancient Pataliputra, which was the capital of the Kingdom of the Mauryans, and has appropriately gone back to her roots for her first book.

She graduated with honours in Economics from Delhi University's Lady Shri Ram College, and has a Gold Medal in Sociology from the Delhi School of Economics. After a stint as a bureaucrat in the Government of India, she now lives on the shores of Lac Léman in Switzerland with her husband and two children pursuing her long-cherished dream of writing to bring the beauty and nuances of ancient India before the world. Ancient Indian history and classical Sanskrit literature have been her lifelong passions.

She is working on her second book on the Mauryans, researching a long term project for a series of books on the kingdoms of ancient India, and doing her best to learn French and Sanskrit!

OTHER INDIAINK TITLES

Anjana Basu	*Black Tongue*
Anjana Basu	*Chinku and the Wolfboy*
Anjum Hasan	*Neti, Neti*
Anuradha Majumdar	*Infinity Paper: A mysterious quest, an unforgettable adventure*
A.N.D. Haksar	*Madhav & Kama: A Love Story from Ancient India*
Boman Desai	*Servant, Master, Mistress*
Chitra Banerjee Divakaruni	*Shadowland*
Claudine Le Tourneur d'Ison	*Hira Mandi*
C.P. Surendran	*An Iron Harvest*
Haider Warraich	*The Auras of the Jinn*
I. Allan Sealy	*The Everest Hotel*
I. Allan Sealy	*Trotternama*
Indrajit Hazra	*The Garden of Earthly Delights*
Jaspreet Singh	*17 Tomatoes: Tales from Kashmir*
Jawahara Saidullah	*The Burden of Foreknowledge*
John MacLithon	*Hindutva, Sex & Adventure*
Kalpana Swaminathan	*The Page 3 Murders*
Kalpana Swaminathan	*The Gardener's Song*
Kamalini Sengupta	*The Top of the Raintree*
Madhavan Kutty	*The Village Before Time*
Pankaj Mishra	*The Romantics*
Paro Anand	*Pure Sequence*
Rakesh Satyal	*Blue Boy*
Ranjit Lal	*Bambi Chops and Wags*
Ranjit Lal	*The Life &Times of Altu-Faltu*
Ranjit Lal	*The Small Tigers of Shergarh*
Ranjit Lal	*The Simians of South Block and Yumyum Piglets*
Raza Mir & Ali Husain Mir	*Anthems of Resistance: A Celebration of Progressive Urdu Poetry*
Sanjay Bahadur	*The Sound of Water*
Sanjay Bahadur	*Hul: Cry Rebel!*
Selina Sen	*A Mirror Greens in Spring*
Shandana Minhas	*Tunnel Vision*
Sharmistha Mohanty	*New Life*
Shree Ghatage	*Brahma's Dream*
Sudhir Thapliyal	*Crossing the Road*
Susan Visvanathan	*Nelycinda and Other Stories*
Susan Visvanathan	*The Visiting Moon*
Susan Visvanathan	*The Seine at Noon*
Tanushree Podder	*Escape from Harem*

FORTHCOMING TITLES

Lavanya Shanbaoug	*An Imperial Friend*
Tanushree Podder	*On the Double*

SUMEDHA VERMA OJHA

First published in 2014

IndiaInk
An imprint of
Roli Books Pvt. Ltd
M-75, Greater Kailash II Market
New Delhi 110 048
Phone: ++91 (011) 4068 2000
Fax: ++91 (011) 2921 7185
E-mail: info@rolibooks.com; Website: www.rolibooks.com
Also at
Bangalore, Chennai, & Mumbai

Cover Design: Turmeric Design
Layout Design: Sanjeev Kr. Mathpal
Production: Shaji Sahadevan

ISBN: 978-81-86939-78-9

Typeset in Abobe Jenson Pro by Roli Books Pvt. Ltd
and printed at Devtech Publishers & Printers Pvt Ltd, Haryana.

Contents

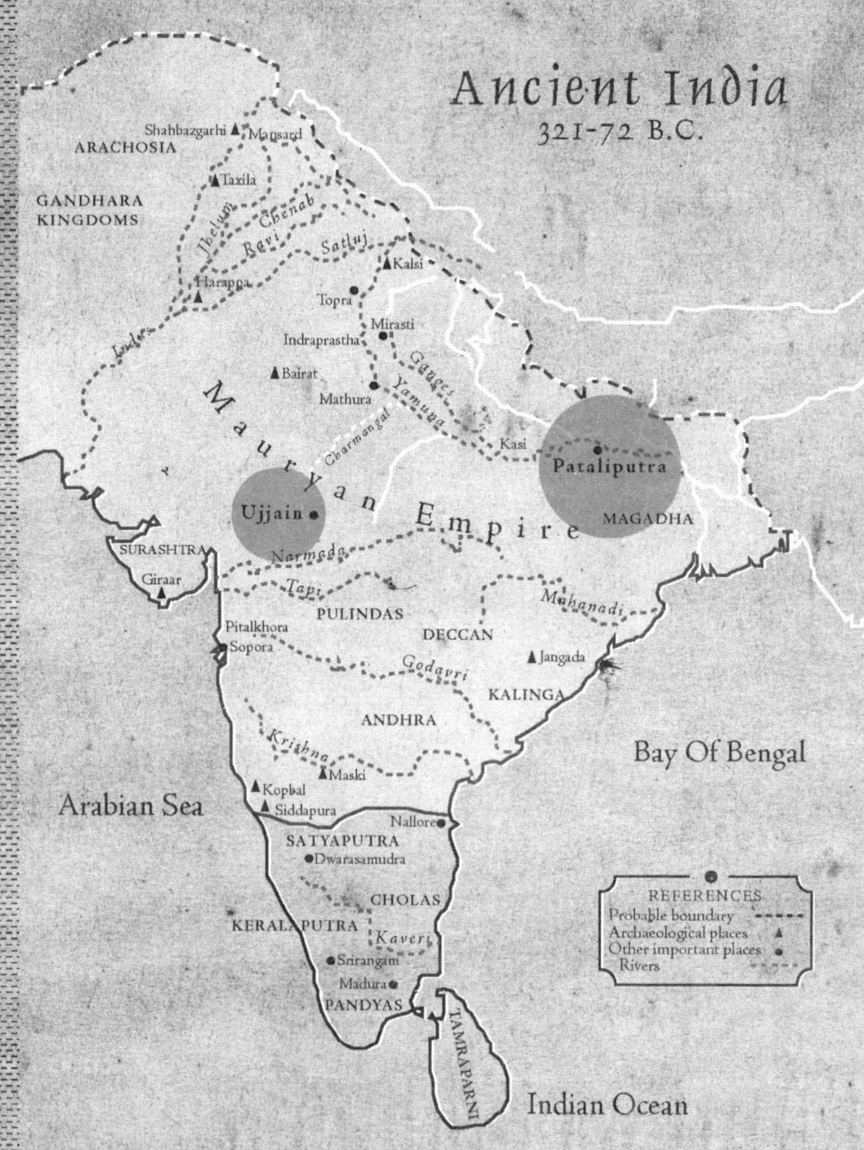
Ancient India
321-72 B.C.
Shahbazgarhi
Mansard
ARACHOSIA
Taxila
GANDHARA
KINGDOMS
Jhelum
Chenab
Ravi
Satluj
Kalsi
Harappa
Topra
Mirasti
Indraprastha
Bairat
Mathura
Ganges
Yamuna
Maurya Empire
Charmangal
Kasi
Pataliputra
MAGADHA
Ujjain
SURASHTRA
Narmada
Giraar
Tapi
PULINDAS
Mahanadi
Pitalkhora
Sopora
DECCAN
Jangada
Godavri
KALINGA
ANDHRA
Krishna
Maski
Bay Of Bengal
Kopbal
Arabian Sea
Siddapura
Nallore
SATYAPUTRA
Dwarasamudra
CHOLAS
KERALAPUTRA
Kaveri
Srirangam
Madura
PANDYAS
TAMRAPARNI
Indian Ocean
REFERENCES
Probable boundary
Archaeological places
Other important places
Rivers

Prologue

It is 326 BCE... Alakshendra, the legendary warrior of the Yavanas has defeated the Paurava king and run rough shod over the big and small kingdoms of the north-western part of the Indian subcontinent, Jambudweepa. The established power centres are smashed and open the way for a young adventurer, backed by the powerful intellect and towering personality of his guru and preceptor.

An army of volunteers, soldiers, and mercenaries is collected from all across the Gandharan region; first the Yavanas who remain after the departure of Alakshendra are subjugated and driven out. Then the great power of Magadha is attacked. But that too fails. The kingdom is too strong to defeat.

The young adventurer, Chandragupta and his preceptor, Acharya Chanakya, are forced to rethink their strategy. They form a grand alliance with five potent kingdoms of the north including Paurava of Kaikeya and Abhisara of Kashmir.

This time, there is a military and covert attack on Pataliputra and due to the infighting between the Nanda princes and the treachery of their senapati, Bhattaraka, Pataliputra is vanquished. Chandragupta takes over the city in a bloodless coup stage managed by Acharya Chanakya.

Consolidation is the order of the day, a marriage is proposed between Chandragupta and the Nanda princess, Dharini, to bring the two dynasties together; important officials of the Nanda regime are reappointed and shown favour, the populace is sought to be soothed and calmed.

The land is thick with intrigue and Chanakya, the power behind Samrat Chandragupta, nurtures a terrible and efficient secret service which weaves a gossamer web of deceit and deception the Urnabhih covering the entire kingdom and is harnessed to the expansion of empire.

This time, between the sixth and the fourth centuries BCE is an Axial Age when radical new ways of social and religious thought arising out of dizzying changes in material technology change the world beyond recognition. An explosion of change is making the radical re-ordering of society seem imminent. Pastoral and nomadic ways of life are giving way to a settled agricultural community and the bringing of the forest land under the plough is the main aim before the state.

From the heart of the Gangetic plain, is also being born a dream; a vision of an empire that would unite vast tracts of the Indian subcontinent and central Asia. The far-flung kingdoms of the fabled 'Jambudweepa' are to be strung on to the thread of a vast empire; a subcontinent of peoples has to be melded into a civilization.

Misrakesi, an orphan, courtesan extraordinaire, a ganika from Ujjain, has come to Pataliputra to avenge the death of her sister... but she finds herself caught up in all these events which sweep her off her feet and take her towards her destiny...

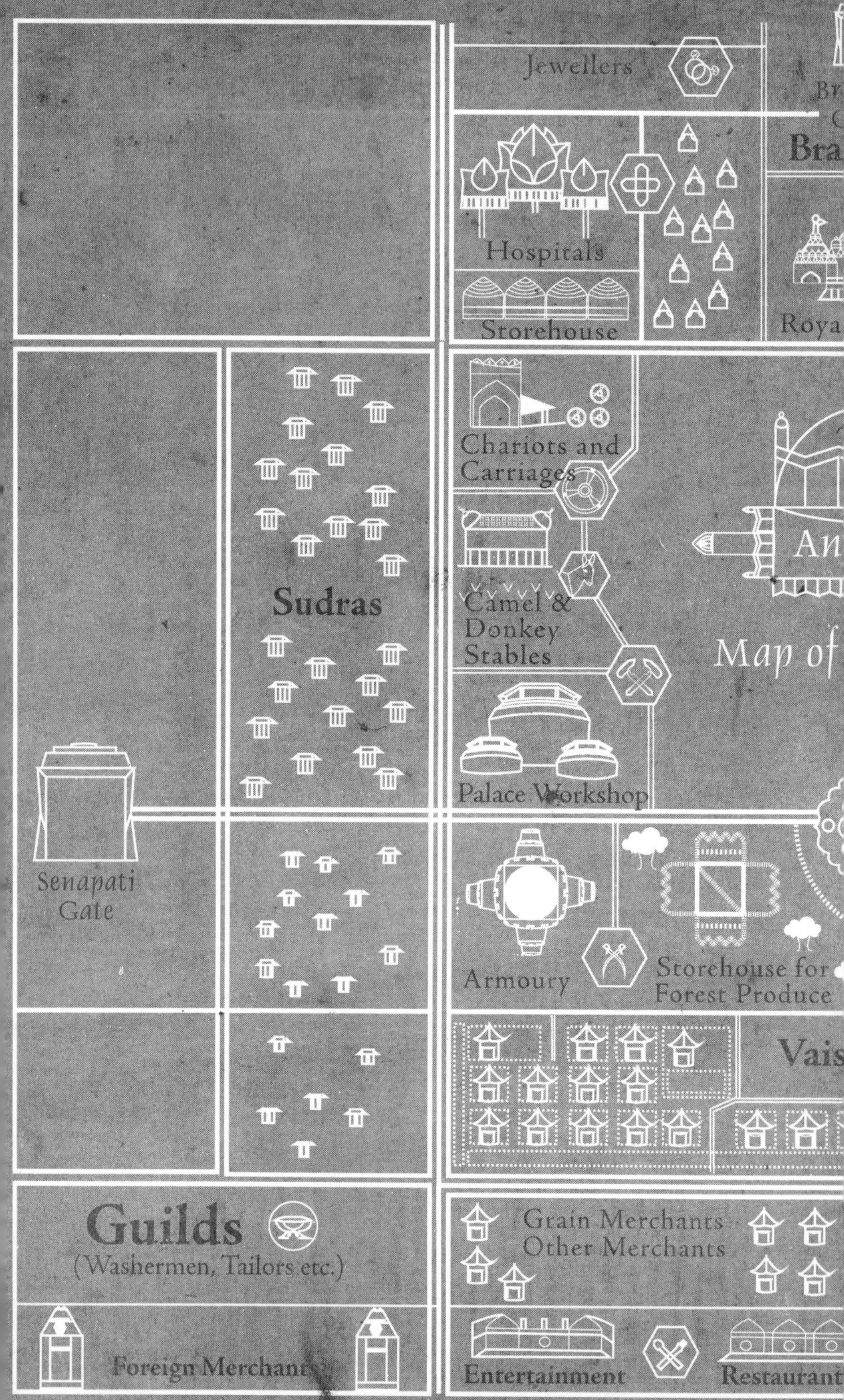
Jewellers
Hospitals
Storehouse
Sudras
Chariots and Carriages
Camel & Donkey Stables
Palace Workshop
Map of
Senapati Gate
Armoury
Storehouse for Forest Produce
Guilds
(Washermen, Tailors etc.)
Grain Merchants
Other Merchants
Foreign Merchants
Entertainment
Restaurant

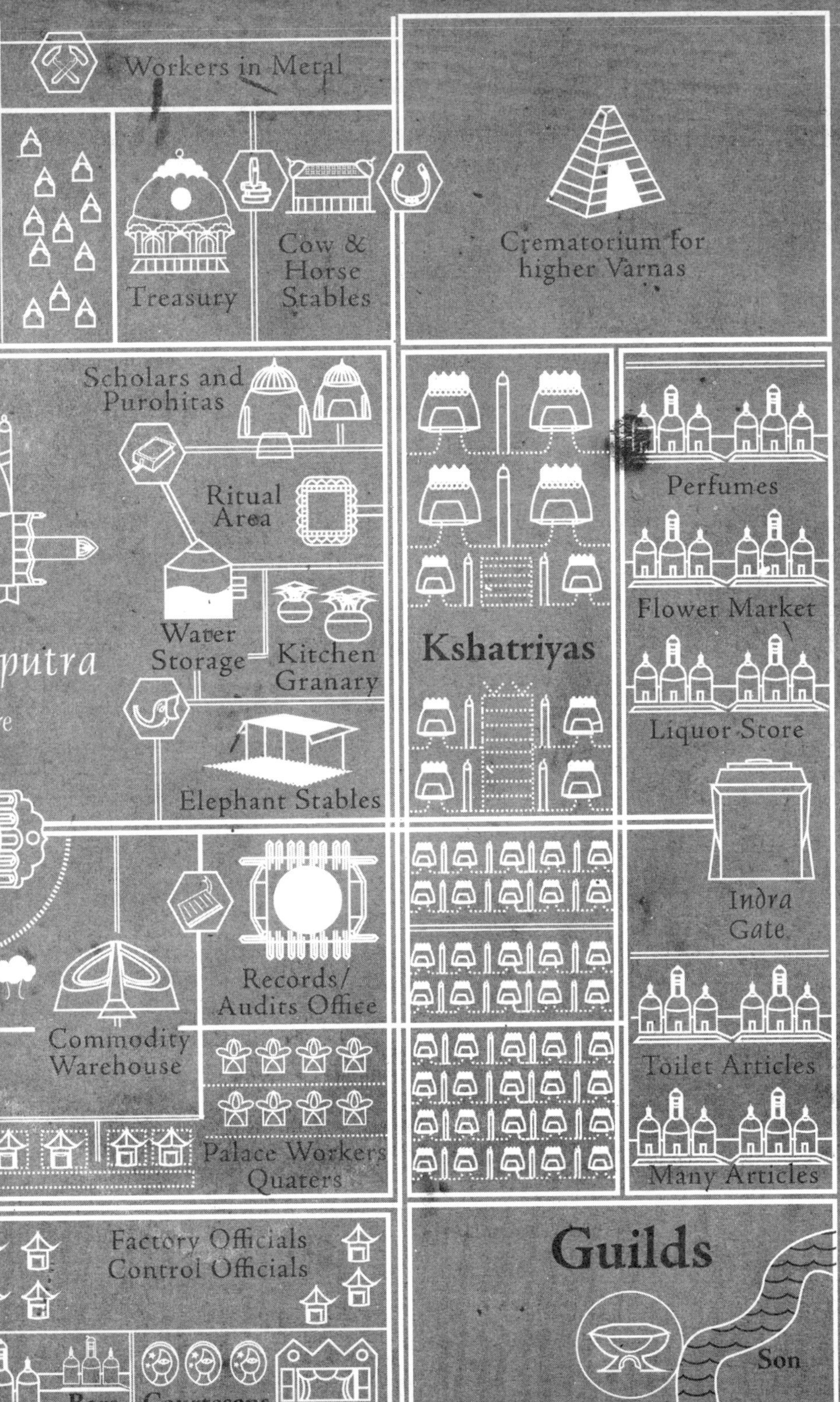
Workers in Metal
Treasury
Cow & Horse Stables
Crematorium for higher Varnas
Scholars and Purohitas
Ritual Area
Water Storage
Kitchen Granary
Elephant Stables
putra
Kshatriyas
Perfumes
Flower Market
Liquor Store
Indra Gate
Records/ Audits Office
Commodity Warehouse
Palace Workers Quaters
Toilet Articles
Many Articles
Factory Officials
Control Officials
Bars
Courtesans
Guilds
Son

Plan of Sugaang
Servants
Chikitsagriha
Pond
Chariots
Water Tank
Elephants
Horses
Guards
King's
Bedchaml
Dressing
Counc
Audi
(Up
Attendants
Admn.
Office
Rampart

asaad
Servants
Women's Quaters
(Misrakesi)
es
Princesses
Alankarbhoomi
Ladies
Maternity
River
Female
Guards
Kitchen &
Stores
ber
Prince's
Tutor
ll
Guard's
Qtrs.

Misrakesi

Send thy spies forward, fleetest in their motion.
Be not deceived by him who, near or far is bent on evil.

The Rig Veda

~

She stood quietly inside the great pool filled with marigold petals, while her body was rubbed down with sandalwood and turmeric and her hair washed with perfumed water. It was a great day: the accession of Chandragupta, the goatherd, who should rightly look after cows and goats, to the throne of Magadha – the richest, most prosperous and strongest Janapada, the mightiest kingdom of the world; and ready, if the wily and wise old Chanakya had anything to do with it, to extend itself over all of Jambudweep and more.

Misrakesi looked around at the beautiful inner courtyard – which was deep within the Sugaang Praasaad, the royal Mauryan palace – with its delicate paintings on the walls of the corridors surrounding it. She had come here but recently, not even a fortnight ago. Her throat tightened when she thought of the reason. Her sister, Sukesi, the leading ganika and exquisite dancer, the jewel of the Magadha court... was dead... and dead by her own hand. All because of Vishnugupta Chanakya.

Well, she would exact her revenge today. She was to dance after the rajyabhishek, the anointing ceremony, with all the new power and bureaucracy of Mauryan Magadha surrounding her. As the guide and preceptor of the samrat, Chanakya would surely be there. She would take care to hide her tiny poisoned dagger in the folds of her richly embroidered silk mantle, and then she would strike. Killing the samrat's guru in the open court would expose her to the most acute retribution and she would probably die a terrible and lingering death but... Sukesi had to be avenged.

A celestial vision unfolded: a graceful nartaki, like a blue lotus in full bloom swaying with the breeze, came in and exhibited her flawless skill and precision leaving the audience dazzled. It was the culmination of years of practice and devotion, a gruelling routine that would have defeated a lesser woman. The dance ended leaving the assembly, especially the male portion of it, asking for more.

Misrakesi retired to the palace room that had been specially arranged for her. She lay back on the low wooden bed and reached for the polished black clay pot which held cool water. There was some gur beside it and she absently crumbled it between her fingers. Her next move was to look for Chanakya in the huge wooden palace complex. He had not been present at the dance performance. She had no idea where to look for him.

'Acharya Vishnugupta was not present at my performance, dasi,' Misrakesi said casually to the serving woman in attendance.

'He does not attend dance or music performances, Devi. He is always busy working and more so these days when things in Pataliputra are so unsettled,' said the dasi conspiratorially, ready to sit down and gossip with this up and coming woman. Who knew but that she might be appointed the Court Dancer one day... and it was always helpful to have well-wishers in high places. 'In fact he must be sitting in the Sabha Griha[1] and doing some paperwork. The heads of all the departments must be reporting to him at this hour of the night, poor things, before the reports formally go before the samrat.'

'I thought Amatya Katyayan had been appointed Maha Amatya. Shouldn't he be looking after the administration?'

'We... ell. Of course he was appointed Maha Amatya with much fanfare but what is the real truth behind it? No one knows the mind of the wily Vishnugupta,' said the dasi, barely able to conceal her hostility.

'My mistress – Devi Dharini, the Nanda Princess – has been convinced to marry the samrat for the same reason as Katyayan has been appointed Maha Amatya. The followers of the Nanda family will now be forced to give up their hostility and provide support to the samrat. But, I think I have spoken too much. I am just a humble dasi of Devi Dharini who has sent me to you as a mark of her favour and appreciation. What do I know of politics or diplomacy?' the dasi recollected herself and fell silent.

She had indeed spoken too much and it was a sign of the times that dasis had the temerity to be so free in their views. The Nandas had gone but the Mauryas had not yet arrived. Anything could happen in the hiatus.

The approach to the Sabha Griha was through the open quadrangle at the front of the palace complex. It was a bare, functional apartment with an austere majesty and gravitas of its own. The throne, set on an elevated platform reached by four steps, dominated the room. Six wooden chairs in two rows were set before the throne. With the dissolution of the Nanda Mantri Parishad[2] and the sole appointment of Katyayan, there were no ministers to meet with the samrat and advise him on affairs of the state. The Sabha Griha was waiting, expectant and empty.

Ordinarily the artist in Misrakesi would have been captivated and stunned by the paintings on the walls. Almond-eyed beauties in attendance on a handsome and godlike king, all aspects of courtly activities displayed in loving and precise detail. Creative freedom and imagination were in full flight. The brush strokes were masterly and revealed their oneness with the sculpting on the wooden pillars and window embrasures. Such examples of the art of painting rarely appeared before the eyes of ordinary mortals. They were the domain of the royal and the rich. Today, however, Misrakesi had eyes only for her prey as she moved across the palace seeking the acharya.

She had never killed anyone for all her training in the art and science of killing; this would be her first time. Her hand tightened on her dagger and then trembled. She could hear her guru intoning in her beautiful voice, 'Put your arms around him and rest your head on his shoulder. Stroke his back to disarm and relax him. Your right hand should then access the dagger with the left not ceasing its movement. In a flash the dagger should be in below the left breast bone for instant death.' There had been experts in the class to illustrate the precise point of entry. She knew the theory better than most. Now was the time for practice; but the Sabha Griha was empty. There were only shades and echoes of past meetings. The ghost of Dhana Nanda seemed to brood over the space.

As Misrakesi looked around, she saw a small door behind the throne platform which stood partially open. There was a little earthen lamp alight in the room as flickering shadows fell across the throne and made it shimmer in the uncertain light. She pushed at the door to enter, but a voice made her halt in her tracks.

'Come in, Misrakesi, I have been expecting you, my daughter.'

In front of her was a short spare figure with stern eyes and the mien of an ascetic. The voice had so much affection and understanding that tears sprang unbidden to her eyes. Was this the greedy, grasping, and cunning villain she had sworn to kill? This thin and care-worn old man with just a coarse dhoti around his waist sitting on a grass mat surrounded by bundles of bhojapatras?[3] The light of the single lamp lent a dim illumination to the scene and missing was the pomp, ceremony, and grandeur which was by popular description, ascribed to Chanakya.

'Come and sit in front of me. You and I have much to talk of.'

Misrakesi had recovered from her surprise and could contain herself no more. 'Sukesi,' the cry burst from her. 'Why did you have to arrange for her killing? She was the most intelligent, lovely, and accomplished of us all. You were the one who trapped her in your political games and caused to commit a dishonour which forced her to take her own life. Typical Kautilya tactics!' Her voice was bitter and tearful. 'She was a lotus in full bloom and you cut her off in her prime. Can you absolve yourself from this sin? Will you ever be able to forgive yourself?'

Tears were now coursing freely down her cheeks. Unable to withstand his compassionate gaze she sank down on the grass mat, her movements graceful as a deer, not forgetting her training even in a moment like this.

'You must believe me, Misrakesi, when I say that no one could blame me more than I do myself. No one was more hurt and disappointed than me when she took this extreme step. I had sent her a reward and a letter. You can read the letter if you so wish I have it here.' The acharya's voice was quiet as he passed her a bhojpatra with his writing on it and parts of his broken seal still clinging to the parchment.

> My felicitations to you, Sukesi. You have at one stroke accomplished both the destruction of Samrat Chandragupta's most powerful military enemy, Paurav, and the neutralization of the most powerful ideological one, Katyayan. You have established the future prosperity of the state of Magadha. Devi, do not burn in self-recrimination, do not even think of taking the step you are contemplating. Magadha needs your life, not your death. Please accept this vaiduryamanavaka[4] as an inadequate token of the state's gratitude.

Misrakesi read this through a haze of tears. Then, she said in a hard voice,'Acharya, Katyayan had hired Sukesi to kill Chandragupta. You have made him the prime minister because he is a powerful and capable man. Sukesi, who betrayed him to you to save Magadha and then even killed King Paurav on your instructions, is dead. You knew very well that she would not be able to live with the shame of breaking her word and betraying Katyayan.'

'My daughter, Sukesi herself came and told me of the plot even before my spies could do so. She knew that Katyayan was blinded by his desire to revenge the overthrow of the Nandas. Otherwise he would never have contemplated this unwise step. Killing Chandragupta at this moment when his rule hangs by a thread was tantamount to declaring civil war in Magadha. No true citizen of Magadha would do so.'

With a pause calculated to let the words sink in, he went on,'She was a true daughter of Magadha. Can you live up to the standards set by her?'

At this Misrakesi, who had been staring sadly at the bhojpatra with her head bowed, looked up at him in surprise. She had not expected this.

'Why do you think I made arrangements for you to be chosen for this performance and come to Pataliputra from your Training Centre?' said the acharya, smiling slightly.

She gaped at him, unable to reply as she had been under the impression that she was the one who had schemed and clawed her way to being the choice for this prestigious performance.

'There were many students at the State Training Academy who were senior to you, more beautiful than you or even, perhaps, better dancers,' the acharya went on, clinically discussing her attributes and precise ranking at the centre. 'None have your drive or determination, a personality which lets nothing stand in its way. I have had my eyes on you for some time as indeed I had had on Sukesi.'

'I am authorized by Samrat Chandragupta,' he went on formally, 'to offer you an appointment in the newly constituted Gupt Varangana Sena of Magadha. It is a secret army of warrior women. You are to be a moving agent in the secret service of the empire. At the moment you will report only to me through a supervisor. Some reports cleared by me will have to be sent to the samrat through his chief personal attendant and bodyguard, Shrunottara.'

'No, she will not in any way be your superior,' said the acharya correctly reading the stiffening of Misrakesi's expression at the mention of her contemporary and rival at the Ganika Prashikshan Kendra in Ujjaini where she had learned her craft for many long years. Shrunottara had been picked up a few months ago and appointed the chief personal bodyguard of the samrat which had caused quite a stir since there had been nobody powerful behind her to further her career.

'And the salary will be 1500 karshapans.' Misrakesi was staggered by the number of karshapans offered. These silver coins of the realm were riches beyond her imagination.

'You will have to work in close cooperation with the Nagarik Suraksha and Guptachar Vibhag. Your supervisor in the security and spy department will be Pushyamitra, the chief of this vibhag.'

This was the hated and feared spy department of Magadha

whose existence and working was shrouded in mystery, but whose reach was from the palaces of the rich merchants to the fields of the farmers and the dice of the gambling dens. Pushyamitra Sunga, the younger of the formidable Sunga brothers (the elder being the senapati of Magadha) was rumoured to be the head of this department, but no one was very certain.

Misrakesi stood silent. Her fingers played with the ring Sukesi had given her while her mind wrestled with a medley of thoughts: revenge for Sukesi, disloyalty to her, a chance to fulfill her own ambitions, the dangers and riches of the job. This was a chance to join the centre of power, to influence important decisions of the state, to practice politics as she had been taught. As Sukesi had been doing. And now was her own chance, ironically appearing as a result of Sukesi's death.

'You are not being disloyal, my daughter,' said the acharya. 'You will only further that ideal of service for which Sukesi gave her life.'

Misrakesi had made up her mind.

'I agree to take up the appointment, Acharya, but I too have one condition. I expect to be freed of my obligation to provide pleasure to the royal family and bureaucrats at their summons.'

The acharya was as taken aback as it was possible for a man of his temperament to be. A courtesan trained at government expense was an income-earning asset of the state and she was not allowed to remain idle without adequate compensation to the state. Misrakesi was, in effect, asking for a raise in her salary and a status different from all the others. But he was an astute man.

'Let this wish of yours also be fulfilled. Devi Misrakesi, you are now appointed to the Gupt Varangana Sena. Here is your royal appointment order.'

Misrakesi bent down and touched his feet.

'Yashasvibhava, may glory be with you.'

And the acharya was gone leaving her alone in that room full of shadows.

Pushyamitra pushed back his hair with an impatient gesture. He was often edgy with himself these days. His complete failure to anticipate and neutralize the machinations of Chanakya and prevent the Nanda dynasty from annihilation would always be his biggest failure.

Anyway, that was the past and this was the present. Chandragupta was the samrat and the strings were being pulled by Chanakya. It was now his job to look for Chandragupta's enemies and demolish them.

He had always worked with people outside his department using whatever instrument came his way. People were just that for him, instruments. This new recruit he had been informed about at the previous night's briefing, Misrakesi, seemed promising. If she was anything like her sister Sukesi, she would be excellent.

Misrakesi and Pushyamitra had their first meeting in the Sugaang Praasaad itself. It was a business-like meeting held in one of the inner and secret apartments of the palace. Misrakesi had dressed carefully for the appointment. She wanted to convey the impression of a serious and prosperous young matron, not a glamorous nartaki. Gone were the kancala-kundala earrings, the satlari necklace, the golden mekhala and, indeed, the flamboyant jewellery for each part of the body as well as the elaborate dhammilia hairstyle in pearls and jewels[5] which she had worn. The crimson silk antariya, her lower garment, and the heavy gold-embroidered muslin dupatta which had enhanced her dance performance were replaced by a sombre blue kaseyyaka, a silk lehnga, with a white Muga silk uttariya embroidered at the borders draped over her head and shoulders. Brilliant blue phalaka[6] sapphires glowed on her kayabandh and at her arms, neck, ears, and forehead.

She was already pacing restlessly by the time Pushyamitra came in. The delay was not an assertion of his superiority but due entirely to an urgent summons from the head of the criminal police regarding a foreigner who had been caught under suspicious circumstances. Whatever the reason, Misrakesi was not happy at being kept waiting and could not help being slightly acerbic.

'Arya Pushyamitra? Pranaam Deva. I am extremely grateful to you for taking out the time to meet me.' The tone of her voice and the expression which went with it made it amply clear that gratitude was very far from her mind.

He saw a slender young woman in front of him with lustrous golden skin and limpid brown eyes set slightly aslant hinting at mysteries below, her bee-stung lips were red as a bandhook flower. He was surprised at the intellectual forehead, in striking contrast with the sensuous persona. Her face and body were in perfect and voluptuous symmetry as befitted a nartaki. Her gaze was alluring but Pushyamitra was in the business of assessing people at a glance and he could sense the resolve beneath. There was, intriguingly, a mixture of hauteur and a certain vulnerability in the set of her lips and the angle of her head. He let his mind run over the briefing he had been given about her as she sat down with feet tucked together sideways, her hands clasped, and head slightly bowed. She looked the picture of submissive womanhood but Pushyamitra was amused as he noticed her back, stiff with irritation and chagrin.

'Young – and immature too,' he thought, as he accepted her greeting and sat down on the other sumptuous asana; there was a low wooden table in between, laden with fruits both fresh and dry. She was letting her irritation show too plainly, and that too on her first day of work.

Her credentials were impressive. She was not an ordinary veshya, a courtesan; but a ganika, a courtesan deluxe, a class apart. As a ganika she was the most talented, beautiful, and virtuous of her compatriots in the Ujjaini Training Academy. She was skilled in all the sixty-four arts with dance, music, painting, poetry, and languages being her specialities. Her formal education was as good as his, with the Triveda, Vedanga, Anvishaki, and Danda Niti[7] all being taught to her apart from the art of writing. Her mental and physical development had been taken to an extraordinary level; she should be useful to his department.

Misrakesi had also been unobtrusively studying the man in front of her who would play an important role in her life as her supervisor.

'Not a very auspicious beginning,' she thought as she castigated herself for her petty outburst.

She saw a tall, lithe man dressed like a courtier but with a broad flat sword with cross straps on the sheath suspended from his left shoulder. The kaccha-style silk antariya[8] and the uttariya[9] flung around his shoulders accented rather than hid the swell of muscles on a superbly fit and solid body with an almost animal-like vitality to it. His most striking feature was his silky black hair which he wore unbound and which was styled in a gurnakuntala; it was curled and hung loose below the shoulders kept back from his face with a pearl headband.

His face was sharp and arrogant although he could have been a model for the portrait of a Gandharva[10] with large luminous eyes, a classic nose, and moulded lips. His gaze was both penetrating and threatening and Misrakesi was reminded of all the tales of torture and beating that surrounded this man like a miasma. She felt a sudden spurt of relief that she was an assistant and not an adversary but quickly suppressed it; she was not in the business of being intimidated.

'I will skip the preliminaries, Misrakesi, as you have been briefed by none other than the acharya.' There was a slight mocking smile on his face as if he could see what was going on in her mind. 'Let me go on to what I want you to do, starting immediately.'

He got up in a graceful movement and started pacing the floor. Misrakesi was to learn that this was his inveterate habit during any meeting, but this leonine pacing in the small room was unnerving to say the least. Only the lashing tail was missing thought Misrakesi.

'There is something going on in this palace which I do not like. On the face of it, everything is quiet and there are no more protests against the marriage of Devi Dharini with the samrat. But the calm surface hides a whirlpool somewhere. And it is your job to find out what it is,' he turned and faced her.

'Is there anything specific to start with?' asked Misrakesi.

'No, nothing. It is the gut feeling of a man experienced in such matters. The same feeling I had in the days before the coup...' Pushyamitra spoke the rest of the sentences almost to himself.

'The first thing I need to do, Arya, is to establish some kind of reason for staying back in Pataliputra. Then I should look for a house of my own or get rooms in the palace,' said Misrakesi briskly, ignoring the last half-muttered sentences which sounded uncomfortably like treason, and Pushyamitra's face snapped back to attention. It was not for them as royal employees to ponder on the justification of the current administration, thought Misrakesi; they were only its instruments. She could not help wondering however, how Pushyamitra had adjusted to the change from being a pivot in Dhana Nanda's court to being an employee of Chandragupta and Chanakya, his most implacable enemies. Was there no dissonance at all?

'For the moment I think it best that you stay in the palace. I have made the necessary arrangements. The date of the marriage has been fixed for one month from today, during the shuklapaksha,[11] on the auspicious muhurat[12] of the Shiva–Parvati vivaha.'

'I know the importance of this vivaha. It is to consolidate the samrat's position and call in the vast money and power of the Nanda clan to his side. After all, this is not a change from the grass roots but from above. The instruments of wielding power have come into the hands of the new comers, but not power itself, at least not as yet,' said Misrakesi.

Pushyamitra looked at her, surprised at her correct and perspicacious reading of the situation in spite of the fact that she was an outsider and had been here for a very short while. The acharya was right about her intelligent and analytical mind.

'It is people like you and me, Arya, who will decide the fate of the Mauryas. If we fail to win the underground war, the dynasty may remain a dream,' said Misrakesi, smiling slightly.

This was getting too close to the truth for his comfort. The basics of devotion to the royal cause were not up for discussion. Pushyamitra knew that there would have to be a deep bond of trust between Misrakesi and himself but only time would build that. In the meanwhile circumspection was the best option.

'As I was saying, there will definitely be an attempt to disrupt the marriage and maybe even kill the samrat. Although the attempts will definitely be from within the Nanda clan, the samrat and the acharya are in the gravest danger, there is no guarantee that the future queen is safe.'

Pushyamitra paused and took out a bronze seal ring, 'Before I forget, here is your mudra. Guard it with your life. Mark all communication on the bottom left corner.' He passed over the seal ring with four snarling lions standing back-to-back facing all the four directions engraved on it.

Misrakesi placed it in a secret slit in her waistband hidden by the phalaka sapphires it was embellished with.

'I think you had better get to work now. Rooms have been organized as I told you. Trust no one but try to build up a network of loyal people. Anything you want to ask?'

There were a thousand things she wanted to ask but it did not seem as though Pushyamitra was willing to spend any time on her doubts and hesitations so she said nothing, merely rising and folding her hands in a farewell; watching him stride away with a slightly bemused expression in her eyes.

The Vivaha

This woman will I now marry to acquire the wealth of Dharma and Praja.

Vedic Vivaha Mantra

Misrakesi watched the dasis setting out her possessions in the palace rooms allotted to her and pondered over her immediate future. The entire palace complex was abuzz with preparations for the marriage. 'Dhana', riches, Nanda's vast treasure – had been co-opted by the Mauryas and some of it was definitely being spent on the marriage. Kings from afar, both allies and vassals; prominent merchants and traders, the setthis; learned acharyas and famous courtesans; village headmen and clan members; all had been invited for the festivities.

She decided to spend some time familiarizing herself with the palace complex. The palace itself was a series of light wooded structures, ornamented, palisaded, and colonnaded with large airy fronts opening out to the breeze from the massive flowing River Ganges along the side. It was set in extensive pleasure grounds with ornamental groves echoing to the call of peacocks and the twitter of birds. Channels had been cut through the moat and there were artificial water ponds as well as small streams filled with fish among the trees and creepers. Already awe-inspiring, it was being redecorated and made into a structure unrivalled in the known world.

The women's quarter where a room had been provided for Misrakesi was at the back of the complex. It was separated from the administrative offices and the Sabha Griha as well as the royal court by the quarters for the queens, princes, and princesses. The Alankarbhoomi, a storehouse for toiletries and the Chikitsagriha were nearby and the Prasavakaksha, the maternity house with its store of medicines was set at the back.

The samrat's quarters were in the centre of the complex heavily guarded by a division of female bodyguards headed by Shrunottara. A restricted area, Misrakesi was not allowed entry into this. The marriage of the sole Nanda princess was the occasion for an unbridled show of riches, magnificence, and luxury. Jewellery and gems were being distributed from the royal treasury, the Kosagriha. Lengths of expensive fabric, embroidered with pearls and encrusted with gems were being fashioned into costumes for the women. Rich food and wines were there for the asking. Maha Amatya Katyayan had ordered the doors of the Kosagriha and the Koshthagars, the warehouses, to be thrown open. It was a time for royal benediction to be felt by all. The prisons had also been thrown open. Thousands of Brahmins were being fed every day. The accumulated wealth of the Nandas was on full display albeit by the Mauryas.

One more new face, even a beautiful one, did not excite any comment in all this hustle and bustle. It was assumed that she had stopped for a dance recital during the marriage ceremonies. She talked to as many people as possible and was struck at the still to be loosened iron grip of the deposed king. The criticism of the upstart Maurya and his temerity in marrying the Nanda princess was in contrast less hesitant perhaps because the nascent Mauryan administration was also far more lenient than the erstwhile king.

Misrakesi had taken to calling the old dasi of Devi Dharini, who had attended her on the day of her first dance, for help with an occasional bath or massage. Her name was Mrinalini and she was originally from Rajgriha. She had been sold as a dasi as a child and her innate beauty and wit had caught the eye of Dhana Nanda's father, the terrible King Mahapadma Nanda. During his life she had more or less been a favourite of his and was later tolerated as a fixture by his son. She looked on Dharini, the princess, more as a grand-daughter than owner and would spend hours talking to Misrakesi about her which was exactly what Misrakesi wanted. Mrinalini also told her details of the working of the palace. The dasas, dasis, how people and supplies were routed from outside and where they went, who was in charge of what. All this was invaluable information for Misrakesi.

'My daughter is not happy,' she said sighing deeply one day as she massaged oil into Misrakesi's long, thick, black, and lustrous hair. It was early in the morning and Misrakesi was going through a ritual bath.

'I mean the princess. I have always thought of her as the daughter I never had and have looked after her since she was born. The Rajmahishi never had too much time for her. Too tied up in that worthless young man who proved to be the ruin of the entire dynasty.' Mrinalini shook her head sadly as she carefully parted strands of Misrakesi's hair and oiled each of them separately, gently rubbing the black silk between her fingers.

'She thinks of Chandragupta as her father's killer but all her family and well wishers have urged, indeed coerced her into agreeing with the marriage, and she had to give in. Poor child, she even contemplated suicide.'

'She is a royal princess,' said Misrakesi, 'this is not the first and will not be the last time that a princess has had to marry for political reasons, and to save her family from destruction. Surely she would know her dharma at a time like this?'

'It is not as simple as that, Devi. Is Chandragupta saving her family by marrying her or is she casting a mantle of protection over him by becoming his wife? Chandragupta has only his own valour and courage to call upon. Dharini can call upon the vast and powerful network of her father.'

Sticks of chandan had been lit and were spreading their heady fragrance in the room. The rectangular water bath in the middle of the room was reached by descending three steps. The water was cool and strewn with fragrant yellow and white atimukta flowers and bath oils. Misrakesi slid into it and reclined against the side upon an ivory peedah, caressed by the perfumed waves that came up to her breasts. The atimukta bark paste applied on her body was massaged and rubbed off expertly by Mrinalini, leaving her skin soft and burnished. Mrinalini ran a wooden roller with knobs at both ends over her back and continued.

'Then there is the Rajmahishi, her mother, who constantly gives her mixed signals. Exhorts her to do her duty and then changes her tune to say that Dharini must wait for deliverance which will certainly arrive. I cannot understand who this deliverer is. The royal Nanda women themselves are surrounded and isolated, spied upon; what can they do?'

Misrakesi was floating peacefully, lulled by the soft drone of Mrinalini's voice talking as if to her own self, the lapping of the scented water, the gentle touch of the atimukta flowers and the pressure of the wooden roller on her back. The morning sun was not yet up but the sky had lightened and the stars were disappearing into an incipient rosy dawn. Chandragupta and Dharini would also be up in their respective apartments. Misrakesi had been told that the samrat followed a punishing routine, one that would crush any ordinary man; but then he was no ordinary man; he had made himself a samrat from a goatherd.

Misrakesi's mind plucked at the kernel in the old dasi's random wanderings. Was there a basis for the Rajmahishi's hope of deliverance? Or was it just the vain hope of a tortured mind? She decided to look for methods to further her acquaintance with the Rajmahishi.

She was casting about for ways and means to approach the royal women when her reputation and skills came to her rescue. Having heard that a nartaki from the famous Ganika Prashikshan Kendra at Ujjaini was in the palace, an elder royal lady sent her a message asking if she would prepare the Lodhra flower unguent which was a must for any bride. It was a difficult process and the women of Ujjaini were reputed to know of certain secret ingredients which increased the efficacy manifold. It would add the final touches to Dharini's shringar for her vivaha.

Misrakesi was only too happy to be called in and involved with the preparations for the marriage. She even took with her some of her own special beauty ingredients which were a closely guarded secret. Something she would never normally have done, but she was now engaged in a job which would certainly require some sacrifices! She had not been called to report on her activities, but given the acharya's omniscience, she had no doubt someone was keeping an eye on her and was anxious to make some progress.

The princess had taken to meditating alone in a room set aside from the rest. She had expressed a desire to be alone, to think upon her soon to be changed status and purify her body and mind for the forthcoming sacred ceremonies.

Misrakesi was led to an adjoining apartment where the Rajmahishi was sitting with some senior women of the family. The furnishings were sumptuous. Misrakesi was impressed. The pillars were intricately carved and floor laid with silk. There were soft semal cotton cushions to recline on. Mrinalini was there, gently massaging the queen's feet with mustard oil. The Rajmahishi was holding forth in loud tones, informing everyone of the grandeur of her marriage with Dhana Nanda and decrying the current preparations as nothing in comparison.

The Rajmahishi looked up as Misrakesi came in and acknowledged her pranaam with more attention than Misrakesi had thought she would get. Misrakesi professed herself to be ready to make the unguent which had to be dried by the sun's rays for a few days before it could be used. She spread out her ingredients before the admiring gaze of the palace women.

It didn't take Misrakesi too long to notice that the atmosphere in the apartment was openly hostile to Chandragupta and the cunning Brahmin Chanakya. It was fanned by the bitter utterances of the Rajmahishi who bemoaned the fate of her daughter and deplored the lack of help from anyone. Misrakesi could not help wondering at her lack of discretion; such comments with impunity did not augur well for the prestige and strength of the new king.

Beside her and nodding vigorously at every pronouncement was her favourite dwarf, Vamana. He had been a close confidant of the deposed king and had escaped with his life only because he was deemed to be harmless.

The days went by and Misrakesi became a regular visitor to the royal apartments. She was in a fair way to becoming quite a favourite with the Rajmahishi. Misrakesi wove in a few bitter references to Sukesi and her suspicions regarding the acharya's role in her death into her conversation and could see that this made the Rajmahishi thaw.

One afternoon, Misrakesi was applying henna to the Rajmahishi's palms and listening to her rambling speech about the lack of Kshatriya qualities in modern day kings (quite forgetting the fact that her husband had been no Kshatriya, and his father had in fact been known as a second Parshuram, the scourge of the Kshatriyas). No one had come forward to wage war for the Nandas. The acharya had some of them tied up in long-drawn alliance talks and others were simply waiting to see what would happen before showing their hand. Chandragupta's army was not an easy foe. If the marriage went through he would become even more unassailable.

'Let Chanakya think that he has won. Let him think that I have been defeated. He will know...' said the Rajmahishi darkly. She examined the intricate design traced on her palms by Misrakesi and nodded her approval, continuing, 'I am a player of chaupad.[13] The game is not lost till the last throw. Remember, Misrakesi, the last throw... but I have said too much. Go now.'

That night she was called by Pushyamitra to report on her findings. They were in his office room and he was leaning against a carved pillar. Misrakesi noticed him passing a tired hand over his brow. He gave her a bleak look, the pressure on him was terrible, the city had to be opened for the marriage without compromising on security. He could not falter again; the onus was on him to prove his loyalty and his efficiency. He, his brother, Senapati Agnimitra Sunga, and Maha Amatya Katyayan were the three most high-profile Nanda administration re-appointees and the expectations from them were colossal.

'She may be planning something but I am sure she is playing a lone hand. My spies are tracking all her potential allies and nothing in their reports indicates that they are doing anything to help.'

Misrakesi was pondering over this when Pushyamitra spoke again, 'The only time she will be in contact with the samrat is during the marriage ceremony. Great care is being taken to segregate the royal Nanda women within their own quarters till then. I can guarantee that there will be no lethal weapons there and also that she has no access to any in the women's quarters.'

'What about the people who pass in and out of the royal ladies quarters? Something could be smuggled in, especially some kind of poison.'

'There are only a few women allowed in from outside, regular access is only for the washer woman and the barber woman. Some others come in as and when needed. They are searched by the guards at both the entrances before coming in or going out.'

'Wait,' Misrakesi spoke hesitantly, 'Might not the Devi Dharini be involved in this, too? Maybe she is preparing something in her solitude?' It sounded unlikely that a new bride would kill her husband but Misrakesi knew that the past was littered with such instances. The Nanda dynasty itself stood on the murder of a reigning king by his queen on the inciting of her paramour.

'You can be sure that the acharya has thought of that. The royal couple is not going to be left alone together till Devi Dharini is above suspicion.'

Some marriage this was going to be, thought Misrakesi cynically. It was good that marriage was out of the question for someone like her.

Pushyamitra told her to persevere and disappeared, he seemed to be everywhere at the same time these last few days and Misrakesi was left wondering whether the man had any human limits at all. If she had stopped to think, she would have realized that this was a man fighting for his life and his future.

Misrakesi's room was behind the quarters for the princesses and was separated from the Alankarbhoomi by a scattering of big Ashvath trees which were also reputed to act as a protection against poisons. The Alankarbhoomi held a staggering variety of ingredients to make all kinds of lotions, unguents and aids to beauty known to man or woman.

Misrakesi had made it a habit to sit outside under one of the trees, absorbed in preparing a beauty lotion but keeping a careful eye on the entry to the royal ladies chambers. After some time, she had come to recognize the regulars, the washer woman, the barber woman, physicians, and of course the chosen traders and merchants.

She couldn't help but notice that the most popular visitor with the guards was the sparkling, flirtatious, and curvaceous barber woman who, interestingly enough, was always accompanied by her young daughter, about ten or eleven years old, her head covered by her uttariya. It seemed to be a peculiarity of hers. The child was mostly ignored but the older woman was always thoroughly searched to the accompaniment of roguish comments and squeals. She was a provocative woman whose full lips were always red with the juice of the betel leaf and her uttariya almost never covered her full breasts. The guards loved it.

There was every opportunity for Misrakesi to study both the mother and the daughter in great detail. A few days before the wedding, she was taken aback when her eyes wandered down to the young girl's feet, she had seen the face before and it was a comely one. But the feet seemed to be large, flat, and ill formed. What a misfortune. It would be very difficult for her as she grew up.

The mother-daughter duo went out, not towards the river but to the opposite side, towards the Chikitsagriha. Misrakesi frowned and got up, following them through the trees. It was getting to be evening and the light was not very good, but enough to follow them discreetly, keeping a distance between them and her.

She kept herself hidden behind the trees as much as possible though the two women she was following seemed unconcerned and were walking comfortably towards the Chikitsagriha. Perhaps they were just taking a different route to the servant's quarters behind the Chikitsagriha?

She decided not to give up, however; she would see where they went and then return. A few minutes later, she saw another shadowy figure detach itself from the adjoining trees and walk ahead on the path before her. It was Pushyamitra with his characteristic animal lope. She put out a hand and tapped him lightly on the shoulder intending to tell him what she was doing.

And the next moment found herself in a nightmare where she was pressed against a tree trunk, her hands twisted behind her back and an unrelenting iron band against her neck choked the breath out of her. She could only watch with dilating eyes as Pushyamitra, lips pulled back in a snarl, blood lust on his face slowly but inexorably strangled the light out of her. As the darkness fell in the last thing she heard was a harsh exclamation.

She came to, coughing and sputtering, her senses swimming, propped up on a decorative seat with water from the nearby fish pond sprinkling her face and a grim Pushyamitra looking steadily at her.

'What was the meaning of this, Misrakesi? You could have been dead by now.' There was not even a hint of apology in his voice, only remembered anger.

She could only glare up at him with streaming eyes, not able to speak.

'This is the first regnal year of Samrat Chandragupta, barely a few moons after a palace coup that killed almost an entire royal family and administration. I am a survivor of that administration. And you come out of the dark and accost me from the back. If I took any chances on such events I would not be alive now. Don't ever do such a thing again!' His voice was inflexible but his hands were gentle as he raised her head with gentle fingers, brushing across her neck and jaw to check for the bruises forming on her neck.

'Come; let us find something to rub on your bruise while you tell me what it was you wanted to talk about.'

He took her in to the Chikitsagriha and Misrakesi sat down shaken and bewildered, she knew that her job would be a dangerous one but to be attacked by her own chief! She gingerly rubbed a balm on to her neck and sipped a warm cordial to ease her croaking voice.

Pushyamitra sat across her and looked at her seriously.

'Before you say anything, let me bring you up to date. The situation has become more serious than we thought. We have intercepted messages from the palace asking some specific close allies of the Nandas to keep themselves and their armies ready for an instant attack on Pataliputra on the morning of the wedding. This can only mean an attempt on the samrat's life. "They," whoever "they" may be, are expecting to throw the city into a panic and want allied armies to take advantage of that to take over Magadha.'

'But how did the message go out of the palace? And who sent it?' asked Misrakesi.

'It was a cloth merchant from Kosala. He had come to the women's quarters in connection with the marriage festivities. We have our people in place in all the merchants' retinues. The concerned setthi is a trader not a political player and he was only too glad to tell us everything and escape with a whole skin.' Pushyamitra gave a thin smile and Misrakesi wondered how whole the skin actually was.

'The origin, of course, was the Rajmahishi. A close confidant of hers conveyed the message to the setthi.'

'So what do we do now?' asked a worried Misrakesi frowning.

'Our army has been placed on high alert and the samrat will be guarded day and night. You must intensify your efforts. The weapon will definitely be poison. It fits in with the occasion. What must be discovered is the source. And we have only a few days left. As for the Rajmahishi, nothing is going to be said to her as the acharya does not want any rupture between the Nandas and Mauryas to come out into the open. The administration is poised very delicately and nothing can be allowed to disturb its equilibrium. Discretion is all important.'

He stood up and then turned and asked, 'What did you want to tell me?'

'I was keeping an eye on some suspicious movements from the royal ladies quarters.'

He shrugged, 'There is no harm in that, but since they are searched rigorously and anyway only a few people are allowed in I do not think you will get anywhere. Keep up your vigilance with the royal women.'

The discussion was over and he left to talk to two of his men who were waiting outside. Misrakesi was left nursing a sore throat and a bruised ego.

She spent as much time as was possible with Mrinalini the next two days but without any luck. Mrinalini was abstracted and downhearted, keeping silent unless spoken to. Misrakesi spoke to her of the future of the Mauryas and Dharini's shining future as the queen of all Jambudweepa and could see that this threw Mrinalini into deep thought. But she did not say anything.

Misrakesi was slowly but surely failing in her first assignment.

It was just two days before the wedding. Misrakesi was frustrated and unable to think of any strategy. The threat remained and the sources had not been identified. She was sitting under the shade of a tree and desultorily chatting with a few women from the Ranivas who were bubbling with excitement about the ceremonies which had already started and their new clothes and jewellery.

There was a sudden interruption from the wilderness near the Chikitsagriha as a huge cloud of parrots rose up into the air, wheeling and chattering excitedly and flying round in a low circle. The women shaded their eyes and looked up wondering what was happening. Before they could remark on it a flock of brahminy starlings twittering madly went flying out towards the horizon. An unearthly shriek went up from the trees; it was a group of fork-tailed shrikes.

The women were silent now, worry writ large on their faces. These were not good omens and spelt the presence of danger. Misrakesi was the only one who got up to investigate. The others slunk quietly back to their rooms.

But there was nothing in the trees, the birds had all flown away and the wilderness was empty. The only figures that could be seen were the barber woman and her daughter who were walking towards the servant's quarters behind the Chikitsagriha. Misrakesi looked after them, frowning. A small nugget was revolving in her mind. Why were the birds behaving so oddly?

That night, the entire palace was on edge, it was as if they were all collectively holding their breaths, waiting. Pushyamitra was like a savage panther prowling the corridors daring anything to happen. Misrakesi had retired early.

Misrakesi woke up suddenly. She was silent and still, only her eyes searched the dark and shadowy apartment. There was still some oil in the night lamp and the wick was burning steadily casting a pool of light near the bed. She was wearing only a soft cotton dhoti and was considering whether to wrap an uttariya around herself and get up when she heard a sob and saw a shadow behind the pillar just inside the door. The figure was huddled against the wall slowly sliding to the floor.

She got up in a flash and approached the figure with her dagger in hand; there was no point in taking chances.

'Mrinalini! My dear, what is the matter? Why are you crying? Has something happened in the palace?' Her dagger was lowered and her mind ran immediately to assassination and death.

'No, No. Nothing has happened… as yet,' said Mrinalini sobbing uncontrollably, her body shaking.

'But I can no longer be silent. I cannot let this happen to my daughter… a widow before she marries!' Mrinalini raised a tear-stained face to a bewildered Misrakesi.

Misrakesi made Mrinalini sit and gave her some water to drink. Mrinalini had suspected something all the time but tonight the Rajmahishi had spoken to her and asked her to spirit Dharini away on the morning of the wedding to a waiting ally. She had not specified what would happen but Mrinalini could guess that it would involve the death of the samrat and she was horrified. The death and destruction that would ensue and the sudden eclipse of her darling's bright future were intolerable to her. She thought of asking Misrakesi for help.

Mrinalini had stopped crying and was in deadly earnest now. She looked Misrakesi squarely in the eyes, 'I do not know who exactly you are but I am certain you have some connection with the current administration. Who will listen to a poor dasi like me? But I swear to you on the head of my daughter, Dharini, that I am telling the truth. And you can do something, you can stop this tragedy from happening. I implore you, please do something…'

Misrakesi believed her implicitly and her only thought was to inform Pushyamitra at once. Without replying directly to the question of who she was and what she would do about the assassination plot she asked Mrinalini to stay in the room, dressed herself and raced through the dimly-lit corridors to reach the chamber from where Pushyamitra operated. She had been instructed to report there in case there was anything of import. Her bare feet made no sound on the wooden floor and the flames of the mashaals whipped by as she rushed across to the other side of the palace where the administrative chambers were housed.

There was no one in the room except Vrishni, an old and trusted dasa of Pushyamitra's. But he knew where Pushyamitra was to be found. He was inspecting the main quadrangle of the palace where the marriage ceremony was to be performed. It was a beehive of activity with the sacred fire burning, musicians playing and auspicious songs already being sung. The officiating priests had arrived as had some of the guests; it was a royal wedding, after all. The atmosphere resounded with the chanting of sacred Sanskrit mantras and it was redolent with the smell of the havishyan.[14]

Pushyamitra was standing at one side and Misrakesi caught him in the act of upending an earthen pot of water on his head, probably to wake himself up. He looked at her questioningly with the water dripping from his hair and over his shoulders; she called him away from the quadrangle and conveyed Mrinalini's information. His eyes focused and he drew her away to a secluded room so that they could discuss the matter in private.

'Many of my people have been giving me indirect indicators of the same thing but your input is the most direct yet. But what about concrete details about what is being planned? Did she give you any information on that?'

Misrakesi shook her head.

'Then it leaves us where we were. As long as the acharya has forbidden me to question any of the palace women, my hands are tied.' He took a hasty and irritated walk around the room. 'And I am supposed to provide foolproof protection to the king!' there was irony in his voice.

'There are a thousand ways in which poison can be introduced into the king's food, clothes, personal items, ointments… so much to protect. We think we have done all we can but one small loophole and the deed is done.'

Misrakesi was silent, going over all the ways in which poison could be used and feeling very disheartened.

'Go into the royal ladies' quarters and spend all your time there. Keep your eyes open for everything. The smallest thing may be vital. I can only ask you to do the best you can and report on every suspicion.'

Pushyamitra took Misrakesi by the shoulder and looked gravely into her eyes, 'Remember, the safety of the samrat and the empire could depend on what you do for the next two days.'

The next morning saw Misrakesi at her post in the Rajmahishi's retinue. There was absolutely no problem in that since she had become a regular visitor for the last many days and excitement levels were running high.

She sat near the Rajmahishi and concentrated on her. The erstwhile queen was mostly silent but Misrakesi felt there was an unholy glimmer to her eyes, or was she imagining it? Vamana was always the jester, but today he seemed to have lost all control. He was giggling, scratching at the ground and cracking his knuckles till Misrakesi was on edge. He was looking pale and emaciated, repeatedly fingering the hair on his head. He was glancing from one person to another but not replying to any questions, laughing to himself with his high-pitched giggle. Or he would start off with a string of pointless nonsense, only falling silent when the Rajmahishi would sternly rebuke him.

Misrakesi looked at him covertly and his behaviour struck a chord within her mind. She found herself going back to what she had been taught about poisons and poisoners by her Ayurved guru. Were these not classic behavioural patterns of poisoners? But where was the poison?

Beneath the excitement the atmosphere was not a very happy one. Too many of the smiles were forced and the laughter artificial. Some of the young girls brought in their pet animals to play with but this did not help matters. A chital fawn was sharply ordered out when tears started out of its eyes and it keened in sorrow. Vamana was jumping up and down in excitement and another small monkey started away in alarm and in fact opened its bowels right there to screams of disgust. The atmosphere was suddenly sombre, these were not good omens.

A dasi was immediately summoned to clean up and Misrakesi happened to be nearby. When she saw a black seed roll towards her she automatically called out to her to pick it up but then suddenly stopped herself as she took a quicker look at it. It disappeared into her waistband.

She had come back to her room to take her meal when she suddenly remembered he black seed and took it out. The single seed pod had a sharp deflexed beak and she gasped as she saw the split pod and the scarlet seed inside and threw it off in a hurry. It was the kala-kuta seed, one of the most notorious poisons known to man! And it was in the royal women's quarters! Misrakesi stopped to consider whether it could have been carried in by one of the animals which had come in since it did grow in the wild. It was certainly a probability, but could she take chances?

'Definitely not,' she decided as she scrubbed her hands clean. The seed pod had rolled off somewhere and she spent sometime looking for it and wrapping it in a piece of cloth.

'I should be allowed to search and question everyone in the ranivas on the basis of this,' said Pushyamitra bitterly as the seed pod was lying on his palm some time later. 'But the acharya is inflexible. He wants no open scandal to mar this auspicious occasion. I have to use all my skills he says to keep the samrat safe. He has sent me into battle with my hands tied behind my back. I only hope his gamble will not...' the sentence was left incomplete but Misrakesi did not need any explanation.

'You suspect Vamana?'

Misrakesi nodded her head. There was something else at the back of her mind scratching away but not able to come to the surface.

'The seeds can be ground and put in anything. I will double the checks on all the items which will come anywhere even remotely near the samrat but he is a difficult man to control. A life led on the battlefield has not taught him to be careful and he laughs away all threats to his person. He will often pick his food even before the cook tastes it.' Pushyamitra shook his head hopelessly.

It was night but Misrakesi was on full alert. She sat outside her room keeping an eye on all kinds of movements. There were still a few comings and goings because the normal night curfew inside the palace grounds had been relaxed, last minute preparations were still on and figures moved to and fro in the flare lit darkness. There were a few areas of darkness; Pushyamitra had taken special care of that.

The Alankarbhoomi was witnessing a flurry of activity as last minute unguents and mixes were being prepared. The barber woman and her daughter were in full flow, coming and going and using the stone mortars and grinding stones constantly. Misrakesi kept a vigilant eye on everyone.

Her eyes followed the woman and her daughter and she suddenly stiffened. Wasn't the weaving about of the head, the scratching of the hair and the cracking of knuckles familiar? Where had she seen it earlier? A high-pitched giggle escaped the child and Misrakesi was struck by a bolt of enlightenment. It was not a young girl but the dwarf Vamana, of course! She had been seeing the two in different guises everyday and the fact had been niggling away at her. And the misshapen feet! They belonged not to the young girl but to Vamana. He was the one who had been slipping in and out of the royal palace without being searched. The birds flying away in fear, the animals reacting strangely and his own odd behaviour – it all fell into place and Misrakesi turned around in an unthinking bid to catch the two. But they were nowhere to be seen.

Instead of wasting time she should immediately inform Pushyamitra, there was very little time now. There was only one muhurat to go before the samrat would get up and start getting ready for the ceremonies.

In no time at all she found Pushyamitra and told him everything. The barber woman and Vamana were immediately taken into Pushyamitra's custody and questioned. Shrunottara had also been called in and she and Misrakesi were trying to pinpoint the threat to the samrat.

'The problem,' said Shrunottara biting her lips worriedly 'is that the field is wide indeed. Poison can be introduced in anything and we have no clues except for the fact that the seeds must have been ground into powder or paste which can be mixed with anything. Can you think of something specific from your ranivas visits?'

'No, not really.' Misrakesi's face was drawn while her mind worked furiously reaching no conclusion whatever.

'Call that dasi of yours and let us see if we can get anything out of her,' said Shrunottara. 'And quickly, there is no time to lose.'

Pushyamitra had come in to join them, his body tense, eyes hard; and he shook his head at the two of them.

'They do not know how the poison will be used. My assistants are continuing the interrogation but I have no hopes from them. We will have to figure it out ourselves.'

Mrinalini came in, scared and hesitant and stood at the side. Pushyamitra signaled to her and Misrakesi drew her away.

'Mrinalini, tell me anything you can which will help us to find out where the poison will be used. Think. Think.'

Mrinalini shook her head hopelessly. They talked for a while about all that the Rajmahishi had said to Mrinalini which was of no use. Time was slipping by, the night was lightening and they were still no nearer to the solution.

'Tell me anything that you may have heard the Rajmahishi say to Vamana.'

'She would always talk to him away from the others and mostly about the old king and her life with him,' said Mrinalini shrugging.

'In the last few days she had been repeating that the new king was sleeping on the same bed as the old one and people were forgetting that she had also shared it for years. I don't know whether all this nostalgia is of any help.'

'Wait...,' said Pushyamitra slowly, his eyes abstracted. 'The bed, yes, the bed. Shrunottara, doesn't it have a hollow pillar on one side which has a staircase inside? Are you sure that this pillar has been blocked?'

Pushyamitra and Shrunottara were suddenly galvanized into action and left the room at a run. Misrakesi and Mrinalini were left looking at each other. What was the matter?

They were soon to know. After some time they saw a contingent of women soldiers headed by Shrunottara entering the samrat's quarters and soon after there were manic shouts emanating from inside. Misrakesi and Mrinalini watched, frozen, as the Rajmahishi was led out struggling and screaming. Mrinalini made a move as if to help but was warned by Misrakesi's strict glare. This was not a small matter and no one could afford to get involved on the Rajmahishi's side.

And so it was, that a scant hour before the wedding ceremonies were to begin, when the bride and groom were taking their auspicious baths, Misrakesi was busy helping the samrat's mother, a quiet mousy woman who still seemed in awe of the palace and not at all aware of her status, to prepare the aarti which would welcome the groom to the wedding. The Rajmahishi's manic screams and shouts were still echoing. Dharini was trembling with shock. Mrinalini had taken over her shringar and was trying to soothe her enough for the ceremonies. Dhana Nanda's second queen, Sunayna was to take over the Rajmahishi's ritual role.

Shrunottara had informed them briefly that the poison had been mixed with the kesar and sandal paste that the groom would put on his body. The paste prepared by the rajvaidya was to be substituted by the Rajmahishi. She had simply walked through the passage which connected the hollow pillar on one side of the royal bed with her apartment. The clay pot would have been switched in an instant without disturbing either the sleeping king or the guards who were at a deferential distance from him. All she needed to do was to extend one hand through the pillar and put her poison on the bedside replacing the original. She had been caught by Pushyamitra in the act of extending her hand with poison.

Soon it was all over. The wedding was successfully solemnized and Dharini was Chandragupta's wedded wife. In an elaborate ceremony witnessed by hundreds, Dharini was also crowned the Pattrajmahishi i.e. the queen consort of Samrat Chandragupta. The samrat and samragyi were seated upon the throne of Magadha and the reign of the Mauryas began in earnest.

Back to Pataliputra

The greatest city in India is that which is called Palimbothra in the dominions of the Prassians where the streams of the Erannabaos and the Ganges unite. It is 80 stadia in length and 15 stadia in breadth. A ditch encompasses it all around which is 600 feet in breadth And 30 cubits in depth and the wall is crowned with 570 towers and 64 gates.

Megasthenes' Indika

The group of riders thundering across the Rajmarga[15] were unaffected by the rain, darkness, and slush underneath. The gusts of raindrops beating against their faces and the sheet of water blocking their way were but minor irritants. On they went, traversing the wide royal highways with the same efficiency as the narrower countryside, forest and chariot roads along the Dakshinapath.

As the morning drew closer the group stopped for rest and a meal. One of them pulled off the thick Gandharan rainproof uttariya covering the head: she was an upstanding young woman with the bearing of a soldier and the grace of a nartaki. Yes, it was Misrakesi, on her way back to Pataliputra.

A year had passed. She had been given small assignments, but nothing major till the instructions to conduct the Love Test on the man who was being sent as the Provincial Governor and protector of the samrat's interests in the western Avantiratha area of Jambudweepa.

It had already been a part of the Nanda kingdom and this expedition was to establish the first Maurya as the suzerain. Ujjaini, already a pre-eminent city, was to be established as the western provincial capital, the first of what would, Mahadeva willing, be a series of provincial capitals in all four corners of the land. For this western part there were plans to extend the kingdom to the Surashtra and Bharukacch area; Ujjaini would be an appropriate base for this exercise.

She had been sent to Ujjaini as part of the governor's convoy with the brief of making him fall in love with her and then testing his loyalty to the samrat by inciting him to rebel and set up his own rule.

The governor had passed the test without a glimmer of doubt but she herself had been left bruised by the deceit and lies the entire episode had necessitated. She had resolved not to get involved in a Love Test again; she did not have the temperament for it. It only remained to discuss this with her chief and she had no idea how he would react. Would it merely be ignored as impudence? She did not know to what extent spies were allowed their freedom. She was determined to define her own.

Once her report on the Love Test had been received by Pushyamitra, Misrakesi had been relieved to receive an order in Ujjaini summoning her back to Pataliputra. She had been staying in her Prashikshan Kendra in Ujjaini and the atmosphere was too quiet for her liking. The world of academics was far from the world of politics. Having once left the academic world for politics, it was difficult to adjust to quiet days spent in the study of shringar, or the sixty-four arts essential for women, or even the all important study of 'Kama'.[16] The precepts guiding the practice of Kama as well as the social rules which governed them were of overweening importance. These were thoroughly taught to each and every pupil.

Misrakesi had gone through the exacting course herself and was counted as extremely proficient. However, an effort had recently been initiated to collect and collate these practices from all the Janapadas into an authentic manual, a 'Kama Sutra', and Misrakesi was drawn into this. Academic discussions on the art of living and making love were all fine but when it came to their cynical usage for entrapping men they became distasteful to her, still smarting as she was from the episode of the Love Test.

Misrakesi had been instructed to wait for the next caravan heading east from Ujjaini to Pataliputra, but she was too impatient. She preferred instead to join the royal messengers as they thundered through the Rajmargs carrying important messages in the shortest time.

And so a cold rainy winter's morning found her back in Pataliputra, not in the palace now but in temporary lodgings with a goldsmith's family; one of the many eyes and ears of Pushyamitra in the city.

The first thing to do was to meet Pushyamitra but this was easier said than done. Hiranyalabha, the goldsmith with whom she was staying, had conveyed Pushyamitra's message that she should wait for further instructions and make no move in the meanwhile; which meant no move to seek him out, also. It had been much easier when she was staying in the palace next to his official chambers.

This was at a distance from the palace, near the Brahma Gate inside the city walls in the jewellers and goldsmiths' part of the city. It was off one of the three main royal roads running from north to south. The other three royal roads ran from east to west. The city itself was surrounded by three separate moats filled with both lotuses and crocodiles and massive ramparts made of compacted earth and planted with thorny bushes. It was at the confluence of the River Ganga and its tributary, the Sona and therefore plentifully provided with water apart from being a favourable trade vantage point.

Pataliputra was a bustling, prosperous and grand city[17] of more than a hundred thousand inhabitants; there was no place in the entire Prithvi to compare with it. It was well provided with public amenities, parks and beautiful residences, dancing houses, shops selling necessities and luxuries brought from all corners of the world and whatever else the heart could desire. At the centre of the city was the incomparable palace complex, the centre of the earth. Ubiquitous were the Patal trees whose scarlet flowers gave the city its alternative name of Pushpapura. The Mauryas were taking it to greater heights with their continuous improvements and attention to every aspect of urban life.

Misrakesi had decided, after much thought and introspection, to settle down as the proprietress of a Dancing House, a matrika, in Pataliputra and make that her cover as a spy, if permitted. She was too young for such a position but she would have to make up in personality what she lacked in years. Or she could look for a slightly older partner. But society was in a state of flux and the breaking of yet another tradition would not be such a sacrilege. The important question was how to convince Pushyamitra, whenever she was allowed to meet him.

She had saved a large part of her salary for the past year and was in a position to buy a house in the city itself. If she fell short she could always borrow the necessary karshapans.

With this end in mind, one day she initiated the topic with Hiranyalabha during the evening meal, or rather, after it. He and his wife, Sreelekha and the entire household had eaten but Misrakesi was eating a little late. They were all sitting in the kitchen while she ate her little pyramid of boiled rice with watery lentil poured over it and vegetables and spicy fried venison pieces on the side. This was all to be followed by a pot of milk.

'I am thinking of buying a house and settling in Pataliputra. Do you think there are any good houses to be bought in the city, as close to the palace walls as possible? If not, any good location will do.' She started off after a dasi had brought water for her to wash her hands and had taken the soiled utensils away.

'That, as always, depends on...' and Hiranyalabha raised his tufted grey eyebrows to smile.

'Money, of course. Everything does.' Cut in Sreelekha, settling her ample hips more comfortably on the mat and preparing to dispense advice as an experienced merchant's wife. She had her reservations about Misrakesi, a young woman making her way in the world alone, successfully, but could never resist the temptation of doling out advice, to just about anyone on any subject under the sun.

'Would you want a garden and groves, maybe a small artificial lake, maybe a double storied house? But no, what would you do with a large house and how would you afford it as a young girl! I think you should make do with a much smaller house without any grounds or maybe share a half with someone else.'

Misrakesi, who never believed in making do with anything less than what she wanted raised her eyebrows at this and pursed her lips, signs that were not lost on Sreelekha who was annoyed that this callow girl should not be happy with her advice.

Hiranyalabha interrupted before any of them could make their displeasure felt. He was a peaceable man, who had also been instructed to render all help to Misrakesi. 'You should not decide in a hurry. I know of many properties and you should consider all factors very carefully before you decide.'

He was obviously very well informed about the city. He suggested the eastern part of the city after entering through the Main Gate as a desirable location. Misrakesi decided to visit the Samaharta the next morning to look at layout maps of the area with the houses and empty areas on the shores of the river marked out.

Sreelekha was not satisfied. 'What will you do with a large house, live alone in it?' She asked with a mocking inflexion which raised Misrakesi's hackles.

But all she said as she got up to go to sleep was, 'Think of it as insurance for my old age.'

She had decided to visit the Samaharta's office in the morning and look at the available properties, maybe put in an application for one. So she dressed carefully for the day. To proclaim her prosperity she wore a white brocade lehnga and a deep pink linen uttariya embroidered with gossamer silver threads draped over both her shoulders. She also dressed her hair in a graceful bun at the back of her head, a pearl band pulling it away softly from her forehead letting a few artful curls escape. The white cloth tied over her breasts was edged with pearls to match with the kunda white satlari necklace from Tamraparni that swung gently with every movement. The silver, pink and white against her honey coloured skin made her look like an ethereal painting etched with loving strokes by a master painter.

Sreelekha was not pleased, 'There she goes, off to entrap another hapless man.' She muttered to herself. Hiranyalabha gave her a helpless look but said nothing. He rather admired Misrakesi's initiative but knew it was useless to say so; and so he held his peace. He had, over the last few days, helped her strengthen her proposal of setting up her dancing house with necessary facts and figures from the city and was hoping she would succeed in convincing Pushyamitra whenever she met him.

As she stepped out into the street with her das, Urmil (hired for her by Hiranyalabha), holding her embroidered chattra, an umbrella, over her head, a mounted messenger suddenly rode to a stop before her and handed her a letter.

It was from the Samaharta commanding her presence in his chambers to discuss certain matters pertaining to her visit to Ujjaini. The Samaharta was a very high official, almost at the head of the administration and was next only to the king, royal family, Purohit, and the senapati. Misrakesi had not expected to meet him, but here was a message from him!

He probably had some questions pertaining to trade on the Dakshinapath since, apart from law and order in the countryside, he was also in-charge of revenue collection for the kingdom. Before Acharya Chanakya took the secret service under his purview, Pushyamitra had informally reported to the Samaharta himself. She would be only too happy to answer all questions to the best of her abilities, and ask about properties for sale at the same time. It was quite a coincidence, all the same, and Misrakesi was puzzled.

The Samaharta, a grizzled and patient looking man of fifty odd years, was dealing with the entry of foreigners into the city, questioning them, finding out the purpose of their visit to the city and deciding whether they should be given the permission papers, the Pravesh Patrika. His decision was normally final but he worked in close cooperation with the Nagarik Suraksha Vibhag of

Pushyamitra. Suspicious characters were led away by soldiers of this Vibhag and it was anybody's guess as to what happened to them – questioned rigorously, beaten, perhaps even tortured if they were suspected to be spies.

His office was near the main senapati gate since he kept a strict eye on the entry of traders and foreigners into the city. The citizens of Pataliputra were allowed to use all sixty-four gates but outsiders had to mandatorily use only this one.

Misrakesi entered after asking permission and greeted the Samaharta respectfully. He was busy examining certain identification papers at a low wooden desk and gestured smilingly at her to enter a door to the side – to wait, presumably, till his work was done. She went in.

'My greetings, Misrakesi,' Pushyamitra entered from another door as Misrakesi turned with a small shock of something like pleasure.

'Pranaam, Arya.' This time Misrakesi was not going to reveal any sign of her impatience at waiting all these days. She had realized that she was a small fish in the big river where Pushyamitra was a crocodile. She put on her most winning smile and gracious manner.

Well, well, the young woman is growing up and learning, thought Pushyamitra, secretly amused because he knew very well from Hiranyalabha how impatient she had been to take the next steps into her future.

'So, how are you Misrakesi? The trip to Ujjaini seems to have suited you. You look well.'

'You are too gracious, Arya.' He was looking good, too: bare-chested with a fine yellow silk antariya and a brown muga[18] uttariya wound around his neck. His kanthahaar[19] was of gold and Misrakesi noticed that a strange ochre bead was tied around one muscled forearm. He always wore this bead and Misrakesi had often wondered why. The sword slapping against one thigh also had a hilt of gold. The Mauryas seemed to be treating him well, he seemed to be in control and supremely confident of himself. The intervening months since the royal wedding had obviously seen his position strengthened and consolidated.

He had fallen into his inevitable pacing up and down and Misrakesi eyed him warily. She had to convince him of her proposal today and she wanted his mood to be receptive.

He stopped suddenly and came to a halt in front of her. 'Well, Misrakesi, the time has come to decide what to do with you.'

As if I am the fifth wheel of an ox-cart, thought Misrakesi, a trifle annoyed, but keeping the winning smile pinned firmly to her lips.

There were the beginnings of a sarcastic smile on his face as he went on, 'From certain indications in the reports you have been sending, I have gathered that work such as that which you had in Ujjaini is not to your taste.'

His voice became even more cutting and Misrakesi stiffened, wondering whether she should postpone putting in her request to a more propitious occasion.

'I really do not know how we will function if each of my guptachars wishes to decide for himself the nature of his work. Perhaps you will also instruct me in this matter?'

Misrakesi flushed at his words, but she was also angry which drove her to say, 'It is not himself but herself in this case. You are forgetting, Arya, that I am not part of the Nagarik Suraksha Vibhag. I was appointed to the Gupt Varangana Sena and surely a new organization can decide the contours of its work and how it is to be done?'

She softened her voice and went on, 'I am only asking for a chance to do something different which will suit my temperament. You must agree that each person should do what they can do best, and I think I am not suited for the Love Test.'

Pushyamitra had been given a pause when she reminded him about the Gupt Varangana Sena. Strictly speaking, she was right and it did not improve his temper. The Gupt Varangana Sena was an organization with a different structure and head and Misrakesi had been appointed to this organization, not his Gupt Achar Vibhag. It was a coincidence that Misrakesi had worked all this time under his directions. He would take care of that administrative detail; she would most definitely be working under his directions at present and in the future. He could even dismiss her on the spot if he so wished, but because he was a fair minded and honest man he decided to discuss the matter with her.

'Forget about the Varangana Sena,' he said briskly, 'you will continue to work with me. What is it that you wish to talk to me about?'

'Surely there are many other ganikas in Magadha who will be able to do the work of the Love Test more effortlessly and better than me?'

'You did not do too badly yourself. From what I have been told, the governor still seems to be pining for you,' Pushyamitra said, his face devoid of any expression.

An indefinable expression flitted across her face and she said, almost to herself, 'Perhaps that is what I object to.' Then she looked up and said, 'Will you at least listen to what I have to say before you reject it outright.'

Pushyamitra nodded at her to continue. He could see the shadow on her face and was wondering at it. Had she involved herself with her target and was that the reason for her present refusal? But then why had she come back? She could have stayed with him. Was it some genuine feeling of regret at her deception? Then she could as well leave the profession immediately. Deception was the way of life she had chosen.

Misrakesi took a deep breath and looked up at him. She had been sitting with her head bent and as she raised her face up to him he noted the sweep of her lashes, the beguiling eyes and the graceful line of her neck, the swell of her breasts and the delicate waist emphasized by the mekhala, with multiple dark-pink garnet strands hugging the shapely hips. She was quite an eyeful and armful, he thought dispassionately; no wonder she had had taken in her target so easily and completely. He had given her a few months' time but she had finished her work in weeks.

'Arya, I do not find myself able to work in situations where I have to forge fake intimate relationships. Very honestly, I am afraid that I may even end up compromising myself.'

'I admit,' she said quickly before Pushyamitra could speak, 'that deception is part of my work and I cannot get away from it. But perhaps in a more impersonal atmosphere?'

'Go on, I am still listening.'

'Arya, just between you and me and speaking within these four walls, is it not true that theft, murder, and lawlessness have been on the rise since...'

'Perhaps you mean since my stewardship of the city?' interposed Pushyamitra silkily, 'Please do not hesitate to say so.'

'Arya, please do not get angry. This is in no way a reflection on you. The confusion inherent in a change of kings, the general amnesty offered to all prisoners on the occasion of the royal wedding, the fact that the Mauryan administration will take time to settle down, all have their role to play. The release of all kinds of criminals may boost the popularity of the administration but it is not going to help the law and order situation and was bound to make your task very difficult.'

Here was yet another painful truth, which no one had had the courage to say to his face. This woman had definitely come here with a death wish, but he decided to hear her out, now that he had come this far.

'There may be some truth in what you are saying but how do *you* come into it?' he asked with compressed lips.

'You would be more aware of this than me, Dev, of the fact that most of the trouble seems to be coming from a particular quarter of the town, that which has the eating houses, actors, veshyas, natyashalas, and rangshalas.[20] This is also next to the area where all the rich merchants live. Robberies and assaults on them have increased.'

Pushyamitra sat up and listened intently. He had been worrying about this trouble spot for some time now and thinking of ways and means to improve the situation. How did this chit of a girl know so much about the city?

'How would it be if you had your very own person established there to keep an eye on the area and provide you with information to neutralize the troublesome elements in your own way?' Misrakesi looked at him anxiously to see the effect this had on him.

'And what makes you think we do not have anyone there?' asked Pushyamitra frowning.

'Arya, I have toured the place last week with Hiranyalabha Kaka. You do have some isolated spies but there is no establishment which can act as a magnet for the rich and poor alike. You do not have a dancing house, for example with a ganika like me and a few others which will act as your extension and pick up all the information necessary.' There, it was out, her proposal, and Misrakesi smiled up at him hopefully.

Pushyamitra started pacing up and down, as was his habit when he was thinking. He was impressed. This was no uninformed and emotional young woman. She had done her job well, recognized a need, and put forward a proposal to address it, with the requisite background check too. He would have to look at her twice now.

Misrakesi's hands were clenched and she was willing him to say yes. Why should it be that her future depended on a decision to be taken by this man on his own whims? Here, however, she was doing him an injustice; he did not work on whims. He might not be happy with her but would not gainsay the truth of what she had said.

He listened to her detailed proposal and said, 'Hmm. There is something in what you say. I have my people amongst the gamblers and dancing girls, but no place which can act as their meeting point. And you think you can do this?' he asked, turning and standing facing her.

It was a genuine question, not an attempt to mock her; so she replied, 'Yes, I can. I have thought about it. I may not be a typical matrika who is past her dancing days but I have the backing of the Prashikshan Kendra at Ujjaini from where I can get other dancing girls as well as advice from my guru who is also the directress. If you think I am too young to head it I can take in an older woman.'

Could it be that she had succeeded?

'No, you should head it yourself since no one else must know the true purpose.' He was still in thought.

Misrakesi ventured hesitantly, 'I also am willing to use my own savings to set it up but I may need a loan from the treasury or I can take it from the market.'

He seemed to come to a conclusion and came out of his reverie, 'All right, Misrakesi, you can establish yourself as you have no doubt planned. You do not need to tell me all the details but it must serve the purpose we have just discussed. Get a few more nartakis from Magadha or from Ujjaini as you wish. Hire or buy a house as seems convenient, get the requisite dasas and dasis and set it up. You can ask Hiranyalabha for help. He will be invaluable. You can leave your savings alone. I will provide the necessary finances from our secret service resources. Be lavish, I want a top-class establishment which is beyond suspicion. The only condition is that, if it does not work out, the costs will be recovered from you.'

Misrakesi's face was transformed into a blooming lotus as she smiled, revealing white teeth like beautiful Kunda buds. She could have hugged him but happily for her, she desisted. They discussed a few more details and then the meeting was over.

Just before he left, he added, 'I shall be amongst your first guests in, say, three months from now?' and he was gone.

Misrakesi almost danced home. She had succeeded with her dreaded chief and was going to do what she wanted. Had anyone ever been so fortunate!

Knowing that Hiranyalabha was Pushyamitra's man, she did not hide anything from him. As the dancing house had to be set up immediately she wanted advice from him. He was not surprised at Misrakesi's success. It was a sensible and workable plan and the important inputs had come from him.

But she had to face the arrows of Sreelekha's ire.

'Done well for yourself, haven't you? What is the secret?' She asked.

'My beautiful face?' said Misrakesi flippantly and regretted it almost immediately at Sreelekha's nasty smile. This woman also brought out the worst in her. She decided to ignore her but she was muttering.

'Only some of us are *lucky*.'

Before Misrakesi could ask her what she meant, a perplexed Hiranyalabha asked his wife, 'But my dear, why do you say that, what is it that you lack?'

'Nothing, nothing. Forget it. Let us concentrate on getting Misrakesi her dancing house. After all, you have been instructed by Arya Pushyamitra to help her, haven't you?' and the subject was closed. Misrakesi was left feeling uncomfortable at Sreelekha's knowing expression and unpleasant tongue. She decided to be cautious around her, but soon forgot all this in her excitement.

Misrakesi spent the next few days combing the lanes and bylanes of her chosen area. It was not too far from the eastern flank of the palace complex and was crowded with food shops, gambling and drinking dens, houses of small time courtesans and actors, as well as a couple of rangshalas. Adjoining these were the splendid houses of the rich merchants along the River Ganges which was the most overpowering presence in the entire city. Both king and commoner could think of it as their own.

Misrakesi wanted one of these houses with groves of trees leading down to the waterfront, and perhaps her own private boat for going up and down the river. She could even stock the groves with deer and birds and have small artificial ponds with duck and teal. But maybe she was being too ambitious. None of the houses she saw appealed to her and she was thinking of a compromise when Hiranyalabha found her the bargain.

Hemguna, one of the leading merchants of the city, was planning to shift from Pataliputra and settle down in the holy city of Kasi. He was looking for someone who was ready for an immediate purchase with karshapans so that he could leave at once.

Misrakesi was happy to hear this as her search had not yielded anything. It only remained to see the place and also find out what the catch was. The house was located in the prime area by the side of the river, and had extensive woods attached to it. Why was such a property on the market with no one to buy it? There had to be some problem.

She was sitting with Hiranyalabha in the evening and discussing the finances of setting up a high-class dancing house; the number of dancers and dasa, dasis she would need, the fitting up of the house with furnishings and decorations, the sourcing of the food and wines and the innumerable other details. Hiranyalabha was an invaluable resource, he knew all the right people and could make the most difficult thing easy.

As she had been meaning to for some time, she asked him, 'You have not really told me everything about the sale of the house, have you, Kaka?' She had taken to calling the affectionate old man Kaka, which means uncle; completely honorary, of course. She had never known who her father was, leave alone his brother. And she would, equally of course, not have dreamt of calling Sreelekha 'Kaki'! She tried to get by without calling her anything at all!

Hiranyalabha sighed and then smiled wryly at her, 'I knew you would not rest till you had heard the details from me. But you must not think that I am getting you into a bad bargain. There is nothing wrong with the house and land or the transaction. In fact the price is a bargain.'

'Then what is the catch?' Misrakesi asked as he paused and looked sadly out of the window.

He spoke in a low voice, 'I have known the family for a very long time, you know. I was there at Chandramukhi's birth twenty-five years ago and I count the Setthi Hemguna amongst my friends. It saddens me to see what the family has come to.'

The story was a sad but not unusual one, what was unusual was the aftermath. Chandramukhi was the adored only daughter of Hemguna and had been brought up as the darling of the entire household. Her father and four brothers pampered her and indulged her every wish. As she grew up into a beautiful and accomplished young woman, her father could not bear to marry her to someone who would take her away to his own home, perhaps to a different city. A handsome young man working in one of his warehouses caught his eye. He was an orphan from Kalinga with no family ties. He seemed eminently suitable to Hemguna and was, as expected, amazed at his good fortune. Chandramukhi was married to him and they settled down happily in the family home.

A few months after the wedding, Chandramukhi and Shreedhan, her husband, expressed a wish to go on a pilgrimage. Permission and means were readily made available and the couple started off with their retinue.

And then, tragedy struck. Ten days' journey from Pataliputra they were set upon by robbers, looted and killed. Only an old servant survived long enough to send word back through a group of travellers who came upon him in a half dead condition the next day.

The family was devastated.

And then, some months later, Chandramukhi's mother started to have visions of her daughter; she claimed that her daughter had returned. She would 'talk' to her daughter and insist on providing food, clothes, and luxuries for her. Hemguna, himself inconsolable, tried hard to cure his wife of her delusion but it was of no use. His wife soon developed a complete obsession with her 'daughter'. Priests were called in and the 'preta' tried to be exorcised but to no avail. At his wits end, Hemguna decided to leave the city full of his daughter's memories and shift his business and home to Kasi where his wife could get some spiritual succour.

'That is why the distress sale,' concluded Hiranyalabha smiling hesitantly as if he expected Misrakesi to raise an objection. 'I am sure that a sensible young woman like you would disregard these stories of spirits and manifestations. The house is a great bargain, you know.'

Misrakesi was not too certain that she wanted this bargain. She had a healthy respect mixed with dread for the world of the dead and wanted to maintain a distance from bhoot-pret-pishach-churail.[21] However, she decided to go ahead and take a look at the house before refusing as Hiranyalabha had taken so much trouble for her.

That was her undoing. She lost her heart to the house as soon as she saw it and the part of her which wanted to refuse was forgotten.

It was located at a reasonable distance from the palace complex and was a sprawling, two-storeyed house built by a rich man as a statement of his mark on the world. The structure was massive and made of teak wood from the nearby forest. There was a wooden palisade around the property and the gateway led to an entry courtyard with an ancient peepal tree on the left and steps leading to the upper storey and the terraces on the right. The building was in the shape of a square with four projecting covered terraces supported by pillars with animal head capitals, a lion, an elephant, crocodile, and bull. There was a huge hall right in front across the gateway flanked by smaller rooms leading out from it. The inner courtyard was a huge private space for the house. Perfect for her purposes thought Misrakesi; the hall would be the main area for the dance and entertainment while the upper floor would serve as the private quarters for her and the other nartakis.

She went through the rooms and all the terraces noting that there would be enough space and more for her household. The view was breathtaking. The Ganga stretched out in a seemingly endless expanse of shining water and green banks in the distance with boats going up and down. Boats had a special fascination for Misrakesi as symbols of adventure and horizons unknown and she found herself falling into a reverie before Hiranyalabha's voice asking her to look at the other rooms recalled her to her surroundings.

She could also see a small grove of trees with a shrine to the Goddess Shree who Misrakesi considered her guardian goddess, yet another pull towards the house. Both beauty and prosperity were in the power of the goddess. The terracotta figure of the goddess in the shrine stood on a full blown lotus with two elephant figures on both sides saluting her with lotus flowers in their trunks. The shrine was scrupulously clean and well maintained; an offering of fresh flowers lay at her feet which made Misrakesi wonder a bit.

On the other side a veritable forest of trees stretched down to the shores of the channel skilfully cut out from the river to provide a water source inside the city walls. Part of this land went with the property but it was difficult to mark the exact boundary with the naked eye though it existed meticulously on paper. The Magadhan administration was very jealous of its land resources. Misrakesi could see shal, kadamb, ashoka, neem, peepal and banyan trees but the most numerous of all were of course the patal trees after which the city had probably been named. They were the city's most noticeable feature. The beautiful red flowers which decorated the hair of goddesses and maidens alike were in full bloom and rightly was Pataliputra also called Kusumpura or Pushpapura after these flowers. A kind of path had also been beaten down to the river side and a boat was moored there.

The entire property was in excellent condition and the owner was even ready to throw in the luxurious furniture, the carpets, curtains, paintings and other miscellaneous items. Misrakesi would actually live, if not like a queen, very near to it.

She had come to inspect the property with Hiranyalabha and Chitalkar, an agent of the Setthi Hemguna. He was a scrawny fellow who looked scared out of his wits. He walked on tip toe and looked over his shoulder every now and then keeping close to Hiranyalabha and Misrakesi. He was in a hurry to finish the inspection as soon as possible and was impatient with Misrakesi's lingering over the views and appointments. She finally took pity on his scared face and chattering teeth and said, 'I have seen what I wanted to see. Will you come to Hiranyalabha Kaka's home with us so that we can discuss the final payment? Since I have to pay immediately, perhaps there could be a further reduction...?'

Behind Chitalkar's back Hiranyalabha nodded and beamed. They were getting the property at a throwaway price, but a little more bargaining never hurt!

They went back together, but the day was almost gone before the transaction was complete. In spite of hours of discussion Chitalkar did not budge on the price. He may have looked boneless and witless when confronted with the other world, but he was tough as nails when it came to money.

'Forgive me, Devi but I think you are well aware that this is a distress sale due to certain tragic circumstances. Otherwise you would not have got such a property at this negligible price of 20,000 karshapans. Is not asking for more concession tantamount to taking undue advantage of a respected family's grief?' he asked softly after hours of arguing back and forth.

This effectively silenced both Misrakesi and Hiranyalabha, especially due to the accusing look he threw at Hiranyalabha: a friend of the family behaving like this. Both of them felt vaguely guilty which, as Misrakesi realized later, was exactly what the clever man must have intended. Appearances had been deceptive; he had not let them best him at all!

Misrakesi was very happy with the property and the price she had to pay for it. It was almost within her savings even if she had to later forfeit the price as per Pushyamitra's condition. But she had no intention of failing in her undertaking; he would see the success she would make of it. There was a lurking apprehension about the 'ghost' or vision or whatever it was but she effectively pushed it to the background. After all the Goddess Shree was there to look after her as was the Yaksha[22] of the peepal tree.

The payment was being arranged through the royal treasury through the good offices of Hiranyalabha. Misrakesi's own money was also deposited with him and he had been advising her on ways of investing it in trade so that she would get a regular income separate from her dancing career. It would make her feel much safer, financially speaking.

She had written a letter to the directress of her academy in Ujjaini asking for three or four nartakis for her dancing house. As she had visited the academy recently she was able to offer a few names for consideration but she was content to leave the final selection to the directress. The letter hinted at a kind of semi-royal appointment and promised a generous salary. The generous salary was courtesy the treasury and would help in attracting dancers from Ujjaini and provide a cachet to the dancing house.

The selected nartakis had been asked to come immediately to Pataliputra without waiting for the selection to be approved by Misrakesi herself: there was no time for that if the deadline given by Pushyamitra had to be met. If anything, Misrakesi was determined to beat it and was ready take shortcuts. Buying a compromised house even if she had fallen in love with it, and appointing nartakis sight unseen, were both shortcuts and she hoped she would not regret it. The house could not be returned but the girls could always be sent back if they were unsatisfactory. There should be enough at the moment for the dancing house to function.

Since the house was more or less furnished and in good condition, there was not too much to be done. What was needed to convert it into a dancing house, for example, partitions into smaller private apartments, the decoration of the main hall and changing some of the carpets and curtains was being done apace. Some special furniture was also necessary and was being made. The men and materials were sourced by Hiranyalabha and personally supervised by Misrakesi.

She had thought of moving in immediately since Sreelekha was not a very benign presence to live with, but then she decided to suit herself. An unacknowledged dread of living there alone may have also played a role in this decision, but Misrakesi would never admit it. She finally decided that the dasas and dasis could move in first and she would move in when the other nartakis arrived. Supervision of the household was still a problem and she was wondering what to do about this when a solution appeared unexpectedly.

After the deal was finalized and it was confirmed that her dancing house was going to be a reality in some time, one day Misrakesi decided to go to the palace to pay her respects to the Samragyi. As an ambitious royal employee it would not do to let herself be forgotten by the palace and she was reasonably certain of being granted an audience with Devi Dharini. She was received in a separate chamber. Misrakesi noted that the shy young girl had been transformed into a woman with a royal and gracious manner. But Misrakesi was still in the royal good graces and she was met with smiles.

It was also politic to meet all her acquaintances from her time in the palace. She took time to seek out Mrinalini with real pleasure which was reciprocated. While she was talking to Mrinalini, Misrakesi could sense that there was something she wanted to say but was hesitant. What could it be?

It came out when Misrakesi was about to leave.

'Devi, I have something to tell you… umm… ask, maybe request you…,' said Mrinalini looking at the floor and not meeting Misrakesi's eyes.

'Yes?' Misrakesi looked at her with her eyebrows raised.

'Do you think you could take me to live with you? No, no, you do not need to buy me from the palace, I have more than enough money saved and anyway my daughter would gladly let me go anytime... but I had nowhere to go.'

Misrakesi looked surprised and Mrinalini continued a trifle desperately, 'You are opening a dancing house. I could help you there; I have years of experience in the palace as you know and I am good at organization. I don't want any money; I want something to do... somewhere to go.'

'But will the Samragyi let you go? You have been like a mother to her.'

Mrinalini looked at the floor again, 'Now that my dear daughter is happily married and busy with her new duties, I have nothing to do. Her future is settled.'

From which Misrakesi gathered that the 'dear daughter' was busy being the feted queen of the Mauryas and had no dearth of confidants. Mrinalini must have become an undesirable relic from the past who brought back unhappy memories.

It did not take Misrakesi more than an instant to make up her mind. Mrinalini would be a godsend, taking the routine and tedious household duties off her hands. She was dependable and experienced and, moreover, her ties to the palace would always be an advantage.

'Mrinalini! That is a wonderful idea. You will be a great help. Consider yourself hired and make arrangements to move in as soon as you can.' She was moved to hug the older woman who flushed with happiness and gratification.

They decided that Mrinalini would move in straight to the house in a fortnight, by which time the nartakis from Ujjaini would also arrive and Misrakesi would also move in. There was only a month's time before the dancing house was to open.

Chandramukhi or the Ghost

The soul is not born, nor does it die;
It is not even that after being once it cannot be yet again.
It is constant, eternal and primeval;
Even if the body dies it does not die.

Bhagawad Gita 2.20

Misrakesi moved into her new home. It was ready to live in and to fulfill its function as a dancing house. She had decided to call it Apsara Sabha, an assembly of celestial nymphs! Mrinalini was in her element as the doyenne of the establishment and Misrakesi congratulated herself on her good luck.

In no time at all she was standing at the gate and welcoming four travel-weary women from Ujjaini along with their retinue and... a little boy! He was probably around ten years of age and was the son of one of the nartakis. Misrakesi was thrown off guard. She had little experience of children, but they definitely had no place in a dancing house. What had the directress been thinking of? Perhaps the sealed letter handed over to her would have the answer.

The four women were Manjari, Chitralekha, Ratibhama, and Chandrakala. The names jogged a memory and it suddenly came to Misrakesi that some whimsy (probably the directress!) had named them after magical nymphs in an old Paisachi Prakrit[23] collection of stories 'Bada Kaha'[24] written by Gunadhya centuries ago. They were probably not their real names. No matter, it was a charming idea;

maybe Misrakesi could carry this idea forward with future nartakis of the Apsara Sabha.

All the nartakis were despatched under the wing of Mrinalini to settle down in their new quarters. No doubt she would also make the necessary arrangements for the child. Misrakesi sat down to read the letter. It gave details of the skills and learning of the women. Manjari was the mother of the small boy and Misrakesi was adjured not to be bothered about the child. Manjari would take care of him and he never came in the way of her work. Manjari was a very capable woman and had been sent as a kind of second-in-command, if needed. Misrakesi trusted her guru implicitly and was therefore content to wait and see how Manjari and the child – in fact, all of them – settled down.

All the elements of the dancing house were now in place and ready to function. Misrakesi was more than satisfied with what she had achieved. It was rich and luxurious, yet elegant and understated, different from the usual gaudy red and gold of dancing houses. She was determined that the nartakis would be equally different and had spent some time explaining this to all of them. Apsara Sabha would have her stamp on it, for better or for worse. Each of the nartakis would be a byword for beauty, aesthetics, grace, and dignity. Hers would be no ordinary dancing house. The food and wine, like the rest of her supplies, were being sourced from the suppliers to the royal household and were therefore exclusive; thanks to Hiranyalabha and behind him the hidden hand of Pushyamitra.

But a dancing house needs above all, clients. It was also, therefore, necessary for Misrakesi and Mrinalini to meet all the people they knew and spread the word around. Misrakesi went to Hiranyalabha's house to tender a special invitation to him for the first evening which was to open with a dance performance by her. She was repeating the recital she had done at the Rajyabhishek so the value in terms of novelty and exclusiveness was high. Hiranyalabha greeted her with a conspiratorial smile. He was so much a part of the preparations that it was as if they were in this together even though the success or failure would not affect him as it would Misrakesi; it could be the making of her... or the ruin.

'Daughter, you know that I do not normally go to dancing houses. Sreelekha would have something to say to that... but I will try. My blessings are with you. I know you will succeed.' She touched his feet and he blessed her with a smile.

She went yet again to the palace and met the Samragyi who was pleased to take an interest in her activities. There were a number of people in her court and Misrakesi was only too happy to explain what she was doing in answer to a query.

'Your own dancing house! At such a young age! You are a woman of initiative,' Devi Dharini was surprised. Opening a dancing house was something nartakis did after retirement, not when they were glowing with youth and beauty like Misrakesi. Performing as well as managing a dancing house could be a very demanding task.

'All your blessings, Agramahishi,' said Misrakesi with bowed head and folded hands. Curiosity bubbled in all those who were present and Misrakesi left after a while, well satisfied that here was a group who would definitely talk of her. She did not yet know that being in the public eye was a double-edged sword. She had arrived on the public stage of Pataliputra but only the future would reveal the results of her performance on this stage.

Mrinalini had come with her and when they met to return to Apsara Sabha, Misrakesi found that publicity need not have worried her. Pushyamitra, or his network, had been at work. Extravagant rumours mixing fact with fiction were afloat and curiosity was rife about Misrakesi as the latest sensation in Pataliputra. The fact that she had performed at the Rajyabhishek was a great pull factor and rumour also hinted that there was some powerful man behind her, otherwise how could she set up such a dancing house so soon. Whose mistress was she?

Misrakesi was unaware of the stories being bandied around and Mrinalini did not feel the need to enlighten her. She knew that rumours had their own life and hoped that these would disappear when the next new story hit the city. In the meanwhile it was good for business and she was now committed heart and soul to the success of this venture. And so it happened that three months to the day after the fateful meeting with Pushyamitra, Misrakesi stood at the door of the Apsara Sabha welcoming her first guest, Pushyamitra himself. He had come early to look around and Misrakesi's heart was beating loudly in apprehension. She showed little of this, resplendent in a golden jamewar ensemble, glittering jewels and elaborately plaited hair, looking like a veritable goddess come to earth.

Pushyamitra was looking every inch the powerful and rich man that he was, a part of the elite of Pataliputra, a good cross-section of which would be present here today; he had done his best to ensure that. A thin, soft-yellow silk antariya was tied with a gold embroidered and vaidurya, ruby-encrusted flat kayabandh over his ridged abdomen. The swelling muscles of his forearms were emphasized by twin serpentine bajubands, armlets for upper arm, and a gem encrusted filigree necklace covered most of his chest. The ivory-coloured kausheya[25] uttariya was draped stylishly over both his arms. A twisted gold band with a huge ruby studded in between had replaced his trademark pearl headband.

They looked at each other for a moment. As always, when the moment of truth arrived, Misrakesi wished she had never thought of a dancing house and was sitting safely and quietly in Ujjaini. She felt certain that it was a mistake and she had wasted time, money and effort, but there was no escape now.

'Shall we go, Arya?' she said smiling painfully and swallowing. They went around the dancing house together and he inspected everything. Misrakesi had been inspired by her visits to the erstwhile Rajmahishi's Palace rooms while decorating the place.

The main hall was a huge one and, as was the custom, open to the breeze wafting in from the Ganga, as it had no walls. It was arranged around a central open space where the dance recitals would take place. All around, intimate groups of low couches with semal cotton stuffed mattresses and cushions were placed with small tripod tables within easy reach. The couches had delicate, intricately carved feet and were covered with silken coverlets embossed with flowers and decorated with tassels. The cushions ranged from as large as half a man's body to small enough to fit comfortably into the crook of an arm. Dominated by shades of blue, the atmosphere was luxurious and cosy.

The pillars in the hall were intricately carved with the likenesses of creepers with leaves, flowers and birds peeping out. This style had been popularized by the palace itself and Misrakesi had called in the same wood carvers for her own decorations. The illusion of being out in the open with the sky above and a garden all around was skilfully projected.

The seating arrangements were interspersed with carved statues of yakshas and yakshis and large flat brass water bowls with fragrant, multi-hued Atimukta, Ketaki, Yuthika, Maulasri, Akunda, Champak, Malati and other seasonal flowers scattered on them. Flowers were also scattered on the couches and around the dancing area. It was indeed an assembly fit for heavenly beauties and their admirers as the name of the place denoted.

The only partitions in the hall were the flowing curtains ranging from ivory mulmul to lilac and pale blue brocade. These were cleverly suspended so that they could be drawn in or opened at the request of the client. Silver edging to the cushions and curtains furthered the image of the night sky twinkling with stars.

Contrary to custom, the serving area of the tall, carinated clay pots of wine and the cups and bowls in which they would be served was kept in one of the connected rooms on the side. There was nothing to break the harmony of the hall as the food would also be brought in from one of the smaller rooms.

The small rooms leading off the main hall were decorated on a smaller and more intimate scale since they were meant for clients who would retire there with the nartakis or even the dasis if they so wished. They offered much more privacy and would also be useful for the hidden purpose for which Apsara Sabha had been established.

~

Misrakesi was walking a little ahead of Pushyamitra with her fists clenched nervously, looking back into his face every now and then to check his reactions as she showed him everything and explained the reason behind the arrangements. As they finished looking around the ground floor she moved to lead him upstairs but he held up a hand.

'No, no, I do not wish to inspect your private quarters, they are very much your own business.'

'Well?' she asked, as he said nothing, noting to herself that he had this infuriating habit of not letting his reactions show on his face.

He broke into a congratulatory smile and took her by the shoulders, shaking her gently.

'Misrakesi, you have done well. You have surpassed my expectations. I like it. I like your sense of style and the way you have put things together. The stage is set. Now you only have to use it as we have decided and the venture will be a success. Go now and prepare for your dance. It should be irresistible. I am going now to talk to your guests and mingle with them. I may not be able to stay for your performance, but do accept my best wishes. We shall speak in a few days.'

He patted her shoulders encouragingly and let her go, smiling again before he disappeared in an instant, as was his habit. Misrakesi watched him go, disappointment tempered with relief. At least he appreciated her hard work!

As she cast a last look around the main hall she suddenly found herself looking at an arrangement she had definitely not done. A graceful statue of a Yakshi adorning her hair with a mirror in her hand stood surrounded with numerous bowls of flowers and also draped with fresh flowers. It was looking well enough but she wondered who had had the temerity to change the arrangement done by her? Maybe it was Manjari.

In the bustle and excitement of the opening dance Misrakesi forgot about this incident. Hiranyalabha had decided to attend, much to her gratitude. Between them, he and Mrinalini were subtly instructing the dasas and dasis about the seating arrangements which were crucial. The guests had to be seated according to their status; any oversight could put off the concerned person forever. Mrinalini's knowledge of the subtle hierarchy between the leading citizens of Magadha had been garnered over years and was ably supplemented by Hiranyalabha. Mrinalini was no longer a dasi; she had bought her freedom and was a full-fledged member of – perhaps even the manager of – the household. She was appropriately clad in both clothes and manner and was fulfilling her responsibilities admirably. Misrakesi peeped in and was well satisfied.

She had decided to do her solo piece followed by the four others joining her for a group dance. Her gold Jamewar was complemented by the copper and earth toned dresses and jewellery of the other nartakis.

She took a deep breath and stepped to the centre; the encouraging faces of Mrinalini and Hiranyalabha beamed at her. Pushyamitra was there too and was looking at her quizzically. As always, Misrakesi was never apprehensive when she had to dance. She was a born dancer and forgot herself completely once she started, becoming one with the dance. Her drive to make Apsara Sabha a success inspired her and there was a stunned silence when she finished. The audience barely had time to react when she was joined by the four other nartakis; it was a feast for the rasikas and the uninformed alike. The five beautiful women, the ambience, their dancing prowess all came together to make this a memorable evening for the Magadhans gathered there.

It was a wonderful start. Men came in to gawk at the beauteous nartakis and stopped to eat the delicious food and sample the intoxicating, exotic liquors and wines. Apart from the high quality asavas, arishtas and maireyas, there were also suras of many kinds including svetasuras and sahakarasura[26] made from mangoes. Madhu[27] from Kapisayana and Harahuraka in the Gandharva Pradesh and beyond had been sourced with utmost effort. For those who did not want liquor, there were phalamlas and amlasidhus made from fruits and molasses. For the special guests the madhu was mixed with a decoction of sugar, datura, meshashringa, and powders of certain herbs and flowers including the blue lotus which made each kumbha[28] of this drink fit for a king. In fact the exact composition was known only to the royal kitchen from where it had been coaxed out by Mrinalini.

Meat of animals and birds had been prepared in innovative ways with pot herbs, oils, and ghee. There were also vegetables and all the dishes were served with rice or barley gruel or wheat rotis. Dainties, sweetmeats, and delicacies were limited only by the cook's imagination and Mrinalini's unlimited expertise.

Those who could resist these attractions were tempted by the roll of dice and the gambling and spent the night happily engaged in tumbling away their coins into the welcoming coffers of Apsara Sabha. Misrakesi had hired some professional gamblers to come in during the evenings and leave at its close. She was yet to make up her mind on offering them board and lodging. As with the rest, she would see how it worked out.

In the midst of all this, of course, were Misrakesi and her four nartakis moving like flashes of lightning among the guests, meeting and captivating all. Each of the dasis had also been chosen for her personal attributes, sweetness, and charm of manner. The women were like the suhaga which increases the glow of gold. Misrakesi was left exhausted but thrilled at the end of the night. It would work, it definitely would. She just had to build on this triumphant beginning.

As the days passed, Apsara Sabha's popularity grew and in a surprisingly short time it became a landmark in the area. Prosperous merchants and traders, royal officials, idle and pampered sons of rich fathers, foreign visitors from outside Jambudweepa, as well as travellers from other areas of the growing empire mingled with professional gamblers and enjoyed the music, dance, and flirtation available in plenty at Apsara Sabha. Officials of all levels who also had to be kept under observation ranging from the Prasastri and Samaharta to the Paura and Dandapal also made it their regular haunt.

Misrakesi had never worked so hard in her life. This was her venture, to win or lose and she was leaving no stone unturned to set her dancing house on firm foundations as opposed to being a mere passing fancy. She instituted a custom of selecting a few favoured clients every evening by offering them gold vark[29] covered betel leaves with her own hands and taking them to a separate room for a select Tambulagoshthi. This became a rage and clients fought for this honour. Misrakesi managed to make it something to boast of and many came to Apsara Sabha only in the hope of being selected by the fascinating Misrakesi for her personal attentions. Solo as well as group dance performances were frequent as she wanted the dancing house to have an artistic and cultural reputation as well; it was a personal vanity of hers. This meant concentrated practice and composition of new recitals. Soon, her Ujjaini dancing and music instructors joined her in Pataliputra. They would be crucial to keeping up the quality of the music and dance.

The daily administration of this complicated household was no mean task and Misrakesi blessed the good fortune which had inspired Mrinalini to throw in her lot with them. Fractious dasas and dasis, cooks, cleaners, helpers and suppliers were all kept under her amiable but firm thumb. Manjari and she had struck up an instant rapport and the two of them were an invaluable support for Misrakesi. She had spent her entire life in an institution for women run by women so this was familiar and comfortable for her with the added advantage that she was the one whose writ ran in this little fiefdom! Men were the focus of the dancing house but they had no presence on the top floors of the establishment, an irony which often amused Misrakesi.

The only man who mattered was Pushyamitra and he rarely ventured into the place. She had asked him for some time before Apsara Sabha started on its basic function of information gathering because she wanted the outward functions to be put on a firm foundation first. He had agreed. Misrakesi had also decided to keep men out of her own personal life. Professional flirtation ended with the session in Apsara Sabha and her bed was most strictly a single one. She was tired of men and wanted no personal relations for as long as she pleased. Her salary and its wise investment in trade was the security which gave her the option to exercise this choice apart from the promise she had extracted from Acharya Chanakya.

~

One morning Misrakesi decided to take some time off and relax. It was early and the sun was just rising over the far banks of the river, a soft inviting breeze was blowing in and she thought she would take a walk down to the river-bank. There was no need to dress up so she asked her personal dasi, a young and perpetually worried girl of sixteen, for her oldest red rain-proof Gandharan wrap and deer skin sandals.

Time went by without the appearance of Madlekha and Misrakesi was annoyed. She went into her chamber to find Madlekha feverishly going through her clothes. She was on her knees before the wooden trunks that housed Misrakesi's various precious garments. They were open and the contents were all out on the floor.

'What is the matter, Madlekha?'

A scared face was turned up to her: 'I cannot find your wrap, Mistress, nor the sandals,' was the hesitant reply. This was unbelievable. Stealing by any of the household was out of the question so the reason for the missing items would have to be Madlekha's carelessness.

Misrakesi picked up another wrap, sharply commanded Madlekha to find the wrap and shoes and went out seriously ruffled. She had often found her room untidy with her things looking as if they had been rifled through and she was inclined to blame her dasi for it. She would have to speak to Mrinalini about this.

A few minutes of walking down the riverbank and she felt considerably calmer. The wilderness was profusely dotted with both patal and shal trees and the red flowers of the one made a bright contrast with the white delicately scented blooms on the other. There were birds swooping amongst the trees and down on the water and she could make out Saras cranes standing on one foot amongst the pebbles in the shallow water and pecking for small fish and insects. Peacocks called to each other in the forest while parrots wheeled in a chattering green cloud above the tree tops.

Against this background, she gradually became aware of other sounds, a diffuse singing and the tinkling of anklets. The sweet voice of a woman singing of separation, loss, and heartbreak came wafting over the treetops. It was a local Magadhi folk song and Misrakesi was intrigued. Who was singing in the forest? Maybe one of her girls; but they were all Ujjainis and none of them knew the local dialect let alone a folk tune. Misrakesi was puzzled and she found herself dwelling uneasily on it even as she returned and started her daily shringar routine. She wanted to explain away this feeling of disquiet, but could not.

She called Mrinalini in to tell her to speak to Madlekha about being more careful, otherwise her dasi would have to be changed. The frequency with which she found her possessions disturbed was not acceptable. Mrinalini heard her out in silence and was about to say something when Misrakesi remembered the singing.

'Oh, and Mrinalini have you any idea who could be singing down on the riverbank below our house? It was a beautiful, trained voice not someone humming to pass the time. I heard it when I was walking down there in the morning.'

'My dear daughter, for someone of your intelligence you can be very blind at times. Your missing clothes, disturbed possessions... the singing; of course it is Chandramukhi,' Mrinalini said calmly and with so much certainty that Misrakesi was silenced for a minute before finding her voice.

'What do you mean? And how do you know about her? Who told you about her? Anyway, she is dead. She died months ago. Are you suggesting that...?'

Mrinalini interrupted in the tone of one explaining something to a small child, 'Of course, I know about her. All of us here do. The poor child's unquiet spirit wanders around this entire area, the house, the shrine, the groves, the woods, and the river. Where else would she go? She died suddenly and violently far from home, there were no proper last rites done to speed her soul's journey to Baikunth,[30] her body was not cremated. How can she be at peace?' Mrinalini nodded her head sadly.

Misrakesi was upset. She had not wanted the strange story of Chandramukhi to get about and here it was: under her very nose with everyone in her own household believing in it. Added to which were these disturbing... should she call them manifestations?

'Why do you say that, Mrinalini? Have you seen...?' her tongue faltered over the words. Could you actually see a dead person? She knew and implicitly believed in the immortality of the soul but that was a spiritual essence, not a physical entity.

'Mrinalini, sit down and explain what you are trying to say.'

'Daughter, the rooms which you live in at the moment were Chandramukhi's. Her presence here is natural and is the reason for the disturbances you are blaming Madlekha for.'

Misrakesi was silent and Mrinalini went on unchecked, 'Many of us living here have noticed a figure flitting in and out of the rooms and around the house. We have also heard the singing. In fact we leave offerings for her at the foot of the peepal tree. And they are always gone...' she finished impressively.

'Nobody sees her come or go but her presence is always there,' Mrinalini repeated in a grave voice.

Misrakesi had recovered herself by now, 'This is all nonsense, Mrinalini, and you seem to have affected the rest of the household also. This must stop immediately. The last thing we need as a dancing house is a reputation for a resident ghost. It could harm us by scaring off our clients. Please stop the talk and the offerings. I am leaving it to you.'

'But you do not understand, daughter, she is not an evil presence, but a benign one. She is here to help us, not harm us.'

Misrakesi stopped herself from asking how exactly Mrinalini knew this fact because she did not want to get into a pointless argument. Really, Mrinalini could be very aggravating at times. Reiterating her instructions she sent Mrinalini away but from the obstinate looks she was receiving she had doubts about whether they would be obeyed. It seemed that food, drink and clothes to appease the spirit would find their way to the foot of the peepal tree.

But she was restless and did not know what to make of it. To set her own mind at rest she sent out a group of men who searched each corner of the house and grounds. After that they searched the forest down below along the riverbank, half a kosa to the left and right. They came up with nothing.

That evening saw Misrakesi perform a newly composed solo with as much precision and skill as ever but her mind was elsewhere, worrying away at the 'spirit' and trying hard to explain everything to her own satisfaction.

After the performance she was, as per her usual habit, moving amongst the clients, talking, smiling, and inviting some of them to the special Goshthi with her golden Tambula. Apsara Sabha, as Misrakesi wanted, was becoming one of the centres of the arts in the city. That particular evening there were a few royal officials, rich merchants and a sprinkling of foreigners. A soulful young man was declaiming his latest poetic effusions to a critical audience.

As Misrakesi moved around the hall with a mechanical smile on her lips, her mind struggling with Chandramukhi, a new group of men entered and was respectfully seated by the appointed dasis. She soon became aware of one of them watching her with a peculiar expression on his face and the beginnings of a smile. Who could he be?

He seemed like the answer to a maiden's fantasy – tall, carelessly handsome with a rangy physique; a sparkle in his eyes and a witty jest on his lips for all who spoke to him. She could not have said what he was wearing but he stood out amongst all the men in their finery. He effortlessly drew attention to himself and Misrakesi could see Ratibhama already draped around him smiling coyly. She was the most beautiful and luscious of the four nartakis and was fast making a special niche for herself. She was also the one consistently on the lookout for herself and Misrakesi was almost certain she would not last long in Apsara Sabha. Who was she paying so much attention to?

And then it came to her. Could it possibly be… Siddharthak? One of Pushyamitra's most able lieutenants and a star of the Magadha Spy department. He specialized in disguises and his contacts in the world of gambling, drinking, and actors as well as indebted unfortunates were legendary. Misrakesi had heard innumerable stories about him from her sister and had in fact often wondered whether Sukesi had been half in love with him. She and Siddharthak had worked together on the last fateful case which had taken her life.

But this was not the time to dwell on the past. As soon as she realized who he was, she moved towards him with a practiced smile and a gracious welcome.

'Welcome, Arya Siddharthak,' she said softly, only for his ears, as she bent her head and then brought her palms together in a greeting, smiling into his eyes. Siddharthak looked slightly taken aback, thus addressed by name, but recovered at once.

'Charmed to meet you, Devi Misrakesi,' his smile was magnetic and Misrakesi found herself responding at once to his undoubted attraction. A part of her mind was busy with the fact that he had probably been sent by Pushyamitra and her grace period was over. The serious work of the dancing house now had to begin.

Madlekha was at her side with the platter of Tambula and Misrakesi offered it to him which he took with a significant look at her. She gestured to Ratibhama to escort him to the goshthi and indicated that she would join him there later. She was wondering whether she should withdraw with him into one of the curtained enclaves so that they could talk in solitude.

Her mind was still in a whirl when she had her second – and far more serious – shock of the night. Entering from the main gate was an old, gaudily dressed up man. With complete disregard for his age and stage in life he had a complicated pearl encrusted red pugree on his head and his uttariya was of the most expensive purple jamewar worn by brides, even his soft deerskin shoes were studded with sapphires. His eyes were lined with kohl and bright yellow marigold flowers adorned his neck and arms. Most of his teeth had rotted away but those that were left were being exhibited in horrible lecherous smiles at the nartakis and dasis. It was difficult, almost impossible to recognize him... but she did. It was Acharya Chanakya!

This could not be happening, she thought, desperately gathering her wandering wits together. Why was tonight the night when Apsara Sabha was being inspected; the very day when she was at her most absent-minded and worried? She had to give a brilliant account of herself. Everything should work as smoothly as a length of muslin running through a finger ring. Pushyamitra had told her that the acharya often disguised himself and moved around to keep his finger on the pulse of the city, but she had never expected him at the dancing house.

She started to move towards him but then recollected herself. He would have to wait his turn for her attention like the others. If she gave him away even inadvertently through any action of hers she would be thrown out of Pataliputra tied on a runaway horse. *So, careful, careful, Misrakesi,* she admonished herself. Not by any expression or gesture did she exhibit any recognition of the acharya. She asked Manjari to escort the old man to the special soiree. He accepted with a great show of pleasure, chuckling and flirting with Manjari and even presenting her with a ring from his little finger, *which was probably a fake,* Misrakesi thought to herself. Such gestures were completely in keeping with the character of the elderly roué that he was playing.

After a suitable interval had elapsed she went in and spent time with all the selected clients she had invited. The acharya she treated with the distant courtesy mixed with hauteur that she reserved for elderly lechs. She could have sworn she saw a flash of approval in the kohl-ringed eyes.

Misrakesi relaxed. After all, the dancing house was well organized and ran smoothly no matter who the visitors and she could hardly be quizzed on matters of state or policy in this setting.

She received extravagant compliments on her beauty and accomplishments and the wonder that was Apsara Sabha from Siddharthak. He did not have to work hard at attracting women, it came naturally to him and Misrakesi found herself responding, perhaps for the first time in her life, to a man who had set out to charm her. It was usually the other way around!

The evening passed away quite easily without any move from the acharya's side. Siddharthak left after telling her that both Pushyamitra and he would come late in the night the next day to set down the modalities for the actual function of the dancing house to start.

When the last reluctant client had been politely sent away and the deep malas extinguished plunging the main hall in darkness, Misrakesi went up to the terrace to sit down, calm herself and think about the day's events.

Misrakesi had filled the crocodile capital terrace[31] outside her room with shrubs and flowering vines and tiny, multi-hued, trained Himalayan Love Birds who lived among the leaves and perfumed flowers. There was a huge, comfortable chair with its back carved in the likeness of a peacock's tail which had been skilfully made to allow it to rock back and forth, and smaller matching chairs and tables. The eastern side had a door which led to her personal shrine to Goddess Shree where she prayed morning and evening. A few steps led down to the river bank where she was fond of walking.

She sat and sipped her nightly maireya of amla, triphala, meshasringa, jaggery, and pepper[32] and enjoyed the subtle scent of her favourite atimukta flowers which grew on the terrace. Misrakesi applied a paste of the dried flower petals and bark of the thick vine mixed with chandan every day to keep her skin soft, burnished, and glowing and give her a fragrance peculiarly her own.

What did the acharya's visit mean? She was certain that this inspection would lead to a summons in the near future for some specific assignment. She and her work were under observation. The acharya was known to not waste any time on inessentials and he had spent a good part of the night in Apsara Sabha. Siddharthak's visit meant the end of her grace period and it appeared that she would have to work in close contact with him. Misrakesi smiled to herself... that could be interesting. Her smile disappeared when she thought of Chandramukhi. What was she to make of it? Was there something in what Mrinalini had said?

The river was inky in the night, and merging into the formless horizon. There were no boats plying and a stillness hung over the busy routes interrupted only by the rustling of the trees and the soft movements of the nocturnal animals. Misrakesi had been staring sightlessly at the quiet river but suddenly her gaze focused and her eyes narrowed; was it a boat she could see on the riverbank? It was being rowed by what appeared to be a female figure with flowing hair below her waist. The figure was a grey indistinct blur and she could not make up her mind whether it was real or imaginary – a product of her unquiet mind. She got up and to go down and investigate but when her eyes went back to the river the boat was gone. Where in the wide expanse of the water had it disappeared?

Misrakesi came as close to being frightened as she had ever been in her life. In vain she tried to reason that it had all been a figment of her imagination brought about by Mrinalini's nonsense but the flowing hair and the bangles on the woman's hands stayed with her. She made her way as fast as possible, in fact she almost ran to her own chamber where Madlekha was yawning and waiting for her. Reassured by a human presence she asked Madlekha to sleep in her room for the night and then retired to sleep. But sleep was a long time in coming.

The morning brought no wiser counsel as she woke up feeling tired. No explanation for the phantom boat had occurred to her and she did not want to mention it to anyone for fear of fuelling more rumours. She went down to examine her own boat but could not find any sign of disturbance, no signs that it had been moved.

The evening was to bring her first formal meeting in Apsara Sabha with Pushyamitra and Siddharthak to finalize the functioning of the secret side of the dancing house, and her mind was feeling like a ball of cotton. This was not the time to give up on her hard work to make her venture a success. She would have to concentrate.

Siddharthak came early and engaged himself in a corner room in gambling with a few selected men who seemed to be his contacts, guessed Misrakesi. There was no sign of Pushyamitra till very late when most of the clients had left except the compulsive gamblers and those who were spending the night with their chosen nartakis. Misrakesi who was on edge, had put on a serene and confident face but was troubled by the incident of the night before as well as apprehension about the coming meeting.

The dasi at the door was dozing, but Misrakesi was there to welcome Pushyamitra in and take him straight to Siddharthak's chosen room. The other gamblers were dismissed immediately and Pushyamitra sat down silently. He was tired and irritated and wanted nothing more than to snatch a few hours of sleep. He had been chasing a band of robbers in the forests just outside Pataliputra since dawn and had not been off his horse for twelve hours. They had been tracking this group for a couple of days and the worrying part was that they had a cosy hideaway tucked away in the forests within easy access from the city. It was all too well organized to be the idea of a crude band of robbers and he had to find out who was behind it. The truth was being beaten out of the survivors while he had come here. It was high time that this started functioning as a centre of intelligence gathering as it was intended to. A number of the clients would bear investigation.

Misrakesi could see the fatigue on his face and signalled to Madlekha who at once produced a pot of flower infused water and washed Pushyamitra's feet and hands with it. Other dasis came in with food; rice gruel, fried meats, fruit, and wine. Siddharthak had been drinking steadily but Misrakesi knew that Pushyamitra was not too fond of liquor and she had an invigorating and cooling mango phalamla offered to him.

Without realizing it Pushyamitra relaxed and felt more able to cope with the meeting than he had thought. The relaxation showed on his face. Misrakesi thought complacently that this was after all a dancing house, meant for the relaxation and entertainment of men and it was only fitting that Pushyamitra should also appreciate this.

She was sitting in her usual graceful posture with her feet tucked under her and body inclined and waiting for her instructions. The two men in front of her were a contrast, one was inscrutable and expressionless, his personality kept him at a distance, while the other was a veritable Kanha in Brindavan, who was wrapped in the warm cocoon of his regard and enticed women into his embrace.

Siddharthak was half reclining on a low couch with a cup of prasanna[33] prepared with a decoction of madhulika and sugar in his hands; he always made it a point to sample all the wares on offer at Apsara Sabha. Pushyamitra was also on a couch but sitting upright with his hands on his knees, head angled, expression abstracted and looking out into the night.

Misrakesi would have been surprised to know what Siddharthak was thinking as he looked at her making a beautiful picture of alluring womanhood. He was going over his conversation with Pushyamitra. Siddharthak had wondered why the establishment of such an important centre had been entrusted to a woman and that too somebody new in the city and the department.

Pushyamitra had raised his eyebrows and said,'No one else came to me with this proposal. You will not deny that such a meeting point was a need crying out to be fulfilled. She put in words and proposals, a need which I had been subconsciously thinking of for some time. It was Hiranyalabha behind her, of course. He is my oldest and best spy in the city. She told me details which could have been supplied only by him. She won his confidence first and that was what made me decide in her favour. And don't be taken in by her looks, she is a clever and determined woman. She is at her toughest when she looks her most submissive.'

When Siddharthak looked unconvinced he said, 'The dancing house has come up very well and if she cannot run the intelligence side well enough I shall give it to someone else. You will have to use it as your centre of operations for now. Information, money and supplies to your contacts as well as some of our meetings may also take place there. Meet me there tomorrow night. Come with details of what you want from her establishment. You should know best what you want.'

What Siddharthak wanted first was to sleep with her. He was a committed connoisseur of women; the only one who had made any kind of lasting impression on him was Sukesi, and here was her sister. He would look forward to this particular conquest with interest; he did not doubt that it would happen. He had not yet met any woman who could resist him and Misrakesi had responded satisfactorily to him in their last meeting.

'So, Misrakesi, the time has come for you to start functioning as a centre of information gathering. And also act as a centre for my guptachars operating in this part of the city. Are you ready?' Pushyamitra began by patting her back encouragingly.

'As ready as I ever will be, Arya,' responded Misrakesi calmly although she resented this patronizing back-patting Pushyamitra sometimes indulged in. She was not a child, although she was a novice. Time would soon show him that.

'From what we discussed initially I have gathered that you want me to do the following,' and she went on to spell out the specifics that she assumed Pushyamitra wanted from her: lists of the clients, their kin and contacts, their businesses and properties, any changes in their habits or income, all indiscreet boasts and whatever they confided to their mistresses in the grip of lust or drink. Since all the nartakis or dasis could not be openly asked to do this she had decided to institute a kind of collective discussion with all of them every morning so that she herself could pick up the necessary nuggets for passing on.

As for acting as the headquarters for disbursals to guptachars she had been in touch with Hiranyalabha who was the accountant for secret operations of the Nagarik Suraksha Vibhag and she had a request, 'Arya, since I am the only one who is to know about these activities it will be very difficult for me to keep an account of all the money or supplies handed out. Either you allow me to take one of my nartakis in confidence or send one of your men for the disbursal each time. Otherwise the details may get lost in the general accounts of Apsara Sabha. In case of an emergency of course I can oblige. And again, I assume that the lion seal will be the code. You will not be able to convey passwords to me every time they change.'

She stopped with an enquiring look on her face. Pushyamitra, who was smiling faintly as she went on, straightened up with his smile now more pronounced and said, 'You leave me with nothing to add but that yes I will send my own man for the actual disbursal. Siddharthak?'

There was a further detailed discussion between Misrakesi and Siddharthak and Pushyamitra got up and went to stand near the billowing curtains and look out over the river. There was a faint elusive perfume in the room which always brought Misrakesi to his mind – atimukta. He took a deep breath and savoured the suddenly peaceful moment, leaving the discussion to the other two.

Siddharthak, in the meanwhile was going through a very strange experience. Not only did he have to revise his opinion of the novice, but also had to contend with being the third in a situation where Pushyamitra and Misrakesi seemed to be enclosed in a diffuse circle of reactions to each other which kept others at a periphery. He was preternaturally sensitive to women and he found to his chagrin that this one was conscious of only one man and that was not him; not something he was used to. He was also, however, a rasika, a man ready to play the strange game of love and was amused when he realized that they were unaware of their own behaviour. The future could be interesting.

The meeting was over with the decisions taken and the two men left. Misrakesi made her way to her own bed hoping there would be no nocturnal distractions and was happy to sleep straight through the night.

Apsara Sabha continued to put down firm roots in the city of Pataliputra. The quick success also meant new problems. The interrelationships between the existing nartakis aside, which Misrakesi left to Mrinalini, there was an urgent need to hire more dancers as the present number was inadequate for the number of clients who made their way to Apsara Sabha every day. The house itself had enough space to accommodate this extension. The ever-resourceful Mrinalini had come up with a list of nartakis from Pataliputra itself, since calling them from Ujjain again would be complicated and even unnecessary given the popularity already enjoyed by the dancing house. Misrakesi decided to sit down with Manjari and Mrinalini to finalize the list. There was little fear of the invitation being turned down given the reputation, salary and prospects of nartakis in Apsara Sabha.

The decision was made and messages dispatched to four fortunate young women: 'Leelavati', 'Kamkandala', 'Kamda' and 'Pushpavati', as Misrakesi had already named them after the nymphs in 'Bada Kaha'. They would start work immediately.

With the new dancers finalized, Misrakesi introduced the topic which had been bothering her for some time.

'Mrinalini, do you know the exact circumstances of Chandramukhi's death? I mean, was her body ever found?' she asked, as she had decided to find out as much as possible about the dead girl and her murder.

Mrinalini gave her a knowing look before replying, 'They had stopped at an old abandoned vihara for the night. I believe that a band of robbers attacked them at night with a huge force. They were all killed and their bodies thrown down a nearby well. Then those paapis ran off with all the valuables. As you know, only an old servant survived the night to send word to the family through another band of travellers who arrived at the vihara the next morning.'

'But were any of the bodies recovered?' persisted Misrakesi.

'I don't think so although I do not know all the details. But they would all probably have drowned in the deep well.'

So no one had seen the corpse of the 'ghost'. A point to note, although to what effect Misrakesi did not yet know.

Manjari, who had been listening carefully to all this said, 'Sister, I think while we are on the subject I must tell you something that has been bothering me. My son, Som, has told me that he has made friends with the "ghost" and often speaks to her. Now I don't know if it is his imagination influenced by all the talk that goes on here or ...'

There was a short silence while Misrakesi digested this; Mrinalini did not look surprised while Manjari looked worried.

'Perhaps I could speak to Som, that is, if he will not be upset by it?' asked Misrakesi.

'Oh, no! He is never upset by anything. He will be happy enough to chat with you. I will call him here.'

'No, don't. I will go out where he is playing,' said Misrakesi getting up.

He was sitting outside in the sun and playing with mud making clay figures. A few horses and carts were drying in the sun and he was busy trying to fashion a dancing girl out of mud. The figures were in fact very good for his age. Maybe he had a future as a sculptor. She had not really spent much time with him but found him a very engaging child with a solemn face and round eyes and cheeks. She sat down beside him and started making mud pies not knowing exactly how to start. It was a surprisingly absorbing past time.

'How do you like your new home, Som?'

'It's alright,' he hunched a shoulder and went on, 'but I don't have anyone to play with. I had so many friends before,' and he opened his arms wide to show Misrakesi the extent. She smiled and pulled his cheek, 'Don't worry, you will make new friends here, too. Very soon.' She said nothing else, hoping he would mention his friend without her asking, but he went on with the dancing girl's figure.

'Your mother said that you have made a new friend,' Misrakesi introduced the topic cautiously.

'Oh… yes I have.' He remained busy with the little figure; he was fashioning a hand held up in a kind of dancing mudra. He looked up from it finally and said without a pause for breath, 'She doesn't really play with me and she doesn't have any face or hands or legs and she is white but she tells me many nice stories.'

Trying to keep the alarm and confusion out of her voice all Misrakesi could manage was, 'No arms or legs?'

'Yes, but she has a voice, so she can tell me stories.' Tiring of her questions he got up and ran in to the house.

Taken at face value this could only strengthen Mrinalini's view of the business as her expression only too clearly said. Manjari was disturbed and worried, wondering what to do. But she was a sensible woman, not prone to panic or instant decisions. They discussed whether they should call in priests and conduct a yagya for purifying the house. Misrakesi was not in favour of doing so. It would cause a great deal of avoidable speculation and her imagination also baulked at accepting the presence of a ghost. They decided to wait.

Mrinalini was reassuring, 'Do not look so worried, daughter. I told you she was a benign spirit and will only keep a watch over all of us.'

Misrakesi was too disturbed to reply.

As the days went by, however, she was forced to admit that Mrinalini was right. There were no calamities or instances of any disturbances by the 'ghost'. Apsara Sabha easily fell into the habit of invoking Chandramukhi as an ishtadevi, a benign guardian spirit of the place. They had all been cautioned against talking about this to outsiders so their reputation remained intact and they continued to prosper like the waxing moon.

But Misrakesi was uneasy. She often had the feeling of being watched, in her room or even out in the wilderness or on the riverbank. Her possessions still suffered and some things would go missing every now and then. She had the distinct feeling that the 'ghost' was targeting her. She would often wake up in the night to an absent presence in the room as if someone had just left. She had started sleeping badly and it was beginning to affect her temper.

It extended itself to the dancing house. One night, as Misrakesi was entertaining a client, he asked her where the dasi called Chandramukhi was, who had entertained him with interesting stories the last time he had come. Misrakesi was so shocked that the beryl-encrusted cup of Harahuraka[34] Madhu fell from her nerveless fingers and splashed the silk wrought carpet. The liquor had been procured at great expense and each drop was worth its weight in gold, to say nothing of this display of clumsiness from a renowned nartaki and the ruining of the carpet. She made a smiling excuse and motioned to Chitralekha to take over.

Misrakesi woke in the middle of the night from a troubled sleep with her heart thudding wildly; she was certain that someone had just touched her face. But there was no one in the room. The terrace curtain was billowing in the breeze but there was no sign of any human.

She sat up, completely awake now, lit the lamps and did some hard thinking. It was between her and the 'ghost' now. Either she believed in its otherworldliness or she believed in the evidence of her senses. She was convinced there was a human agency, a girl out there in the forest who was managing to disturb her and become a hindrance to her peaceful existence, evading all attempts at discovery. Going on like this was impossible so she sat up all night thinking of ways and means to flush Chandramukhi out. Her hideout, wherever it was, was skilfully hidden and not amenable to exposure; so she would have to be forced to come out in the open. But how?

The next morning, a bleary-eyed but determined Misrakesi called the superintendent of all the dasas in Apsara Sabha, a brawny and burly man in his fifties (whom she suspected of being Pushyamitra's man; she had no illusions that her household was not infiltrated by him), and gave him certain orders. By the afternoon, the news was all over Apsara Sabha. Misrakesi had asked for permission from the city authorities to cut down the wilderness behind the house and extend the building as the business was increasing by leaps and bounds.

Mrinalini came to her with a grave face and said, 'Don't do this, my daughter. There is nothing to be gained by disturbing the spirits of the dead.'

Misrakesi merely gave her an exasperated look and refused to engage in any discussion. It was very difficult to counter Mrinalini's illogical arguments and quotations from the Sutras. She had noticed in Mrinalini a certain tendency to be complacent if not downright dictatorial. The change from being an old dasi to the doyenne of an establishment of young people was showing. Misrakesi, however, had grown to be really fond of her, she had a heart of gold and her advice was generally useful. But Misrakesi was not ready to take it this time; that was all.

The permission asked for came in due course. Misrakesi set about hiring the necessary workers to supplement the men in her establishment. In the meanwhile, the spirit sightings had become more numerous and sometimes the offerings seemed almost to be snatched from the hands of the devotees. So the ghost was getting upset, thought Misrakesi, chuckling inwardly. She was by now convinced that it was a girl out there: one, moreover, who had something special against her.

It was now a war of nerves between her and the ghost. She did not have the money or the resources to clear the entire wilderness and could only hope that the possibility and appearance of cutting down the forest would force Chandramukhi to show herself. In actual fact, although the Apsara Sabha was doing well it was also an expensive place to run and there was no question of having generated enough profits to plan extensive additions. It was a lie which would have to work for the 'ghost' to appear in front of her.

Another week went by, but no ghost. It was now time for the next move, to actually cut down the trees and clear the undergrowth. Misrakesi could afford very little of this, it was a trick of the last resort. Thus, the place where the cutting down would start was of vital importance. After consideration she decided to start with the area where she had sometimes seen a flash of red from her terrace.

The next day saw at least twenty men at work there from dawn to dusk. A nice little clearing was accomplished by the time the men put down their iron axes. Maybe she could use fire to clear the area, it would be considerably cheaper but very dangerous; not only the ghost but also the house itself could be in danger. She abandoned the thought and went in to get ready for her performance.

This was the night – either Chandramukhi would reveal herself tonight or Misrakesi's trick would fail because she could not afford to spend any more on cutting down the forest. Of course, even if the ghost did exist and lived in some hideout in the forest she could just choose to go away. But somehow Misrakesi did not think that any ghost would like to give up such a comfortable and well provided existence. If she did exist... Misrakesi's entire strategy was based on this assumption. Sometimes she did not know whether she was ridding her home of a ghost or could not bear to lose in what was rapidly becoming a battle of wits between her and Chandramukhi.

Misrakesi sent Madlekha off summarily that night without indulging in the usual leisurely chat she had with her about the day's events. She had made a habit of this since it would never do to have Mrinalini being the only conduit for information on household affairs. She asked Madlekha to light the tapering deepmala in one corner which illuminated the entire room and leave. She sat down to wait.

The night darkened and then started lightening. Misrakesi was pacing up and down. It would soon be morning and she would have wasted a great deal of time and effort for nothing. She heard a slight rustling but it came to nothing... maybe a small animal outside. The curtain moved... but it was only the breeze from the river.

Tired of staying up and worn out with pacing up and down, Misrakesi lay down on her bed and closed her eyes.

She awoke with a start, her room was a blaze of lights, all the lamps had been lit. And then someone stepped out from behind the shadows,

'You win, Misrakesi.'

The Ghost's Story

Thieves should not be trusted.

Chanakyasutra 251

~

The sudden blaze of light hurt Misrakesi's eyes. She raised her hand to shield her eyes and saw a figure detach itself from the shadows and stand before her.

So this was Chandramukhi! There was not even a vestige of a pampered setthi's daughter in her appearance. She looked like a tough, coarse forest dweller. Her clothes (some of which were extremely familiar to Misrakesi!) were torn and frayed in places, especially the uttariya. Her hair was long, below her waist and hung in unevenly cut ringlets. But she walked with a swagger and there was no self-consciousness in the once-beautiful features. There was a dagger slash across her left cheek, a horrific scar which ran down her neck and disappeared or perhaps continued across her back. This was no ghost but a girl of flesh and blood.

'You win, Misrakesi,' she repeated when the former was mute, looking up as if transfixed. She came forward and sat down at the edge of the bed and said aggressively, 'So what are you going to do now that I am out in the open before you? Denounce me? I hardly think so.'

She smiled as if she had the upper hand over Misrakesi and started walking around the room pretending to admire it. 'Hmm. You have kept my room well. You do know that this was my room for more than twenty years? I grew up here. I know every corner like the palm of my hand.'

Misrakesi shook herself out of the sudden shock and spoke up at last, 'Chandramukhi, why have you been haunting and terrorizing my household? Why are you here? You were obviously not killed by the robbers? What happened?'

Chandramukhi chose to ignore the last few questions, 'Haunting and terrorizing? Not really!' She gave a short unamused laugh, 'I have been your protective spirit. And I know this house better than any of you. I can slip in and out as I wish.' She picked up a banana and peeled it, eating it as unconcernedly as if she were indeed the daughter of the house.

Misrakesi was losing control of the situation. She had not envisaged such a confident and insouciant Chandramukhi. 'Why have you come here?' She repeated.

'Why have I come here?' echoed Chandramukhi with a furrow between her brows, 'Where else would I go? This is... well, *was*, my home and family. And you drove them away,' she shook an angry finger at Misrakesi.

The untruth of this struck Misrakesi forcefully but there was no point in fruitless argument. It was important to talk to this girl and convince her to go away for her own good; maybe she *would* if threatened with disclosure.

'Now that they are no longer here, what do you gain by staying? And why, in the name of Goddess Shree are you leading this peculiar life?'

'I see. You will not rest till you have my pitiful story out of me. All right, come with me.' She moved onto the terrace in a lithe movement and jumped off onto an overhanging branch of the Patal tree nearby shinning down it before Misrakesi could react. 'Come on,' she whispered urgently.

No wonder I could never catch her in the room, thought Misrakesi as she followed through the more conventional route of the steps. *Not only does she know the house and its surroundings intimately, she is also very fast and agile.*

Chandramukhi led the way through the trees and dense undergrowth, glancing back at intervals to see if Misrakesi was following her. It was not a very long walk from the house. Under a large Patal tree she stopped and pulled up a woven mat of grass and creepers disclosing an iron cover to an underground passage. The woven mat had been completely indistinguishable from the forest floor and Misrakesi could have spent years combing through the forest without finding it. Chandramukhi beckoned to her and lowered herself into the passage. Misrakesi followed in silent surprise.

The passage was small and led into an underground chamber. Misrakesi entered and gasped. It was a small but self-sufficient room furnished comfortably, not to say luxuriously. She could recognize a number of things which had been missing from the house as well as some that had been offered to the spirit haunting the house.

Misrakesi turned to her accusingly but Chandramukhi only laughed and gestured back, asking her to sit. 'I had this secret underground chamber built some years ago on a whim. No one except one of my brothers knew about it and he must have forgotten about it long ago. It was a passing fancy like many of my other passing fancies. Little did I know that it would be my home and sanctuary one day.'

'Do you mean you have been living here for the past year without being discovered?' asked Misrakesi disbelievingly.

'It is, or was, not very easy to find me. If I had not been carried away and come into my old room too often, mingled so much with your household, I could have been a ghost living in my secret room for as long as I wanted. If indeed anyone can *want* to be a ghost and live such a life.'

Chandramukhi was quiet, sunk in some obviously ugly reflections, her face a mirror of her thoughts.

'What happened, sister?' Misrakesi asked, gently, moved by what she saw.

'I do not have and have never had a sister so you can spare me the pity,' said Chandramukhi sharply. 'Any way, you may as well hear what happened to me. It may serve as an object lesson to someone, anyone...'

She resumed after a pause.

'You would know that I was the adored and pampered daughter of my father and the sister of four loving elder brothers. There was nothing in the known world that I wanted and did not get. Then I was married, to Shreedhan. And it seemed that I was the favoured of the Devas because he fell into the pattern too. There was nothing he would not do for me. The day began and ended with me and if he neglected his duties in the warehouse, Pitaji was only too happy to ignore it because I was happy. But distrust your destiny when it seems to be giving you too much.

'I do not remember whose idea it was to visit the temple at Kasi. Mine perhaps, but certainly suggested by something he had said. We set off, amply provided with the means for the journey and, of course, much more gold with me in case I wanted to buy something when Pitaji was not there to indulge me. My personal jewellery, both what I always wore and that which I carried with me was worth a king's ransom. Shreedhan encouraged me to take more than I needed. I love... loved... finery and it was his duty to indulge my every wish. It was all too good to be true. What a husband I have lost!

'The first few days passed pleasantly. In spite of my pampered life, or perhaps because of it, I had been out of the city only on rare occasions and I enjoyed the sense of freedom. The armed men with us were not from my father's entourage but had been chosen personally by Shreedhan and so I felt secure. They looked very alert and efficient.

'On the ninth day, Shreedhan suggested that we should make a detour and stay the night at an old ruined vihara reputed to have been made for Bhagwan Buddha himself two hundred years ago but long since abandoned. Some of the murals on the walls still survived and were highly reputed. I wanted to see them so I agreed. We reached there in the evening and set up camp. It was late and I was tired so I thought I would see the murals the next day and went to sleep early.

'I suddenly woke up somewhere in the middle of the night. Shreedhan was not beside me. As I lay there, drowsy, half in and half out of sleep I could hear some whispers. I was not really listening but I heard something which shocked me into wakefulness. "Kill them all," someone was whispering. I was too scared to move. Opening my eyes slowly I could make out that most of our camp was asleep except for our armed escorts and they had been joined by some twenty or thirty armed horsemen who must have come from the forest. They were discussing how best to kill us all and run away with the loot.

'As you can imagine I was scared numb. I looked around desperately for Shreedhan but he was not there. I then tried to look for Kirat, an old and trusted servant of ours. I could just about see where he was sleeping but before I could reach him the killing began. Soon the whole camp was a mass of agonized screams and throttled death rattles. I panicked and ran, I do not know where. One of the horsemen caught me and dragged me back. He quickly tore off my jewellery and raised his sword to kill me. I am not ashamed to admit that I begged for mercy. I promised him much more money than he had ever imagined if only he would let me go to my father. He appeared to waver... but he said he would have to ask his chief.

'His chief... as I waited, cowering, a man who had tied the end of his pugree around his face so that only his eyes were visible came up on a magnificent black horse, which happened to be mine. My captor spoke to him and he came up to me. He removed his cloth mask and spoke to me.

"Let you go back to your father? No, my dear wife, how can I do that?"

'It was Shreedhan. It was all his plan... from the beginning to the very end.

I looked at him, dazed, unable to utter a word. He laughed – an ugly sound – and planted the tip of his sword on my neck, "You know you have to die, don't you... you have had a short but lovely and pampered life, my darling wife," and with those words he pushed me into the well behind me. As I turned to try and save myself his sword gashed my face, neck, and back. I still have the scar to remember him by. I struck my head against the side of the wall and lost consciousness. The last sound I heard was of the horsemen riding away.

'To his misfortune, however, what he did not know was that the well was dry and I did not drown. In fact they had thrown a few more bodies in before me and so my fall was cushioned in a way. But I had cracked the back of my head open.

'I do not know how long I lay there. When I opened my eyes, I was in a Jain ashram. A group of shramans passing by had heard my groans and rescued me. Their medicines and care brought me back from certain death. I stayed with them till I was able to take care of myself. My health improved… my spirits… I have probably lost them forever.

'Those months of slow recovery were torturous. I had never known anything but love, affection and care. To receive such a betrayal from my husband, who I had learnt to care for after marriage and who had given me every reason to do so, was beyond my wildest nightmares! And then… my scar. What you see on my cheek and neck is just a part of it. My back is even worse.'

Chandramukhi moved and Misrakesi flinched.

'No, don't worry, I am not about to show it to you. Just trying to explain what I felt and why I could not bring myself to send word to my family.

'But why am I telling you all this? This is the first time I have spoken of this to a living soul… having started I find I cannot stop. Everything is coming back to me… I thought I had got over it…

'Anyway the next part is where this house, my home and later, you, come in. After my physical wounds had healed I could not keep myself away. I just wanted to see them all, my father, mother, brothers, nieces, and nephews. The shramans would have gladly let me stay with them for as long as I wanted. But I am not cut out to be a sanyasini.

'When I came here I could not muster up enough courage to go in front of them, the wreck that I was. Perhaps they were better off thinking I was dead. I remembered my secret room and started living here. I spent my days in the forest learning the ways of the water front folks and the forest dwellers. The shramans had also taught me a great deal about self reliance and the world of plants and animals.

'As time passed I could not resist the temptation to talk to my mother who was almost mad with grief. I would not reveal myself fully to her and she thought I was a spirit. This suited me and I encouraged her to think so.

'I was desperate to go back to my family but could never bring myself to do so. On innumerable occasions I came this close to revealing myself,' Chandramukhi held up her hand with the finger and thumb touching to emphasize her point.

'But it was precisely that which was my undoing. As you know, my father was so worried about my mother that he took them all away to Kasi. I was left alone and sorrowing... because you bought the house. If no one had bought the house maybe they would not have gone away.

'Anyway, I managed as best as I could in the forest and along the waterfront. And then you and your household came along and became a source of food, clothes, other necessities and also a kind of human contact. I forgot myself so much as to talk to Som for hours. But I would wrap myself in a white uttariya and never show my face. It was as if I had found one of my little nephews again. And...that's about it. That is my story. What are you going to do about it?' the challenge in her voice jolted Misrakesi out of her sympathy.

Misrakesi did not know what to say or indeed what to do. As she had been listening to the story she found her anger and irritation with the ghost melting away to be replaced by shock and then gradual sympathy. It was a gruesome story of greed and betrayal. What kind of man must Shreedhan be?

She was silent for a while considering what to say. The look on Chandramukhi's face warned her against expressing all her sympathy and pity. It would be repulsed, she was certain. Finally she said gently, 'Your story is a very shocking and sad one but what a woman you must be to have come out of it alive and to have managed all these months as you have.'

It was clear that Chandramukhi had not considered this aspect of her life before and a surprised smile lit up her face, 'Yes, you are right. There must be more of my father in me than I realized. You do know that he came from a poor family and became rich only through hard work and persistence, all his own efforts. He would often tell me stories from his past and he definitely never gave up in the face of adversity. And he always said that he would make sure that I never had to face anything tough in life.' Her laugh was richly ironic.

'Chandramukhi, it is so clear from what you say that you love your parents and family very much. Nothing that happened is your fault, you were a victim. Why are you torturing yourself and them by keeping away? Just imagine how happy they will be to find that you are alive and well.'

'Alive, yes. But well? No, no, I can never go back to them in this state. My father would never forgive himself for what happened to me. He had chosen Shreedhan. How would he live with the result of this choice before him all the time? As it is, all of them will forget me and get over their sorrow in time. You don't understand but I can never go back.'

'I know I can never understand. How can I? I never had a mother or father, only a sister who is now dead. Both my parents died when I was a baby and my relatives sold us to the Training Academy. I have no family but I am sure if I did I would go to them no matter what,' replied Misrakesi.

'Spare me the emotional appeal,' said Chandramukhi harshly and turned away dashing her hands across her eyes.

'But what am I to do?'

'Do? Absolutely nothing. You are going to do nothing. If you try to do anything about me you will regret it. The whole of Pataliputra will know just who you are and what goes on here under the cover of a dancing house. You are a spy in the pay of the kutil Chanakya... and Apsara Sabha is nothing but an elaborate trap set by you and that Pushyamitra.'

She laughed triumphantly at the look of surprise and dismay on Misrakesi's face and came to stand threateningly before her.

Misrakesi was stunned. She had never expected Chandramukhi to discover the reality below the singing, dancing, and beauty on the surface. And here she was, almost, one could say, in the power of this strange, solitary, and probably unbalanced girl.

'Ghosts know everything.' Chandramukhi said mockingly, 'And they use it to their own advantage too!'

There was a small silence and then Chandramukhi got up, hustling Misrakesi before her.

'And now, Devi Misrakesi, I think it is time for us to seek our beds. You have your dancing house to run and I have my reputation as a ghost to consider! Remember, not a word to anyone.'

Misrakesi walked back slowly to the house. She had a lot to think about. Sleep was a long time in coming. What a tragic story and what a strange and bitter girl. Of course the experience was enough to twist anyone's character. And she was in the power of this girl. It was an unstable situation. How long could Chandramukhi remain hidden in her underground room? And how could she be trusted with the truth about Misrakesi and the establishment. Not to mention what Pushyamitra would say if he found about Chandramukhi. It was too much... Misrakesi drifted off to sleep and into strange and disjointed dreams about Shreedhan and a threatening Pushyamitra who enveloped her in his arms and whose gaze she could not meet.

The next morning she gave orders for the clearing of the trees to stop, saying she had changed her mind about the extension. No one except Mrinalini and Manjari was really concerned. On being accosted by Mrinalini she gave a garbled account of a visitation in the night which had led to her change of heart. Mrinalini did not notice the sarcastic glint in her eyes and went away well satisfied as Misrakesi had known she would be.

That took care of the household but did not solve the problem. Adding to her worries was the impending next assignment she was certain was coming. With Chandramukhi's presence haunting her wherever she went she found it difficult to concentrate on anything. For the first time even her dance suffered; she missed the taal[35] while practicing. The censure in the eyes of her accompanist served to pull her together but she remained deeply worried.

The expected summons came in the form of an invitation to Hiranyalabha's house. Chandramukhi had not put an appearance for the last few days. Maybe she had been warned off but certainly not permanently. Her hold over Misrakesi was very strong and she knew it.

Misrakesi had thought it would be an individual briefing but it was very clearly not. It was a huge affair in honour of the birth of a son to the younger brother of Hiranyalabha. Sreelekha was in her element welcoming the guests, bullying her sister-in-law and directing the proceedings in a loud voice. She welcomed Misrakesi, too, but her smile stopped just short of being cordial. Hiranyalabha met her with his customary affection and introduced her to his honoured guests. She was aware of a twinge of guilt, since Apsara Sabha had established itself she had seen very little of him. He should not feel that she had made use of him and when she had no further need of him, dropped him. She resolved to come and meet him more frequently.

Hiranyalabha's house had extensive grounds as befitted a rich setthi; there were trees, shrubs and plants, vines and creepers, colourful, perfumed flowers and even fruit orchards. These were interspersed with water fountains, small lotus ponds, and swings under the great mango trees. It was a festive assembly with different kinds of entertainment including buffoons, jugglers, mimicry artists, and singers. The guests were eating dainty dishes, exotic meats and drinking intoxicating drinks. They were a mixed assembly, a cross section of the powerful and the prosperous. Misrakesi could see many of her rival establishment's ganikas gracing the assembly, although none of the matrikas could hold a candle to her as far as youth and beauty were concerned. They had mostly long since retired, but the most accomplished and fascinating nartakis were very much in prominence looking for prospective clients or just flaunting themselves in front of an admiring crowd.

There were family groups, too. Misrakesi could see a shy young girl accompanied by an elder woman, maybe her mother or sister being introduced to a prospective bridegroom and his family and she watched the little play, interested.

This was the first time Misrakesi had attended such an assembly and she was an object of much curiosity, comment, and covert glances. Many of the male guests wanted to appropriate her company but she had the misfortune of being stuck with the head of the Goldsmiths Guild, a short, fat, self-important man named Prajapati who impaled her with his glance and thought that he was making a wonderful impression on this new star on Pataliputra's firmament by instructing her in the business of goldsmithing.

Misrakesi was fairly caught, unable to get rid of him, a polite smile fading on her lips, eyes hunting desperately for escape.

Pushyamitra was also there, standing apart from the others and watching everything that was going on with an aloof look in his eyes. The nature of the day's proceedings was such that it was an official necessity for him to be here. Otherwise he was in no need of any briefing nor was he needed to conduct it since that would be done by someone else.

He noticed Misrakesi cornered by one of Hiranyalabha's most pompous and painful setthi-friends and the frozen look on her face. Amused, he beckoned to a dasi and picked up a goblet of mango Mahasura, walking over to her and offering her the drink, at the same time smoothly detaching her from Prajapati.

They walked away to a little nook under a mango tree where a swing hung from the boughs and Misrakesi sat down with a sigh of relief.

'Thank you for the rescue,' she said standing up, and looking at him with tentatively smiling eyes as he propped himself against the tree trunk.

His was a compelling personality, she thought, it was difficult to remain indifferent to him. He led an active, not to say physically punishing, life and stood out in the contrast of his hewn muscles and animal grace. But it was also an angular and dangerous personality. Misrakesi would not have approached him of her own volition, but she had responded to the invitation in his smile and walked up with him.

So the two of them stood a little apart from the others and conversed lightly of unimportant things. Misrakesi was standing gracefully with her left hip lightly flexed and head gently inclined. Her blue transparent mulmul uttariya fell in delicate folds over her back caught up by her left arm, and the dhoti style antariya – alternating in sky blue and saffron – emphasized her slender waist and shapely thighs. Her kayabandha was a flat patti and tied low on her abdomen, deliciously framing her navel. Her jewellery today was lapis lazuli and carnelian. She raised her right hand to tuck in a stray curl and the artist in Pushyamitra was captivated by the perfect pose of a sculpted dancer's body.

It was dark and the illumination provided was by the oil cloth flares flaming against the night sky and swaying in the breeze. Pushyamitra was only a dark silhouette with the light in his unfathomable eyes.

There was a slight pull of antagonism between them and Misrakesi tilted her head up to give him a swift smile with challenging brown eyes. She would not have done it if she had known who was watching and what it would lead to in the future. As it was she knew nothing of the future and imagined no harm in a light flirtation with an attractive man who was responding in kind. If she had seen Sreelekha's eyes boring into them and her gestures and signals to her cronies she would have stopped, and that would have been a different story.

There were groups around them playing different games and there were loud voices and squeals of laughter, the guests becoming merrier as the levels in their goblets went down.

Misrakesi plucked a few flowers from the atimukta vine around the tree and absently started making a complicated garland.

'How do you do that so easily? I cannot make a garland to save my life,' said Pushyamitra curiously.

Misrakesi's musical laugh pealed out, 'You cannot make a garland? How can you claim to be a civilized man? Have you never ever woven a garland for a beautiful woman's hair?'

'No... not yet,' he said smiling slowly.

'Then I would say it is far too late to start now. Or should I teach you how to make a simple garland?' Her deft hands made a small but perfect circlet and gave it to him, 'There you are.'

He took it from her and there was an electric pause as he held her hand with the flowers in his own. He was about to tuck them behind her ear but a dasi interrupted and the moment was gone.

There was a little commotion and Acharya Chanakya walked in accompanied by his friend, Acharya Attri and his wife. Misrakesi and Pushyamitra's attention also focused there. It was time for the briefing to begin. Misrakesi had completely forgotten her troublesome ghost by this time and was enjoying the company and the food, looking forward in anticipation to the briefing and directions that would surely come now that the acharya was here in person.

'Stay with me. The acharya will call the selected people here while the others will go on with the bhoj,' said Pushyamitra quietly.

The acharya took his seat under a huge banyan tree nearby and a group of about fifteen-twenty guests gathered around unobtrusively, pretending to be engaged in nothing but conversation and games. They were mostly men, but also a few women who would be a part of the Stree Varangana Sena but were kept strictly apart from each other. Misrakesi had only seen a couple of them with Siddharthak at times.

The acharya sat erect and in a padmasan, the lotus posture, as he always did, his hands placed on his knees in a yogic posture of concentration. He was silent and his face was at rest but the entire group fell silent in a few moments. There was a sudden brooding atmosphere of foreboding. She was affected by the atmosphere but Pushyamitra looked unmoved, his own normal self. He patted her back when he saw her face. Misrakesi pulled herself up sharply, she did not need any support, she was here to do her bit for the protection of Magadha. So she moved away slightly and concentrated on the acharya. It was too late to escape Sreelekha's censure but Pushyamitra let her go without protesting.

The acharya's voice fell like shards of crystal in the silent room. As she had expected, he spoke at length about the political challenges facing Magadha before he went on to the actual work expected from them.

'All of you may not know this but when we, the samrat and I, made plans for the liberation of Magadha from the Nandas we took the help of an alliance of five kings of the mountainous regions of Gandhara.[36] The smaller kingdoms there including the tribal confederations and the Aratta were subdued or co-opted into our army during our extensive years of campaigning there. But there are still three threats to us from there.

'The first two are not very serious – the weak and collapsing Upper Indus Greek Satrapy of Eudemos is the most minor. He is ruling in the name of Peithon, a general of the dead Alakshendra and he has now been reduced to a minor irritant after the collapse of Yavana power in the area. Ambhi is on the throne of Taxila, but we have friendly relations with him. He has only to be watched till the time comes to extend our suzerainty over him.'

The acharya paused to emphasize the seriousness of what he was about to say. The actual threat: 'The kingdom of the elder Paurav. As you know, the younger Paurav was with us in the campaign to free Magadha but was treacherously killed by unknown persons in a tragedy which I wish I could have prevented.'

Misrakesi felt her face tighten at this disingenuous reference to the incident due to which Sukesi had lost her life and she bent her head to hide her expression.

The acharya continued: 'Now Malayketu, the son of the younger Paurav, his kingdom between the Asikni and Parushni[37] restored to him under the over-lordship of his uncle, is inciting him to act against us. The elder Paurav rules in the Vitasta[38]-Asikni doab and it is today the most powerful kingdom in the area and indeed perhaps in the whole of Jambudweepa. He is today the de facto Satrap of the

Upper Indus, coexisting in an uneasy relationship with Eudemos and Ambhi.

'Malayketu has advised his uncle to ask for his share of the spoils of the Magadhan war; and yesterday we have received a message from him. What he is asking for is no less than half of Magadha and what he has sent is nothing but a politely couched threat of war.'

There was a weary silence amongst the acharya's audience. War was a familiar animal for them. It meant danger, disruptions, death; but it was their duty to be in the forefront, even before the soldiers.

'I cannot over-emphasize that this must not go beyond those of you who are here. No panic can be allowed to be spread amongst the nagariks. War is not imminent, maybe we can also avoid it; but any hint of it will slow down the process of setting up an efficient administration in Magadha. That must and will go on as before. I am not pulling out any people from there. Other resources will be made available to you as you need them. But it is you and only you who can foil the enemy's machinations.'

All of them were listening carefully. They knew what this meant. There would be an increase in disturbances, an effort to break the kingdom from within. Enemy spies would already be walking the streets of Pataliputra, sowing dissension, inciting disloyalty, creating a climate of fear and distrust in the city, shaking confidence in the samrat and his ability to rule. Such a kingdom was always easier to defeat. They would have to be on the lookout for all kinds of stratagems.

The acharya continued, 'It has been a very strict rule of mine that you should all work alone or in groups of two or three, and report only to your appointed superior. Your secrecy and privacy have always been upheld. But circumstances are different now. It may be possible that some or any of you could need help at short notice and not have the time to go through your supervisor. It is therefore now imperative for all of you to know each other. I have selected you all on the basis of the work that you are doing.' He concluded, leaving unsaid the fact that many more spies and secret agents remained unknown and faceless, his to command. He was never one to disclose all his stratagems.

'I have called you here to explain the situation and ensure that all of you are on alert. Remember, any… any unusual activity or unusual movement or event must be investigated thoroughly. No matter how minor it seems. The movements into and out of the city are naturally being closely monitored.' He looked at Pushyamitra who nodded grimly.

Misrakesi was listening carefully to the acharya when an unwelcome thought struck her, Chandramukhi was an unusual – very unusual – circumstance. What had she done to investigate it? Absolutely nothing. That would have to be rectified and some solution to the problem would have to be found. Although she could not imagine even a remote connection between Gandharan plots and plans and Chandramukhi, she would have to be conscientious and do her duty.

'You know our goal; Samrat Chandragupta will be Chakravartin,[39] he will rule over Jambudweepa and God willing even beyond. We have started our campaign in the west, and some of you have been involved in the push towards Ujjaini and the sea ports of Sopara and Bhrigukachha. Our governor there is establishing the provincial capital of Suvamnagari.'

Misrakesi listened with an expressionless face but she bit her lips; involved, yes indeed!

'Anga, Panchal, Kasi, Kosala, Vajji, Malla, Chedi, Vachchha Machchha, Kuru and Shoorsen of the central region of Jambudweepa have also found peace under the Mauryan flag. Eastwards, Kalinga was a vassal of the Nandas and we shall reestablish our suzerainty over them. Expeditions to the south are also being sent. The most pressing and immediate problem, as I have told you, comes from the north. The stage on which this will be played out is your own city of Pataliputra. So be vigilant, all of you.'

The acharya was coming to the end of his directions. He ended with a shloka exhorting them to do their duty and then folded his hands and stood up in dismissal. Acharya Attri and his wife had been waiting, and the three of them left together almost immediately.

The entire group could not leave at once so they spread out and started leaving in twos and threes. Sreelekha smiled cynically when she saw Pushyamitra seek Misrakesi out, but she was doing them both an injustice. The light mood of flirtation and the tug of attraction had passed and they were talking because Pushyamitra's finely honed professional instinct had sensed something.

'Misrakesi, I would like you to meet me in my palace office after Basantotsav is over and give me a report on Apsara Sabha. And be on the alert. It is exactly the place where foreign agents try to strike up friendships with rich and foolish nagariks,' said Pushyamitra crisply.

She summoned up her most confident and efficient expression, 'As you wish, Arya. I shall be there.' And then she left.

But she was in a bind. She had been ignoring the insistent voice inside her head which told her that the Chandramukhi incident should be reported to Pushyamitra, telling herself that it was not important enough. There was no need for any knee-jerk reaction and she could mention the incident at the time of her regular report. Well, here it was, time for her regular report. There were no excuses left; not mentioning it now would be a breach of duty she could be dismissed for. Maybe no one would ever know, she argued with herself; there were so many rumours of ghosts and spirit visitations. This could remain one of them.

She was in a tight place. Not reporting, she risked dismissal, and if she did report the threat of exposure of her secret spy status would effectively again mean the end of her career. Could she shift the day of reckoning, pretend to be ill or offer some other excuse for not going? Lying to her supervisor and risking him finding out would have exactly the kind of consequences she did not want. In any case it was a cowardly way out merely postponing the inevitable.

She was in an agony of indecision for which she was bitterly ashamed. Where had all her quick-witted decision-making capabilities gone?

Chandramukhi, missing for all these days, chose to make an appearance that night. She startled Misrakesi by appearing in the room just as Misrakesi was falling off to sleep.

'So... all well, Devi?' The harsh voice jerked her out of sleep and she found Chandramukhi hovering over her as she lay on the bed. She sat up in silent anger.

'No, no! Please do not disturb yourself on my account. I do not want to disturb your beauty sleep,' Chandramukhi said with a distinct sneer.

'I am glad you have remained silent. I came to remind you of the consequences if you should change your mind. Remember, all this luxury, this opulence, and your occupation of my ancestral house will vanish like smoke as soon as I open my mouth.' She stared threateningly at Misrakesi and shook a finger to emphasize the point and vanished as suddenly as she had come.

Misrakesi's life was quite complicated, but she resolved to forget it for a few days and enjoy the festive season of Basantotsav. It was a time for joy and enjoyment, an uninhibited indulging of all the senses, a celebration of a successful harvest and the coming of spring. The entire city would be decorated with silk flags, banners, decorative gates and flowers, masses of them at every step. Decorative swings were hung under the big trees. All citizens were allowed to manufacture and drink unlimited alcohol for four days.So the mood would be uplifted, to say the least.

Musical troupes would move around giving performances. All the nartakis were required to give public performances and mingle with the general public. Apsara Sabha had already been given its schedule and all of them had been busy with the preparations. The weather was beautiful with the advent of Vasant[40] ritu and Kamadeva[41] would be everywhere with his bow of flowers. Colours made of roots, leaves, flowers and fruits of various plants, especially manjittha, nil, tesu, harsingar, saffron etc. would be smeared on everyone, on rich and poor, powerful and weak, young and old alike. It was a festival that knew no boundaries, a falling down of barriers for a day.

The samrat and his samragyi had been blessed with a son, the heir to the throne and the first sprig on the Mauryan tree. He had been named Bindusara. There was an atmosphere of jubilation and

Pataliputra was celebrating the festival with an extra enthusiasm and verve. After the uncertain and dangerous year that had gone by, there was a desire to forget the past and move into the future.

Apsara Sabha had also made special arrangements for the festival, with vast quantities of food and drink to be offered to the public and all the nartakis putting on their best performances at various places. Many would also go to the palace to felicitate the samrat who was making a rare public appearance.

It was going to be unadulterated pleasure and Misrakesi had every intention of forgetting her troubles for a day and letting herself go.

And she did. It was a beautiful day, their arrangements were perfect, with Mrinalini in charge of them. There were quite a few of her regular clients who thought this new mood would finally, after months of waiting, land them in her bed. But Misrakesi waved all of them away and went her own way.

She was making her way back home accompanied by Manjari and Som. The others were just behind them, Ratibhama having acquired a dedicated band of admirers which was following her back.

Just before they entered Apsara Sabha they were hailed by a rollicking Siddharthak who was drunk, in wonderful spirits and accompanied by a sober Pushyamitra. Siddharthak was smeared with colours, but Pushyamitra had just a tilak on his forehead which must have been applied by his elder brother. No one else would have had the courage to play.

Siddharthak caught hold of Misrakesi at once: 'Hold her, Bandhu.' He shouted jovially to Pushyamitra. 'We will not let her go today. She will have to pay the penalty.' Before she could say or do anything, Pushyamitra had obediently caught her hands and twisted them slightly behind her back, holding her immobile against his body. Siddharthak came forward to rub her with the flaming yellow-orange of saffron while she squirmed and twisted and laughed, trying to free herself. But she could not break free from Pushyamitra's hold.

Pushyamitra was tall but so was she and she reached quite above his chin. He had turned his head while she was pressed up against his length. Her eyes were closed and she was breathless with laughter. Manjari was laughing with Siddharthak and Misrakesi, but she watched with a sudden arrested look in her eyes as Pushyamitra's impersonal hold slowly turned into an embrace and Misrakesi was held close in his arms, still laughing.

The others had come up by now and Misrakesi called to Ratibhama to save her. As she had expected, that diverted Siddharthak at once and he was set upon by all the nartakis of Apsara Sabha and was soon in the centre of a melee, enjoying himself immensely.

Misrakesi took the opportunity to twist free and said threateningly to Pushyamitra, 'That has taken care of him. Now you wait and see,' and she ran off.

Pushyamitra was watching Siddharthak's antics with the women and waiting for him to finish so that they could leave when a small boy came up to him and pulled at his hand insistently. Puzzled, he followed him inside the palisade of Apsara Sabha. Som pulled him towards the lotus pond to one side and pointed. As Pushyamitra looked in, caught unawares, Misrakesi suddenly came up from behind the peepal tree where she had been hiding and gave him a shove which sent him sprawling in amongst the flowers, leaves, and floating roots in the water.

His first reaction was anger, this had not happened to him since he was a boy. But then he saw Misrakesi and Som holding hands and laughing till they were bent double, and his face broke into a reluctant smile. Misrakesi was careless, standing too close to the water's edge, and he simply stretched out a long hand and pulled her in. She came in and sputtered before surfacing to beat his chest in mock anger. But she enjoyed the joke, and as Som ran off to his mother, they were left alone in the lotus pond with the water lapping softly around them and the flowers screening them in.

Misrakesi was lying on top of him, her chin on top of his head. She slowly slid down till their lips met. Her mouth was sweet and passionate and her hands moving slowly down his back seemed to be soothing an eons-old ache in his body. When had any woman kissed him like this?

'You taste of fire and wood smoke,' she said, raising her red and inflamed eyes to his. Her lips were rosy and swollen with the kiss and her face was dreamy.

'And you of honey and ginger. *And* you are drunk.'

'Yes, I am. You should try it sometime.' She twisted away and then suddenly came back and pushed his hair away from his face, 'You are a beautiful man,' she said seriously, taking in his dark eyes, thick eyelashes, sharp nose, and chiselled jaw and running a thumb down his curved lips.

'These are meant for loving and kissing, not commanding.'

'Maybe I never found anyone to love.'

'Nonsense, you just did not look hard enough.' Her mind was free and floating somewhere removed from its moorings. She was hardly aware of what she was saying or doing. Perhaps that is why she had kissed Pushyamitra and was presuming to advise him on some very private matters.

She pulled herself out of the pond and gave him her hand to pull him out. Then she pirouetted around and started making her way inside the house.

'Stop, don't go.' Pushyamitra had this mad urge to give in to the Madanotsav[42] and make her his own right then and there.

But alarm bells were ringing in Misrakesi's head. She was drunk and not in control of herself; she would be best off in her own room and in her own bed, alone. So she merely smiled and walked off. Pushyamitra watched her with mixed feelings till she disappeared from sight.

Mrinalini caught hold of her as soon as she went in and clucked over her wet and bedraggled state. She was rushed into a cleansing bath and then into dry clothes. Although the festivities continued, Misrakesi had had enough and soon she slept, perhaps due to the copious quantities of wine she had imbibed. Misrakesi woke up suddenly before dawn the next day, with a raging headache, a dry throat and a very hazy memory of the last few hours. She could only remember a succession of dances and pots of wine and colours, a riot of them. Madlekha was waiting with a cooling and reviving drink and Misrakesi felt a bit better after drinking that. She tried to concentrate and soon gave up in despair although there was a niggling feeling inside that there was something important she should remember.

Was it something to do with Pushyamitra? Probably not, it did not seem possible and where would she have met him anyway? Probably one of the strange fantasies she had been increasingly prone to these days. And so it was left at that. Manjari was perhaps the only one who could have enlightened her, but she kept her own counsel.

The Solution and Other Problems

Goods are from the countryside, from the city and from foreign lands. That on goods going out and on goods coming in is duty. On goods coming in the duty shall be one-fifth of the price.

Arthashastra 2.22.1 to 2.22.3

The palace glittered in the blazing sun. The carved and polished wooden columns and façades were being inlaid with gold and silver. The palace had belonged to the Nandas and it was incumbent upon the first Maurya to make it even more opulent and magnificent to impress the nagariks of Pataliputra. The gardens and groves outside were cleverly reproduced in the golden creepers and foliage twining around the columns with little silver birds peeping from behind the golden gem-studded leaves. Peacocks, which were the symbol of the Mauryas, strutted unhindered and proud in the palace and gardens, their harsh calls echoing; any harm done to a peacock was punishable with death.

Misrakesi had heard that exotic animals from all over the world were being brought to stock the gardens and that the designing of the trees, vines, and creepers was something to be marvelled at. There were shady groves and pasture grounds planted with new and exotic trees, the branches of which were interwoven by the art of the royal woodsmen. They twisted and shaped the branches into complex and wonderful designs as the trees grew.

It was a wonder of the world and it would be no surprise if future generations exclaimed and thought that it was a race of supermen who had built it. The magnificent palaces in the Persian cities of Susa and Ecbatana paled in comparison.

Misrakesi left Urmil with her chhatra in the outer courtyard of the palace where all the visiting chariots, horses, and attendants waited for their owners to transact palace business and return. Urmil would be well engaged in picking up gossip and who knew when little nuggets would come in useful.

Misrakesi was in a very unhappy frame of mind. After the festival, she had decided to report the entire Chandramukhi incident to Pushyamitra, not only because it was her duty, but also because he was bound to find out the truth. If he found out her secret from some other source not even Bhagwan Vaijayanta[43] would be able to save her from his wrath. She was very apprehensive especially because she had also decided to tell him that Chandramukhi was threatening the entire espionage establishment of the city.

They met in the same secret chamber where she had met him for the first time. He was in a brisk and business-like mood. He greeted her perfunctorily, gestured at her to sit down and started questioning her immediately. Misrakesi did not remember enough of their last meeting to react in any way, and he had never been one to show what he was thinking. He had actually put the episode away as an aberration because of Basantotsav and the wine. If he had warmed up to her too much in their last few meetings, he was now back in his secure armour of her chief.

The antecedents of all the dancers and household staff, their conduct and activities were the first to be discussed. Next was the issue of the finances of Apsara Sabha. Neither Misrakesi's nor Pushyamitra's mood improved when he chose to remind her about the interest payments on the amount advanced as loan from the royal treasury for the establishment of Apsara Sabha.

Misrakesi replied in a carefully unoffended and even tone, 'You may rest assured about that, Arya. The excess of net earnings over the monthly one and a quarter percent interest payment are being used to pay back the principal; I am not taking my salary till it is repaid in full.'

Pushyamitra looked unimpressed, 'Good. And I hope I don't have to remind you that the expenses should be kept to the minimum and within the budgeted items. The luxury is a bait which should be used as such and not wasted on... anybody.'

Misrakesi bit her lips to keep herself from making an angry rejoinder, but her eyes flashed; what was he implying? But she thought better of pursuing the argument, given that she had to deal with a far more difficult issue very soon in this briefing.

She went on to give a selected list of clients at Apsara Sabha who she thought would bear investigation. Chief amongst them was Ugrasala, the younger brother of the dead senapati of the Nandas, Bhaddasala. Ugrasala did not hold any official position in the royal administration, but all the wealth collected by his brother was now his to fritter away. He was a bitter and opinionated young man who felt that his obvious merits were being ignored by the current administration due to bias. Bhaddasala's family had been influential and very close to successive Nanda kings for two or three generations, and the current lack of power and patronage rankled. If it had not been for the policy of appeasement followed by the Mauryan administration towards the Nanda network, which still seemed to be in operation, he would have been killed and his property confiscated a long time ago. However, he was very much at large in the city and importuning Mahaamatya Katyayan for a royal position in one of the many departments which were being set up under the directions of Acharya Chanakya.

Pushyamitra listened carefully to the report. His deputy, Sumant, was also present and they had a short discussion which also included some hangers on of Ugrasala, mostly the sons of minor court officials and rich setthis, while Misrakesi was silent preparing herself for her 'confession'.

'There is something else, isn't there, Misrakesi?' said Pushyamitra looking directly at her.

'Yes, there is.'

'Well?' He asked, raising his eyebrows.

Misrakesi swallowed and glanced at Sumant.

'All right, Sumant, you can go. Start the actions we have discussed and report if you find anything significant,' Pushyamitra nodded at Sumant, a grizzled and silent individual who was known to open his mouth on very rare occasions. He went out, surprised at what Misrakesi could have to tell Pushyamitra which would be a secret from him; but he was not one to indulge in fruitless speculation and soon put it aside.

Misrakesi did not know how to start but did get it all out in the end, starting with the rumours of a ghost, the curious incidents in Apsara Sabha, her own deductions and ending with the trap she had set and Chandramukhi's appearance and story. She had been speaking without daring to meet Pushyamitra's eyes but when she risked a quick look she could see that his face was thunderous and the ever-present harsh glint in his eyes had become pronounced, they were almost shooting flames.

Pushyamitra, to put it mildly, was furious. He had entrusted a particularly important job to a newcomer – a young woman – against received opinion, based entirely on his own evaluation of her abilities and here she was, making mistakes and jeopardizing the entire network of guptchars; and he had only himself to blame.

When Misrakesi finished and looked up, his voice cut through the silent room like a whiplash and made her jump, 'That is wonderful. I congratulate you! No sooner have we set you up in a dancing house with great trouble and expense that you come up with this woman who will ruin all our efforts and reduce them to nothing, a shoonya. You have brought a disaster upon yourself and perhaps all of us.' He was striding up and down the room and he whirled suddenly to come to a stop in front of Misrakesi.

She had been about to add the fact that Chandramukhi had threatened to expose them all, but she thought better of it. In fact, anger overrode guilt at this unfair speech. After all, most of the effort and a good deal of the expense had been hers and she would be the one hit the most if Chandramukhi did execute her threat. She was not responsible for Chandramukhi's tragedy or appearance. Perhaps she should not have bought a haunted house, but what about the bargain she had got and the short time she had been given in which to set up the establishment?

'Please calm yourself, Arya,' she said in anything but a calm tone herself. Furious eyes met stormy ones and neither relented. After a few moments Misrakesi took a deep breath and striving for a reasonable tone went on, 'This was all in the nature of keeping you informed. It is in no way a problem. In fact,' she was thinking desperately, 'I have won her confidence and am planning to use her as a source of information about the waterfront where she seems to have many contacts.'

Pushyamitra looked at Misrakesi with narrowed eyes. 'I see,' he said, still suspicious. 'And what gave you the impression that she can be trusted and will cooperate?' He was still standing in front of her, in an almost threatening stance over her.

She stood up, forcing him to move away from her, and said, 'All of us have to cultivate our own informers and make our own judgments; this is mine. Then again, she has very few options as long as she is adamant about not going to Kasi. Why would ṣhe like to create unnecessary trouble? At least give me some time to try her out. Otherwise I can always persuade her to change her mind and go to her family.' She was thinking gratefully that Pushyamitra had not met Chandramukhi and did not know just how prone she was to make trouble just for the sake of it and exactly how 'amenable' she was to persuasion. Maybe she would get away with her story.

It seemed to be working, at the moment, at least. Pushyamitra gave her his grudging approval but said, 'I am not going to allocate you any additional funds for her. You can build up your network but till this girl proves to be of any use, no extra pans can be spent on her.'

They parted on the worst of terms and Misrakesi was seething, as she made her way back to Apsara Sabha through the crowded streets resounding with the sound of horses, chariots, palki-bearers, and raised voices.

She was in such a fury and walking so fast that she upset a clay waterpot being carried by a hapless woman and scattered to the four directions her husband's bundle of cotton. She narrowly missed being knocked down by a horseman who turned out to be Siddharthak and who gave her a quizzical look as she stormed off without noticing him in the white cloud of cotton. An enlightened look crossed his face and he smiled. He was going to meet Pushyamitra and knew that Misrakesi had been called before him. Sparks must have flown!

Urmil had been left to deal with the irate couple Misrakesi had bumped into, who had collected a crowd in their support by then, as best as he could. Siddharthak added another soothing note before riding off for his meeting. He and Pushyamitra could definitely be classed as old friends, that is, if Pushyamitra had any friends and he, Siddharthak, could afford any. They had both come this far by placing their careers first, but they did see eye to eye on many issues and had the comfort of a very long association stretching back to their brahmachari days in the Takshshila gurukul

In Siddharthak's opinion, Pushyamitra was a peculiarly focused and grim character who had no time for the lighter side of life. He had spent most of his life in the army and then having discovered a bent for the secret service, he had moved to the Nagarik Suraksha Vibhag where he had risen to head it in a phenomenally short time. His elder brother and sister-in-law had married him off early but his young bride and her firstborn had died in childbirth within the first year of marriage, and since then, he had had very little to do with women. His private life was very private and no doubt he had the normal male urges, but no one had ever seen him associated with any woman. Perhaps it was time that Kamadeva should send a Misrakesi to him. Siddharthak chuckled to himself, much amused.

Disguised as a compulsive and poor loser in a gambling house, Siddharthak created such a ruckus that the soldiers had to be called in and he was thrown into the nearest Nagarik Suraksha outpost where Pushyamitra was waiting for him. This was one of the ways in which he could meet Pushyamitra secretly, as he was a lone operator and had not even been called for the bhoj at Hiranyalabha's house.

Pushyamitra, in keeping with his image, had taken a supple bamboo stick to beat the trouble out of this troublemaker. He came in and kicked the door shut. In between slashing around with his stick, carefully avoiding Siddharthak, their conversation was conducted in low voices interspersed with roars from Pushyamitra and shouts of mercy from Siddharthak.

Siddharthak found Pushyamitra shaken out of his usual calm; he had already seen the reason some time ago on the road. He did not ask any questions but gave Pushyamitra the information he had. It was slightly peculiar.

'All the gamblers and gambling houses in the city are flush with funds. I have never seen Pataliputra so full of coins. And most of the supply seems to consist of Masha, one-sixteenth of a pan, small enough to not attract undue attention, but still with some value. I have brought a sample for you to see what you can make of them.' Siddharthak passed a handful of Mashas to Pushyamitra.

They were the standard copper coins struck by the Nandas with their symbol of a dog and a rabbit perched atop a mountain on one side of the coin, and the Lakshan of the Lakshanadhyaksha[44] on the reverse. Those were being struck over with the peacock symbol of the Mauryas, and being included in legal tender. These particular coins had not yet been struck over with the Mauryan peacock, but would soon enough reach the royal treasury and be so marked. These were copper coins although there were also silver Mashas in circulation. Pushyamitra kept them away for examination by the Mint officials.

'There is another fact you should consider very carefully. Gambling, drinking, and whoring have increased suddenly and appreciably amongst the soldiers in the standing army. Apart from the question of where they are getting the money, it does not speak well of their alertness and preparedness. It can and must be stopped immediately before the problem spreads.' Siddharthak added gravely.

Pushyamitra nodded grimly. The Magadhan army did not know it, but things were going to get very busy and tough for it from the very next day – soldiers would have no time to waste. The senapati happened to be Pushyamitra's elder brother; so there would be no trouble in passing on the information and getting it acted upon. The sources of the extra flow of coins would have to be found, and he asked Siddharthak to continue his investigation.

Misrakesi, in the meanwhile, had reached home dusty, hot, and thirsty. She had not even had the benefit of her chhatra for most of the way as Urmil had stayed behind. But Madlekha was waiting in the front courtyard with a claypot of cold well water sprinkled with kewra petals and gently washed Misrakesi's face, hands and feet with it. Misrakesi threw off her uttariya and clad only in a thin dhoti and a cloth tied around her breasts went out to sit under the shade of a tree on the riverbank. There was a soft breeze from the river, which combined with the sound of the water on the stones near the shore, soothed her as she thought over the meeting and her instructions. Madlekha had also brought some sugarcane juice in a painted black pot and she relaxed and sipped it quietly.

She had some breathing time with reference to Chandramukhi but she was stung by Pushyamitra blaming her for Chandramukhi's appearance. It was definitely not her fault. And now she had not been given funds for using Chandramukhi as a new informer – that was the worst of all. Pushyamitra was not to know that she had made it up on the spot, so what was the reason for not giving her the necessary funds?

He was turning out to be a most unpleasant chief. To deny her legitimate expenses was unheard of; spend hundreds of Pans on setting up Apsara Sabha and then deny her the few Pans needed to pay Chandramukhi! Anyway, she would manage; she had enough savings of her own. She had bought a share in a trading boat that plied up and down the Ganges and was comfortably placed as far as her own finances were concerned. But why should she fund informers for the all-powerful and rich-beyond-imagination Mauryan state?

Even more unwelcome was this insistence on cutting costs when she was already operating carefully and on a constrained budget given the kind of impression she was supposed to maintain! Mrinalini, Manjari and she were very careful householders. From where had he got the idea that she was wasting Pans in idle luxury? Apsara Sabha was a sugar heap for ants, the ants would not be able to resist the attraction and then could be crushed at leisure. She was not spending the money on herself, no more than was necessary to keep up appearances. But she remembered a few barbed remarks at Hiranyalabha's bhoj about her lifestyle, clothes, and jewellery and thought... Sreelekha! She had probably been spreading these rumours and she happened to have his ear. Well, 'she', Misrakesi, had no idea how to stop vicious and ill-natured gossip. She would just have to hope it would go away, but it left her feeling uneasy and vaguely apprehensive. Public opinion was a very strong weapon. It was all getting too much. Maybe she *was* too young to run a dancing house.

She sighed and leaned against the tree trunk, stretching her hands above her head. Som's tutor, who was leaving the house after the morning lessons, was brought up short by the vision in front of him. He was a brahmachari, but he was also a man and could not but appreciate the picture she made. Her shapely arms were raised above her head throwing her beautiful breasts imperfectly covered by a thin cloth into relief, her dhoti had ridden up to her thighs and her slim waist, inviting abdomen and long legs were clearly visible. If she appeared like this in the evenings, he wondered how the men restrained themselves. Against the sylvan background she looked like a painting etched in the new naturalistic style being developed. He shook his head but went away with the image firmly held in his mind's eye.

Unaware of his scrutiny, Misrakesi went off to her daily dance practice. A long conversation with Chandramukhi was now in order, but how was she to meet her? Chandramukhi came and went of her own will.

After some thought, she decided to go and sit near the little shrine to the side of the house. She knew that Chandramukhi often came there to collect the offerings made to her. She had also noticed that people from nearby houses had also started invoking the protective spirit and leaving offerings. Who knew, it could save her the necessity of spending money on Chandramukhi's upkeep?

Misrakesi waited for sometime, but nothing happened. So she sent for her expensive blanket from Nepal, which was so skilfully woven that it kept the rain out, and left it as an offering along with some fruits. It seemed suspiciously like a bribe but there appeared to be no other way of contacting Chandramukhi. Some way, preferably a little less expensive than a blanket, would have to be established or she would soon be unable to afford her pet ghost.

That night, Madlekha was sent away early and Misrakesi sat on the bed hugging her knees and waiting for Chandramukhi to appear. Thankfully, she did appear, climbing up the tree under the terrace and swinging into the room.

'I appreciated the gift, *sister,* and also correctly understood that that you wished to see me. What about?' She asked as she made herself comfortable on the floor cushions and flicked through a bundle of bhojpatras with Misrakesi's poetry inscribed on them.

Misrakesi had planned her speech carefully and launched immediately into her argument. She had realized that Chandramukhi was unaffected by preliminaries and appeals. 'Chandramukhi, we must come to some agreement on how we are to go on. You know very well I am not a private nagarik who can do what she likes. This entire establishment and I personally am accountable as a royal employee. We must decide what is to be done and I shall then expect your support in that.'

Chandramukhi, who was listening with an unconcerned expression on her face, now started tinkering with a lute hanging on an ivory stand, 'I feel sure that you have already decided what is to be done and are only waiting to inform me of it. I am ready to listen.'

So far so good. Now for the difficult part, thought Misrakesi. She looked directly at Chandramukhi and said rapidly, 'I had gone to meet Pushyamitra today. And I have told him all about you.'

'What?' Chandramukhi started up with an ugly look on her face, the lute forgotten, 'You will pay for this, Devi Misrakesi. I will see you ruined.' And she started out of the room.

'Wait, wait, it is not what you think,' whispered Misrakesi running after her urgently. 'It is not what you think. I have asked for you to be employed as an informer by the Spy Department.'

Chandramukhi had already reached the grounds and Misrakesi had been hissing as loudly as she dared from the top of the terrace, but she stopped at that. 'I think you had better come down. We can talk about it at the river bank.'

Misrakesi hastily wrapped a blanket around herself and hoped that nobody would see her. Then she went down after Chandramukhi. They walked to the river bank and sat down together. The silence was anything but companionable.

'Well, tell me. What have you planned for me? Me, a royal informer. Hmm... that has an ironic flavour,' and she laughed at a private joke and then turned to Misrakesi, 'So how much am I going to be paid?'

That was a knotty question which Misrakesi would rather not have answered. As it was, she temporized and said, 'Let us first do something, shall we? We will consider the payment after that. I will take care of whatever you want in the meanwhile.'

Chandramukhi did not look very happy but had to agree when Misrakesi refused to budge on the issue. 'Well alright. Just for some time. But do get some good dhotis and uttariyas for me. The blanket you have given me will do for the moment. And I would like some of your shringar ointments and unguents.' She looked at her chapped hands and touched the rough skin of her face.

Misrakesi was quite agreeable. Clothes, even new ones were not a problem and skin unguents and hair washes were in unlimited supply in a household of dancing girls. In a burst of gratitude at this easy way out she decided to ask Mrinalini to get the special sandalwood bathing coolant as well as the aloe vera, saffron, and cream mixture which was a luxury Chandramukhi must have been used to. Camphor and musk hair scents would also be appreciated she was sure. She also knew of a medicinal ointment which would help to lighten her scar. She would do all she could to make Chandramukhi a new woman, or rather, the old Chandramukhi.

'Now that we have decided on that let us get to some serious work. There are two things I want from you. The first is all that you remember about your attackers so that we can start trying to trace and punish them,' said Misrakesi.

Chandramukhi sat up, 'Punish them? Is that really possible? If my darling husband came before me again I would not let him go alive. I have learnt many ways to kill in this past year. They were for survival but will do very well for his end,' she said sharply.

'It depends on the information you can give me. Do you remember their faces? Perhaps if I gave you some colours and bhojpatra you could paint their faces or at least your husband's face.'

Chandramukhi looked intrigued. 'I have never heard anything like it. Of course, I have learnt to draw and paint from the best gurus in Pataliputra but those were imaginary or mythical figures from the Ram Katha or the Mahabharata. To draw a real person from memory is... I don't know. But I can try. The same principles will apply. Then again I have learnt to draw and paint murals on the walls. I am not too sure about a bhojpatra. Will the colours stick on the surface? I know the technique of making a terracotta plaster in two layers. Natural fibres and various coloured stone mixtures and sand are mixed; glue and sares are used. Let me not go into the technical details. I will try, you must get me the materials I need.'

Chandramukhi had never been so animated. Perhaps it was the desire for revenge or the interest in painting, or both. It was very welcome, and if a likeness did emerge, it could be of help.

Misrakesi now moved on to the more important issue. 'The second thing, Chandramukhi, is that I would like you to take me down to the waterfront one of these days: especially the docks where the boats from all over come down the river. There are the official docks which are in public view and then there are the secret landing places where only those in the know can go. This is a fertile area for smuggling of goods without customs duty and for spies from our enemy kingdoms.'

Chandramukhi was silent and Misrakesi went on a little desperately, 'Just consider, Chandramukhi, it is impossible for anyone to enter the city overland without being checked at the entry point, the city is securely encircled by the walls on all four sides. I know that the riverbank is a conduit for smuggled goods. I feel sure that you know the way these goods enter the city.'

Chandramukhi twirled her fingers around a long strand of hair, looked down at the grass and still did not say anything.

'Look, this is not some plan to give you up to the Nagarik Suraksha Vibhag, I need your help in my work and you will have to trust me.'

'Misrakesi, many of the kevats and unloaders are my friends and have helped in my time of need. I cannot betray them,' said Chandramukhi unmoved by the appeal.

This left Misrakesi in something of a quandary. Avoidance of customs duties was not really her business and she could ignore it, picking up only relevant information. But she doubted if Pushyamitra or the Samaharta would share her views. As a royal employee it was not correct for her to suppress information which would lead to an augmentation of revenue for the state and plugging the loopholes. She thought a compromise would be best.

'Let me put it this way. I do not wish to know about the smuggling. I am interested in the news from other kingdoms which travels up and down the river. None of your friends will come to any harm through me. But all the people involved cannot be your friends. If, and I am saying *if*, I see the need for passing on any information, I will check with you first. Is that fine?'

Chandramukhi nodded, satisfied, but Misrakesi was left feeling uncomfortable; she had no right to give any such undertaking and was sure she would have to break her promise. Anyway, that was best left to the future.

Misrakesi procured some discarded uniforms of soldiers, and two nights later, stole down silently to the tree where Chandramukhi had her lair. She had tied up her long hair in a male-style turban, and was wearing an old patched soldier's tunic with a dhoti. She also had a sword tied ostentatiously at her hip, but a small and lethal dagger hidden in a slit in the tunic in a far more accessible position. She wore knee-length boots. Her face was masked with the end of her turban.

Chandramukhi was waiting. She raised her eyebrows and pursed her lips when she saw Misrakesi, 'Why are you dressed like a man? Let me assure you there is no need to do so. There are many women on the waterfront, and if anyone makes any unwelcome advances, you just have to be able to defend yourself. I have now cut open too many men with my dagger for anyone to try anything with me. And I will look after you.'

Smiling, Misrakesi said, 'I will depend upon you for that. But I also need to keep my identity a secret, so don't mind my disguise.'

They walked on, Chandramukhi leading and Misrakesi following. It was a moonlit night and there was enough illumination to see the way. They went to the Yama gate and followed a silent procession of people leaving the gate to go outside the city. There were no sounds except the occasional wailing and beating of breasts, and Misrakesi realized with a shock that she had joined a procession of people going out of the city to cremate their dead. The cremation would take place in the morning, of course, but the crossing of the gates was being done at night.

There was a beaten path through the trees and they went on for some time and came to a place where the river turned in and then divided itself to gush forth in its own tributary, the Son.

There were, in the desolate night, many huge fires smouldering and as they neared, Misrakesi understood that they were crossing the crematorium near the Yama Gate. The fires were burning the mortal remains of the lower varnas living in the city. In death the higher castes lay on their funeral pyres to the north near the Indra Gate.

She suppressed a superstitious shudder and Chandramukhi laughed mockingly. The Chaandals, who supervised the crematorium, were busy handing over the collected ashes to relatives after sifting them of valuables, stoking the fires so that the smoke rose up grey and black in the air, making sure that the bodies were fully burnt. There were also the Aghoris[45] who were to be found in cremation grounds and Misrakesi had to stop herself from clutching at Chandramukhi at this surreal and frightening scene.

To her relief, they soon moved into the trees adjoining the river bank and the scenery became as normal as it could be during the night.

'For your information,' said Chandramukhi, 'that is how the smuggled goods get into the city and out, none of the guards want to enquire too closely about the bodies and ashes of the dead. The ox-carts go in and out with the payment of a few judicious bribes.'

As they approached, Chandramukhi asked Misrakesi to stop and wait behind a tree. 'There must be something big happening tonight. There are many such landing places along the Ganga but there are generally only one or two boats and five or ten unloaders. Informal word goes out and there is a kind of roster system for them. They come here to make some quick money. But look at the number of people today, must be more than fifty. You wait while I ask one of the kevats if you can also come in.'

So Misrakesi waited behind a tree while Chandramukhi walked off. She obviously knew one of the kevats very well because she walked up to him, greeted him familiarly and talked to him for some time. The scene was one of controlled confusion, with medium-sized jute bags being unloaded from the boats and on to waiting bullock carts. The bags seemed to be quite heavy for their size and not even the brawniest man present could carry more than three. The bullock cart drivers were standing apart and not talking to anyone, the others were a hubbub of activity.

After some time, Chandramukhi came back and told Misrakesi that she would not be allowed to join the unloaders. Apparently tonight was not a good time for a newcomer to join. The owners of the goods were extremely careful and had personally vouched for each of the unloaders. Chandramukhi could be allowed in as she was vouched for by her friend, the kevat, but Misrakesi was out.

Misrakesi agreed to wait for Chandramukhi to earn some Mashas and spent the time trying to look carefully at the cart drivers who would deliver the smuggled goods to their destination in the city. She did not gain much as they had their faces almost completely hidden. If she could have memorized any face it could have helped since these were the men who would know the secret warehouses from where the goods would be sold to other setthis willing to take the risk for the profit. The Magadhan State did not take kindly to being cheated and the rules had recently been tightened.

Misrakesi was left feeling disappointed. The idea behind disguising herself and coming down to mingle with the smugglers and unloaders had been to talk to them and pick up nuggets of information. This was a hidden underclass of Pataliputra with whom very few people had any contact. But they were the first to feel the effects of any impending earthquake and were certain conduits of information from other parts of Jambudweepa. The boats that plied up the river took news from Magadha, Kosala, and Kalinga to the important cities of Uttarapatha. Equally, boats coming down from Hastinapur, the first river port on the Uttarapath, brought down the icy winds of the mountainous kingdoms of the Gandharan region, Iran, and Afghanistan.

So much for the careful disguise! All a waste! But she could try to convince Chandramukhi to let her at least meet the kevat. The unloaders were the usual poor hangers on at the gambling houses and eating houses earning some Kakanis[46] to drink and gamble away. They were mostly clad in coarse cotton loincloths and nothing much else, though some of them did have dhotis and uttariyas. The indifferent illumination from the moonlight did not give Misrakesi much of a chance to memorize anyone's features. Even if she had, the city was too huge and it was too easy to lose oneself in the lanes and bylanes. Where would she look for anyone?

The mosquitoes were out in full force and she had to swat them away continuously. It was close and airless and she moved to stand under another tree which was slightly in the open to get some relief, but the insects were as bad as ever; even the impassive bullock cart drivers were troubled by them.

It was some time before Chandramukhi returned jingling some coins in her hand and laughing at what her friend the kevat had said. She looked in good humour and emptied the coins into Misrakesi's hand, 'Here, take this. Now that I am in your employ, I don't really need this, do I? You are going to take care of all my needs. These few Mashas are yours!'

Misrakesi put them away and the two of them started back. Chandramukhi shrugged away all Misrakesi's questions and finally said, 'Look, I kept my promise and brought you here, didn't I? I did not promise to answer any interrogation. So don't ask me questions about the boats and the goods and the people involved, I will not give you any answer.'

So the questioning had to perforce be abandoned and there was no information gathered. *Never mind,* thought Misrakesi, *I will slowly win her trust and then the information will flow. Patience, patience!*

The only concrete results of the evening were the few Mashas she had got from Chandramukhi. She was looking at them the next morning, turning them around to look at both the sides. They were Nanda coins, she noticed, and the overstamp of the peacock symbol had not yet been put upon them, they were still acceptable as payment of course. Since she had not got anything else out of the expedition she decided to send these to the Mint for close examination. She was hardly an authority on coins and could make out nothing from a physical examination.

She tied up the coins in a strip of cloth and sealed it with the lion ring. She then called Urmil and told him to take the small bundle to Hiranyalabha's house with a message that these should be sent to the Lakshanadhyaksha.

That evening, she decided to cultivate Ugrasala and his cronies. They were regulars at Apsara Sabha but she had never shown them any special favours. Today, however, she selected them for her Paan Goshthi. After that it was an easy step to get him alone. A few languishing glances and captivating smiles and the thing was done.

He was highly flattered and encouraged by this behaviour which he thought of as only his due and happening quite late in his acquaintance with Misrakesi. Foolish, vain, and rich enough to believe that he was irresistible, he had always been certain that it was only a matter of time before the ravishing young patroness of Apsara Sabha would fall for his many charms and become his mistress.

Overflowing with Harahuraka, the green grape wine of Afghanistan, he expanded like a bubble in the breeze of Misrakesi's appreciation. He boasted to her of his money, his good looks, and his connections in high places. He was not fully appreciated in Pataliputra he admitted, because of the bias of the powers that be, but there were other kings who understood and appreciated his good qualities and were anxious to get his support.

This made Misrakesi prick up her ears but his drunken ramblings took him off in another direction, about how he was going to become richer than ever in the next few months. Money, according to him, was positively going to rain on him. And he promised to shower a good bit of it on her if she agreed to become his mistress.

Misrakesi smiled and gave him a non-committal but encouraging response. She was going to find out more about the source of the money. Overcome by wine and lust, Ugrasala tried to take Misrakesi in his arms and he fell flat on his face when she neatly side-stepped him. Unable to get up, he was soon snoring on the floor.

Misrakesi asked his men to take him home while she went about smiling, talking, and flirting with other customers, making each one feel special. She also kept a sharp eye out for the quality and wealth of her clientele and had no compunctions about throwing out undesirables.

For example, she did not like the look of a down-at-heel gambler who was sidling in trying to avoid the attendants who stood at the door to greet the guests. He probably did not have enough money to gamble and she was sure he would soon be importuning others for a small loan. He would drink too much of the free wine provided by Apsara Sabha, and then become belligerent and start a brawl.

She was about to get him thrown out when the gambler caught her eye and she realized with a shock that it was Siddharthak. He was really good! Not only his clothes but his hair, eyes, expression, the way he held himself, the cunning and servile look on his face, all betokened a down-and-out gambler.

The persona fell away from him like a discarded blanket once they met alone in a secluded room. It was Siddharthak standing before her.

'Pranaam, Arya,' she said smiling, 'my humble abode is enriched by your presence.'

His smile acknowledged her greeting, but he was in a serious mood. He took out a small bundle from his dhoti which Misrakesi recognized as the one she had sent for examination by the Lakshanadhyaksha.

'What are you doing with these?' She asked surprised.

'More to the point, Devi, where did *you* get these? Do you know what they are? They are the small seeds whose flowers could poison our entire kingdom and force it to die a slow death.'

'What do you mean? They are just coins.'

'Not just any coins. These are counterfeit coins,' said Siddharthak quietly.

Misrakesi could only gape at him in silence while the singing and dancing went on around them.

Too Many Coins

The Mint Master should cause to be minted... copper coins with one quarter sustenance (of an alloy), of the denomination of one masaka, a half masaka, a kakani, and a half kakani.

Arthashastra 2.12.32

Misrakesi had withdrawn herself from the Tambula goshthi and was sitting out on her terrace with Siddharthak trying to take in what he was explaining.

'Misrakesi, where did these coins come from? If your dancing house is being used as a place from where to spread these counterfeit coins, it is a very serious matter. No matter how difficult it is you must find out the clients who are trying to put these in circulation.'

'Please wait. It is not Apsara Sabha from where these coins come. That is a different story altogether. But what do you mean counterfeit? Who, apart from the royal treasury, knows the method and has the means to produce coins? Not even the richest setthi would have the resources to say nothing of the fear of the stringent punishments handed out. Who would dare? And what about the stamp of the king?'

She picked up the coins and looked at them closely, 'In any case, to my untrained eyes this looks like any other copper coin. Then how do you know that they are counterfeit and what does this mean anyway? They have the Nanda king's stamp.'

'I can understand your confusion. I am not an expert on coins either but I have picked up some arcane knowledge along the way and have just been given a comprehensive lesson by the Lakshanadhyaksha himself. Let me explain.'

He picked up one of the thick, squarish coins and weighed it on his palm, 'Using only our hands we cannot estimate small differences in weight but on checking with the appropriate instruments, the mint officials found out that not only has the copper content been diluted, but that the weight is half of what it should be.'

Misrakesi found the whole idea incomprehensible. She had heard from old people of her grandmother's generation that there was a time when individual merchant guilds issued coins and operated an elaborate system of checks and balances to keep them in circulation at the correct weight, but those days were long gone. Ever since the days of the Shishunag kings, the move towards a centralized issue of coins had gained ground and the Nandas had institutionalized it. It was the basis for their vast wealth. Acharya Chanakya could be trusted to put it on a more sound, and less personal, basis. A thirty member committee divided into six groups had been set up for the regulation of all aspects of urban governance including coins and coinage, weights and measures, and indeed many other social and commercial aspects.

Who, then, could issue coins single-handedly and what was the purpose behind it? Misrakesi shook her head and looked at Siddharthak helplessly. It was too complicated for her.

'All right, let me try to explain as simply as possible, Misrakesi. Coins are issued with the royal insignia on one side followed by the stamps of the mint authorities; central, provincial, district, and village level. You can make out from these signs exactly which mint they have been coined in.'

When Misrakesi looked disbelieving he said smiling, 'I don't mean you or me or the ordinary nagarik. This is a very specialized and secret area of knowledge. It is set down in a manual called the Rupasutra and guarded so closely that most of us do not even know of its existence, leave alone what is inside it.'

'I believe you. Go on.' Misrakesi picked up a coin and squinted at it trying to see what signs were struck on its obverse. There was a hill with a rabbit, the sun, a six-sided geometrical figure, a mountain and a bull. She knew that the hill with a rabbit on top had been the Nanda royal insignia and was familiar enough with it. The other signs were a mystery.

'You do not need to know all the details, but the other signs are of the royal mint officials in descending hierarchy. Now turn it over on the other side, the reverse,' said Siddharthak as he produced another copper coin from his own bag of coins.

'But there is nothing on the other side, the surface is plain and shining,' protested Misrakesi.

'Exactly. Now look at this coin,' he handed her the coin he had taken out from his bag.

As Misrakesi took it out and held it up to the light of the branched terracotta deepmala set beside the chair, she saw that the obverse was the same as the coin she had examined earlier. The same five symbols were struck on to the surface.

'Turn it on the other side. You will see that the surface is not plain,' instructed Siddharthak.

'I can see a number of symbols struck but they make no sense to me. They seem to be some four or five strange symbols which are very different from the symbols on the front side,' said Misrakesi peering hard at the coin.

'You find them incomprehensible because you have never been instructed in the symbolic language of the Rupasutra. I do not know the meanings myself because I was not given the key but I believe they are simplicity itself when you read it with the key.'

'But what is the purpose of these symbols? All the royal and mint symbols are already on the other side?' asked Misrakesi perplexed, her eyes were hurting and head spinning with signs and symbols.

'Again, let me try to be brief and simple. But the topic itself is very complex. These strange symbols on the obverse are punch marks struck there by "Rupadarshaks", the officials appointed by the mint to oversee coinage. They are put there periodically by the

"Rupadarshaks" within the circulation period of each individual coin after checking that the weight and the specifications are up to the set standards. They are a kind of guarantee of the purity of the coin and its intrinsic value. So that the user of the coin and the trader know that they are not being cheated. Merchants know how to read these punch marks.'

'I see. I think I understand something now. In the suspect coins, the guarantees are missing and also as you say they are not up to the set standards of weight and metal,' said Misrakesi thoughtfully.

'Yes, if we had not had the coins checked, the lack of symbols on the reverse side could have meant simply that the coins were new since it is only after a certain period of circulation that the coins are checked. But in this case, the explanation is not so innocent.'

Misrakesi rose and paced around the terrace, deep in thought. Then she looked at Siddharthak and said, 'Shall we stop for a minute and think about what we have understood. Can I offer you something to eat and drink? I think we are going to be here for some time.'

Siddharthak watched appreciatively as she poured a kumbha of special maireya into two round beryl cups and offered one to him with her graceful dancer's movements. She also offered him a platter of fruits which he declined. He sipped his wine and watched her meditatively. Even as he mulled over the problem in front of them, one part of his mind was busy planning her seduction. Her subtle scent and delicately moulded body combined with the ambience of the night to make his desire for her quicken.

'Tell me,' said Misrakesi after thinking for a while, 'if the Lakshanadhyaksha can understand from the symbols which mint the coins were struck in, can some enquiries not be made there?'

'That is a very good idea. So good, in fact, that I have already thought of it and sent some men there for enquiries, or rather the Lakshanadhyaksha has.'

'So we wait for them to come back and tell us what they have found?'

'That part is being handled by the Mint authorities. They will not even tell me where the concerned mint is for fear that I will start deciphering the secret code of the Rupasutra. They are a secretive and suspicious lot. But it cannot be too far since they are going to report in about a fortnight.'

'This may be a part of the enemy machinations against Magadha but I must say that I do not see how it fits in. Somebody somewhere has found a way to make himself very rich. It can hardly be the Pauravas,' mused Misrakesi.

'It is, you must admit, a most unusual circumstance and must therefore be looked into. The Lakshanadhyaksha is so agitated, outraged, and worried that I feared he would ascend straight to swarg without the benefit of even a pushpakviman,' Siddharthak put down his wine cup and stretched. The atmosphere was right for his next move.

The breeze gently stirred the loose tendrils of Misrakesi's hair as she smiled at him. He pulled her up into his embrace and tipped up her chin to catch her lips in a full and expert kiss, which made women melt into his arms. She automatically encircled his shoulders with her arms and gave herself up to the kiss but with only half a mind, the other being on the coins. In spite of his laid-back looks, his body was iron hard and virile beneath her fingers.

Siddharthak raised his head after a while and shook it, smiling, 'One of these days...' and let her go.

'No, wait,' he said turning back, 'you and the wine have turned my head. What about the source of these coins? I know where my lot came from and I will pursue the wretched gambler who gave them to me. Not that I expect anything much as he is a broken-down old drunkard. What about your coins, Devi, where did they come from?'

Misrakesi looked away and said nothing. She had no intention of divulging her ghostly problems to Siddharthak when it was not necessary. She would report only to Pushyamitra and that too because it was important.

'Well?' repeated Siddharthak.

'You pursue your enquiries, Arya Siddharthak, and I will pursue mine,' said Misrakesi smiling sweetly and folding her hands in a pranaam.

'If that is how you want it,' and Siddharthak left with an offended laugh.

Misrakesi thought a little ruefully that she had probably just made another enemy when she desperately needed friends in Pataliputra. If Chandramukhi's problem had not been involved, she could have talked to him and also taken his advice. It was late, so she decided to go to sleep and leave all decisions for the morrow.

The morning saw her determined to speak to Chandramukhi and, in a change of mind, with Siddharthak. She left a blue lotus at the feet of the Goddess, which was the signal she had arranged with Chandramukhi, and sent Urmil to look for Siddharthak on the pretext that he owed Apsara Sabha some money from the last night.

Chandramukhi appeared at the height of the noonday sun when the household was dozing in the afternoon heat. Khus curtains were hung at the windows and doors and Madlekha had had them soaked with water so that the fierce loo winds which were blowing turned into a cool breeze by the time they came through the curtains. The interior of her room was therefore cool and perfumed with khus with a welcome dappled darkness as opposed to the glare outside.

Misrakesi flinched when Chandramukhi pushed the curtain aside as the sun struck her straight in the eyes. She gestured to Chandramukhi to come in and drop the curtain back in place.

'Aha! Is it not wonderful to be a famous and rich nartaki and not wilt in the heat and dust outside,' was her only greeting, sarcastic as ever. *If she misses her comfortable life why doesn't she go back to her parents,* thought Misrakesi, irritated. Apsara Sabha would be nothing compared to the luxury and opulence of Chandramukhi's parental home.

Masking her irritation she said, 'Rest a while, we can talk later. And here, have this drink. It is made of Bel and will cool you down.'

To her annoyance Chandramukhi took her at her word, drained the Bel drink and then happily spread herself to sleep for half an hour. Misrakesi was left fuming and on guard to stop anyone from coming in. Thankfully, they were all asleep and she had also asked to be left alone till the evening.

The afternoon and the comfortable half-darkness in the room combined to make Misrakesi also fall into a light doze when Chandramukhi woke up and said, 'That was refreshing. Good to know that our industrious nartakis get their rest in such comfort.'

Misrakesi did not say anything and after a moment, Chandramukhi shrugged her shoulders and said, 'You may as well tell me why you called me. I cannot take you down to the riverfront again till the next shipment is due, which will probably take some time. As for the portrait, I have all the material you gave me but I am still experimenting and that will also take time. So what is it?'

'It is those coins you gave me,' replied Misrakesi.

'Yes, what about them? What does someone like you want with a few copper Masakas? You must be worth your weight in Karshapans,' sarcasm again.

'Leaving my riches aside, those coins would not make anyone rich. They were counterfeit.'

'Counterfeit?' said Chandramukhi frowning. 'Do you mean that the copper content was diluted or that the weight was less than two rattis?'

Misrakesi was impressed. This girl knew her coins. In fact, she exhibited the most unexpected skills at times; case in point, the portrait she was making. No matter how much her father had indulged her, he had also been very careful with her education. Surprising, since Chandramukhi was the youngest daughter and hardly likely to take over the family business.

Chandramukhi smiled at Misrakesi's look of surprise. 'My dear sister,' and the term did not hold any affection, 'I am the daughter of a merchant, commerce runs in my blood.'

'To get back to the question at hand, Chandramukhi, where do you think the kevat would have got them? What is his name, by the way?'

'Oh indeed, I am such a fool as to tell you his name so that you can get him traced by those rakshasas of Pushyamitra's and beaten and tortured,' snapped Chandramukhi.

Since Misrakesi was not sure that Pushyamitra would not do exactly that, she let it go and waited for an answer. Chandramukhi prowled around the room popping badaams in her mouth and scrunching them. After some time, she shook her head.

'It cannot be him. He would not spread counterfeit coins, I am certain. And he would never cheat me; someone else must have cheated him. I will go and meet him and find out. And I will go alone; I am not taking you to him unless it is absolutely necessary. You are too dangerous.'

This left Misrakesi perversely amused, her feelings about Chandramukhi were exactly reciprocated! And she was certainly very sensitive about the kevat, was there some affair of the heart brewing? It would be most inappropriate for a merchant's daughter. She pulled herself up short; Chandramukhi was no longer a merchant's daughter but a person without any existence, without any place in the social hierarchy. But Misrakesi could not help thinking wistfully that if the kevat took Chandramukhi away, her life would certainly be less complicated.

Urmil had come back from Siddharthak's hovel with the message that he, Siddharthak, did not think he owed Apsara Sabha anything but maybe he would come along sometime, when he was free, to discuss the matter. Misrakesi had to be content with that. Perhaps this was his way of telling her that he was offended. She would try to win him over when he did come. She had been foolish the previous night as she could easily have told him about the visit to the riverfront and referred to Chandramukhi simply as an informer. Keeping the identity of an informer secret would not have occasioned any surprise or offense. She would have to become more adept at playing this game of chaupad.

She had however, done Siddharthak an injustice. His voice was heard raised in drunken and slurred indignation at her gate early that evening. He was defending himself loudly against charges of cheating Apsara Sabha and demanding to see Misrakesi herself. She asked Urmil to bring him in. The evening had just begun, so a number of the private enclosures were empty; but they did not want to take any risk. So they met briefly and Misrakesi asked him to come to her terrace at midnight.

'Pushyamitra is also going to be there. We will come up together,' said Siddharthak just as he was about to leave and watched the almost imperceptible flow of emotion across her face. She said nothing, merely inclining her head and gliding gracefully across the room to do her duty in the dancing hall.

Her foremost duty these days was Ugrasala. He was a thin, weedy young man with lank brown hair straggling across his shoulders and an unprepossessing leer on his face. He was now firmly of the impression that he was Misrakesi's favourite. His inflated self esteem made even a small encouragement go a long way.

He swaggered in confidently, exuding wine and lust in equal quantities and greeted Misrakesi familiarly. She smiled charmingly, giving no hint of the dislike she felt for him, and led him off to a sustained interrogation cleverly disguised as a flirtation. Ugrasala's stock amongst his circle was rising; to be the object of interest of the latest beautiful ganika in Pataliputra was indeed an achievement.

Misrakesi was painstakingly compiling a list of his family, friends and contacts, trade interests, and properties. This was under instructions as Ugrasala was exactly the kind of disgruntled element, rich and powerful in the Nanda regime that the Mauryans distrusted the most.

Ugrasala was basking in her attention and losing no opportunity to slide an arm around her waist or put his lips close to her cheek or her ears to whisper. Misrakesi knew he was working up to kiss her and responded coquettishly. The list of his contacts she was supplying to Pushyamitra increased with each session.

This was her work and she did it without a second thought but she was conscious of a feeling of relief when one of the dasis appeared and requested her presence in another part of the hall as there was a situation which required her attention. Misrakesi gestured to Manjari to take over and escaped with fulsome promises to be back as soon as possible.

The 'situation' turned out to be Pushyamitra who had appeared a few minutes ago and was demanding to be entertained by the proprietress herself. He was the most dreaded man in Pataliputra and so a dasi had been hurriedly dispatched by Mrinalini to call

Misrakesi while Ratibhama did her trembling best to entertain him, all her languishing glances and come-hither looks forgotten.

He was reclining on his side with one powerful arm resting on an upraised knee, looking completely at ease while he took in the perfume of the white Yuthika flowers strewn on the couch. This was more than could be said for Ratibhama who had an apprehensive look in her eyes and was offering him Madhu in a silver cup with a timid smile and a hand trying not to shake.

Misrakesi was amused at the sight and since whatever she felt for him it was definitely not fear she hastened to meet him with a smile, ignoring the fact that their last meeting had left her raging and angry. He remembered it, perhaps, because he greeted her with a restraint only she understood. However, they were in their roles as ganika and client and both of them knew how to enact those roles to a nicety.

Pushyamitra never disguised himself while moving around the city and Misrakesi had often wondered why that was so. Here, too, he was present openly as the chief of the Nagarik Suraksha Vibhag. It was probably because he was too distinctive in his looks. Every child in Magadha knew those handsome but harsh features; the cruel lips, penetrating eyes and the silken hair with the jewelled headband, it was no use trying to hide them.

The three of them met at the appointed hour in Misrakesi's private quarters. There were no dasas present but wine and food had already been kept on the terrace. Drinks, barley gruel and meat, fruits and sweets were there in abundance. There were beautifully wrought silver bowls with matching stands kept for the guests. Siddharthak flung himself across the larger rocking chair while Pushyamitra sat upright on one of the smaller chairs. The two men were hungry and helped themselves to the fried meats and fruit. Siddharthak was also drinking heavily as was his habit while Pushyamitra confined himself to a Mango Mahasura. Misrakesi excused herself and went into the room to take off her heavy jewellery.

She was partially visible from outside as she moved around shedding jewellery. First her small and delicate feet were placed on the bed as she undid her ghunghrus. The mekhala at her waist was then followed by ear rings, nose ring, armlets and bangles and the long satlari around her neck. But she was stuck at her kanthahaar; it was always removed by Madlekha. In response to a murmured request Pushyamitra went in and untied the string which held it close while she stood with her back to him holding her heavy swathe of hair away from her neck. She slipped off her heavy embroidered uttariya and donned a thin blue one affording Pushyamitra a beautiful glimpse of her.

'My apologies, but I am ready now.' Her neck and arms were bare and the blue mulmul around her shoulders only accentuated her cleavage. Her skin always had a warm golden lustre but this was the first time Pushyamitra had really appreciated it. Her only remaining jewellery was the flat sapphire bindi just below her hair parting. She looked fresh, soft, and inviting and was smiling at him with her head slightly raised.

This was also the first time he had entered her room. It was whitewashed with a black and red floor and a large soft bed dominated it. There was a small niche just above the bed with fresh atimukta flowers in it. The entire wall above the bed was taken up by a stunning fresco depicting an amorous Gandharva couple in different positions of love making. The room in which she actually slept was further in, but this too was her personal space and bore her stamp. Her jewellery and clothes were strewn around as were her lute and bamboo flute. A garland of atimukta flowers was waiting to be finished. She had obviously been trying her hand at poetry as a half-finished bhojpatra fluttered on the bed.

Pushyamitra's hands were still on the bare skin of her back as his eyes moved inadvertently from the fresco on the wall to the flesh and blood woman shivering slightly to his touch and the cool breeze from the river.

Siddharthak's voice broke their reverie, Pushyamitra's hands dropped and the two of them came out on to the terrace.

Siddharthak had been watching them through half-closed eyes and compressed lips over his cup of wine. In his long years with Pushyamitra, he had never seen him attracted to or involved with a woman. This was partly why he had such a spotless reputation; any mud thrown at him had fallen off that sparkling surface.

That was changing now and the mud seemed to be sticking. People, in the plural, led by Sreelekha and a reluctant Hiranyalabha in tow were talking; that he was in the toils of a beautiful ganika from Ujjain and was misusing his power and influence to set her up. Only a handful of people knew the reality of Apsara Sabha, to the others it was a mystery how had it sprung up and established itself so soon and that too with a new and unknown ganika as the patroness? Sreelekha knew the truth, but that did not stop her from setting about malicious rumours, a skilful mixture of half truths and lies. And once the fire was lit, very little was needed to keep it going.

He also wondered whether it was just Sreelekha's malice or whether there was some truth in the rumours. Attraction, mutual, was certainly there but his experienced eyes told him that they had not yet slept together. He had seen Misrakesi shiver and tense when Pushyamitra had touched her back while undoing the kanthahaar. As far as he was concerned, he was fast giving up on sleeping with Misrakesi. Her response to him left a lot to be desired and he was not one to force himself on a woman. There were enough willing ones for him to choose from. Misrakesi seemed to be sleeping in a lonely bed at the moment, from choice, he had no doubt. It was her assignment in the spy service which gave her the luxury and courage to make this choice.

It was ironical that his failure seemed to be due to competition from the most unlikely quarters: Pushyamitra, whose strength had always been in scaring women off rather than attracting them!

He shrugged his shoulders and decided that he was not going to interfere. They were guptachars after all and should know what the public was saying. Pushyamitra would not thank him for interfering and Misrakesi had given him no cause to love her. He turned his attention to Pushyamitra who was speaking.

'The three of us have to put our resources and information together and decide what to do next. I will be coordinating this case myself with the two of you. If any extra help or resources are needed you can ask me.'

'But why?' asked Misrakesi wrinkling her forehead below the sapphire bindi, 'What is so important about these coins to merit your personal attention?'

'Not just mine, Misrakesi, but also Acharya Chanakya's,' said Pushyamitra quietly. 'He is taking a weekly brief from me about developments. He wants us to trace the source and stop their dissemination and eliminate the source behind it. The mint officials are also going to issue a royal proclamation that all new Nanda coins have to be exchanged at the treasury, they will not be acceptable as payment till further notice. But all this will take some time to take effect and for all the coins in circulation to be gathered.'

Misrakesi bit her lower lip and said dubiously, 'If the acharya himself is taking an interest and instructing us, it must be important, but I ask again, why?'

'Let me explain, if I can. The acharya has a keen and intelligent mind that sees far beyond ours can. Once he told me why he was so concerned I was also convinced,' said Pushyamitra, his mind going back to his meeting with the acharya.

Pushyamitra had met him in the small anteroom behind the royal throne which had become his de facto work room. The acharya habitually sat in a Padmasana with his back straight as a spear. His shabby low wooden desk was before him with a deepak burning for illumination. There were no other furnishings in the room except for kusha grass mats to sit on. There were bundles of bhojpatras for his perusal. The acharya was possibly the hardest working man in the kingdom with the possible exception of the samrat.

'Pranaam Acharya. You had summoned me.'

'Aayushman bhava. Sit down and wait while I finish looking at these accounts,' said the acharya, raising his eyes briefly.

Pushyamitra sat down on the grass mat in a Padmasana which, even if not as perfect as the one in front of him, was passable. He wondered which hapless official was having his accounts examined at this level. This was normally the work of the accounting and auditing department, and there must have been some serious problem for it to reach here. Someone was definitely going to be punished in the near future.

The acharya was often heard saying that royal officials were like fish in water. Who knew how much water the fish drank as it swam in the water; similarly who knew how much royal officials appropriated from royal revenues. He was forever vigilant, setting up inspection departments and rules and regulations to counter this. He had recently set out a list of behaviour patterns that the inspecting officers were to look for in isolating corrupt officials. Detailed and stringent punishment was also prescribed.

The accounts were examined, annotated and put away. The acharya turned his severe gaze on Pushyamitra who concentrated his attention.

'This is with reference to the matter of the counterfeit coins. It is a very worrying and serious situation. It could shake the foundation of the empire we have started to establish, and lead to ruin.'

Pushyamitra was listening silently. He could not understand why the acharya was so worried but was waiting to be enlightened.

'You see, Pushyamitra, our traditional methods of trade and payment have changed in the last hundred years or so. Barter and payment in kind are being replaced by the coinage system especially in the cities. Coins were earlier issued by the merchant guilds but again, this has been taken over by the royal authorities. The coins are backed by the king and are accepted as long and as far as his writ runs. It has facilitated the explosion of agriculture, trade, and commerce as you see before your eyes because of its acceptability and convenience. But do not forget,' he held up a finger impressively, 'the coin is only a piece of metal. The entire system is a delicate one. Trust and acceptability of its value in terms of goods depends upon an entire social contract.' The acharya stopped and looked at Pushyamitra to see if he understood.

Pushyamitra was still confused. Where was this leading to? He knew that the acharya was a renowned professor of Politics from Takshshila and was engaged in writing down the principles of Arthashastra or the science of wealth. He was compiling the wisdom of centuries which had been in his family's keeping for many generations. His father had passed it on to him. He had no one to pass it on to but was compiling it for posterity. This was probably a chapter from this compilation. Pushyamitra had received lessons in political economy in Takshshila, but could not honestly say that he had spent any time thinking about these issues after that.

The acharya went on, 'The value of goods as expressed in coins is a complex matter of give and take. If a trader keeps his price too high, he will find few buyers and will perforce have to lower the price. If it is too low, he will find it difficult to sustain his activities but since there will be multiple buyers, he will find it possible to raise his price. He will adjust his price till his costs are covered and there is something left over as profit. Again, the element of how much profit is sustainable is dependent on a number of factors which I will not get into. Suffice it to say that supply and demand play a major role in fixing the price of goods.

'Look at the current situation. There is a sudden influx of below-par coins from outside our system. The total goods in our kingdom have not increased by any significant amount in the short run. The people with these fake coins are willing to pay more and more for the same goods thus driving the prices up, too much money chasing too few goods. With the increase in prices the average nagarik will be adversely hit. He will be discontented and dissatisfied. It is always easy to incite a rebellion of the dissatisfied.

'Others will soon discover that the coins are below par and faith in the coinage system will be shaken or even shattered. There could be a move back to barter. This would be a retrograde step. I am trying to increase the production of an agricultural surplus through the clearing of large tracts of forest and their conversion to cultivation. This surplus can only be encouraged through monetization and enlargement of trade which go hand in hand.

'Then again, we maintain a standing army with payments made in the same coins to soldiers. If their faith in the coins is shaken it would be fatally easy to destabilize the army.'

The acharya lifted his hands and placed them on his desk, 'I cannot let all this happen,' he said in a cold and flat voice.

Pushyamitra said hesitantly, 'Acharya, for all these consequences to follow the scale of the influx of these coins would have to be really large, wouldn't it? A few coins here and there would not have much effect.'

'You are right. And which is why we must find out their source and extent of circulation. I will take care of the latter with the help of the Lakshanadhyaksha. You concentrate on the source.'

He smiled suddenly, a rare occurrence which lit up his austere face. 'Are you wondering how I have outlined the entire plan and its consequences with so much precision? Let me tell you something that happened in the Gurukul of Takshshila twenty-two years ago. A group of ten students were graduating from the Gurukul. They were asked to form groups of two and submit their final dissertation; the topic was innovative methods of secret warfare. The two students who graduated as the first and second had prepared the plan I have just been detailing.'

There was an electric pause. Pushyamitra ventured, 'One of them was you, Acharya.'

'Yes. And the other was Narsingh Dev, the current Maha Amatya of the Pauravas…' the words fell like pebbles into a pool of silence.

'Narsingh is a brilliant man. Yes, we had made this plan together. In the whole of Jambudweepa, he is one of the few men whose intelligence I recognize. And I fear for my motherland…' the words were spoken almost in a whisper. Pushyamitra was silent as the acharya stared unseeingly before him.

'So, Pushyamitra,' said the acharya, rousing himself from his abstraction, 'find the source and stop the dissemination of the counterfeit coins. Go now.'

As Pushyamitra joined his palms in a pranaam, he said somberly, 'Vijayibhava.'

Pushyamitra had left the ante room with the words ringing in his ears. For the sake of Magadha, they had to win.

On the banks of the River Ganges, on the flower-laden terrace of a dancing house there were two silent people who looked on as Pushyamitra finished and fell silent.

The silence was broken by Siddharthak. 'So! Where do we start?'

The Course of the Coins

Things should be examined with reference to facts patent and latent, and inferences.

Chanakyasutra 132

It was a pertinent question which merited an immediate response. Both Pushyamitra and Misrakesi were putting their thoughts together and had no quick answer to give.

Siddharthak had decided, for his own reasons, to break the mood of harmony between Misrakesi and Pushyamitra.

'Let us first put all our information together. That is, if Devi Misrakesi has no objection?' Siddharthak sat up and directed a pointed look at Misrakesi who flushed slightly.

'What is all this about?' asked Pushyamitra shortly.

'Nothing at all, except that Devi Misrakesi very rightly refused to report any thing to me yesterday. After all, I am not her superior,' said Siddharthak smiling affably at both of them and embarrassing Misrakesi just as he had intended to.

The look on Pushyamitra's face said that he understood perfectly and had himself experienced her obstinacy but he contented himself with saying, 'Now that I am here and am directing both of you to work as a team there should not be any problem.'

Misrakesi felt like a recalcitrant child put in her place and rebellious thoughts of paying Siddharthak back in his own coin arose only to be suppressed. She was relatively new in the department and the two men before her were battle-hardened veterans. Let her establish herself and then she would see who would embarrass who.

She composed her face and thoughts and gave Siddharthak a brief account of how the coins had come into her possession. She referred to Chandramukhi only as her informer and was grateful when Pushyamitra did not interrupt to elaborate. The fewer people who knew about her ghost the better. She flashed a grateful smile at him and he nodded back, her secret would remain a secret for now.

Siddharthak caught the smile and nod and was seriously annoyed. *Either they are keeping something from me or there is indeed something between them,* he thought angrily, Maybe that old witch Sreelekha is right after all! Pushyamitra is ganging up with someone else against me, after we have worked together for more years than I can remember. Women! He would make it his business to find out what exactly was there between the two of them.

'As I see it,' said Siddharthak, 'the riverfront where the boats land should be surrounded by soldiers the next time they land. Catch the men and beat the truth out of them.' Secretly he was also rather impressed and jealous of Misrakesi. He had been trying for years to cultivate informers from the waterfront with indifferent success as they were a very closed and suspicious lot. And this new woman had achieved a breakthrough in a matter of months. There must be something behind that desirable body and beautiful face.

Pushyamitra was completely in agreement with Siddharthak's suggestion, but Misrakesi was furious. Could they think of nothing beyond torture and beating? She had given her word that nothing would happen to the kevat.

She interjected heatedly, 'Could we stop for a moment please? You seem to be forgetting that my informer has told me all this and taken me to the exact place of landing on condition that we would not touch the kevat! I cannot betray her.'

So the informer was a woman, Siddharthak thought. It was getting more and more intriguing.

Pushyamitra said sternly, 'Misrakesi, please keep your emotions in check. You are new to this profession but soon you will learn that our word depends on circumstances. You will have to get used to your word depending on expediency because Magadha comes first.'

'Magadha comes first for me too, Arya. I am only objecting to your method. We can do it my way. What credibility do I have if I betray an informer just when I am trying to establish a network? Beating is not the only way of obtaining information.' Misrakesi was vehement. Was she never to have any degree of professional freedom but always be a puppet dangling from Pushyamitra's fingers? Siddharthak said nothing but gave Pushyamitra an eloquent look and then started whistling soundlessly with elaborate unconcern as if to say, this is your problem, solve it.

Pushyamitra looked scornfully at Misrakesi and said, 'Do you think that in the more than ten years of espionage work I have done I have not seen all methods of extracting information? And it is fear that works every time. Let us leave your sensibilities and your relationship with your informer out of it.'

Misrakesi had well and truly lost her temper now and she threw discretion to the winds. 'Don't throw your experience at me. And as far as my sensibilities are concerned I am afraid they are here to stay. You hired me to do a job, and I will do it my way.'

It was only the two of them confronting each other in the room now, Siddharthak was forgotten.

Pushyamitra stood up and said thunderously, 'Be careful of what you say, Devi. Are you putting your informer before the information?' He towered over where she was sitting and glared down at her. His anger was so palpable that Misrakesi moved back as if struck; but her expression did not change and her voice did not falter when she looked back fearlessly into his eyes and said, 'Yes, I am. My informer can be reached only through me and I will not lead you to her and the kevat so that you can torture them.'

Both of them were in the grip of an irrational wave of anger and Siddharthak could only look at them with his eyebrows raised. This entire discussion could be carried out in a more reasonable manner although he felt that the fault was more Misrakesi's: she was going too far in questioning someone who was after all, her chief.

Pushyamitra's voice was as cold as a Himalayan mountain stream when he sat down again and said in a dangerously silky voice, 'So, as an intelligence officer, you are refusing to turn over information and an informer who has been working against the kingdom of Magadha. Am I to take this as a formal refusal in front of a witness?' he jerked a hand towards Siddharthak.

'You are mistaken Arya Pushyamitra,' replied Misrakesi in an equally cold voice, 'I am not refusing to turn over anything. I will merely do it my own way. I undertake to provide you with the necessary information regarding the source and destination of those boats and any connection they have with the counterfeit coins in a fortnight's time. If I fail to do so, you are free to act as you wish and I hold myself ready to accept whatever punishment may be imposed on me.'

Pushyamitra snapped, 'You have a week,' and walked out without another word. Siddharthak got up, shrugged, gave Misrakesi an ironic pranaam and left, too, thinking, *She may have peculiar ideas but she also has the guts to stick to them.*

As he caught up with Pushyamitra marching out in a temper he could not resist saying, 'This is what comes of trusting an untried young woman with important work. Her inexperience and emotion come in the way.'

Pushyamitra's face darkened. 'I will take care of her emotions,' he growled, 'maybe I will have her thrown into prison and beaten for defying the directions of a royal official and acting against the interests of Magadha. Then we will see whether she saves herself or her kevat. Don't be surprised if I regret the time I have given her and beat the truth out of her tomorrow.'

Siddharthak was mildly disapproving after considering the idea, 'She is not just any nartaki, you know. She has the personal blessings of the acharya and it might not work out, especially if she says nothing. But then again, you are Pushyamitra and can get away with actions others might not be able to get away with'

Pushyamitra cast him an impatient glance and soon left to continue the extensive combing operations he was conducting in the outskirts of the city.

He had little intention of doing what temper had made him suggest. He was in a cold rage, frustrated, thwarted in a way he had never been before. Why did he have to face so much trouble from Misrakesi, why couldn't she just listen to his orders and do things the way they were supposed to be done, not in some unconventional and emotional way which had the element of uncertainty. He had given her too much professional freedom and she had over reached herself. Who was she after all but a petty spy in his pay, how could she defy him? His mood was savage and his men, always sensitive to his mood were apprehensive and quiet with none of the cheerful badinage which accompanied their work.

He was too ruffled to continue his supervision and came back leaving Sumant, his deputy, behind. It was early morning and he decided to go to the one place where he always found peace and rest. The home of Kaumudi, the wife... no, the widow of Veerbhadra, the only man he had ever called friend, and their seven-year-old son. He was always certain of finding a welcome there. Veerbhadra, Kaumudi and he had been childhood friends, then the two of them had married but the friendship between the three had remained the same. Now he and Kaumudi were close friends and occasional lovers. He had also been thinking of giving in to his brother's increasing pressure to get married and who better than his old friend?

The household was up and Kaumudi was happy to see him although she could see at a glance that he was upset and not his usual self. When she held his shoulders and looked a question, he grimaced and smiled, 'Nothing, it is just a new recruit at work. Don't worry, perhaps I am a little stressed.' They had left it at that; Pushyamitra thinking yet again that as soon as he had settled this problem of Misrakesi, he would ask Kaumudi to marry him.

Misrakesi, on the other hand, sat rooted to her seat after the two men left, waiting for the pounding of her heart to subside. She was feeling sick and shaky, she had lost her temper and made claims she could not possibly fulfill.

Sunk in her own thoughts she did not even notice a shadow detach itself from the tree outside her terrace and enter her room. It was a strangely subdued Chandramukhi who came and sat next to her and patted her shoulder clumsily.

'Thank you *sister*.' The word was not a sarcastic one this time. 'I have heard everything. Perhaps I have misjudged you. You have put yourself in danger by defending us.' Her voice was low and sincere.

Slightly recovered, Misrakesi got up and drank some water and turned to smile faintly at Chandramukhi. Truth be told, she had considered nothing while giving her undertaking to Pushyamitra and did not know how she would manage to wrest any information from Chandramukhi or the kevat. Perhaps with Chandramukhi in this strangely sympathetic mood she could make a start.

She was taken by surprise.

'Misrakesi, I will take you to meet my friend, the kevat. His name is Basant. He is originally from Hastinapur but his grandfather came down the river looking for work and they have been Magadhi for three generations now. He does help traders evade customs duty and makes his living from that. But I don't think he would go so far as to help the enemies of the kingdom. That would be rajdroha.'

This was cooperation indeed. So far all the information Misrakesi had managed to extract from Chandramukhi had been as tough as filtering gold from the legendary streams of the north; and here it was, positively gushing forth like the rivers of the plains flooding in the rains!

'Keep yourself ready tomorrow night. If I can find him and if the time is right, I will take you to talk to him. Be patient till then.' And Chandramukhi was off.

Left alone, weighing her options, Misrakesi realized she was fighting for her future. Fate had conspired to put her in situations which had allowed her to exercise more freedom in her actions than would normally have been possible or allowed. The results had been useful, so she had not faced any adverse reaction. She was now in direct confrontation with her chief and she felt anything but brave and confident. In fact she felt lonely... defenceless. She imagined herself back at the academy in Ujjain, a failure. Her directress would always treat her with sympathy and she would have a place there, but her political career would be dead almost at birth.

She sat hugging her knees as she reflected dully that unless Chandramukhi really did do what she was promising and some useful information was obtained, she was doomed.

It was imperative to get rid of her, the weapon of disclosure she held in her hand was too dangerous and was bound to be used sometime or the other. It would have been better than fighting with Pushyamitra to get Chandramukhi and the kevat captured and out of her way. But would she have been able to take such a ruthless step against a girl who had anyway been at the receiving end of fate?

She sighed and got up, preparing to go to sleep. But sleep was far from her. Her mind ranged over all kinds of issues trying to solve them or make sense of them. She would, for one, have to lighten her duties at the Apsara Sabha, the personal appearances and daily performances would have to go for some time, one of the other nartakis would have to take over. She could not trust the new Magadhan girls yet, Ratibhama would have to step into the breach.

The organization was in the capable hands of Mrinalini. Manjari was a very reliable second in command; she had the knack of sympathy and drawing people out so maybe Ugrasala could be handed over to her. It would keep him occupied till Misrakesi had either surmounted the current crisis or... well, if she could not find a solution to her current problems there would be no need to worry about Apsara Sabha at all! It would be taken over and given to someone else.

She had come face to face with Pushyamitra in his true professional colours for the first time and it was a revelation. The face he had put on before her had always been calm and controlled, she had forgotten the methods he was reputed to use to extract information. She had never thought about the use to which her reports on the men who frequented Apsara Sabha were being put. She wondered now what retribution had fallen on them. Although she had no specific sympathies for any of them it was better not to conjecture along those lines. She finally went to sleep with the thought that she would perhaps like to see Ugrasala with his wandering hands and loose mouth being tortured to death!

The next morning she joined Mrinalini and Manjari as they sat surrounded by the ingredients for a sandalwood body lotion. She was also reminded of her promise to Chandramukhi and quickly gave a list of items to be put in her bath. She would give them to Chandramukhi if and when she came in the night. There was no harm in giving the kevat something to think about by helping Chandramukhi regain her beauty!

Misrakesi was trying to be optimistic about her situation. After all it was not the end of Kaliyuga if she was to stop being a spy and go back to Ujjain. She could have a career as a nartaki there, too, it was not a backwater but a centre of art and culture for centuries. In fact, it was Pataliputra which was the upstart city.

As she sat down with Mrinalini and Manjari, however, she realized she had started to enjoy her life here and was slowly, for the first time, beginning to call a place home. A sense of permanence had been seeping in. Now, it was all in jeopardy.

Her face must have reflected her thoughts because Mrinalini asked her sharply, 'What is the matter, daughter? Tell us. I am sure we can help.'

Misrakesi had been thinking about how much to tell them and the answer was, obviously, nothing. There was no need to increase the number of players in her personal drama.

'Yes, there is a problem but I cannot tell you what it is. Can I trust you to take what I say without any explanations? I can tell you only that I need help,' she said finally.

Mrinalini's emotional answer was backed by Manjari's quieter, but heartfelt offers to help. Misrakesi felt a little comforted, she was not alone, the whole of Pataliputra was not against her, only one, or was it three, of its inhabitants?

'Mrinalini and Manjari – I want both of you to completely take over the supervision and running of Apsara Sabha for the next few days. I will not be able to discuss anything with you. After that, I am either out of the trouble or out of Apsara Sabha.'

She shrugged resignedly at the shock on their faces. 'I told you, I am in a difficult situation but do not ask me anymore. Manjari, I also have a specific piece of work for you. You know Arya Ugrasala who comes in almost every evening?'

Manjari nodded. She had seen Misrakesi with him and wondered at the closeness. Misrakesi was gracious, even flirtatious, with most customers but with him it was something more. She could not believe it was attraction – there were men with more money and personal attraction than him. In any case, Misrakesi had never behaved like a ganika out for money since the opening of Apsara Sabha. Manjari had often wondered at the fact that she was nobody's mistress. Youth and beauty were ephemeral, they had to be used while they were there, what was she waiting for? Anyway, it was not for Manjari to question her.

'Take him over from me and keep me informed on what he says and does. Make him forget me and become your slave, you know how,' said Misrakesi, smiling faintly at Manjari. 'Then, either we discontinue the solo dance performance I give, or someone takes over. Do you think you and Ratibhama could divide it between the two of you?'

They looked dubious, Ratibhama was difficult, cooperation was not on her priority list and at any indication that she was becoming more important to the dancing house she would demand an immediate increase in salary.

'Shall we wait and see? If you are going to be away only for a few days maybe we can do without it. We will have to have a story to tell the clients. We could tell them that you have gone on a pilgrimage to Urubela[47] and will be back in a few days,' said Manjari.

'But you are not going anywhere, are you?' asked Mrinalini anxiously.

'I will be in Pataliputra but could be moving around within the city very frequently so I want both of you to take over, do not wait to consult me on daily matters.'

Mrinalini was clearly preparing to ask many more questions so Misrakesi stood up in one fluid movement, thanked them with an eloquent look and left.

She spent the day waiting for Chandramukhi, planning the questions she would ask the kevat, Basant. If Chandramukhi came and if she took her to him and if he answered any questions and if he knew anything at all to tell... the list of ifs was very long.

The sun had gone down across the river and Misrakesi was still waiting. She had not expected any developments during the day, but now her impatience reached fever pitch. Chandramukhi had almost promised to come but there could be many hitches. Misrakesi tried to think over where Basant would probably live and how easy it would be for Chandramukhi to contact him. Above all did she really mean to? What if she had a change of heart?

The moon and stars now shone bright but still no Chandramukhi. Misrakesi knew she should go to sleep but was rigid with tension and expectation; sleep was impossible. She sat on her terrace and focused on the tree from where Chandramukhi normally made her appearance.

She stood up suddenly. She could spy a figure making its way through the trees. Yes, it was Chandramukhi and she was in a hurry. She came and stood below the terrace and called in a low voice, 'Misrakesi, are you ready? Let us go immediately.'

As Misrakesi got up and Chandramukhi took a look at her she hissed, 'You cannot go like that! Your clothes and jewellery will be snatched off your back before you know it. Where is that ragged soldier's dress you had on when you went to the water front that first night? Change fast, fast, you understand?'

Misrakesi nodded her head and vanished. In a few minutes she was down with Chandramukhi who led the way, not towards the river bank or the forest but towards the city. In fact, she was moving towards the outskirt of the city past the royal stables, the settlements for the secondary artisans, weavers etc, the vaidyashalas,[48] the grain stores of the city and the animal houses. The ornate sculptured stone temple to the Lord Vaijayanta came up. Misrakesi stopped and offered up a short but heartfelt prayer for help to the God of Victory. His blessings would be needed.

They had come to the ironsmiths' houses, all huddled together but the prosperous households differentiated from the poorer thatched huts. A narrow lane disappeared into the darkness; Chandramukhi carried on confidently after looking around carefully for an instant. Misrakesi swallowed her uneasiness, fingered her poisoned dagger, and went in behind her.

Wooden flares were casting an uncertain light over the lane and groups of people could be seen sitting outside the huts in the heat of the night. From the raised voices, raucous laughter, and strains of Magadhi songs floating in the night air Misrakesi could guess that some form of madira must also be flowing. She could hear drums, cymbals and lutes. There were female voices and laughter, too. Far from the glitter and blaze of Apsara Sabha this was nothing but the same thing happening. Misrakesi wondered whether these basic establishments had a license and paid the requisite fraction of their earnings to the state. Drinking and gambling houses were being strictly regulated by the state, no doubt the inspectors would reach this remote lane in time. She gave herself a mental shake and returned to the task at hand.

Chandramukhi gave a low whistle and entered one of the huts which had a single deepak burning at the door. There were a series of these single roomed, circular structures of wattle and daub down this lane which showed none of the organization and cleanliness exhibited by the other more prosperous areas of the city. She moved aside the reed curtain and motioned to Misrakesi to follow her in.

The light inside was a little better. There was also a fire burning in the little circular hearth by a low wall with clay storage jars next to the cooking fire. A wizened old woman was making some rotis on a flat iron griddle. There was some boiled daal in a clay pot: the meal was waiting to be eaten. The kevat was sitting in the other half of the room with an expectant look on his face. He got up as they entered. Chandramukhi and he exchanged looks but he joined his palms and greeted Misrakesi formally. He looked surprised, as well he might; he had been expecting a beautiful ganika from Ujjain and what he could see looked like a young, out-of-work soldier.

He was a short but solid young man with an open face and a dogged determination about him but looking worried at the moment. All three of them sat down cross legged on the floor and there was an awkward silence. 'Can we talk freely in front of her?' Misrakesi finally broke the silence as she jerked her head towards the old crone.

'Easily. She is stone deaf and cannot hear anything even if you want her to. I do not think she understands anything much of what goes on around her,' replied the boat captain.

'Nevertheless, I think we should keep our voices down,' said Misrakesi who had her doubts about whether the old crone was as stupid as she pretended to be. Her beady eyes were sharp and black and she was throwing constant glances at them over her shoulder as she rolled out the flour and made the rotis.

'Basant,' Misrakesi said softly and seriously, 'We – Magadha needs your help.'

His pleasant and open face became even more worried. His voice was uncertain as he spoke, 'Devi, from what Chandramukhi here has told me, I seem to be mixed up in something I want no part of. I confess at once that I have been helping people smuggle goods into Magadha without paying customs duties but that is all. Rajdroha is unthinkable. I am ready to do whatever you like but I am afraid I do not know anything much.'

'Tell me whatever you know,' urged Misrakesi.

'Well, about a year ago, the same time as I met Chandramukhi for the first time wandering around the riverfront,' he smiled reminiscently, 'a man from Hastinapur, who I know in the way of business, approached me. There were some boatloads he wanted landed in Pataliputra. Without sounding immodest, let me tell you that I know the river banks for a few kosa up and down the river like the back of my hand. And we have often put work in each other's way. So I agreed. I would meet the boats upstream, somewhere between Kasi and Pataliputra. My friend, let me not take his name, piloted the boats from Hastinapur, which, as you know, is the northernmost port on the Ganga near the Gandharan kingdoms.'

He paused to take a sip of the coarse prasanna he was drinking from a clay pot. Misrakesi had declined but Chandramukhi joined him and was listening to him anxiously, holding her pot in both hands with her eyes fixed on him.

'That is all I do. I have never been told or thought to enquire about the bags I bring ashore. There are always a few heavily armed and frankly, ominous looking, men with the boatloads and I have never wanted to interfere with them. They are none of my business. I get my payment, and a very generous one at that, as soon as the boats are unloaded. And that is all,' finished Basant.

'How many times have you brought boatloads for these people?' asked Misrakesi, her ears pricking up at the mention of the Gandharan kingdoms.

Basant considered the question and counted laboriously on his fingers, 'About five or six times, I think.'

Misrakesi was dismayed. If indeed these were coins, quite a substantial number would already have been brought into Magadha.

'When is the next consignment planned?'

'I do not know, but I have been called by my contact to meet him today. Tonight actually, any time now.'

Misrakesi was taken aback, 'Then why are you... I mean, why have you not gone there yet? And why did you call me today of all days.'

Basant smiled diffidently and said, 'I thought you may want to come with me?' Misrakesi thought swiftly; catching the men in charge of the shipment, would that be a better idea than catching the shipment itself? If the men could be questioned properly the shipment, its source and destination could all be extracted from them. But would she, Chandramukhi and Basant be able to capture them? Three armed and dangerous men? Basant was a brawny young fellow and she and Chandramukhi could take adequate care of themselves but capturing the men would take some reinforcements. Who could she call?

It had to be either Pushyamitra or Siddharthak, and Pushyamitra's home was nearer. Never mind what had happened the last time they had met. This was very important for her if she was to vindicate herself and fulfill the promise she had made.

In less time than it took to separate all the strands of thought Misrakesi had made up her mind. She stood up and was at the entrance, 'Where do you have to meet them?' she asked.

'In the drinking house at the end of this veethi, the last mud hut on the left of this lane,' said Basant automatically but with a confused look on his face.

'Basant, I am going to get some reinforcements. I will take at least an hour, probably more. Try and delay going to meet them as long as possible so that I get as much time as possible,' said Misrakesi decisively as the other two stared at her uncomprehendingly.

'Reinforcements? But, but… it is too dangerous. They know I am here. If I don't arrive at the drinking house they will be suspicious; what can I say to them? How will I explain the delay?' stuttered Basant.

'Think of something,' snapped Misrakesi turning back to tell him, 'you are slow. In Chandramukhi you have a ready-made excuse. Tell them or show them that you have been engaging in love play and they will have no more questions.' As the two of them turned red Misrakesi said impatiently, 'This is no time to be squeamish. Get to it. And do not let them get away before I come back.' With this final adjuration she raced out into the night

She walked as fast as she dared, breaking into little runs whenever she could. Anyone running across the roads of Pataliputra at night would soon attract undesirable attention. She was trying her best but was not making good time when she suddenly had an idea. Why not take help from the Nagarik Suraksha Vibhag! Its soldiers would be patrolling the city on horses. If she could find one of them and get him either to lend her his horse or more probably take her to his chief's house she would save valuable time.

Luck favours the audacious. Five minutes later she saw one of the riders and hailed him. It was the work of only a few seconds to show him the mudra and ask him to take her to their chief's house. The soldier was probably used to such events since he did not comment but just dropped her in front of her destination. Sitting close to him on the horse must have made it clear that she was not a man but he only gave her a speculative look as he rode off.

Getting inside the dreaded chief's house was simple. Fear itself probably kept people away since there were no guards or soldiers to bar entry. There was a solitary old daasa dozing outside who let her go in as soon as she showed him her mudra and said that she had urgent business with his master. He motioned her in and she crossed an outer courtyard to enter the inner one.

And was brought up short by an unexpected sight. There was an ornamental pavilion in the middle of the courtyard next to a small lotus pond and the trees and creepers. It was open on all four sides and was reached by three small steps whose sides were embellished by lion heads and the roof was decorated with frescoes of plant motifs.

It was not the pavilion which brought Misrakesi up short, it was Pushyamitra; but as Misrakesi would never have imagined him to be. He was sitting on a low couch and lost in playing a veena. His right leg was tucked under his left thigh on which the large resonator of the veena rested. The smaller resonator was near his left shoulder and his left arm lovingly encircled the veena and played the frets while his right hand plucked the strings. He was playing the Sama Gana from the Sama Veda which had been systematized by the Sage Yagyavalkya during the time of the Buddha. He was wearing a thin white mulmul antariya with a plain gold kayabandh tying it in place across his muscled stomach. His hair was unbound and flowing gently in the breeze and against his chest as his uttariya had been flung aside. His eyes were focused on the horizon but his gaze was directed within; such an expression of peace on the face of such a man!

The music and the vision in front of her enthralled her. The combination of the rippling muscles and the sangeet sent something knifing through her which she acknowledged as a visceral attraction, a knife thrust of pure lust. So that was it, the reason for the antagonism between her and Pushyamitra, the oldest reason in the world between a man and a woman.

Misrakesi was standing, leaning against the wall, unwilling to interrupt. Jolted by Kama's arrow she raised her eyes to his and saw... nothing. Pushyamitra stopped playing when he saw Misrakesi approach. It took him a minute to recognize her and put the veena away. Her presence, in disguise, at this hour of the night in his house could only mean an emergency. The musician gave way to the soldier and he got up asking sharply, 'Misrakesi! Is everything alright?'

Misrakesi had also recovered herself and returned to the urgent situation at hand. 'Arya, you must come with me at once along with any other available soldier. I have the kevat holding the taskers of the boat loads in the ironworkers' colony. I will tell you everything on the way. We must leave immediately.'

'All right. Just let me pick up my sword.' It was hanging on a hook and he had it tied on in an instant. 'There is no one here but I will send a message for the nearest contingent to reach the ironworkers' area as soon as possible.'

They were walking out and Pushyamitra spoke rapidly to his dozing daasa who was now alert and awake. There was only Pushyamitra's horse tethered outside the house and he sprang on to it taking Misrakesi up in front of him. They galloped away to the ironworkers' area while the daasa made his way rapidly to the nearest soldiers' encampment.

Misrakesi filled Pushyamitra in on the details while they were engaged in a mad dash to arrive in time to catch the men Basant and Chandramukhi would be desperately holding.

The horse was tied up some distance from the lane and the two of them approached the hut silently on foot. Misrakesi had opened her hair so that she no longer looked like a soldier but an oddly dressed woman; the better to disarm the taskars.

Misrakesi entered first and in the flickering light of the earthen lamp she saw that the room was empty but for the crone. Where were they? Pushyamitra was behind her with his hand on the hilt of his sword. A cracked voice piped up from the hearth before they could say anything. It was the old crone, 'They have gone to the drinking house down the lane. All of them. And you had better go there quickly too if you want to save Basant and the girl.'

Pushyamitra looked at Misrakesi, a question in his eyes. Misrakesi was quick to respond: 'Yes, I know the place Basant explained where it is. Let's go.'

It was a down-at-heel place and Chandramukhi and Basant could be seen dimly in the darkest corner, hemmed in by three menacing looking men. They seemed to be angry and questioning Basant threateningly.

Misrakesi drew a deep breath and thought, *This is it.* Then she stepped forward, Pushyamitra behind her trying to look as small as possible. She had opened not only her hair but the top of her tunic and began weaving a carefully drunken way to the corner.

'Greetings, Basant,' she called out in a slurred voice as she neared him. 'How are you Priye? How have you been? You have been ignoring me all this while. See who I have got to meet you?' She weaved her way closer.

The three men stood up, suspicious. Basant who was looking frightened but dogged started to say something but one of the men intervened.

'What is this? Who is this woman?' The sword was at Misrakesi's neck and he raised his arm to strike.

It was over, all over in instants. They were no match for Pushyamitra's sword and swiftness.

Three men lay dead on the floor and the drinking house had erupted in alarm. The proprietress came hurrying in to stop short at the sight of Pushyamitra with a sword dripping blood.

'My felicitations, Arya. This is indeed a wonderful night's work. You have three dead men and nobody to answer any questions or give you any information.' Misrakesi's voice was honey sweet and tone poisonous. This was a dead end.

There was a thunder of horses' hooves outside and the contingent of soldiers arrived. Pushyamitra instructed them to dispose of the bodies but keep the personal effects for examination.

In the melee no one noticed Chandramukhi. She had picked up a silver dagger from the waist of one of the dead men and was holding it up with a face as white as death.

The Silver Dagger

The territory of the texts extends only so far as men have dull appetites; but when the wheel of sexual ecstasy is in full motion, there is no textbook at all and no order.

Kamasutra 2.2.29

It was a quiet and thoughtful two people who made their way back from the drinking house. The captain of the contingent of soldiers had taken over the nitty gritty. Basant and Chandramukhi had simply disappeared. Misrakesi had made no attempt to look for them and, she noticed, nor did Pushyamitra. They had proved their loyalty and usefulness. Although perhaps circumstances had forced him to kill their sources of information and he had in fact, perhaps saved Misrakesi's life, it was also a fact that they were at a dead end. Not because of Misrakesi or Chandramukhi but Pushyamitra himself, they would have to look elsewhere for progress in the matter of the coins.

Carried along on Pushyamitra's horse, Misrakesi suddenly felt very tired. The last two days and nights had been hectic, both emotionally and physically. They had resulted in a reprieve for her certainly, but what else? She sighed and let herself relax against Pushyamitra's solid chest. Her silken black hair was open, caressing his arms and shoulders, and filling his senses with an intoxicating perfume.

The look Misrakesi had given him while he was playing the veena had struck him with a devastating impact. He, too, had understood himself in a flash; the reason for his strong and ambivalent reaction to her. He was only better at concealing his feelings than Misrakesi and he had let nothing show, but there was not much else that he would like better than to carry her off to his couch and play the Kamadeva to her Rati.[49]

A fine misty rain was beading their faces and bodies, a reminder that the season of rains was upon them. A time for love and dalliance… Pushyamitra bent his head just as Misrakesi raised hers and their lips met. It was the first time he had kissed her of his own volition and he was lost, but his hands on the reins did not falter. He continued to guide the horse along the correct path in the darkness which was relieved only by flares lit at intervals.

Misrakesi wriggled out of her tunic exciting innumerable frissons in him as she moved. She could feel his thighs burning hers and she arched her back slowly to catch the falling droplets. Both the reins were transferred to Pushyamitra's right hand while his left hand stroked and caressed her abdomen and waist. She was moaning softly under her breath.

She would have liked to be an alluring apsara clad in jewels and diaphanous garments which he would have slowly removed. He would have teased out the strands of pearls from between her round, tight and high breasts and slid his fingers in between rubbing her into taut desire. She would have let him nibble them to his pleasure and her own. She would have wrapped her legs around him and taken him to an unimagined swarg; instead she was in the garb of a ragged soldier and hampered by a horse.

Pushyamitra's left hand was wandering increasingly urgently all over Misrakesi's body. She moaned and squirmed more than ever and could feel him pressing into her back.

A rueful voice, thick with desire, said into her ear, 'Misrakesi, I cannot do this on a horse. Have pity on both of us and let's stop, just now.' She barely managed to nod her acceptance when she found herself lying on a bed of soft wet grass under a tree. Her remaining clothes were tossed to the rain and Pushyamitra proceeded to demonstrate just what it was that he had been unable to do on a horse.

Their bodies met with a hunger sharpened by the edge of all that had happened between them. Misrakesi's body was covered, squeezed and melded into his. She gave bite for bite and caress for caress; sucking on those curved and cruel lips which had softened for her, as if she would draw his essence in.

She was more than ready when he entered her with a thrust that went straight to her core and pierced her heart. What was she going to do, she thought, as she turned her head from side to side in a frenzy of wanting and wrapped her legs around his waist to pull him even closer; this man was becoming much more than she had wanted any man to ever become.

Then she lost her thoughts in the wave upon wave of climax that struck her as Pushyamitra stroked her in and out, in and out till she let out her release in a hoarse scream renting the silent night. Pushyamitra covered her open mouth with his and found his own release as he bit her lips till she bled.

It was impossible to move as she lay cradled in the grass and flowers; her body covered by her lover's with the rain beating down on both of them. It was cool and delicious and she licked a few drops from the chest against which her nose was pressed. She smiled a smile of pure animal satisfaction and turned him on his back. She pinned his arms with her hands, straddling him and looking down into his eyes with an expression which turned his bones to water and then held his gaze as she slowly raised herself and took him in grinding their bodies together.

The night passed but their passion for each other was not spent. It was as if they wanted to tear each other apart and make themselves one body from two.

The morning found them both in Misrakesi's bed. The room was witness to their love play and they were lying spent and asleep when Madlekha walked in with Misrakesi's morning tulsi drink. Finding your mistress in an intimate position with a man in her bed should not surprise you at all if she happens to be the proprietress of Apsara Sabha, but Madlekha was young and inexperienced and had, moreover, not seen a man in Misrakesi's bed in all the months she had been there. The naked man in her bed also happened to be the dreaded chief of the Nagarik Suraksha Vibhag; so she gasped and let fall the bronze pot.

The sound woke up two people. Two pairs of eyes flew open and looked at her, irritated.

'What is that noise, Madlekha?' said Misrakesi yawning. 'You really must try to be more graceful. Clean it up and bring something to drink for both of us.' Madlekha fled.

She stretched and sat up with a feeling of well being which suffered a sudden though slight diminution when she found the cause lying next to her, larger than life. Pushyamitra was on his back with his head pillowed by his hands and was looking at her with his eyes glinting. The hauteur and arrogance of the man was back. Last night he had been unrecognizable, a gentle considerate loving man from her dreams. Well, if he thought that a night with her was going to give him an upper hand over her he would have to be told that he was mistaken. In fact, given who she was, it might even give her more confidence in dealing with him.

She smiled back trading glint for glint and opened her mouth to speak when there was another interruption. It was Chandramukhi from the terrace. She walked in, saw Pushyamitra and raised her eyebrows. 'I see. A reward for saving her life, is it? Misrakesi, I will come again when you are not busy,' and walked out.

'Do you always get so many people walking in and out of your room in the morning?' said Pushyamitra amused by the look on Chandramukhi's face; sleeping with the enemy, it said clearly. 'And was it really a reward for saving your life? I have saved the lives of many beautiful women but so few have seen fit to reward me so well.'

Misrakesi raised her eyebrows and said, 'I thought it was an apology from you for having killed off my sources of information?' and had the satisfaction of seeing his expression change.

Madlekha brought in the tulsi drink in silver cups and they sipped their drinks quietly for a while. Both of them were silent. Misrakesi turned on to her stomach and put her chin on her hands staring at him seriously, *What now? Where do we go from here*, she thought.

Pushyamitra got up and tied his antariya with the kayabandh over it. The sword was next and the uttariya was hung on one shoulder while Misrakesi watched with images of the night chasing each other in her expressive eyes. He did not wear any of his jewellery except for the ever present bead tied on his arm and his hair tumbling over his brow softened his face.

'It is farewell for now, Devi.' He said, standing over her as she lay on the bed. Before he could go, Misrakesi gave him a kiss which tried to express all her mixed up feelings. He strode off well satisfied with the night's work. Now, perhaps, he would be free of the thorn which had lodged itself under his skin. Misrakesi knew better… and she laughed to herself as she settled down to sleep for another two hours. She knew this thorn better than any man and most women; the more you try to work it out the more it gets under your skin!

It seemed only a few moments before she was being shaken awake urgently. She awoke wondering how Madlekha could have the insolence to shake her but it was Chandramukhi; and a very agitated Chandramukhi it was, too.

'Wake up Misrakesi. I have to speak to you immediately. I cannot wait any longer.' For the second time that morning Misrakesi sat up reluctantly. 'I have come to tell you that I am prepared to do anything, anything at all to help you to get to the root of this matter. Who are these taskars, from where do they come and what do they want to achieve?' announced Chandramukhi in a voice full of suppressed emotion.

Misrakesi could only gaze at her, surprised. Such a show of support from someone she had hitherto considered a stumbling block was too much to swallow. 'Why, what has happened?' she asked confused.

'This,' and she threw a small dagger with a silver hilt inlaid with jewels into Misrakesi's lap. It was fashioned with the face of Skanda, the god of war and studded with precious gems; altogether a beautiful and valuable piece. Misrakesi picked it up and fingered the edge.

'I do not understand. You will have to explain more clearly. What does this dagger have to do with anything?'

'You were too busy last night to notice anything,' said Chandramukhi in her old sarcastic voice. Since Misrakesi did not see what her personal choices had to with Chandramukhi she merely pursed her lips and waited for her to continue.

'You know the three men killed by your... killed yesterday? Remember the one with the yellow uttariya? I found it tucked in his waistband and picked it up because I recognized it. It is, or was, mine.'

Misrakesi's attention was engaged at once. Had this man come to Apsara Sabha and picked it up from here? Many of the erstwhile owner's possessions had been left for her when she had bought the house. She had, however, not seen the dagger before, she was certain of that. It was an exquisitely fashioned and valuable piece which would not have been forgotten or left lying around for anyone to pick up.

'Do you think it connects him with Apsara Sabha, that he was one of our customers and had stolen it from here?' asked Misrakesi wrinkling her forehead.

'No, no. It connects him directly with my dear husband, my pati parmeshwar who loved me to death, remember? I gave him this dagger as a gift. It was with him when he robbed me and threw me into a well to die. So there is a definite connection between him and the people you are looking for. Now it is not only you looking for them, but me too.' This was said through clenched teeth.

Misrakesi was sympathetic and relieved, too, that Chandramukhi, for whatever reason, was now so strongly on her side; but she did not see how it would help. They had no idea where Chandramukhi's husband was or who his associates had been. He could even have sold the dagger or it could have been stolen. He could be dead or alive. It was a very slim and tenuous link but it seemed to have stirred up very powerful latent emotions in her who was prowling around the room like a cheetah after prey.

'Chandramukhi, we will work together, even harder now. We have to look for new sources of information. And whatever you can remember and share with us will help.'

•

'It is my only aim in life: to catch up with my husband and... kill him,' this came out in a harsh whisper and Chandramukhi's eyes were like flints.

She struggled to regain her composure, 'I stayed up all of last night and have almost completed the sketch of my husband. I want you to come and look at it, also your new lover and the other man who is part of your network, Siddharthak, is that not his name?'

Misrakesi interjected, 'What about your condition imposing secrecy on me?'

'That is a thing of the past. Nothing matters now but finding Shreedhan. My life, existence and safety are all unimportant now. Call them. I will take them all to my secret room and show them the evil face I am looking for.'

It was a positive development, thought Misrakesi as she went through her morning ablutions. She had, on reflection, decided to stay away from Apsara Sabha for another night to add credence to her story of visiting the Urubela Teerth. She decided to take a tour of her household and check on how it was running.

She had always positioned herself as very much the mistress of Apsara Sabha and there had never been any dearth of respect from everyone. Today, however, she could sense a difference; the glances cast upon her were new. The news of Pushyamitra in her bed had spread like wildfire through a forest. The dreaded chief of the Nagarik Suraksha Vibhag, the younger brother of the senapati of Magadha's vast armies – and Misrakesi was now his mistress. From an up and coming nartaki, Misrakesi had catapulted herself into the rarefied echelons of real power. She could see envy in Ratibhama's calculating eyes and approval even in Manjari's strangely anxious face. The other nartakis who were in any case a little in awe of her, seemed to withdraw even more deferentially. There was one exception only and that was Mrinalini.

'Daughter,' she said, catching Misrakesi alone at first opportunity, 'be warned by an old and wise woman and have nothing to do with this man. He is an evil man. I could tell you stories about him that would raise your hair on end. He is a byword for cruelty and was one of the main instruments for the Nanda hold on the kingdom. I will give you the names of other men; they may not be as powerful but will be much better in the long run.'

This was too much to handle but Misrakesi said patiently, 'How do I explain to you that I do not want a man for the long run? I also do not have any relationship or any intention of one with Pushyamitra. Do you think you could leave my choice of partners alone? It is really nobody's business but mine. And can we get back to the list of aromatic oils?'

Mrinalini was silenced for the moment but there was no doubt that Misrakesi would hear more of it in the future. So many ganikas would be sleeping with so many men all over Pataliputra but she seemed to be the only one attracting unnecessary attention. A relationship with Pushyamitra indeed! *Indeed,* whispered a small voice inside her which she instantly suppressed, resolving to concentrate on the matter in hand.

It would be useful to review the developments and see what could be done further. There was still a possibility that some information would be brought back by the minions of the Lakshanadhyaksha who had been sent to make enquiries at the place where the coins had been minted. Siddharthak's gambler had proved to be a complete non starter; he was a broken-down old wretch who could barely remember the time of day let alone the source of a couple of coins. Misrakesi gathered that no amount of beating had elicited any information from him.

This left only the latest tenuous link of Chandramukhi's murderous husband that needed to be explored. It was at best a very improbable source for any progress in the matter but there was perhaps no harm in taking a look at his picture painted by Chandramukhi so that he could be identified if he was lurking in the city. She would send a message to Siddharthak and, since she was a professional in the pay of Magadha with no personal issues, also to Pushyamitra. All of them should also get together to think about what to do next so it would be practical for all of them to see the sketch together.

As it turned out it was two or three days before all of them could come in. Misrakesi was curious about Shreedhan's sketch and had wanted to go down immediately that evening but had to wait for both the men as per what had been decided. On the outside, she was waiting impatiently only to see the sketch, but there was another small fire of impatience which was spreading a warm glow inside her which she refused to acknowledge.

She was waiting in her outer room where she had asked that the two men be shown in discreetly. Madlekha was not experienced enough to show no emotion; she looked knowing at the instructions about Pushyamitra but puzzled when the same were repeated for Siddharthak. Misrakesi laughed and shook her head. It seemed that the members of her household were not going to leave her alone, even those who had absolutely no right to comment on her actions. Madlekha was far from being an ideal servant girl but Misrakesi had become imperceptibly fond of her, awkward as she sometimes was. She had plans of grooming the young girl into a graceful woman.

'Misrakesi,' said a quiet voice behind her, interrupting her thoughts. She turned and it was Pushyamitra looking – to her smitten eyes – even more muscular, fit and good enough to eat in a dark blue and gold ensemble. Breaking her own vague resolve to be cold and businesslike she gave him a warm smile straight from her heart because she was suddenly genuinely glad to see him.

Siddharthak, who had come up behind him, received the full impact of the smile and blinked – the last time he had seen both of them they had not been on smiling terms. As Pushyamitra's back was to him he also did not see the sudden transformation of his face as he returned the smile.

The three of them did not waste any time as Pushyamitra had to return to the palace and Misrakesi was also planning an appearance at Apsara Sabha later that night. Chandramukhi was waiting for them, behind the trees and foliage, and took them quickly to her underground home. Misrakesi had tried to memorize the way and the precise tree under which the room was hidden but was certain she would not be able to locate it alone.

The underground chamber was not meant for quite so many persons. Apart from the four of them, also an uncomfortable Basant was also present, and he looked as though he wanted to melt into the wall when he met Pushyamitra's cold gaze and Siddharthak's questioning one.

'Yes, we decided that he should stay here for a few days; till your people forget him,' with a glance at Pushyamitra, 'otherwise they may have caught him and beaten him senseless before we could do anything about it,' said Chandramukhi aggressively.

No one said anything. No one knew better than Pushyamitra that this reputation of his men was well deserved. Misrakesi was relieved to see Basant unhurt since she still had hopes of squeezing information out of him. Siddharthak was too busy examining the chamber and exclaiming admiringly. He would have loved to have a hideout like this but was not, unfortunately, a setthi rich beyond the dreams of avarice. He had been filled in on the bare details of Chandramukhi's history during the walk and was extremely intrigued by her.

Siddharthak was also given the details of the other night's events and the killing of the three taskars. *More and more curious,* thought Siddharthak, *I know the Pushyamitra who would have cheerfully sacrificed Misrakesi, Chandramukhi, and Basant included, before letting harm come to an informer. Here we have one who kills three men when one of them threatens a single, solitary, expendable woman. Anyway, good enough! I do not really want to see Misrakesi killed, she has certainly made life very interesting.*

Chandramukhi drew his attention to one side of the wall where a small earthen lamp was burning. A meticulously drawn picture of a handsome man with ugly eyes, a sneer twisting his lips and a weak chin stared out at them. 'This is Shreedhan,' said Chandramukhi simply.

'This is her husband. Remember, we found a silver dagger on one of the men which belonged to Shreedhan; so there is definitely a connection between our taskars and this man,' explained Misrakesi and, turning to Siddharthak, asked, 'Have you perhaps seen him anywhere? I thought a painting of his would help either of you – and Basant of course – recognize him.'

Pushyamitra and Siddharthak came up to take a closer look. Misrakesi was standing close behind Pushyamitra and lightly put her hands on his shoulder. Prompted partly by a spirit of pure mischief and partly by a desire to see the forbidding look on his face chased away, she pressed herself against him and leant close to point at the face on the wall, 'It is quite a distinctive face, not very easy to forget.'

Pushyamitra returned to his seat, but Siddharthak's memory was jogged, 'You are right Misrakesi. I think I have seen this man somewhere,' he said, slowly, '... but where?'

Chandramukhi was excited at once. 'Tell me whatever you remember. I will follow up the slightest lead.'

Siddharthak was frowning and silent in an effort to remember but Pushyamitra spoke up, 'Chandramukhi, did your husband have any connection in the northern kingdoms? One of the taskars had exclaimed in Kharoshti just before he died. This language is commonly spoken in the Gandharan kingdoms. Most importantly, we found a few revealing items amongst his possessions. Some coins which were similar to the ones sent in by Siddharthak and Misrakesi; and this seal.' He drew out a ring seal with the mark of the moon, a symbol of the Chandravamsa and the ancient Vedic tribe of the Purus, the legendary ancestors of the Pauravas.

At least two of the people present realized the gravity of the situation and were silent. Chandramukhi was still thinking about the connections with her husband and was oblivious to other ramifications.

She replied thoughtfully, 'Not that I can remember. I do seem to remember, however that the robbers who he had attacked us were tall, fair and light eyed like the Gandharans. I was not really paying attention to their language. The man who spoke to me was speaking in Magadhi Prakrit like me. I do not know Kharoshti, so some others could have been using it, I cannot be certain.' She looked up at him frowning.

Siddharthak was listening to everything carefully, trying to think back to why Shreedhan's face was ringing a bell and, with one part of his mind watching the byplay between Pushyamitra and Misrakesi.

Oh, oh! he thought enlightened, when Pushyamitra picked up one end of Misrakesi's silk uttariya which had become inextricably entangled with his bajubanda and placed it on her bare shoulder, *It has happened finally. That dayan, Sreelekha, is right and they indeed are sleeping together!*

He continued to watch covertly as Misrakesi twitched her shoulder unconcernedly and let her uttariya fall again, exposing her curved and graceful back to Pushyamitra's touch. He thought, chuckling to himself, *Look at her courage, she is teasing him, and successfully, too. Something that has never happened to friend Pushyamitra before! Well, let us see where this takes them.*

Beneath his enjoyment of a novel situation was also an uneasy sense of disquiet. Was Pushyamitra leading himself into something which would be too difficult to handle? The voices of rumour and gossip were doing their work only too well. Here were the two of them before him, their behaviour lending credence to stories which he had hitherto discounted.

Pushyamitra asked Chandramukhi, 'Would your husband dare to show his face in Magadha? Would he not be recognized?'

'We were married for a matter of a few months only. He did not really move in the circles of the rich setthis; so he could risk it with some changes in his appearance. The people who would recognize him would be the ones who he worked with, the warehouse officials, overseers, loaders. Maybe he has grown a beard or a moustache or changed his appearance? He will do anything if he is paid for it.'

'That's it! I know where I have seen him. And it is true, he has grown a beard. I have seen him with the Setthi Devakanta at one of his warehouses. I was there once in the guise of a loader and I saw this man being entertained with great honour. This also connects Devakanta with the whole affair. We will have to go after him.' Siddharthak looked at Pushyamitra who nodded grimly.

Chandramukhi was beside herself with suppressed emotion. 'I

know the setthi too and I could not have believed that he would give shelter to a man like Shreedhan.' She was ready to rush out of the room but was persuaded to wait and discuss the best way of approaching the situation.

After some discussion it was decided that Siddharthak, Chandramukhi, and Basant would take a round of Devakanta's home and business premises to see what they could find. Pushyamitra was also to instruct some of his men to do an in-depth investigation. Devakanta, unfortunately, was not one of those in the habit of frequenting Apsara Sabha. Pushyamitra and Misrakesi were to return to their professional pursuits for the moment.

Misrakesi had stopped to adjust her anklet as the others went ahead. As she walked down the path to her house she found Pushyamitra waiting for her, cross-armed leaning against a tree. She smiled to herself but walked forward unconcerned, coming to a stop in front of him.

'What exactly were you up to in there?' he asked as he took her hands and slowly pulled her closer.

'Nothing. Just trying to see if there is any red blood in you.'

'I see. And what do I have to do prove that?' His breath was fanning her face and she was but a thread away from being enveloped by him. His lips moved over her face delicately without touching her.

She closed her eyes and whispered, 'It is very easy. I will show you how.' The male scent of him mixed with saffron and sandalwood was making her light headed. She swayed slightly and he moved to steady her. She twined herself around him as an atimukta vine around a mango tree, her lips were parted and her sweet breath sent his blood coursing madly along his veins.

They were at one with the cosmic dance of creation as they sank down on the earth strewn with flowers and leaves and slowly explored each other.

'Are women fashioned by Ishwar solely for the pleasure of men?' Pushyamitra murmured as his hands savoured her softness and firmness, curves and mounds and his mouth drank her up like a wine.

Misrakesi was beyond replying as her hands and mouth in turn found his chest, shoulders, his sculpted arms his hardness driving out all her conscious thought, her being was concentrated on the planes and surfaces at her fingers and below her lips.

'No. You have been made for my pleasure. Take me and give yourself to me.'

The force with which he took her shook her out of her stupor; she raised drugged brown eyes to his and drowned in desire.

She sat up in his lap, the slim lines of her waist and long legs contrasting with the solidness of his, his arm across her breasts was a brand burning them together.

'Don't go. Take me up to my room and stay with me tonight.'

He picked her up and carried her up to her terrace and they spent the night in a world of their own.

This became a pattern. He would come to see her dance and it was as if she danced only for him. They would go up to her room and spend the nights together. No thoughts of the watching world intruded.

She would sometimes go to his house under the pretext of reporting to him but they both knew why she came. Urmil and Vrishni soon became good friends after spending nights waiting for their masters to emerge. They would make themselves comfortable after Vrishni had left food and wine inside and gossip for hours drowsing uneasily till the morning sun came out.

Misrakesi and Pushyamitra would be inside talking to each other, their desultorily minds only on each other's body. He would often make her sit on the low couch in the pavilion and sing for her devouring her with his eyes till she forced him to suit his action to his gaze. He had a beautiful and trained voice. Misrakesi was surprised and said so.

'I would have been a musician if I had not joined the army. But in my family I had no choice...' he would shrug and smile.

He was taken by surprise by her hungry passion for him. 'Any woman who is not overpowered by you does not deserve to be called a woman.'

Pushyamitra tried to think of other women he had slept with

but they were a blur beside the alive and all encompassing woman with him.

As Misrakesi knew and Pushyamitra was slowly realizing, making love once is not the end but the beginning of a story. She let herself flow with the current, content not to think but feel. Pushyamitra knew what he was doing, also knew that he should not do it but could not summon up the will to stop. So they stepped on to a path neither of them had imagined traversing, where would it take them?

The Ox-Cart Drivers

A little effort accomplishes the task.

Chanakyasutra 93

The entire issue of the counterfeit coins was assuming very serious proportions. After the proclamation regarding the submission into the treasury of non-punch marked Nanda coins, the sheer quantity of coins flowing in had taken the royal authorities by surprise. The coins were obviously being introduced at a steady rate for some time now and it had only been a coincidence that the scheme had been found out. The Lakshanadhyaksha and the Mint officials were in a frenzy and the seriousness was such that it was also being monitored by the samrat himself.

The Mint where the coins indicated that they had been struck was closed down for a year. An intense but secret search was on for the royal and provincial seals which must have fallen into the wrong hands.

Pushyamitra and his handpicked assistants were in the eye of the storm but they had nothing to report. He had assigned them all separate areas to work on. Siddharthak, assisted, or dogged, by Chandramukhi was to keep Setthi Devakanta firmly under his eyes and report on all his activities, innocent or otherwise. Misrakesi was to keep an eye on Ugrasala and continue to expand the list of his business and personal life.

Basant, their closest link to the actual taskars, spent hours being continuously questioned by Pushyamitra and some of his men.

There was no question now of respecting anyone's confidentiality or secrecy. It would be impossible for Basant to go back to his old work of smuggling goods into Pataliputra without paying customs duties. In fact, he would probably not escape alive if he showed his face on the waterfront. An entire network was slowly being exposed through the information coming to light.

The Samaharta and the board which looked after customs were simultaneously pleased at the exposure of the network and crestfallen at its extent and efficacy. That such an extensive and organized parallel conduit for goods into Pataliputra existed without their knowledge was a blow to them. With the payment of small bribes to minor royal officials the royal treasury was being defrauded of thousands of pans, not to speak of it being used against the king and the empire. The system was now to be completely reformed by the administration which meant the acharya. Corrupt officials were being ruthlessly weeded out.

But this did not solve the problem for Pushyamitra. It was true that no more coins would come into Magadha until the perpetrators thought of an alternative, but there still seemed to be an inexhaustible supply. This meant that there was a store of counterfeit coins inside the city and the network to disburse them was active and effective. The sources and distributors of coins had to be unearthed and demolished.

At Apsara Sabha, Misrakesi's attention was increasingly being focused on Ugrasala. He was rich, weak, dissolute and had a grievance against the Mauryas. His huge business ramifications, the land and trade interests he owned and his contacts inside the army through his dead brother also made him a very suspicious character.

In the days after the incident at the ironsmiths' drinking house Manjari reported that Ugrasala appeared very upset and downcast. On that day itself, one of his hangers on, a minor merchant named Jatindasa, had reported a brawl in which some of his men had been killed. Mere coincidence? Perhaps.

Apsara Sabha had become the informal headquarters for this case. Pushyamitra had also assigned one of his able and rising officers,

Neel, to the case. There were many others who were working on the information being gathered by questioning Basant and Chandramukhi, but Neel was also involved in the actual interrogation and so was initiated into the mysterious underside of the dancing house.

He was a strapping young giant of a man and probably exactly the kind of officer who had given the Nagarik Suraksha Vibhag its vicious reputation. The solution to all matters, according to him, was beating and torture. Physical violence was a reflex action for him. Paradoxically, he also displayed a definite flair for drawing out information from suspects and exhibited a monumental patience and attention to detail.

Pushyamitra called a meeting of all the principals at Apsara Sabha to review the situation and look for further leads. It was to be held in the middle of the night in one of the larger ante rooms off the main hall. They were to pose as a convivial party enjoying their drinks and gambling. Chandramukhi was also to be there with her face veiled. Given the number of visitors and the general level of noise and activity, they would not attract much notice apart from the fact that Pushyamitra was spending the night gambling and flirting with a dancing girl. Misrakesi was a little nervous about eavesdroppers so she had instructed a group of her musicians to take up position just outside the ante room and play their loudest compositions.

They were obliging to the best of their ability when Pushyamitra walked in, the last to arrive as usual. He frowned and raised his shoulders questioningly at Misrakesi. She came near him and whispered, 'I am worried about somebody else listening in.'

'In that case let us remove ourselves from here. It is not possible to do any work in this din,' he replied.

Misrakesi decided immediately that they should go up to her rooms and conduct the meeting in her outer room. Chandramukhi disappeared to appear in there via her tree and in her normal dress, and she took Basant along with her. Siddharthak and Neel left together to be followed last by Pushyamitra and Misrakesi.

The appearance of a convivial party was revived over there with food, wine, flowers, and chaupad. Apart from Neel and Basant the others were of course very much at home there. Neel was enjoying himself immensely; it was all new to him. Visiting a dancing house and working alongside a woman like Misrakesi, appreciating the sights, sounds, and food and drink of Apsara Sabha, to say nothing of the beauteous nartakis; and now this private room of Misrakesi. He had always thought that there should be more to a secret service than just ruffians. Where were all the beautiful women spies he had heard so much about? Well, here they were and with a vengeance.

He was not too enamoured of Chandramukhi, regarding her primarily in a professional light, his personal feelings being more of revulsion at her scars; he had a great deal of growing up to do. Misrakesi was another matter. He was figuratively at her feet from the moment he set his eyes on her. After Pushyamitra's entry, however, he had not needed Siddharthak's slight warning glance to see how things stood between them and had withdrawn immediately. He thought of his chief as next only to the king and admired him with all the intensity of his youth. Pushyamitra was a personification of Magadha for him.

If Misrakesi had realized this she would have been most annoyed, she was certainly not ready to think of herself as any one's property, not even Pushyamitra's. She was not ready to become a Sita to any Laxman. She was, however, so wrapped up in Pushyamitra's presence that she missed the subtle signs of her own entrapment.

With the help of Basant and Chandramukhi, many of the loaders present to transfer the bags at the waterfront had been identified and questioned but had added nothing to the answer of the two most vital questions, where was the store of coins and who was the mastermind behind the dissemination of the coins?

Pushyamitra and Neel were, for the umpteenth time, taking Basant through every step of his transactions with the Gandharans, for now there was no doubt that they were Gandharans and were involved in this act of financial war against the Magadhan State.

Misrakesi was, for the first time, privileged to see Pushyamitra in action, demonstrating his sharp intelligence, ability to collate facts and organize the work of his behemoth organization to cast an invisible web of protection around the city. It was a pointer to his meteoric rise within the Vibhag although being the brother of the then up-senapati would certainly have helped.

She was there mainly as the informer who knew the most about Ugrasala and had updated Neel on the latest information she had, which was not much. The only interesting bit was that Ugrasala and Devakanta had recently had some business transactions, the exact nature of which was not clear, a fact confirmed by Siddharthak's enquiries. She was listening to the questions and answers and was casting her mind back to her own maiden visit to the waterfront. She had already been extensively interrogated by Pushyamitra but had been unable to contribute anything beyond what had already been revealed by Basant and Chandramukhi.

'Neel, what it boils down to is that we are going to get nothing from the loaders,' said Pushyamitra. 'The taskars Basant was meeting are dead. We only have suspicions of Devakanta but nothing concrete. All his warehouses as well as those of Ugrasala and his group that we have information on have been examined by the Warehouse Inspectors.'

'Find my husband and you will find the ringleader,' said Chandramukhi. Pushyamitra let this pass since they had no real evidence of Shreedhan being behind it all and in any case finding him was easier said than done.

'Have you considered the ox-cart drivers? They would certainly know the destination of the bags,' asked Misrakesi.

'Yes, we have. We have gone through it innumerable times with both of them,' Pushyamitra looked at Basant and Chandramukhi, 'but have not gathered anything that can help us locate them. They were a secretive lot and spoke to no one. They kept themselves muffled up so that we do not even know what they looked like.' He got up and sat down in front of Misrakesi concentrating his formidable personality on her.

'Let us try again with you. You told me that you had taken a look at the drivers. You had gone there with the express purpose of gathering information on all the people present there, you must have observed everything carefully.'

Misrakesi shook her head and replied, 'I have already told you everything I could remember. I was also not allowed to go near the actual centre of the activity but was watching from behind a tree. Yes, I did look at the drivers but they were muffled up and unrecognizable.'

'The ox-cart drivers were standing apart from the boats and loaders. They were probably closer to you than to any of the others. Let us go through everything again. Close your eyes and imagine yourself back at the waterfront. I will take you through, step by step, do not ignore anything. Tell me everything that comes to your mind, even the smallest detail may be of vital importance. Shall we start?'

'I suppose so, although I am not certain we will accomplish anything.'

'Try your best.' He smiled encouragingly and took both her hands in a decided clasp. Misrakesi could feel his determination and steadiness flowing into her.

'Right. Now let us start with your first view of the scene. Describe it to me.'

'It was a moonlit night although there were many trees which made the place intermittently dark. I saw four... no, five big boats anchored at the river bank piled with gunny bags. There were many people milling around, could have been twenty, thirty, even more. Confusing in the beginning before I realized that they were all busy unloading the gunny bags from the boats as fast as possible. One group was unloading from the boats to the land and another group was putting them on to the waiting ox-carts. There must have been ten or fifteen carts lined up the drivers were in a group, all standing apart.'

'Good. What happened next?'

'I stood and waited behind a tree while Chandramukhi went up to ask if I could be allowed to join the loaders. I tried very hard to look at the loaders and memorize their faces but they were too far and the moonlight was not enough to make them out clearly.'

Misrakesi went on, her eyes closed, her hands held between Pushyamitra's, her mind on the banks of the River Ganges in a forest washed by moonlight.

'Chandramukhi came back and told me that I would not be able to join the loaders and went back. I was very disappointed as the entire purpose of going there that night seemed to have been defeated. I stood there for a while batting the mosquitoes and insects away. Finding them very irritating I moved to stand under another tree, closer to the group of drivers.'

Pushyamitra exchanged a glance with Neel; Misrakesi had not remembered this move in her earlier answers.

She had fallen silent and was trying to remember anything else that she could.

Pushyamitra asked her quietly so as to not disturb her concentration, 'What could you see?'

'As I was brushing and swatting the insects away, I could see one man standing apart from the others, he seemed to be their leader.'

'What was he wearing?'

'I could not see anything. He had a coarse blanket wrapped around him. It was wrapped also around his head leaving only two glittering eyes revealed. The blanket covered him up to the knees. He was barefoot.'

Pushyamitra was disappointed, this was just what she had told them the last time and it was of no use. There had to be some distinguishing mark, of dress, appearance, jewellery, anything that would help to mark out the identity, region, or community of the man. The blanket could have hidden anything and that was probably why it had been used. They had also, probably under instructions, not mingled with anyone else. He persevered, however, because he had nothing, no other lead to pursue.

'It was stifling, under the trees and the mosquitoes were eating me up. I remember thinking that the man I was looking at was well protected because of his blanket, but his face was not. I was beating and slapping at my legs and arms. A swarm of them settled on his forehead and he raised an arm to brush them away.'

Siddharthak was looking sceptical, how would all this discussion of the inevitable insects on the river bank help, but he said nothing. Pushyamitra was still concentrating, he never gave up.

Chandramukhi and Basant were talking to each other in very low tones and Neel was listening.

'The moonlight caught at the back of his hand which he had withdrawn from his blanket. There was something on it.'

Pushyamitra held his breath and refrained from squeezing her hands. Was this the breakthrough they were looking for?

Misrakesi opened her eyes and said. 'There was some kind of tribal insignia on it. A long hooded serpent-like figure. The bared fangs were on the back of the hand and the body extended down his arm. He then...'

Pushyamitra slapped his thigh and got up pulling Misrakesi up with him, 'That's it. Neel, come on, we've got it. Let us hope they are still there. Good woman.' And he gave the confused Misrakesi a hug before shooting off directions to an alert Neel.

'Take your division, Neel, and also Nagasena's and Bhoj's. Do you remember our combing operations last month, a few kosas from the city boundaries off the Rajmarga to Rajgriha? There was a settlement of Nagas[50] we had come across who claimed to be here to earn some money from the city? They are the only enclave of Nagas nearby. The serpent mark is only sported by them. It has to be them, staying near the city yet keeping themselves away. They have no contacts with anyone inside the city which is why we were not able to get any leads to them.'

Neel nodded, comprehension and excitement spreading across his face. He was already up and going when Pushyamitra's voice checked him, 'Take as many more men as you like but all the men must be captured alive... alive, you understand? They are valiant and courageous fighters and are also prone to committing suicide with small poison pellets when cornered. They are as dangerous as their patron god, the Cobra, so take care, Neel. No killing. I shall meet you there.'

In another minute both Neel and Pushyamitra were gone with instructions to Misrakesi, Basant, and Chandramukhi to keep themselves ready for identification of the drivers, if needed.

The four people left behind in the room had an overpowering feeling of anti climax. Siddharthak was never happy when anyone else, as in Misrakesi, was the one providing the important inputs. Pushyamitra had not even thought fit to take him to the Naga camp for the capture.

The party dispersed, Siddharthak almost hoping it would turn out to be a fruitless chase despite his desire to see the serious problem of the coins solved. Misrakesi arranged with Chandramukhi that she should keep an eye out for signals from the terrace in case there was an urgent need to go and identify the Nagas as they were brought in. That they would be brought in exactly as Pushyamitra had ordered she had no doubt.

The next day passed with Misrakesi trying hard to concentrate on her work. She practiced her dance and music half heartedly, an ear open and an eye out for any messenger from the Nagarik Suraksha Vibhaga.

In the afternoon she was sitting and talking to Manjari, trying to distract herself with Apsara Sabha business when Som came running in. She had become very fond of him in the time that he had been here, and her love was enthusiastically reciprocated; he had even started calling her Chhoti Ma. She pulled him onto her lap and gave him a kiss on both his plump cheeks. He was a delightful child, solemn and prone to making precocious comments.

'How are your mud statues progressing, my dear? And your studies?'

'The statues are good. I have nearly made an army, but no ganit. Because of you.' And he fixed accusing dark eyes on her. 'You always hug and kiss me but you don't love me or you would not have asked Amma to send away my tutor who was teaching me so much.'

'But, my dear, I did no such thing! Why should I?' said an astonished Misrakesi. 'What is this Manjari? Why did you send away his tutor? And when did I ask you to do so?'

'No, no, of course it was not like that,' replied Manjari carefully, not meeting either Misrakesi's eyes or her son's and hurriedly pulling him from Misrakesi's lap. 'He was just unsatisfactory, that is all. Come now, Som, it is now time for your bath.' And she fled leaving Misrakesi wondering what it was all about.

Mrinalini was not forthcoming either making Misrakesi think that she might be trying her hand at some domestic tyranny. She would have to look into it once she had some time. Perhaps make arrangements for Som to be sent to one of the best gurukuls in the city. He was a brilliant child and would be sure to qualify on the basis of his abilities. In any case the best acharyas were concerned only with intelligence and not varna and jaati. She would ask Manjari to meet Acharya Attri.

It was only at dusk that her nervousness ended, and in the event it was not a messenger but Pushyamitra himself who came riding up, bloodied, dusty and sweaty but exultant. He caught her up and kissed her hard before setting her down and shaking her exuberantly by the shoulders, 'I think we've got them, and it is all because of you. Before we go on I want you, Chandramukhi and Basant to come down to where we hold them captive so that they can be identified.'

'Tell me what happened. Were you able to catch them by surprise?' said Misrakesi, holding on to Pushyamitra to stop herself from falling down.

'We definitely did, Neel is a very bright boy, he had them completely but silently encircled before they could react. The fact that we had been there earlier on a routine combing operation also helped as they did not think that our aim was to capture them. There was some fighting but not much as they were hopelessly outnumbered.' Pushyamitra's usually impassive face was reflecting his relief at the breakthrough today. 'We have at the moment left the women and children in the camp under a strong guard; the men, who are about fifty or sixty in number, are at the prison behind the palace complex. After you identify them we will go ahead with the interrogation.'

Misrakesi was slightly unsure and was not able to share Pushyamitra's confidence. 'How do we go to the prison, all three of us cannot march up there in full view of whoever may be watching?'

'There is a secret way into it. I am sending Neel to escort Chandramukhi and Basant. You must go to the palace on some pretext and wait for me in my palace office and I will take you to the prison. Send Chandramukhi a signal to call her here.'

Misrakesi accordingly waved a red uttariya from the terrace. They did not have to wait for long before she appeared.

'I have sent Neel off to get some much needed rest and come here to ask all of you to be ready. Misrakesi will come through the palace and Neel will meet you and Basant under this Patal tree in a couple of hour's time. You can hide yourself behind it till he comes. He will take you in through a secret passage.' Pushyamitra was brief and to the point. He was, Misrakesi noted, weary and filthy with dust, dirt and dried blood but had sent off his subordinates to refresh themselves and had taken on the duty of calling the witnesses over.

'Misrakesi, I am leaving. Follow me after a decent interval and make some excuse to go to my palace office. Wait for me there.' He left and Chandramukhi also went off to call Basant and wait at the assigned place.

Misrakesi made her way to the palace, more apprehensive than she would acknowledge; how was she to 'identify' someone who she had seen only as a hand and two eyes? She was also certain that she was going to see the violent methods of the Suraksha Vibhag in full swing and her stomach was turning in anticipation. She did not know whether she could bear to see the torture and beating of a fellow man face to face even if he was a rajdrohi and deserved no better. It would not do to exhibit her squeamishness which could be misconstrued as sympathy, she was a royal employee after all.

She had to endure some very uncomfortable moments at the palace. The soldiers who guarded the entry knew her after a fashion but were obviously suspicious of her asking for entry without any stated reason or person to meet. Since she could hardly state her actual reason she was caught in an awkward position and feverishly went over her acquaintances wondering who to name. She finally thought of asking for Shrunottara. The guard was unconvinced and sent one of his men to check with her. Thankfully, he received confirmation from her and Misrakesi was taken to her quarters escorted by one of the soldiers.

Shrunottara dismissed the soldier and looked at Misrakesi a little quizzically. They had met on and off over the last year as part of both their official duties but were not intimate in any sense of the word.

Now, Misrakesi was not sure how much of the case she should divulge to Shrunottara without authorization from her chief and compromised by stating vaguely that she had to meet Pushyamitra in connection with the counterfeit coins case. There were no questions from Shrunottara who was another name for discretion but as Misrakesi thanked her and made her way to the office she was left with the feeling that her explanation had sounded more like an excuse. The hazards of being a spy.

By now she was squirming inside, worried about her coming ordeal, as she saw it, and feeling foolish about her encounter with Shrunottara. She was waiting alone in the palace when her evening performance should have been starting; she had only had time to tell Manjari that it was cancelled for the night, an increasingly frequent occurrence these days.

She was standing there with nothing to do and she began to examine a huge mural which dominated one wall of the small room. It was slightly incongruous, too big for the small room but it had been executed with delicacy and precision. The subject was a scene from a royal court with the king meting out punishment to a cowering prisoner surrounded by royal officials and all the panoply of power. Misrakesi could almost imagine Pushyamitra standing behind him and all the tortures the prisoner must have gone through.

She was carried away by her own imagination and started when the mural suddenly moved; it was there only to act as a camouflage for a secret door which led into the palace prison. Pushyamitra entered and pulled her through, shutting the door carefully behind him. It was unlikely that anyone would enter his room without permission, but it never hurt to be careful.

They walked through a long, dark, uneven passage before it opened out into another structure which was the prison. Neel had not yet arrived with the other two, but Pushyamitra decided that she could see the captured men by herself. She was standing in what could be called the administrative area of the prison from where the Prison Keeper, who she did not know at all, operated. He was a formidable looking man of indeterminate age who could probably wrestle down any would be escapees with one hand. He did not pay any attention to Misrakesi beyond a cursory look and went on with his work which seemed to be the listing out of the latest prisoners and where they would be kept.

Pushyamitra soon sent Sumant to lead her into another part of the building. This seemed to be much older and sunk deep into the bowels of the earth, probably a network of underground caves cut out by the river millennia ago and appropriated by the Nandas for their notorious dungeons – a legacy which the Mauryas were quite comfortable with.

Iron grills had been sunk in front of some of the cave mouths; costing a fortune and the exercise of the exceptional skills that the Magadhan ironworkers were famous for, but which made escape impossible. The ground below was damp and water oozed from the walls, the air was stale and the atmosphere humid enough to make it seem as though one was inhaling water; Misrakesi was already feeling sick.

In one of the apertures, bound hand and foot and secured inside the great iron grills, were the captured Nagas. In the dim light available, Misrakesi could make out nothing more than a welter of human bodies lying on the floor. How and who would she identify?

She shook her head helplessly at Pushyamitra who was standing outside the iron grill. 'It is impossible to say anything. This is not how I had seen them on that day. Remember they were covered with blankets and I saw only the eyes and the snake emblem.'

He looked thoughtful and creases appeared on his brow as he thought about what to do next. His exultant mood was waning.

'They are all silent and will say nothing at all. Of course, we have more ways to make them talk, but the important decision is who to start with.'

He walked up and down outside the grill looking in at the prisoners. One of them was not lying supine but had managed to pull himself into a sitting position. His eyes flashed fire and defiance. His was a handsome face and a dignified persona even under the circumstances. Pushyamitra suddenly came to a decision.

'Bring out that man in the corner. I want Misrakesi to have a close look at him and I want to talk to him.'

Misrakesi took a step back and her bhairnivasini[51] which was already wet and bedraggled around the edges whispered along the stone walls even as her chains on her girdle jingled. She clutched her uttariya tightly around herself and readied herself to face the captured Naga, she did not know what she would see.

'Do not worry, he is perfectly fine at the moment. We have done nothing to him as yet so you do not need to be apprehensive,' said Pushyamitra with a grim smile.

The Naga was dragged out by a couple of brawny men. He was slight and wiry in built but must have possessed phenomenal strength because even two men were not enough to subdue him. He spat at the two men and shouted at them in his own language. Nagasena, who was a Naga and one of the captains in the Suraksha Vibhag came up and sternly spoke to him in his own language commanding him to be silent.

The captive and Misrakesi stared at each other, she examined his face with his slanting eyes, flat cheekbones, and yellowish skin but could not find anything which jogged her memory. His eyes held hers and she found herself at a disadvantage, they were full of a desperate pride and courage and challenged her even as he was a prisoner, beaten and humiliated.

'Perhaps, if I could see his hands...' said Misrakesi hesitantly. Nagasena snapped out a command and the Naga's hands were wrenched and held up for Misrakesi's inspection. The tendons stood out in his effort to free his hands and sweat poured out of his forehead but he did not utter a sound. It was the symbol of the hooded cobra that she remembered the bared fangs on the back of his hand and the sinuous body going down to his wrist. She looked at Pushyamitra and nodded although not with any great conviction.

Neel arrived at this moment with Chandramukhi and Basant who were equivocal in their identification; they had not really seen anything in enough detail to identify the people involved.

Pushyamitra decided to concentrate on the Naga who was still outside held by two men. He directed Neel and Nagasena to question him separately and to make a start while he took a much needed break.

'I am the chief's son. You will never break me.' The Naga suddenly spoke up in broken Magadhi. 'No matter what you do to me.'

'We will see about that.' Neel was incensed and would have smashed his fist into that obstinate face if Pushyamitra had not stopped him with a glance.

'Question him, gently, at first. And see what he tells you. Wait for my orders before you start anything else.' Pushyamitra was thoughtful. He had seen the determination on the Naga's face and was thinking of his best approach. They needed information, not a dead man; and the Nagas were famous for their ferocity and obstinacy.

Misrakesi had retreated till she was alone in front of another iron grilled cave. She did not want to be a part of this discussion.

'Misrakesi, where are you?' Pushyamitra came up to where she stood leaning against the iron grill, a smudged figure in the half darkness.

'What is the matter? Not able to stand the harsh realities of the profession, is it? Never mind, it will soon become routine.' And he came up to where she was standing with her head bent.

They were away from the rest of the people milling around. Misrakesi did not say anything and Pushyamitra took her in a slight embrace. The silence grew and as always, when close to him, Misrakesi was caught up in his physical presence and pulled him close to her.

'Don't touch me, I am filthy.' Pushyamitra stepped back. Misrakesi's only response was to twine herself closer, rub her lips against his and press herself against him. He was breathing hard and tipped up her face to give her a searing kiss which pressed her against the iron grilles.

'Chief?'

There was a call and Pushyamitra turned around to shield Misrakesi from Neel's curious gaze.

Neel gallantly ignored Misrakesi's presence and informed him that they were taking the Naga to the interrogation room. Pushyamitra nodded his permission.

'Come home with me,' Pushyamitra said under his breath. Misrakesi wanted nothing more.

Vrishni, who was the only person at home, was curtly dismissed as soon as they entered. Vrishni shook his head, there they were again, and who knew what would be the end of this? She was the only woman he had ever seen in this house walking in unmistakably encircled in the owner's arms.

He picked her up as they entered his sleeping quarters and laid her gently on his bed. 'Wait for me,' he said as Misrakesi refused to let him go. 'I must have a bath. I cannot come to you in all my dirt.'

The rectangular bath was just across the courtyard and Misrakesi propped herself on some pillows watching him cross over. It was all ready for him, filled with fresh water strewn with Neem leaves. It had a marble seat and silver vessels of herbal scented water, oils and river clay scrub kept on the side. He sat on the seat and poured the vessels of water over himself, arching his neck back to let the water flow all over his body, it was now two days since he had slept and he briefly ran his hands through his wet hair and closed his eyes.

Then opened them to find two soft hands running through his hair and rubbing it with scented myrobalan extract.

'Misrakesi!' he protested softly.

'Shhh. It is your newest dasi reporting for duty,' Misrakesi was smiling mischievously as she took up the little pot of sandalwood oil and poured it on her palms before massaging and rubbing it all over him. It would be washed off with the clay leaving the skin clean, supple and scented.

'You will get wet,' he murmured even as he relaxed against her and let her hands run unchecked over his chest, arms, back and shoulders, and legs. The voluptuous pleasure of her ministrations made him stretch like a tiger before it springs on its prey; and Misrakesi was that prey as she found herself clasped to him regardless of the water.

'I am not the one who needs a bath, remember.'

'Too late,' his voice was abstracted as he removed her uttariya and loosened the nivi-bandh[52] of her antariya. He was stretched out before her, with all the arrogance and glory of his manhood rising in front of her, for her, how could she resist him?

Misrakesi woke up a few hours later. They had made delicious love and then fallen asleep in each other's arms. She was lying on Pushyamitra's bed and he was bending over her in the half light. His long sensitive fingers were caressing her with a warm and possessive touch.

Was she imagining a tinge of desperation in his eyes before they turned into dark pools of tenderness as soon as they met hers?

Pushyamitra raised his head and said reluctantly, 'It is time for me to go back. Come, I will take you back to your home.'

He got up to put on some clothes, tying a fine saffron antariya around himself as Misrakesi lay across his bed, only a thin chadar partly covering and partly exposing her. Her eyes were conveying a laughing invitation which Pushyamitra was hard put to ignore.

He was dressed and standing over her and he held out a hand. 'But I have nothing to wear. I want this.' And she slowly unwrapped the uttariya from his waist looking up at him impishly.

'Misrakesi!' He gave her a bone cracking hug before he actually wrapped his own uttariya around her and then went to dress himself again.

They were finally dressed and making their way to Apsara Sabha on horseback. Neither of them said anything much but their parting embrace in front of the gate said it all. Pushyamitra rested his forehead for an instant against Misrakesi's in a revealing gesture before riding off. He had taken many women in his varied career, but this was the first time he had given himself to one.

Apsara Sabha was up and about. In fact Mrinalini had not slept at all and neither had Madlekha, both waiting for Misrakesi to return. Mrinalini had seen Pushyamitra bid her an intimate farewell and was waiting, her lips tight with disapproval. She started her remonstrations at once, but Misrakesi had too much to think about to listen to Mrinalini's reproaches.

'Do not trust him… his only mistress is his Suraksha Vibhag, no one can come between him and his love, Magadha. You will only regret what you are doing…' Mrinalini's mutters followed Misrakesi as she took the stairs to go up.

That evening Misrakesi performed a solo dance after a long time, electrifying clients and dancers alike. The passion that inspired the dance was reflected in the glow about her which made her compatriots look at her slightly curiously.

She collected a few chosen men for her Paan Goshti, Ugrasala of course being one of them. She and Manjari worked on him together and as the evening went on he would have been ready to gift them with whatever they saw fit to ask of him. The attention of two beautiful women at the same time was beyond his fantasies.

Misrakesi had decided that if at all Ugrasala had anything to do with the counterfeit coins, they would have been stored somewhere in one of his warehouses. Although there was no concrete evidence linking him with the coins, there was plenty of reason to keep him high on the list of suspects. She had thought over his situation and behaviour and was determined to continue her investigations into his affairs.

She had had a detailed briefing with Sumant who – along with the warehouse inspectors – was coordinating the thorough search of all Ugrasala's warehouses. Nothing untoward had been found in any of them. She had a list of all the searched premises and wanted to check if anything had been left out.

Sumant was also being briefed by the Mint officers on their ongoing investigations. A master list of all the seals and their owners did exist, but it was of the Nanda times. Many of the persons mentioned on that list were dead or removed from their posts. It was being updated now. Great care had been taken after the Mauryas' entry into the city to take the Mints and seals into their custody, but who knew where a slip could have occurred in the overall confusion. As far as the royal seal was concerned it was a problematic issue. Only Dhana Nanda could say who he had entrusted with the royal seal. His known favourites were in consideration and that was where Ugrasala came in again, the brother of one of Dhana Nanda's prime favourites, Bhaddasala. Amatya Katyayana had confirmed that it could be possible although the Nanda king had not confided everything to him.

All these facts were buzzing in Misrakesi's head as she smiled and flirted with Ugrasala and served him carefully controlled amounts of wine with her own hands. She did not want him passing out on her.

He lolled on the cushions, smiling fatuously first at Manjari and then at Misrakesi. His caution, never very abundant, he had thrown to the winds and was ready to say anything to these two apsaras who were making so much of him. He would tell them whatever it took to keep the smiles on their faces and keep them sitting next to him. He boasted of his dealings with all the important setthis of Pataliputra and implied that he was indispensable to them. From here it was but a small step for him to be led to Devakanta. Ugrasala's business was expanding so fast that he had recently bought a warehouse from him.

Misrakesi smiled and ran her fingers up his arms coquettishly, 'You are indeed a rich and powerful man, Deva. You had not told me this before, I am very impressed. Maybe you could take both of us to show us your land and properties. We could make a day and night out for that.'

Ugrasala's eyes glistened at that and he said, 'A very good idea. My new warehouse is a little outside the city, towards Rajagriha, it is a beautiful spot and quite solitary. We can enjoy ourselves in complete privacy over there.'

Misrakesi expressed her enthusiasm and readiness suitably and stayed talking to him till he had drunk himself into a stupor. Manjari had been a silent facilitator in all this activity and she did not ask any questions even as Misrakesi got up to leave, merely making arrangements for Ugrasala to be sent back home.

Siddharthak and Misrakesi met the next day to compare notes. Misrakesi was reasonably sure that the warehouse that Devakanta had sold to Ugrasala had not been examined, it had not figured in the list Sumant had shared with her. It had also been kept a secret by Ugrasala. Coincidentally, Siddharthak had also picked up the same piece of information, that a warehouse had changed hands between Devakanta and Ugrasala.

Misrakesi was a step ahead of him and also knew the location, roughly if not exactly. They discussed the significance of this without arriving at any conclusion but they agreed that it should at least be investigated. So they decided to give the information to Sumant who was looking after that part of the case. Neither was willing to give up the initiative to the other so they went off together although at a discreet distance from each other to the Nagarik Suraksha Vibhag headquarters.

The headquarters was such a beehive of activity with all kinds of people being summoned on a variety of pretexts that two more entrants attracted scant attention. Neither Pushyamitra nor Sumant were there but there was a message waiting for Siddharthak. He was asked to bring Misrakesi and Chandramukhi to a destination on the Rajagriha road which would be shown to them by Vrishni. Misrakesi pricked up her ears when she heard the destination. This could not be a coincidence.

In as much time as it took to locate Chandramukhi, the three of them were riding down the Rajmarga to Rajgriha with Vrishni leading the way.

'I believe the Naga chief's son, Kumaril Naga has been of great help to the investigation. You have already seen him, haven't you? You will see him again wherever it is we are headed I am sure,' remarked Siddharthak idly as they were trotting on at a steady pace.

Misrakesi shook her head disparagingly, 'See him! You mean see his remains such as they might be. Your vibhaga would have left very little of him intact.'

'I do not think so. I met him yesterday and he seemed to be not only in possession of all his limbs and faculties but also in full command of his contingent of Nagas who were busy helping Pushyamitra and his people.'

Misrakesi turned her head to look at him disbelievingly, 'You mean Arya Pushyamitra has won him over without the use of force and torture?'

'Yes, why not? Pushyamitra is highly skilled in the art of persuasion and negotiation. He always uses force as only a last resort. Of course some of his men get carried away but you know Pushyamitra enough to understand that now.'

'His reputation is very different,' said Misrakesi shaking her head.

'Reputations can be based on untruths and exaggerations. You, of all people should realize that,' said Siddharthak enigmatically.

When Misrakesi looked uncomprehending he changed the subject back to the case at hand. Very soon Vrishni turned into a narrow track off the road and they came upon Pushyamitra and his men, and they were indeed accompanied by the same Naga Misrakesi had identified who was at the head of a group of his men, all free and looking in fine fettle.

They dismounted and went up to Pushyamitra who greeted them briefly and brought them up to date. This was where the Naga ox-cart drivers had brought the carts and left them, making their own way back to their encampment on foot. The only problem was that Pushyamitra and his men had not been able to find anything here as yet, even though there was a small, semi-abandoned warehouse structure nearby. It was almost empty and showed signs of having been left to its fate quite some time ago.

Siddharthak and Misrakesi exchanged glances. Siddharthak told Pushyamitra about what they had discovered in separate enquiries.

'This must be the warehouse. I don't think much of it. I wonder why Ugrasala bought it anyway. And to think that he has visions of bringing Manjari and me here for a few days of dalliance! I don't think much of it even as a secluded love nest and neither would Manjari,' declared Misrakesi.

Siddharthak laughed and said, 'Oh, I am sure he would have made a luxurious little love nest of it by the time he brought you down. Money can do anything.'

'Can we get back to the matter at hand?' said Pushyamitra, cutting short their laughter. 'My men are busy searching the area for anything suspicious. Can you think of any purpose that this dilapidated structure can serve?'

Siddharthak and Misrakesi were silent, trying to bend their minds to it. Chandramukhi had been silent all this while. Night had already fallen and they were working with the help of mashaals. She was walking around the building quietly examining it and looking at it from all angles. The moon had come out and the structure looked almost respectable in the full moon night. There was an arched gateway with a kalash[53] on the top and her attention was engaged most of all with that. As the others were also walking around and putting forward their opinions she came to a stop in front of the arch and seemed to make up her mind.

'Ask Arya Pushyamitra to try this spot where I am standing. He should find the gateway to the underground chamber where he will find what he wants, if indeed there is anything to find, that is,' she said in a calm voice to Misrakesi.

Misrakesi looked at her, 'Are you sure?'

'Not entirely, but I am making an informed guess. In any case how does it hurt? His men are searching everywhere, may as well do it here.'

'That is true,' and Misrakesi went up to tell Pushyamitra about Chandramukhi's idea. By now Pushyamitra had a healthy respect for what Chandramukhi said, except perhaps for her harping on about her husband as the kingpin of the plot, and he immediately directed a team to dig under Chandramukhi's supervision.

There was only the sound of iron upon the small stones in the soil as a group of men worked away at the spot she had pointed out. Pushyamitra and Misrakesi came to stand and watch.

There was a metallic clang and a shout went up. They had indeed struck an iron trapdoor with a large ring. All of them except Chandramukhi gathered around excited and Pushyamitra, with Neel's help, pulled up the trapdoor. There was a flight of steps leading in and Neel silently handed a mashaal to Pushyamitra before commandeering one for himself. They disappeared into the bowels of the earth.

Each minute was like an eternity for the waiting group outside. There was no sound from inside and it suddenly struck Misrakesi that they could have walked into a trap, an ambush. Even though the two men had swords with them who knew what was waiting for them inside.

However, a few achingly long minutes later, Pushyamitra's head appeared outside. He came out and handed the mashaal silently to Siddharthak, sitting down suddenly on a rock.

He looked up as Siddharthak disappeared inside and said in a wondering voice, 'We have found it. It is like a royal treasury in there. Bags and bags of coins, of silver and bronze, of every denomination. It would have slowly ruined Magadha. There is far too much for us to have been able to stop the dissemination.'

Neel came out exulting and set up a shout. The small camp was soon ringing with shouts and congratulations. Pushyamitra stood smiling with his arm around Misrakesi and slowly let the relief sink in. Chandramukhi who would have been the cynosure of all eyes had disappeared somewhere.

Events moved with dizzying rapidity after that. The swiftest horseman was dispatched to the senapati to ask for a heavy contingent of the army to guard the cache of coins till it could be moved into the treasury. Pushyamitra left Neel for the safeguarding of the treasure and took Sumant and Nagasena with him for the summary arrest of Ugrasala and Devakanta.

There was nothing more to be done there, so Misrakesi also prepared to depart to the secret disappointment of Neel who would have loved to give her a special tour of the underground chamber, alone with her in the dark.

'How did you know about the chamber and its entrance, Chandramukhi?' asked a very curious Siddharthak as the three of them who had come together made their way back. He was not alone, Misrakesi was also aflame with curiosity.

'I am not going to let out all the secrets of the setthis. Suffice it to say that there are some standard formulas regarding the positioning of underground chambers adjoining warehouses and I know some of them. It has to do with the position of the shadow a certain part of the building casts on a full moon night. That is all I will tell you,' replied Chandramukhi.

Siddharthak looked at her with genuine admiration. She was a source of all kinds of knowledge and skills and was courageous to the point of carelessness and an outcast from society to boot.

Chandramukhi did not look happy at the developments although she was the heroine of the day. Misrakesi guessed it was because they had not found any sign of Shreedhan, her wicked husband. Maybe they would, in the future.

In the event, Chandramukhi was proved right in another way. Shreedhan was indeed one of the perpetrators of the secret plan. Ugrasala and Devakanta were caught and subjected to the most terrible interrogation Neel could devise. Pushyamitra gave him full freedom, Ugrasala's actions were indefensible. Even Misrakesi hoped he would die a lingering death. His only motivations had been greed and resentment against the Mauryas.

Devakanta proved to be a more or less ignorant pawn. Shreedhan who had been hired by the Gandharans for his local knowledge of Magadha had known of the warehouse with the secret chamber and approached Devakanta on Ugrasala's behalf for purchase. The warehouse had been sold in good faith. Shreedhan also helped in the local dissemination of the coins along with Ugrasala and his network within the trade and craft guilds as well as the army. They were all caught as the entire contours of the plot were exposed.

Unfortunately, Shreedhan had managed to escape and would have most probably gone to Gandhara. Chandramukhi was morose and refused all credit which a grateful administration was willing to shower on her. She did not want her identity to become more public than it had already become as she did not want her parents to get any hint of her being alive. She did, however, ask for a certain sum of money to help establish Basant in some alternative business and soon after that the two of them disappeared.

Flight

What is not possible by deployment of force is possible by the use of stratagem. The black cobra was defeated by the stratagem of the crow and the golden chain.

Chanakyasutra 124

In all, Misrakesi felt that she had good reason to be satisfied with herself. The solution had come to them through the efforts of a team of people, but her contribution had been substantial. After all, Chandramukhi was *her* informer, and all the information coming from her went to Misrakesi's credit. She felt that she deserved a few days of complete rest and peace, and she took them. These would be the last days of peace and quiet she would have for a long time, but she was not to know that.

The first rumblings became audible when she called Mrinalini to oil and wash her hair and also give her a long massage and bath; something she had almost given up for a long time. She was planning on enjoying the relaxing bath as well as some choice tidbits of palace gossip.

Mrinalini was evasive as she oiled Misrakesi's silken black tresses and rubbed her body with a sandalwood and aloe paste. She was running the ebony roller between Misrakesi's shoulder blades silently, concentrating on the task rather than chattering as usual.

'Come now, Mrinalini, what is the news from the palace? I have not been able to gossip with anyone for such a long time. You must bring me up to date.'

'Nothing, ... there is nothing happening. They are a set of foolish and malicious people who know nothing but say a lot, most of it lies.' She said, shaking her head.

Misrakesi was quite amused because she knew Mrinalini loved gossip and to make entire edifices out of straw. 'Come on Mrinalini. There must be something. You mean to say that no one is appearing in the wrong bed or misappropriating royal funds or...' she stopped when she saw Mrinalini's downcast face and heard her mutter about that vicious Sreelekha.

'It is me, is it not?' she said slowly, stopping Mrinalini with an upraised hand and looking her in the eye. 'All the gossip is about me.' She should have guessed immediately, given the usually garrulous Mrinalini's hemming and hawing

'But don't worry about it. Daughter, I know how to put these foolish chattering women in their place. I told them you had nothing to do with Rudra!'

'But Mrinalini, I really have nothing to do with this Rudra, whoever he may be,' said a bewildered Misrakesi, 'Who is he? What is all this about?'

'He was Som's tutor,' muttered Mrinalini unwillingly. Of course, the young Brahmin who had been dismissed by Manjari! But what did he have to do with her? She had never seen him or spoken to him. It was time to ask for all the answers.

'Call Manjari.' Misrakesi said in a voice that brooked no argument. She poured water over herself and cut short her bath, merely pausing to wash out the oil from her hair. 'I must get to the bottom of this matter now.'

A nervous Mrinalini scuttled off to call Manjari, shaken by the unexpected harshness in Misrakesi's manner.

She had put on her antariya and was braiding her long hair by the time both of them returned.

'Sit down Manjari and tell me exactly what happened that made you send Som's tutor away. If it is a serious matter I should have known of it long before this. One of you should have informed me,' said Misrakesi severely, her hands busy twisting the strands of her hair.

'You see, Misrakesi,' began Manjari hesitantly, 'you were already so worried about so many other things that we did not want to further upset you. This was finally only baseless gossip. They were saying that you had seduced him, a young Brahmin boy.'

'Me, seduce a brahmachari!' cried Misrakesi in gathering indignation. 'Goddess Shree save me from such a sin! How could anyone accuse me of such a terrible act? I do not even know the young man in question.'

'I was equally surprised and shocked, and I could not understand how this particular story could have started. So I called him and questioned him closely. He finally admitted that one day, while returning from his classes with Som he saw you sitting under a tree in your dhoti and kanchuki and was struck by your... beauty. He also admitted that he may have described you in detail and expressed his admiration very warmly to one or two of his friends who jumped to the wrong conclusion. And given Sreelekha's campaign against you, this was more fuel in the fire. I... we, Mrinalini and I decided it would be best to send him away. And to punish him, we did not give him his wages.'

'Oh, give the poor boy his wages,' said Misrakesi exasperatedly, torn between anger and the sheer absurdity of the situation. Accused of seducing a brahmachari she had never even seen!

'What is this woman's problem? Why is she targeting me like this? I try my best to be polite and friendly with her.'

Manjari shook her head more in sorrow than in anger, 'Whether you did anything or whether you were just you, she has her knife into you. When one vicious lie has run its course she introduces a new one. She says she knew what you were like even when you were staying with them, that you tried to seduce Hiranyalabha but he was too clever for you.'

Misrakesi felt bile rise into her throat as she stared at Manjari. How could anyone say that?'And Hiranyalabha kaka, does he confirm that? A man old enough to be my father, even my grandfather.' She flung her plait back angrily and it knocked over a clay pot of sandal paste. Hearing the noise Madlekha came running in.

Manjari gestured to her to go away and started to pick up the pieces herself, going down on her knees. 'No, he does not. But you know him, he is quiet and dissembles, never really contradicting her and so people draw their own conclusions which are usually...' she left the sentence unfinished and got up with the pieces in her hand.

'People always think the worst... ' this was Mrinalini.

Misrakesi was burning with rage. She decided to confront Sreelekha with her lies and had got up to summon Urmil when Madlekha entered with a parchment, which had just been delivered. It was from Pushyamitra, his seal stamped ostentatiously in three places. Mrinalini and Manjari exchanged glances looking even more unhappy than ever. Misrakesi dismissed Madlekha and unrolled the parchment.

It was a congratulatory letter from him, praising her contribution in bringing the enemies of the samrat to justice. It also said that much more important work was expected from her in the future. She rolled it up again and turned to the other two with a vindicated air.

'Let that old vicious woman say whatever she wants, I don't care.' Although she could not tell them that she was happy because her superior, the royal official she reported to, was happy with her work, her expression clearly said that the letter was a welcome support.

When they remained silent, she took a close look at them and understood. 'Hé Devi Mata, I understand now.' And she sat down suddenly, 'It is him, isn't it? *He* is the problem.'

Their embarrassed silence was the only confirmation she needed. 'Tell me the worst. What is the story being spread by Sreelekha?'

Mrinalini did not have the courage to open her mouth. It was Manjari who told her about the entire storm of lies which had been swirling around her unconscious head; that Pushyamitra was smitten with her, that he had set up Apsara Sabha for her, misusing royal funds at his disposal, that they were misappropriating funds from the treasury and to crown it all... that Misrakesi was making a fool of Pushyamitra by wallowing in luxury and using it as a centre for seduction and sexual escapades.

It was a clever structure of half truths and lies blended together with speculation to come up with a picture so vile and sordid that Misrakesi felt physically sick. She was cast as the grasping and greedy nymphomaniac.

She was silent, her stomach churning with anger and disgust, ready to go and do battle but with whom? She could not talk to all the faceless phantoms who were maligning her, but Sreelekha was real. She would definitely get a piece of Misrakesi's mind.

'Misrakesi,' Manjari spoke gently, 'there is more. If it had been just gossip we could have ignored it but we have also heard that there may be a royal enquiry into all this.'

'What? A royal enquiry!' Misrakesi clenched her fists in agony. This meant that someone in a position of authority actually believed this farrago of nonsense. She was tangled in a web of lies. What was she to do? She would have to go and explain her side of the story; clarify her position with facts and figures and accounts. She maintained the account books strictly as per regulations and any audit would testify to her honesty; but the indignity of it!

Manjari continued, 'That is why I was happy, in spite of everything, when Pushyamitra came here that night, before that I knew that there was nothing between the two of you. I thought if you were really his mistress he could perhaps save you along with himself. He is a very powerful man, his brother is the senapati and he has the ear of Maha Amatya Katyayan as well as the acharya. I hear that the samrat also holds him in good regard. These things count.'

'Yes, but not when bhagya is against you,' was Mrinalini's mournful riposte. 'I have heard that the enquiry is going to include Pushyamitra's role in the entire affair and that he may even be removed from his Nagarik Suraksha Vibhag.'

This was worse. She was also going to be the unwitting instrument for the destruction of a fine man's brilliantly built-up career.

'Sister!' This was Manjari. 'I know you want to go and confront Sreelekha but please do not. What will you gain? She will deny everything and, in any case, the issue is now far bigger than her. If you say anything to her she is far more likely to twist it and use it to your disadvantage.'

Misrakesi was forced to agree, Sreelekha was cleverer than her at twisting things around.

'The two of you will have to be my eyes and ears. Mrinalini, be on the lookout for an opportune moment when I can go to the palace and defend myself. I will try to meet the acharya. Do you think you can talk to the Samragyi and ask her to intervene on my behalf? I can try to ask for Shrunottara's help, but I do not know what her reaction will be.'

She paced up and down the room trying hard to think of ways of saving herself though her mind was feeling like a handful of cotton. This was too much to take in at once. She had been living in a bubble which had burst.

Mrinalini nodded with a determined look on her face, 'I shall do my best.'

Manjari said, 'Try not to worry too much. Maybe it is all temporary and will blow over. We must hope for that. We know there is no truth in these allegations, so why should the palace not reach the same conclusion?'

There was emphatically no truth in anything except for the fact that she and Pushyamitra were lovers. But there was no law against that, was there?

~

The next few days were a living nightmare for Misrakesi who was out of her mind with worry and mortification. She wanted to stop going down for her performances but was persuaded not to do so by Manjari. It was much better to keep things going as normally as possible.

Pushyamitra, in the meanwhile, was also going through a strangely rough patch. His solving of the counterfeit coins case had been given a lukewarm reception far from the praise he had expected. His audiences with the samrat had been suspended and even the acharya had not met him for some time. He had never been a very popular or gregarious person, but even his armour of detachment had been pierced by the way people were avoiding him; even Siddharthak, and Hiranyalabha had once positively scampered out of his way when they had run into each other in the palace.

He went on calmly with his work but the alarm bells were ringing in his mind. And then, one day, there was an urgent summons from the acharya. It was a secret, closed-door meeting with just the two of them.

~

A grim and controlled Pushyamitra came out from the small room. He went straight to the senapati's office. His brother was there, as usual, working day and night with Magadha's expanding aspirations of empire and the consequently expanding army.

There was a silent but deep bond between the brothers; Agnimitra was fifteen years older than Pushyamitra and had brought him up almost as a son. They had lived in the same house till a few years ago.

He bent down and touched his brother's feet. Agnimitra pulled him up and clasped him to his chest, kissing his forehead. There was a remarkable resemblance between the brothers. Only, Agnimitra favoured a more conventional hairstyle with his hair drawn back from his forehead in orderly waves, and he was slightly shorter and leaner than his powerfully built and solid younger brother.

With his hands on Pushyamitra's shoulders and looking at him searchingly Agnimitra said, 'Is everything alright, Putra?'

Pushyamitra nodded and bent his head for his brother's blessings, 'Do not worry about me Agraj. No matter what happens, I can take care of myself.'

'Vijayi Bhava, Vatsa,' and Agnimitra placed his right hand on Pushyamitra's bent head. That was all, Pushyamitra left.

A few minutes later, the senapati approved and signed an order to send a contingent of soldiers at the crack of dawn the next morning to imprison the ex-chief of the Nagarik Suraksha Vibhag on charges of misappropriation of royal funds and raj droha.

Misrakesi received a royal summons from the palace to the same effect as she was about to go down to the Dance Hall for the evening. Manjari had brought in the roll of parchment herself when she saw that it had come from the palace, her heart beating in dread. She handed it to Misrakesi, not daring to say a word.

Misrakesi opened the parchment, read it, and let it fall from her suddenly lifeless fingers. This could not be happening to her. She had been named as co-conspirator with Pushyamitra in the defrauding of the treasury and misappropriation of funds through Apsara Sabha. She was directed to present herself at the palace the next morning.

She had been tasting success and flying high since her arrival in Pataliputra. Here was the fall; she had been dashed down. Humiliation, rage and despair washed over her in equal measure, but she said not a word, sitting down heavily on her couch and looking at the floor with unseeing eyes. Manjari left, unable to say anything either, sympathies offered at such a disaster would be useless and puerile.

She and Mrinalini huddled together outside the room wondering what would happen next. Apsara Sabha was to be taken over by the palace officials. What would happen to them?

The evening activities continued downstairs. Sounds of laughter, music and dance; the twinkling of anklets, the sound of the mridangam, the lute and the flute and the ring of metal drinking pots floated up to where the three women sat numb with shock, unable to function.

Into this scene, striding forcefully, who should walk in but Pushyamitra. He did not wait to be announced, shoved aside a dasa who was trying to usher him to the Dance Hall and went straight up to Misrakesi's room. Past two frightened and now indignant women. He went in and shut the door.

'Misrakesi.'

It was Pushyamitra's voice. She had not seen him since the day they had found the underground chamber full of counterfeit coins. She did not turn around because she did not want to see a beaten down and humiliated Pushyamitra instead of the proud, indeed arrogant man to whom she was accustomed. She would not have wished this fate on her worst enemy, let alone Pushyamitra.

'Misrakesi,' he repeated, and came around to kneel on one knee before her. She noted through a haze that he looked anything but beaten; grim and serious certainly but definitely upbeat. He held her by the shoulders and shook her gently.

'There is no time to lose. Roll up a few clothes and necessities. We have to go immediately,' he said urgently.

'Go? But where?' said Misrakesi uncomprehendingly.

'We are leaving Magadha before the crack of dawn. I have two horses waiting and we will be out of Pataliputra before morning dawns.'

'Let go of me, Arya. I am not going away anywhere. Do you want us to prove the charges of Rajdroha by running away? I am not moving, do you understand?' She fairly screamed back at him.

Mrinalini and Manjari heard the raised voice and the last sentence. With one accord they pushed the door open and entered ready for battle. What was this man forcing Misrakesi to do after being the architect of her ruin?

Pushyamitra turned his head from where he was kneeling in front of Misrakesi and snapped, 'Out! Out at once and do not come in before I call you.'

His tone stopped them in their tracks and they withdrew, bewildered and upset.

This served to roil Misrakesi's numbed emotions. He had forced his way into her life, her bed and now her bedroom, and was now shouting orders at the only two people in the world who cared about her. She shook herself free and stood up.

'There is no need to shout at anyone in my... this house, Arya.' She said coldly. 'No amount of shouting is going to make me agree to go anywhere with you.'

'Misrakesi, do not argue, please. There is no time for that. The few hours before dawn have to be used to put together resources for a journey to Gandhara which will require very arduous travel.'

Misrakesi gasped, 'Gandhara! The kingdom of our worst enemy? Are we going to run *there* for refuge? Have you taken leave of your senses?'

'No.' He came up and his fingers bit into her arm as he jerked her close and breathed into her ears, his lips almost on hers, 'I am briefing you about your, our, next assignment.'

'You mean…' comprehension suddenly dawned in her eyes and she clutched at his arms.

'Yes, I do,' he said, 'and now can you understand why I do not want to talk to you here, with two pairs of ears doubtless still glued to the door.'

'But what about this?' Her breath hitched and she pointed at the royal summons lying forlorn on the floor where it had drifted from her fingers.

'Ignore it. It is meant only to deceive any Gandharan spy who may be operating here into believing that we have indeed been banished by the samrat. It will facilitate our reception in the elder Paurava's kingdom. It need not concern you at all.'

The sudden relief felt by Misrakesi led to an upheaval, a murderous rage at his words so great that she did not know what she was doing. She gave Pushyamitra a sudden push which sent him sprawling unawares. Before he knew it she was astride him with her poisoned dagger at his throat.

'Need not concern me, is it?' She hissed between her teeth, 'Publicly humiliated and belittled, the object of lecherous and disgusting gossip for the entire city. Of course, it should not bother me. I am not a woman of flesh and blood but just a vessel for your devious tactics, Arya Pushyamitra. Well, let me tell you…'

'Misrakesi, stop.' The shock in Pushyamitra's voice brought her back to her senses. Her poisoned dagger was a very efficient weapon and she could very easily kill him with it.

She was seized by a trembling she could not control and sank down against the wall with her head on her knees and the dagger still in her hands. Pushyamitra came up and removed the dagger, holding both her hands in his.

'It is not only you, I have also been stripped of my post and publicly stigmatized as a rajdrohi, a criminal and a fool.' He said calmly.

'Arya, you knew the truth before you saw the order from the palace, did you not?' When he did not deny her charge she went on, 'I am just an ordinary dancing girl from Ujjain... I am not used to royal plots and plans, the ups and downs of flirting with power. You were born to this, a part of Rajtantra. I was not. I thought I could do it but I find myself lacking. These charades and deadly serious games are beyond me. The last two months were bad enough but this surpasses everything.'

'You do excellent work,' pointed out Pushyamitra.

'Yes, but to what end? This?' She gestured at the summons. 'You are above public opinion and can brush it off scornfully. I am not. I have been stripped of my dignity and livelihood. What if I chose to stay like this? There are many dancing girls in Pataliputra, take one of them with you if you need someone.'

Pushyamitra was in a quandary. He had not expected this. Unhappy and humiliated she would be certainly, but not to the extent of withdrawing completely. He tried to look for the right words.

'Misrakesi, Magadha needs you. You must live up to the standards of courage it expects from you.' He said in an unconscious echo of her first meeting with the acharya. Misrakesi lifted her head to look at him. Sukesi had given her life for Magadha, maybe she would have to do the same, in a different way. Stop caring about herself as a person and think of herself only as an instrument in the hands of Magadha... or Pushyamitra?

'Serving the motherland in the capacity we do, Misrakesi, is not easy. There is physical and mental pain and wrenching decisions which tear you in two. But you can do it, you will learn as I have over the years to put duty first,' said Pushyamitra slowly. His mind went back over his own career and the terrible period of the Nanda decimation when he had had to choose between two loyalties, his motherland and his samrat. He had put it behind him but it still came back to torment him at times.

'And...,' said Pushyamitra checkmating all of Misrakesi's objections, 'what would the acharya say if I arrived alone at Pataliputra's gate in the morning where he is waiting to brief us and give us his blessings?'

At Misrakesi's interrogative look he repeated, 'Yes, he is waiting for us.' This was a privilege indeed as Misrakesi, too, realized. He was the most important man in the emerging empire, perhaps even more so than the samrat.

Privately Pushyamitra realized that the acharya was a wiser man than him and had understood Misrakesi's probable reaction. Which is why he was taking the time to brief and encourage her himself. Was she so important for this mission? The acharya never did anything without a reason.

'Come on now,' he said getting to his feet and pulling her up with him. 'Have some water or wine and pull yourself together. Collect what you will need.'

When she did not respond he said, 'All right, let me put it this way. Misrakesi, will you elope with me to a Himalayan paradise where we will live happily ever after?'

Misrakesi smiled faintly at his mock romantic tone and tried to reply in the same jesting tone, 'Certainly Arya, but only if we live in a golden palace full of dancing peacocks and all the treasures of Jambudweepa.'

'Right, now that is settled, those two women fainting from curiosity can come in and make themselves useful in helping you to collect what you will need. It had better not be much. We will be travelling light and fast.'

'Just the two of us! Across the Uttarapath to the northernmost part of Jambudweepa? With the rains upon us? Your confidence is commendable but would we survive to reach Gandhara?' exclaimed Misrakesi, suddenly alive to the acute physical dangers of the journey he was proposing.

'Devi, you forget that we can call upon the full might of Magadha's armies. We shall be alone but only ostensibly so. A substantial division of the army will travel both before and after us to keep us safe.

Siddharthak will also be with them. But enough of that now. I will tell you the rest on the way. Call in your protectors and make haste with your preparations. You have to leave with me immediately. We are fugitives now. We will leave and ride straight out of Pataliputra. But remember, not a word of the truth to them, especially Mrinalini.'

Misrakesi went out and called in the two waiting women. Their faces were drawn and worried. The frowns became heavier and tears came to the emotional Mrinalini's eyes when Misrakesi told them that she was leaving Pataliputra immediately, and did not know when she would be back. But they obediently set about packing the clothes and other things she would need when they were told about the long journey.

Pushyamitra was silent, standing to the side and watching the women with hard eyes. He only interrupted once to tell Misrakesi to take as much of her jewellery as possible.

Even Manjari threw him a glance of dislike at this, and Mrinalini burst out, 'Don't go anywhere with him, daughter. Stay with us, we will take care of you.'

Manjari also said in a low voice, 'Misrakesi, we will all go and stay in Ujjain while this enquiry is on. You will be vindicated. It is only a matter of time. Then we can come back or stay there as we wish. There is no need to go with him, we are there for you.'

Misrakesi squeezed her hand gratefully but shook her head in refusal. They were ready quickly, more so under Pushyamitra's impatient gaze. Mrinalini was sobbing openly now and Manjari's eyes were shining with tears.

Misrakesi embraced them tightly before leaving and said in a choking voice, 'Do not worry, everything will be all right, I promise. I will be back and everything will be as before. Take care of Apsara Sabha in my absence and do not leave it in anyone else's hands. I am depending on both of you.' She dashed away a tear and said, 'Manjari, give Som a kiss from me and tell him that I will expect two terracotta armies when I come back.'

That was it. Pushyamitra and Misrakesi rode away into the darkness leaving the glitter of Apsara Sabha behind.

'Who is Som?' asked Pushyamitra casually after they had been riding silently for a while.

'Nobody you need to worry about. He is Manjari's little son, and no, it is not him but his brahmachari tutor I am supposed to have seduced,' said Misrakesi bitterly.

Pushyamitra was silenced and privately agreed that thanks to Sreelekha, the gossip about her had taken a particularly vicious form.

His body was relaxed on horseback and they were cantering along but he was stiff inside, wondering when certain other aspects of unfolding events would occur to her. The moment he had been putting off for the last few months had arrived and he was uncertain as to what it would bring for him.

As if in answer to an unspoken thought Misrakesi suddenly asked him, 'You, of course must have known about this plan from its inception? And did you add to the flames of gossip, judiciously?' Her voice was controlled.

'Well, I did know about it naturally but…'

'And why did you sleep with me? Was it part of the plan made by the Magadhan State or was it your own idea to add reality to a false picture?' asked Misrakesi in a dangerous voice.

Aware that he was in deep and flooding waters he answered with a straight face, 'Nobody directed me. It was what you might call a strong personal inclination. I don't think the plan envisaged such a sacrifice on my part.'

He did get a perfunctory smile out of her but only a very small one; he could feel gusts of fury emanating from her.

'And may I ask why I could not be told of this plan since I have also unwittingly played a major role in your naatak?'

What could Pushyamitra say to that? The truth was not something he could easily admit to; the plan had been mooted at the time when Chandramukhi had made her appearance in Misrakesi's life and Pushyamitra had been deeply suspicious of what the results would be and whether Misrakesi would survive. It was true, he had not trusted her in the beginning and later… He had just not wanted to interrupt their idyll and he had put it off. He had thought that he would be able to explain everything to her, but now that the moment was upon him he was unable to do so.

In the face of his silence Misrakesi supplied the obvious answer, 'Of course I know, what a stupid question,' she said with a cold smile, 'because you do not trust me. I am perfect for some sex and to be played around with, but not to be trusted with anything that really matters, oh no! The chief of the Nagarik Suraksha Vibhag must be very careful about who he trusts...'

'It was not like that Misrakesi...'

'What is there to explain, Deva? I am sure you took the perfect decision for the Vibhag. It always comes first, doesn't it, and it is why we are here after all.' Misrakesi cut in with the same silky and cold voice.

She spurred her horse and went on ahead, only to return and tell him, 'You need not worry, Arya Pushyamitra, that there will be any problem in my performance as a spy now that my position has been made so clear to me. It will in fact increase my efficiency. My performance as a lover is of course another matter.'

'Misrakesi, don't be a fool. Let me tell you...'

She merely spurred her horse again and refused to listen to him. Pushyamitra let her go, it was useless to talk to her while she was in this white hot temper; so he followed her in a slow canter.

They were at the gates of Pataliputra by the time the skies flushed with the dawn. Word of their fugitive status had not been allowed to reach the guards; so they were escorted out with great respect. Another short ride and they could see a spare, solitary figure seated in meditation under an ashvath tree. It was the acharya clad in his coarse white dhoti and uttariya.

He opened his eyes as he saw them come up and await his permission to approach him. His piercing eyes looked straight into Misrakesi's soul as he placed his hands on her head to bless her. She could feel all her resentment and anger falling away. To serve Magadha body and soul: that was the mantra given to her by the acharya and that was what she would do. Her personal scores with Pushyamitra were a different matter.

The three of them sat down to a frugal breakfast of milk and fruits and, when they had finished, the briefing began. The logistics had already been conveyed to Pushyamitra, but their actual role in the Paurava court and Misrakesi's role had to be explained to them.

They were to go as enemies of the Magadhan State and offer to trade inside information, which Pushyamitra had aplenty, in return for a position in the royal court, also hinting that the Senapati Agnimitra, his brother, was willing to betray Magadha and cross over to Kaikeya along with the vast army. However, their real mission was to buy or convince important members of the Kaikeya Mantri Parishad that the ailing and old Paurava, who was without any heirs, should appoint Chandragupta as his successor. All three of his sons had been killed in the epic campaign against the Yavana invader Alakshendra, and there was a question mark on the succession. Malayketu, his nephew, had proven himself to be a coward and a fool and was tolerated only as a dependent satellite, a king only in name.

The danger, however, was that Paurava would call his son-in-law Ambhi, the ruler of Takshshila and anoint him as his successor. And that was where Misrakesi's role came in. Paurava's daughter, Shailanandini, one of Ambhi's queens, was also in Kaikeya to add her weight to her husband's claims. It would be Misrakesi's special duty to target her. Misrakesi's presence was therefore both to bolster the reason for Pushyamitra's flight, and to approach the queen and convince her about Chandragupta's claims.

Misrakesi was, of course, left wondering why the queen would choose the Mauryan Samrat over her own husband but decided to not interrupt and just listen to the briefing. She would learn all there was in the appropriate time, she was sure.

'Putri,' said the acharya, 'take this Hemasutra.' And he gave her a gold necklace with a design of emeralds, sapphires, diamonds and rubies glowing in the rising sun. 'Give it to her at an opportune time and tell her that it comes from me to remind her of her dharma and our shared vision.'

Misrakesi took it but the questions in her eyes were very obvious and the acharya, correctly understanding them, said, 'You will know everything if you succeed in getting close to her. She will tell you everything herself. And, remember, you must introduce yourself as Sukesi's sister. The two of them were as sisters at the Training Academy in Ujjain. You will not remember her as you were too young, but she spent a year there learning the arts.'

Here, thought Pushyamitra, *is the importance of being Misrakesi.* And he marvelled anew at the acharya's grasp of the minutiae that could make or break such a delicate mission.

'Remember both of you, we are ready for war but we want a peaceful victory. That depends on you. Now you must be on your way before the sun rises.'

He blessed both of them. As Misrakesi bent to touch his feet, he said softly, 'Saubhagyavati Bhava, Putri,' at which Misrakesi flushed an ugly red.

'Pushyamitra, Misrakesi, Vijayi bhava. The future of the Mauryas goes with you.'

And their perilous journey began.

Jambudweepa

'Of the Indians, the population is by the greatest of all nations whom we know of...
There are many nations of Indians, and they do not speak the same language as each other.'

The History of Herodotus

~

It began to drizzle steadily before they could go very far and Misrakesi wondered dismally how she would be able to go through the entire journey to Kaikeya. The soil was soft and turning to mud as the rain fell. She had a rain-proof blanket wrapped around her but it merely saved her from the worst of the rain, it did not keep her dry. Part of the necessities she had packed for herself were there in a roll bumping at the horse's flank; the rest had been dispatched with the company of soldiers accompanying Siddharthak who were going to rendezvous with them outside Pataliputra. They went on in a sour silence.

Pushyamitra had spent many years in the Nanda army before he specialized in espionage work and was a hardened campaigner. His provisions were practical, professional, and neat. In fact he was the one who had the dry rations on which they would have to subsist for the immediate future, to be supplemented by whatever game they could kill or fresh fruits they could find. There was dried meat cooked with salt, sugar, spices, yoghurt and oil, barley chapattis and dried fruits. Water, of course, would have to be drunk as and when it was found although he had a small gourd skin of a fortified and spiced arishta, a medicinal extract of herbs, for emergencies.

Initially Misrakesi was in no mood to talk to Pushyamitra. As the day wore on she found herself increasingly incapable of it. Although a young and active woman with the stamina of a dancer, she was not a soldier and had no experience of campaign speed. They were travelling at more than two yojanas a day, more than the best speed of an advancing army.

Pushyamitra sat at ease, almost lounging on his saddle, and his riding was effortless. He hardly looked as though he was doing anything strenuous. For Misrakesi it was otherwise. She had left everything she knew far behind, was venturing into virgin forest accompanied by and thrown into close contact with a man whose very sight was abhorrent to her at the moment and who she felt she could never trust again. There were pitfalls stretching wherever she looked. Her only other resource was a company of soldiers. The euphoria generated by the meeting with the acharya had dissipated and harsh reality was staring her in the face. How would she survive? The physical strain was perhaps slightly less than the mental strain.

Pushyamitra was also quiet, but he wanted to talk to her and mitigate the feelings of anger and betrayal which were so obviously emanating from her. They rode on side by side, but her expression and body language gave him little encouragement and his attempts to talk to her were ignored.

The day wore on and dusk fell. Pushyamitra decided to stop for rest and food. They stopped and ate from the meagre provisions he was carrying. Misrakesi did not vouchsafe any conversation, her head was bent and she spent her time looking at the ground.

Pushyamitra tentatively held out a hand and caught her arm as they were getting up. He would end this situation immediately.

She turned around and shook herself free. Her eyes were red with fatigue and blazing with anger but her voice was cold and expressionless, 'I have nothing to say to you, Arya Pushyamitra. I will try to do the work given to me to the best of my ability. Beyond that, I do not wish to have anything to do with you.'

Pushyamitra's hand fell but her reply ignited his own sorely tried temper, he was not used to being on the defensive. He had been trying to explain the state of affairs to her but if she really did not want to listen he decided that he had had enough of being the guilty party. They were here to do some work and do it they would.

He increased their speed after that, setting a punishing pace which soon replaced the mist of angry tears Misrakesi was seeing through with a haze of tiredness. But she had no intention of remonstrating; she would do whatever he wanted professionally, and nothing at all personally.

~

The next three nights they stopped at sunset, ate the food available and slept rolled up in their blankets. At least Misrakesi would fall into an uneasy, tired sleep while Pushyamitra stayed awake to keep watch. The lack of sleep did not perturb him unduly, he was used to worse. He did not bother to hunt for food thinking that they would get enough to eat when they met up with the army. This again did not bother him too much but was an added catastrophe for Misrakesi. The world had become a grey expanse of exhaustion and she did whatever she was directed to, mechanically.

Pushyamitra was living in a blaze of temper himself and avoided looking at her or registering her presence as much as possible. He missed the tell-tale signs which he would never have ignored in any soldier of his.

This was not true of Siddharthak whom they met three days later. They met at the appointed time, Pushyamitra and Misrakesi had of course arrived before him. They were to go on together and meet the Army Division under Akshay at a day's ride from here.

Misrakesi greeted Siddharthak perfunctorily, wolfed down the food he had with him and rolled herself up to sleep; collapsed into sleep would be a better description.

Siddharthak had not been too pleased to hear that Misrakesi was also going to be such an important part of this crucial mission. She was a newcomer and should first gather enough experience before being allowed to take part in missions which were vital for the empire. However, he had not been consulted and had to make the best of it.

As soon as Siddharthak saw the two of them he realized that something was wrong but he could not understand what it was. Surely Misrakesi could not be angry about being selected for this secret operation? That she could be upset by any of the stories surrounding her departure never even entered his mind, those were the normal requisites of following a career of espionage.

However, he saw at once that Misrakesi was exhausted to the point of no return. His normally unready sympathy was stirred by her drawn face, eyes smudged with black and trembling legs. He had never seen her like this and understood that the pace was too much for her.

He and Pushyamitra had built a fire and were sitting next to it with Siddharthak taking on the first round of guard duty.

'Are you by any chance trying to kill off your partner before you reach Kaikeya?' He asked with a lift of his eyebrows when Pushyamitra said that they would move at daybreak the next day.

Pushyamitra looked at him and shrugged his shoulders, 'Hard riding never killed anybody.'

Siddharthak tried again, 'She is a young woman, bandhu, not a soldier, and you should treat her as such.'

'While I agree that I know less about women young and nubile than you do, you had better leave this one to my management.' Pushyamitra was determined to be obtuse; so Siddharthak let the subject drop, wondering again what had happened. Any rift between Misrakesi and Pushyamitra was very welcome.

When Misrakesi was woken up at daybreak, her first thought was that it would be better to just lie down and die at that very spot. Then Pushyamitra's grim face and the slight hint of scorn in his voice made her get up. It was only her determination not to give up and her refusal to ask Pushyamitra for any concession which made her mount her horse and go forward hour by dreary hour.

By the evening her abused body gave up. Pushyamitra had been riding ahead but Siddharthak was concerned and decided to take a hand. Misrakesi was bending forward resting herself on the horse's neck, barely aware of what she was doing.

He dismounted and went over to her, 'Misrakesi, what is the matter?' He said sharply as she looked white, drained and on the verge of collapse.

She raised her clouded eyes to his but was not able to answer, swaying forward on the saddle. 'Misrakesi,' he called gently, preparing to lift her off.

And he found himself pushed away roughly as Misrakesi distinguished herself by fainting for the first time in her life and sliding down heedlessly into Pushyamitra's arms. He had turned around and come up when he saw Siddharthak dismounting and was just in time to catch Misrakesi.

So there he was, in the middle of a forest with the rain coming down and darkness closing in with an unconscious woman in his arms. He should have listened to Siddharthak, that expert on women.

The expert stood a little away, a quizzical look on his face as Pushyamitra laid her down on his hastily opened blanket, chafed her hands and feet and slapped her cheeks, forcing a few sips of the arishtha down her throat. Her eyes opened and she mumbled, 'I am all right, Arya, I will just get on the horse again,' before her eyes closed again.

'There is only one thing to do, Pushyamitra, take her to the vaidya who will be there at the army encampment. You had better take her up on your horse while I lead hers.' He did not say I told you so, but his tone said it loud and clear.

Pushyamitra covered the rest of the distance with Misrakesi held up close against him. Any memory of a different and more exhilarating ride he ruthlessly suppressed.

Pushyamitra and Siddharthak caused a small sensation when they rode into the encampment past the guards with a beautiful young woman lying in a faint across the horse's saddle. The eyes of the men on guard popped at the sight and only the strict discipline in force prevented them from expressing their admiration and astonishment. That, and the expression on Pushyamitra's face. The entire army knew the senapati's brother and very few would have dared to even raise their eyes to his.

The vaidya was summoned after Misrakesi was laid down inside a tent. He examined her and said that there was nothing wrong with her except for extreme fatigue and lack of food. He was not told all the details except for the fact that she was a royal employee going to Gandhara on an important and urgent mission.

'Whatever the urgency, you will have to take into account her physical capabilities and make your schedule according to that. She will not be able to survive the pace you are setting for the time needed to reach Gandhara,' he said shaking his head after he had administered a reviving draught to her. Misrakesi was conscious now but barely so; otherwise she would have been very mortified at her collapse.

Pushyamitra was irritated; he had realized that temper had betrayed him into an unprofessional act and he did not want a lecture.

'When will she be able to travel again? Also, perhaps you can make some arishtha which will help her improve her stamina?' Reaching Gandhara as quickly as possible remained paramount. The king was old and dying and he would not await their convenience.

'You will have to let her rest for at least three days. She should spend the time sleeping. I will prescribe what she should eat. And, yes, I will make some tonics for her which she can carry. Leave her to sleep now.'

Pushyamitra and the vaidya came out of the tent where Siddharthak and Akshay were preparing to eat the evening meal of meat and rice broth with some fresh fruit.

The vaidya went off to prepare his medicine while Pushyamitra joined the other two men.

'So, is she all right?' asked Akshay in a concerned voice. He was the hand of force for this mission to conquer the Gandharan kingdoms and knew about the role to be played by Pushyamitra and Misrakesi. He was a fierce loyalist of the samrat and did not want anything to jeopardize the mission to Kaikeya. Apart from which he was also a kindly man towards all except his enemies and he had been concerned at Misrakesi's condition.

'Yes,' replied Pushyamitra briefly, 'only fatigued. The vaidya is giving her some tonic and prescribing a diet.'

'Will you have to modify any of our schedules because of this?' further asked the samrat's man.

'I do not think so. We are a bit ahead of schedule as it is. So a short rest of two-three days should not make much of a difference.'

Siddharthak interrupted, even his indifference surprised by the lack of interest in the victim, 'Don't you think you should go and see if there is anything she needs, Pushyamitra? There are no women in this camp, only soldiers. And I don't think our attentions would be welcome. You are the one best qualified, perhaps.'

This was a speech well calculated to irritate Pushyamitra, making it clear that since he was the one who had brought her to this pass, he had better do something about it and reminding him that he could not shrug off his responsibility. Pushyamitra looked unhappy, he did not fancy the role of a nursemaid and was in any case extremely angry with her at the moment, but there was no option.

Akshay looked slightly confused as Pushyamitra got up and went in to Misrakesi's tent. He was aware of many undercurrents but could not understand any of them as he did not know anything of the past relationship between Pushyamitra, Misrakesi, and Siddharthak.

She was lying on a bed of dry grass with blankets thrown over her. Her hair was tangled and clothes dirty with the days of travel, and she was also wet; altogether a sorry scrap of humanity. Pushyamitra thought of the sophisticated nartaki dressed in silks and glittering jewels, redolent with the perfume of flowers and shook his head. The tonic given to her contained a sleeping draught, and she slept on heedless breathing through her slightly open mouth.

The only emergency seemed to be that her wet clothes should be removed. He accordingly did it in a carefully impersonal way and rolled her in a couple of dry blankets, leaving her to sleep away her fatigue.

The other two had finished their meal by the time he came out; so he ate a quick meal and stretched out to catch up on his own sleep while he could, but spent the night mostly lying awake near the fire in a strange mood of introspection.

Misrakesi slept through most of the next day and awoke only as dusk was falling. It was the time of godhuli bela, when all the cows would be coming home from grazing all day. Only this was the middle of a forest, there were no cows and she was alone here. She remembered nothing but the kosa upon kosa of travelling in a daze of complete exhaustion and dripping wetness. She wondered what had happened and was ashamed to think that her fears had come true and she had collapsed. What she needed was the resolution of Sita who had followed her husband Rama into the fearsome Dandakaranya forest with never a qualm and lived there in exile with him for thirteen years.

Her thoughts received a check when there was a sound at the entrance and Pushyamitra walked in. She was not Sita and he was certainly not Maryada Purushottam Ram. Misrakesi had registered the fact that she was rolled up in a couple of blankets and nothing else. Her humiliation was complete. She turned her face away and said nothing.

'How are you now, Misrakesi?' asked Pushyamitra squatting down beside her and looking at her pale face. He decided that he would have to put off being angry with her for later. It would be an unequal contest at the moment.

'I am all right now.' Her voice emerged unwillingly. Pushyamitra took her hands in his and she let them lie there, wooden and stiff; she had no energy to protest.

'The vaidya has had a look at you and prescribed only rest and a few tonics for exhaustion. Why didn't you tell me if I was going too fast for you?'

This was the wrong thing to say as she was put on the defensive about her stamina and capabilities.

'Anyway, rest here for some days till you are fit to travel again and I will see to it that we travel in a more reasonable fashion.' Pushyamitra let go of her hands and became stiff and formal.

'Is there anything else that you want?'

There were a thousand things she wanted to do, starting with wearing some clothes, but where was she going to find the privacy to do so in this encampment? She felt rather desperate as she looked around the tent.

Pushyamitra understood her dilemma and said, gesturing to a corner of the tent, 'There are your things. Dress yourself while I wait outside and then I will show you a little rivulet which runs nearby and you can wash up.'

She dressed herself hastily and wrapped a blanket around herself before emerging on wobbly feet. But some time later she felt like a new woman, clean and properly dressed. Her shringar was absent but at least she was not dirty and bedraggled. She sat inside her tent for a while and then decided that shutting herself up would be impossible for the months of travel which were to follow. Being the only woman in the middle of an army was intimidating and uncomfortable, but she would have to get used to it and then ignore it. She drew a deep breath and stepped outside. A fire was burning and Pushyamitra, Siddharthak, and Akshay were sitting around it engaged in cleaning and polishing their weapons.

She came up and tentatively greeted Siddharthak who asked her how she was feeling. It was also left to him to introduce her to Akshay since Pushyamitra was looking at her intently, saying nothing. Akshay would have had to be a fool of monumental proportions to not guess that Misrakesi and Pushyamitra were in the middle of a quarrel, and also that there was more between them than just a quarrel.

As she sat down, Siddharthak said, 'There is the arishta the vaidya has left for you. He has also ordered you to eat a full and hearty meal and drink some wine.'

The awkwardness of the moment passed as Misrakesi was ravenous and only too ready to do justice to the rice gruel, roasted meat, barley rotis and the wine to go with it. It seemed like a feast and she ate with a will. The food and wine brought the colour back to her face and the amount she consumed amused Siddharthak who said, 'For a nartaki who looks so ethereal you certainly can eat quite a bit!'

'Do not forget that I have been systematically starved for the last week,' returned Misrakesi tartly. The fire turned her brown eyes to black as she turned to smile at him. She had decided to be charming to everyone except a certain person and succeeded so well that after some time even the ambivalent Siddharthak forgot that he disliked her and said admiringly, 'You are a courageous woman, Misrakesi. I cannot think of many other women who would have been ready to undertake this journey even for Magadha. And that too in the company of this human fiend who was ready to ride you into the ground if I had not saved you.'

Misrakesi could not help laughing at this even as the human fiend looked up from cleaning and polishing his Nishtrimsa campaign sword with its curved tip and rhinoceros horn-hilt edged with gold. He was looking at the two of them through hooded and expressionless eyes. He had immediately become alert to Misrakesi's attempts to charm Siddharthak and could not say that he appreciated it. He was wondering at her motives, was she trying to make him jealous or show her lack of concern for him or simply looking for some support? It was a novel experience being out of the centre of her attention. He could remember only too well that, before he had been forced to shatter their idyll, they had existed in a world of their own.

Akshay was a taciturn and self-contained man who was little used to interacting with women. His brahmacharya of the Takshshila days still seemed to cling to him like a second skin although there was nothing in him which would be offensive to a woman. He was tall with the well set up body of a professional soldier to say nothing of a regular yoga practitioner. The habit of command gave him a martial air compounded by his luxuriant moustache and steady eyes. But there was something almost diffident and self-effacing about him. He was not one to put himself forward while talking to anyone. He was content to listen and smile. He maintained his distance from women assiduously.

Misrakesi had slept the day through and was in no mood to sleep, but she had been given strict directions as well as a sleeping draught and was soon yawning. It was a much softened Siddharthak who stood up when she got up and went off to her tent to sleep alone. He was thinking that it would be worthwhile to try and lure her to his bed; Pushyamitra and she seemed to have an on-again, off-again relationship and he could always jump into the gap.

'The lady sleeps alone, does she? You do not seem to be preparing to follow her?' he asked Pushyamitra interrogatively.

'Yes, she is sleeping alone and so am I.' growled Pushyamitra, not in the best of tempers. *And so are you,* said his expression, upon which Siddharthak shrugged and went off. If Pushyamitra was going to act like a tigress with one cub it would be very difficult.

A couple of days passed and Misrakesi felt more than restored.

They were to cover the next stage of the journey along with part of the Army, and they started off together, the four of them at the head of the long column which would break up into smaller groups as they moved on.

Akshay was the Nayaka of the Army Division which consisted of ten battalions under their respective commanders with each of these having ten Patikas under them. The entire force consisted of a thousand units of men and horses; the chariots had to be left behind as they could not travel inside the forest, they would accompany the main army when it came up with the samrat later. There were only a few chariots for the Nayaka and some of the commanders.

It was a huge force and it was an exercise in ingenuity to take it up the yojanas on the Uttarapath leading to Gandhara without warning the Gandharans. Many were the subterfuges, and it would be necessary to disseminate misinformation in the villages along the way. Pushyamitra's men were busy doing that. The battalions moved in a complicated criss-cross fashion, never travelling together on the same path.

The next few days saw a great deal of discussion on the mission they were on, and Misrakesi belatedly realized what a huge privilege it was for her to be handpicked for it. The feedback given about her by her chief must have helped the acharya to make up his mind although he also had his own sources. Her name may even have been suggested by Pushyamitra. She had reasons to thank him perhaps, professionally speaking.

And personally? She had been hurt and shocked by what she saw as his duplicity and deceit; he had used her, she thought, lightly and thoughtlessly, slept with her only for the ends of state policy. Every time she looked at him she saw only her own foolishness.

She was dressed much more sensibly now having taken time to think about it. So she was transformed; gone were the complicated clothes. She was wearing a simple cotton dhoti drawn up kaccha style between her legs for convenience. She had removed all her jewellery and kept it away. There was only a kanchuki around her breasts and a long tulapansi cotton wrap around her shoulders to protect her from the elements. Gone was the elaborate hairstyle with hair ornaments, her luxuriant curls had been ruthlessly shorn to her waist, parted on the side and confined in a tight chignon, a kabaribandh, at the nape of her neck with just one silver clasp holding it all in place. There was a simple rudraksha mala around her neck.

She looked like Shakuntala in the sylvan surroundings of Sage Kanva's ashram with little delicate circlets of flowers around her neck, wrists and waist instead of jewellery; strange and different from her usual decorated and sophisticated self but still so desirable that Pushyamitra's scowl had deepened and Siddharthak's eyes glistened. It appeared as if even the taciturn Akshay had been forced to take notice.

They were still on the plains so the going was not very tough, especially since it had stopped raining and the ground was less slushy. They had to keep to the deep forest and away from the frequented pathways. They were trying to follow a path parallel to the Uttarapath so that they would not lose their way in the forest, but at the same time they had to take care to stay away from the actual path. It was a delicate manoeuvre made possible only because of the experienced scouts with the Army of whom Pushyamitra was also counted as one. Misrakesi found herself riding at his side but neither of them acknowledged the other's presence.

Siddharthak watched them with ill-concealed amusement. He, who had no emotions with regard to anyone, could not understand their stormy relationship and was wont to dismiss it as posturing, or plain and simple stupidity. Why spend time agonizing over anyone when it was better spent sleeping with her? Women were like cooked rice, only to be consumed.

One evening, they had stopped on the way and were watching the setting-up of the camp for the night. Misrakesi and Pushyamitra had been ahead of the group and had reached early. Pushyamitra had wrenched a neck muscle when he had ducked to avoid a low lying branch which had sprung up while he was chopping off another branch coming in Misrakesi's way. His neck was troubling him; he stood and massaged it absently or twitched his shoulders to ease the pain, mentally making a note that he would ask one of the masseurs travelling with them to take a look.

He was in considerable discomfort and Misrakesi was moved to offer her help.

'If you sit down, I can massage the kink out of your neck, I have learnt how to,' she offered in a gruff voice.

Pushyamitra sat down immediately and she knelt behind him. She raised her hands, hesitated, and then placed them on his shoulders. She kneaded his shoulder muscles and her thumbs made slow circling motions at the base of his neck before she laid his head on her breasts and gave his neck a deft rightward twist making him grunt. The kink was out and she pressed and soothed the muscles for some more time.

He was in no mood to end the sudden massage. Her hands, warm and caring, were telling him what her face and body refused to tell him and he was well satisfied. Siddharthak and Akshay were approaching and she got up saying, 'I think you should be all right now.'

He turned and gave her a slow and genuine smile of thanks before joining the others. Misrakesi was shaken; she had thought that she would never forgive him but her resentment was slowly melting away. He was the same as ever, his attitude towards her was also the same as it had been in Pataliputra; once he had gotten over his initial spurt of anger, of course!

Pushyamitra's scowls and grimness had vanished and he was laughing and joking with some of the soldiers as if he did not have a care in the world. When she got up to sleep he gave her another of his newly-acquired heart-stopping smiles leaving her bewildered and staring at him.

Misrakesi was in a thoughtful mood the next day. The path was a little difficult here as there were many small rivulets, which appeared in the rains, to be crossed. It was a wet and muddy business and she sighed when they came to yet another one. This one was a little deep so she got off her horse leaving him to swim across and prepared to wade into the waist deep water. The next minute she found herself off her feet and being carried effortlessly in Pushyamitra's arms as he walked across.

Her arms went up in a reflex action but her hands linked behind his neck as she looked up at him with uncertain eyes, too taken aback to speak.

'Pull up your wrap. It should not get wet,' he said. She pulled it up mechanically as they looked at each other, especially Misrakesi as she had made rather a business of not looking at him for the last many days. Those piercing eyes, the hands and mouth which had pleasured her out of her senses, the hard body against which she had melted countless times, the bead pressing into her shoulders all these were as familiar to her as her own self.

'So Misrakesi, how much longer is this going to persist?' he continued conversationally. 'Have you punished me enough?' he asked, raising his eyebrows.

She continued to look at him with dark and troubled eyes and said nothing. They reached the other side of the rivulet and he stood on the dry bank holding her still. No one else had reached the rivulet as yet, so they were quite alone.

'Put me down,' said her lips as their gazes held, but her hands did not unlink from behind his neck.

She slipped down after a moment. Water was dripping off his chest and neck and back and his dhoti clung to his muscled thighs. She felt herself flush and her throat went dry just looking at him smiling faintly and questioningly at her.

They had reached a mango grove and Misrakesi went and sat under one of the trees to recover. Pushyamitra tethered the horses to a nearby tree. It had stopped raining and the whole world seemed green shaded and freshly washed. The mango season was almost over but some late mangoes were still hanging on the trees. More to give herself something to do than to really eat it, Misrakesi caught at a ripe yellow mango hanging overhead and plucked it.

Pushyamitra was sitting opposite her and enjoying the picture she made. Her ochre wrap had fallen off one shoulder and as she pulled at the mango, a few drops of water fell and tumbled over her bare shoulder and slipped down to disappear. He drew in his breath. Her hair had come slightly loose and one long curl moved idly against her breasts in the slight breeze.

She bit into the mango, spit out the stalk and began to suck at it, her luscious lips pulling out and enjoying the sweet yellow pulp. Then, as she looked up, a lightning message passed between them and the next minute Misrakesi was in his arms, cradled between his knee and shoulder.

He kissed her thoroughly and began feeding her little pieces of the tender and tangy mango. He would bite into the fruit and then open Misrakesi's mouth with his own pushing in the tiny pieces with his tongue, exploring her mouth while she swallowed. She was soon whimpering with passion. He raised his head and looked at her for an interminable moment and then gathered her closer to his heart and back into that driving spiral of passion where there was no one but them, their lips fused and tongues tangled as if they would never stop.

But only for a few heartbeats… a thundering of hooves signaled the arrival of the others who found them sitting apart disinterestedly. Siddharthak was not deceived for a moment.

That night, Pushyamitra opted for the second spell of guard duty and disappeared ostensibly to sleep. Misrakesi had already gone. Siddharthak watched with the eyes of a bored veteran; he knew only too well what they were actually going to be up to. The night passed and Siddharthak settled himself comfortably beside the fire. Akshay was with a different group of soldiers tonight and he was alone.

'Waiting for me?' asked Pushyamitra softly as he entered Misrakesi's tent. She was sitting with her back to him with a small polished silver mirror in her hand, preparing to brush her hair with a fine ivory comb. A thin orange uttariya was around her and the dhoti had been replaced with the soft white mulmul cloth she tied around her hips while sleeping. It was just about enough for a knot to be tied at her hips and left one side gaping with a view of her tapering thigh and leg.

She had just opened her kanchuki so she was wearing nothing else, there was a small earthen lamp burning on the ground beside her and in that dim light Pushyamitra could see the long lovely line of her back, the curve and flare of her figure. He removed the clasp from her hair and it tumbled down in a perfumed and silky cascade. She had closed her eyes and was slowly shaking her head from side to side presumably in denial of his question.

'Liar,' he breathed against her neck as he pushed her hair away and started kissing her back. As his tongue and lips tasted her skin he could feel her tremble and sigh. His hands were none too steady as he held her arms and feasted on her. She moaned when he nibbled at her waist and went down further below.

'Sshhh. Be silent.' He put his hand on her mouth.

'I can't.' She squirmed and strained against his lips. His other hand went around to cup one breast which flowered into his palm. With a muffled exclamation he turned her around and his mouth tugged at her through the thin uttariya. Misrakesi groaned loudly enough to wake the entire army. His mouth cut it off.

'You are mine tonight,' he said fiercely.

'Arya…'

'Shut up. Call me by my name. Say it.'

'Pushyamitra,' it emerged as a husky whisper and sent him into a frenzy. His mouth roamed at will and she repeated his name as the one support in a whirling world. He brought her to fulfillment again and again before embedding himself inside her and losing himself while she sobbed out his name.

He was half-lying on a cushion and she was lying across his chest as he gently stroked her face and hair. 'Misrakesi, it is almost worth it, your being angry with me if you will let me feast on you like this after that.'

'Don't joke.' She stopped his hands, 'I was not angry with you for nothing.'

'Yes, I know, dearest.' And he gave her a contrite hug. 'And I am sorry. I should never have hidden anything from you. Bear with the way I am.'

His apology turned her heart over and she covered his face with small feather light kisses. He had never ever called her his dearest before, either.

'Ummm. This is wonderful but I have to go and take over guard duty from Siddharthak. Come with me and we will finish this off under the stars. You do not need to wear anything else.'

Misrakesi smiled to see that her mulmul cloth was still tied at her hips although the uttariya had been discarded. She yawned and stretched, 'I am sleepy.'

'Come on. I will be all alone and lonely.'

'Alright, you go on and I will follow you.'

A little after midnight Siddharthak heard Pushyamitra walking across the trees to the fire. He came and sat down companionably next to Siddharthak and poked at the fire. His limbs were loose and relaxed and his eyes were those of a satiated tiger.

There was silence for some time. Siddharthak and his insatiable curiosity coupled with the absence of certain grim lines across Pushyamitra's face which had been there for years pushed him to ask,

'So how is the Apsara, bandhu? As good as she looks?'

Pushyamitra considered and then answered, 'As you say, an Apsara from Indra's court. And she is fierce...' before he could continue there was an interruption. Misrakesi had actually followed him after some time and came up in time to hear them talk. She walked up, her face flaming and clapped her hands on Pushyamitra's mouth.

'How can you? How can you possibly discuss my performance with your friend here? I don't believe it, it is...' she sputtered to a stop.

Pushyamitra shrugged, hiding his amusement and his face studiously neutral, 'He asked and I answered.'

'Yes, I did,' put in Siddharthak from across the fire.

'You did, did you?' said Misrakesi narrowing her gaze and looking at him with consideration as she walked across the fire.

Siddharthak eyed her warily. She was looking incomparable but she could also be dangerous. She had only the thin mulmul wrap around her hips and an uttariya flung carelessly around her shoulders. Her fragile collarbone, slim shoulders, and narrow waist looked as if they could barely support the weight of her heavy and shapely breasts. The mulmul clung to her thighs, outlining her long legs and Siddharthak had to blink his eyes before this vision of incandescent passion.

The next minute he found himself pulled to his feet. Looking deep into his eyes, Misrakesi placed her right foot on his left one and then her other foot on his thigh. One arm gripped his back and the other bent his shoulder down so that their lips almost touched, in the classic 'climbing the tree' embrace. Deliberately, she pressed her lips to his and the attack went straight to his gut. Misrakesi finished off the kiss and stepped back to smile wickedly at him, 'You can imagine the rest, Arya Siddharthak.'

Aware of another pair of eyes boring into him, he thought it prudent to remove himself from the fireside. 'Any time you finish with Bandhu Pushyamitra, I am right behind him, waiting.' And he was off.

'Don't ever do that again, Misrakesi,' Pushyamitra said dangerously.

'Yes I will, every time you feel impelled to discuss my sexual performance with any of your friends,' replied Misrakesi as she settled herself in his lap between his outstretched legs and leaned against his chest, making herself comfortable.

He pulled her in and adjusting her contours against his, raised his knee so that she could relax against it. 'Do I get the same privilege? Tell me whenever you want to discuss me with that stupid but ravishing girl you have at the Apsara Sabha, Ratibhama, isn't it? The one with the luscious breasts and banana stem thighs.' Pushyamitra murmured as he ran his hands over her swollen breasts and still trembling body.

The fire was throwing a gentle heat over everything, she was relaxed and snug tucked in against Pushyamitra's body, 'For all your pretence of not being a ladies man, you do look at the women, don't you? But no such luck for you, I may discuss you only with Mrinalini,' and she giggled sleepily at his look of horror.

She was here to help him while away time during his guard duty but soon, her head was falling back on his chest as she drifted off to sleep. He covered her with a blanket and set himself to wait the night through.

This guard duty was anyway in the nature of a formality since regular patrols guarded the territory around the army's stop and also brought news of outlying areas. He and Akshay had decided that one of them, or Siddharthak, should be on hand all night in case of any emergency. He was therefore able to relax.

He wondered whether he should wake her up before Akshay arrived to take over the early morning shift but decided against it. He had not liked the gleam in Akshay's eyes when they rested on her. He and Akshay had a history of conflict during the Nanda days which they had put aside but there was little love lost between them. Siddharthak was of course very forthright about what he wanted, but that was not his problem but Misrakesi's.

So when Akshay walked in just after dawn he was met with the sight of Misrakesi sleeping peacefully in Pushyamitra's arms. Misrakesi would have died a thousand deaths if she had seen the expression on his face, but Pushyamitra was never embarrassed. He got up in a matter of fact way picking her up and taking her to her tent where he laid her down on the grass bed. He looked down at her and then, giving in to temptation lay down beside her and was soon fast asleep himself.

Misrakesi woke up and was taken aback to find Pushyamitra sleeping peacefully next to her, she wondered what the others would be thinking and thought resignedly that it was just like Pushyamitra not to bother. She was the one bothered and stung by public opinion, although she was the ganika here and should be less bothered about niceties.

She soon forgot about it. It was the middle of a forest and they were not out on an expedition of pleasure. She had been concerned with her personal problems but now that they were out of the way, she started to take stock of what they were doing, the area they were passing through, and their ultimate target.

They were advancing up the Uttarapath, the trade lifeline through the northern part of Jambudweepa. Vesali was nearby, the nearest town on the Uttarapath after Pataliputra; the renowned Vesali of the 7707 palaces, 7707 koshthagars, 7707 parks, 7707 lotus ponds and its courtesan, Amrapali. They had to be careful. Villages were numerous here since Vesali was also a Janapada or district in the new administrative nomenclature. The mythical days of the sixteen great Janapada kingdoms of the time of the great Kurukshetra war were over but the names had survived.

The two so-called fugitives and the travelling Army Division had to stay away from the town although a few soldiers would be sent in disguise to pick up news and some provisions.

This was the area around Vesali, scattered villages of five hundred or so inhabitants. As it was varsha ritu or the season of the rains – rice, millet, and udaraka had been sown and were at different levels of growth but not ready for gathering as yet. The sweet ikshu (sugarcane) could also be seen waving their tall heads in field after field. This was the land favoured by the gods, fertile soil was scattered like a blessing on the plains by the River Ganges, soil brought down from the abode of Lord Shiva on which crops grew like magic.

The region was not only well watered by the rains but also had many rivulets, lakes, ponds, tanks and wells for irrigating the fields of crops. There were chakkavattakas[54] as well as other water lifts used to fill the channels in the fields with water. It was a peaceful and prosperous landscape unaffected for generations by the conflicts between kings. It was widely said that in this area soldiers could be fighting a bloody war while farmers tilled their fields nearby unaffected and untouched by the mayhem.

Pushyamitra and Siddharthak were strangely confident and comfortable in this area. They seemed to know the terrain very well and unerringly led their forces through clever shortcuts which were easy to cross and hidden from the village population.

'How do you know this area so well, Pushyamitra?' she asked him one day when he had taken the two of them across through a shortcut which made them arrive at the rendezvous much before the rest of the army. She had stopped addressing him formally because of his insistence although she was not completely comfortable about it. Whatever had happened between them did not change the fact that he was still her chief to whom she reported.

'Oh, I have wandered extensively in these forests during our campaigns against the Licchavis of Vesali. Magadha has broken their power over and over again over the last hundred years, but I do not think we have managed to wipe them out,' replied Pushyamitra.

'The Licchavis of Amrapali the Nagar Vadhu, the chief courtesan who was like their queen,' mused Misrakesi dreamily.

'Yes, the same. But I do not think they have the institution any longer, they are but a shadow of their former glory.'

'She must have wielded real power during her days,' Misrakesi continued, carried along by her train of thought.

'Yes and not only in Vesali. Remember, the then samrat of Magadha – Bimbisara, was at her feet and warred against the Licchavis to try and make her his queen.'

'And then she left everything to become a follower of the Sakya

Muni. A woman who lived in the lap of luxury and was treated like a queen, became a barefoot nun owning nothing but her saffron robe and begging bowl.'

Misrakesi was lost in thought. She had heard many stories of Amrapali, the woman who had both the Licchavis of Vesali and the samrat of the Magadhans under her delicate feet, intrigued between the two, had a son by Bimbisara who became the samrat after his father, but gave up everything to follow the Buddha. The story of the fight between the two old Janapadas of Vesali and Magadha for supremacy in Jambudweepa had been written by her hands. And it was her son, the Samrat Ajatsatru, who had led the triumph of Magadha over Vesali and made the former the most powerful Janapada amongst them all.

'That is what I call a full life.' She said looking up at Pushyamitra as she sat on the spreading roots of an old neem tree while he leant against the trunk keeping an eye out for Akshay and Siddharthak.

'Any ambitions in the same direction?' He asked with a curve of the lips.

'No, but seriously, she is also supposed to be the best nartaki there ever was. It is said that she once danced to the veena of the legendary King Udayana of Kosambi, who could play in all the three grams at the same time.' They were now at a short north-easterly distance from the old Janapada of Kosambi, although they would not be crossing it as it was not on the Uttarapath.

'I did not know that this was even possible, to play in three grams at the same time I mean. Although you know I do play the veena.'

'I have heard you,' said Misrakesi with a smile as her mind went back to the days and nights they had spent together in his house.

They had a feast that night because of the fresh vegetables bought from the village and the fresh meat killed by the shikaris. There was fresh pumpkin made with jaggery and spices, masoor dal, green gourd, and venison prepared with sesame oil and garlic. Crisp cucumbers were a pleasure to munch.

There was good quality Harahuraka and Kapisayana with them as well as svetasuras Mahasura and other acid fruit drinks apart from the long lasting sukta-varga.[55]

Siddharthak had been abstaining from any kind of liquor but tonight he was indulging himself, intoxicated, red-eyed but very much in control. He and Misrakesi were sitting together and enjoying the wine. Pushyamitra had refused to join them, had a quick drink of some sukta-varga and had gone off on one of his frequent rounds of the soldiers.

'You are forcing me to abandon all my finesse and subtlety Misrakesi. Are you sure you are not going to sleep with me?' he asked in a brooding tone.

'Quite sure, thank you, Arya Siddharthak. I don't think I can manage more than the one man I have at the moment.' Her hands were on her upraised knees and she rested her chin on them looking up at Siddharthak as he had propped himself against a fallen tree trunk. Her eyes were dreamy and her thoughts elsewhere.

'How can an experienced ganika like you say so? You should be good at having a string of men dangling after you. I am quite willing to be one of them.'

'But you see, that is where you are wrong. I have very little experience. It was not long after I finished my training that I came to Pataliputra and the rest of my experience, such as it is, has happened before you.'

'Then it is Bandhu Pushyamitra who seems to have killed your career even before it really took off. I shall wait and see what the results are.'

Misrakesi was silent, looking into the fire and thinking about the past three years. Was Siddharthak right?

'Do you know that Sukesi was the only woman I was ever really impressed by... maybe I even...'

A shared sorrow passed between them. This was a different side of Siddharthak. His handsome face was shuttered as he looked into the fire in his turn.

'I wonder what would have happened to me if she had not taken her own life?' said Misrakesi sadly. 'I know I would never have come to Magadha. She was the one who had the ambition, the intelligence, and the beauty. I lived in her shadow and was happy, till she died.' Her eyes filled up.

Siddharthak gave a short laugh, 'If she had not died! The sky would have been the limit for her. She did not have your qualms about what needed to be done. She had the stomach to succeed, no matter what it took. Not that you have done too badly for yourself, but sometimes I wonder whether it is you or just good luck.'

Pushyamitra was coming up to them from where he had been sitting and talking to some of the battalion commanders.

'Look at that man, for example. Never, in all the years I have seen him – and they are too many to count – has he evinced the slightest interest in any woman. Then why you? You are an outsider; you do not yet know how powerful and rooted he is in this kingdom. You have rushed headlong into something you know little about, and it is taking you away from your dharma as a ganika. You have no idea how determined and single minded he is. Who will stop you from being led on by him? Nobody under the flag of Magadha will dare. Sukesi would have talked to you'

Misrakesi had wiped away her tears and was listening to him, her mind still on her dead sister.

Pushyamitra had come up by then and noticed Misrakesi's wet eyes with some concern. Siddharthak was looking grim, almost despairing, as if he had lost something he would never find again.

'What are you making her cry about, Siddharthak?' he asked, sitting down next to Misrakesi and putting an arm around her.

'I was telling her all about you and warning her against you,' returned Siddharthak in the same brooding tone.

'Let me do that myself. Who knows you may leave out some details of my evil career. Come Misrakesi, join me while I take the rounds of the next encampment and I will tell you all.'

Siddharthak went back to his wine cup, facing who knew what spectre from his past.

'What made you cry?' asked Pushyamitra as both of them rode

away to another encampment.

Misrakesi shook her head and attempted a smile, 'He was talking about my sister and I couldn't help remembering her and thinking that I did not ever have the time to mourn her properly. You knew her, too, didn't you?'

'I did indeed, very well. We worked together on a number of occasions, including the one involving the younger Paurava and she was truly impressive.'

'Tell me,' Misrakesi's voice was close to breaking, 'Do you know why... why she did it? I was not there... I could be of no help. I did not even see her body.'

'She lived by a very superior code of morals, Misrakesi. She could not live with what seemed to her a betrayal of her own values although she did it for the larger good of Magadha. It was a tragedy and I wish with all my heart that she had talked to someone before taking this extreme step. I do know that the acharya's message arrived minutes after...'

Tears threatened to flow again but she stopped them. 'And Siddharthak? Was he very close to her?'

'He was. They were working together on this case and had completed it successfully. Siddharthak had never dreamt that she would do such a thing. She did not speak to him or say farewell and he has never been able to come to terms with why she shut him out. He was shattered, and I have seen him picking up the pieces after that.'

'She was the only family I had. Now I have no one.'

As the nights passed and Misrakesi took the rounds and met soldiers from every rank, she realized what Siddharthak had been saying. These were men who were personally loyal to the Sunga brothers. Akshay was the Commander, and a very efficient one, too. Misrakesi had not seen Pushyamitra interfere in the running of the affairs of the army but these men would move at one word from him. It was perhaps both politic and necessary to send him along on this mission.

The extent of the hold of the Sunga brothers on the army was a revelation to Misrakesi.

'Pushyamitra, who have I got myself mixed up with, an orphan from Ujjain? No wonder you do not care what the ordinary people of Pataliputra say about you. It is only people like me who have to care.' She said wonderingly.

'You will learn not to care about what public opinion says. It is mostly uninformed and foolish but of course one has to be cognizant of it and mould it as necessary.'

Misrakesi laughed and shook her head, 'You just do not understand, do you?'

'The army is our life, Misrakesi, and three generations of my family have given their lives to it. I have walked away from inheriting my brother's mantle but of course the responsibility and heritage has not left me. My brother has brought me up, like your sister brought you up, I am his son. I will not take over as senapati from him so he now wants a son from me to take over the family heritage. He has only three daughters.'

'You show no signs of obliging him?'

'I will have to, very soon now. Maybe when and, of course, if, we return after finishing our work.'

'If?' Misrakesi had not thought of the mission in terms of the danger they confronted and she was silent, brought up short before reality.

They were crossing the great plain over which the mighty Ganges flowed unchecked. Vesali had been left behind and they would soon cross Kusinara, Kapilvastu and Savatthi. The area where the Sakya Muni had been born, preached his timeless sermons and died. His presence still sanctified and permeated the area after centuries. Savatthi was still a mahanagar at the crossing of the northern and southern trade routes, one of the most important places in Jambudweepa.

The journey went on, routine-set but enlivened by the dangers and travails of travelling in the forest during the rains. Not only was the ground wet and the skies open all the time, snakes and other slimy denizens of the forests had been forced out of their holes in the ground making it dangerous to set foot on the ground without caution. They were wearing deerskin shoes and riding, of course, and were saved the worst of the trouble. But sleeping at night was a problem for Misrakesi who imagined snakes slithering over her even in her dreams. So she also preferred to stay awake at night and catch up on her sleep during the day.

They were now on the long stretch between Savatthi and Hastinapur. They had passed gramas, ghoshas and nagaras, past a landscape of toiling peasants, cattle and buffalo rearers, industrial guilds and merchants and traders. The fighting between the Janapadas had stopped and the populace was gaining a much needed peace under the peacock flag of the Mauryas. It was a strange medley with a mix of populations ranging from the atavikas and tribal communities in the forest stretches, to sophisticated Brahmins, Shramans, Bhikshus, and urban dwellers in the cities and towns.

Pushyamitra was in his element, sending his men forth to gather information which he listened to, analyzed and was storing up for further use. The spy network had to be extended and properly set up all over Jambudweepa after all.

The journey was not always smooth sailing. The length, difficulties and secrecy which had to be maintained were now getting on the nerves of the soldiers as well as the leaders.

Small fights broke out between the soldiers and it was the job of Akshay, Pushyamitra, Siddharthak, as well as the battalion commanders to keep the peace.

Siddharthak was irritated. He had broken up a fight between soldiers from two rival battalions and had been dragged in the mud because of it. He was wet, uncomfortable and annoyed.

'Here we are, stuck in this useless forest for months with nothing for miles around but a few wild animals and maybe a settlement of atavikas to add to the fun. Why do we do it? Why do we, good solid civilized Magadhans, travel to all these savage and peculiar kingdoms outside? We do not need them. We have everything we could possibly want or need in our beautiful Pataliputra. All this unnecessary empire building, resting on the unhappy shoulders of men like me, of what use is it?' He could be heard grumbling.

Akshay sat close by, stiff and offended at what he perceived as disloyal sentiments, and disloyalty to his beloved Gurubhai and samrat was something he was unable to tolerate. He was a friend and contemporary of Chandragupta and a disciple of Acharya Chanakya. He had no goal in life but to advance the interests of his peer and current samrat. For him, the acharya's word was law and here was someone challenging that word. The samrat was lucky to have a group of closely knit and loyal fellow students from his Takshshila days to support him unquestioningly. Or maybe it was design and not luck, a design etched by that master manipulator, the acharya.

Misrakesi and Pushyamitra realized at once that some peacemaking was in order. Pushyamitra dropped down beside Siddharthak and put a restraining hand on his shoulder.

'How can you, a snatak from Takshshila Gurukul, say so? You owe your entire education to that kingdom,' he observed mildly.

Misrakesi had in the meanwhile, sat down next to Akshay and given him her sweetest smile, forcing him to smile back. His hand moved back from the hilt of his sword.

'What we need is a Gurukul in Magadha so that we do not need to come here. The acharya has done well to identify Nalanda as a potential place for this. After all, those people from the north do not think of us as their equals, we are the easterners, with our funny pronunciations of Sanskrit and mixed heritage. It is only our power and prosperity that they are afraid of.' Siddharthak was not to be stopped so easily.

'We do have a lot to learn from them but I would say that art aesthetics and even pure Vedanga learning are progressing in the east. What you are talking of are very old and outmoded ideas. After all, Shraman Mahavir and Sakya Muni have both emerged from the east. And their followers have gone up this very same Uttarapath,' replied Pushyamitra

'All I say is let us leave them alone and they can also leave us alone.'

'Can we really afford that? In spite of the distance between our kingdoms we are perpetual targets of all kinds of plots against us.

Remember, we were the victims of the counterfeit coin fraud. It is either us or them – no, the entire land has to be under our flag,' interrupted Akshay hotly.

Misrakesi broke in peaceably, 'The more I travel up this Jambudweepa of ours, the more I see its sweep and beauty, the different peoples and regions, the more I feel that there is an underlying commonality. We are all the same and we should forget the differences and emphasize our similarities.'

Akshay looked at her and said in a surprised tone, 'That is exactly what the acharya always says.'

'This land of ours is so vast, so full of diverse people, ways of life, from the permanent snows of the Himalayas to the heat of the plains. Its rivers, valleys, jungles, and plateaus protect and nurture such unimaginably different communities... there has to be a way to knit all these strands, all these glowing colours, into a single beautiful tapestry,' this was Misrakesi again trying to put into words all that she had been seeing for the past days.

Siddharthak was sceptical, 'Yes, but how? How will this large, complex and variegated society be assimilated? What does the sophisticated acharya in Pataliputra debating the nature of the atman and brahma or the ascetic composing chaste Sanskrit sutras have in common with the women dancing around an ashvath tree in a fertility rite or the simple peasant worshipping the goddess of the field? To say nothing of the differences in food, dress, language and culture?'

'I do not know how it can happen, but I am certain that it will happen,' Misrakesi said emphatically.

'Yes, the little traditions will definitely coalesce in or around a great tradition. We are part of this great work which is happening slowly in front of us,' said a thoughtful Pushyamitra.

The discussion could have been acrimonious but it was not, instead veering towards philosophy and literature, and as was normal for royal employees, politics, and they found themselves well in accord.

Pushyamitra and Misrakesi were becoming inseparable as the journey went on, but Siddharthak remained slightly puzzled by their relationship: was it expediency or proximity or something else?

Akshay found himself growing to like her more and more. Perhaps because she was the first woman he had really talked to and spent time with or perhaps it was her open, friendly, and attractive personality. The fact that she was an intense, passionate, and sensual woman also could have contributed to his attraction. He was drawn towards her, both mentally and physically, but was too diffident to ever tell her so. She seemed unaware of this, but Pushyamitra was not, although he never reacted to it.

It became colder as they went up the Uttarapath. They were now near Hastinapur, the magnificent capital city of the Kauravas of yore from where their cousins the Pandava brothers had been exiled. The bards still sang of the war to end all wars which had taken place between them which had arrayed all the heroes of the earth against each other.[56] This was ancient Kuru country where the primeval Kandavaprastha forest had once sprawled. The feat of clearing it for civilization had been done by the Pandavas, specially Arjun and Bheem with the help of their cousin Krishna and it was now dotted with fields of crops and settlements.

Beyond Hastinapur it became hilly as they reached the foothills of the mighty Himalayas. Misrakesi soon realized that a thicker wrap and a bigger fire were now needed. Autumn was spreading its glow over the land. The nights were cosy, either inside a tent or outside, next to the fire. Misrakesi didn't know about anyone else but she was warm and comfortable in Pushyamitra's capacious embrace.

They had now crossed the River Satki as it cut across the Uttarapath and were well on their way towards the River Parushni, then would come the River Asikni. The main army with Akshay was to halt after that as it would be very close to the elder Paurava's kingdom which was in the doab between this river and the Vitasta. A small group with Siddharthak would advance further with them but stop well short of entry into the city proper.

While Pushyamitra and Misrakesi went boldly to operate under the eyes of the administration itself, Siddharthak would activate the old channels of communication and the goodha purushas[57] of

Magadha stationed inside. It could take some time after which he would send a message to Pushyamitra or Misrakesi who would hopefully be inside the city and in an entrenched position to carry out the rest of the plan.

They sat down to discuss everything, arrange signals, codes and time schedules, also emergency plans and escape routes. Information about the area, the people and the royal court was pooled and gone through over and over again. Alternative approaches were discussed and kept aside for possible use. The three men were all familiar with the area. Misrakesi was the one who needed to learn about the locality, which she had been doing through the journey. Since she was the only one who had not been to this area before, she was their weak link. The positive side was that the character she was assuming was anyway not supposed to be familiar with the area. But it would make her vulnerable.

They left Akshay behind with the army and went on ahead. Ten days journey from the gates of Kaikeya, and Siddharthak and his group also said a sombre goodbye and Pushyamitra and Misrakesi set off alone. The break was over, it was now serious, life or death, Magadha or Kaikeya.

Kaikeya

The enemy should be destroyed by rulers by all means at all times: whether by conciliation, concession, dissension or invasion.

Chanakya Rajnitishastra

The town was not very impressive, not like Pataliputra. It was built amidst the mountains and hence very grand buildings were not really possible. The area itself was very beautiful, with wide rings of vast mountains and valleys, blue skies and green trees. The palace and surrounding city structures perched on top of a high mountain, three sides protected by walls and the fourth by a steep sheer cliff.

The ramparts of Kaikeya city's walls were shining in the slanting rays of the setting sun. They had decided to approach the city gates for admission just a little before they closed so that the authorities would not have too much time to ponder before the closing time.

It was a very different couple which rode up to demand admission at the gate. They were back in their old garb as prosperous citizens of Magadha. Pushyamitra had on a silken dhoti and the finest yellow kausheya uttariya. His pearl headband of matching kunda white pearls from Tamraparni was linked with gold chains and the jewelled hilt of his sword hanging from the matching solid gold patta of his kayabandh was the value of five villages' revenues. Seven thin strands of perfectly matched pearls had been twisted into a thick strand and hung aslant against his chest and back-fastened at the shoulder with a resplendent six-pointed sun set with a huge diamond. A similarly woven necklace was around his neck and arms. He looked magnificent and formidable, every inch a soldier, and a man who was used to command, with power emanating from him in waves.

Misrakesi had taken time to turn herself back to a rich and beautiful ganika. Her most valuable jewels were on display as were her undeniable physical charms, with a soft and delicate antariya tied deep below her navel, a short decorated kanchuki barely covering her breasts and a transparent embroidered uttariya. Her hair had grown again and was back in a complex and graceful bun, decorated with a filigree of gold chains caught up in an enamelled circlet at the back. Again seven emeralds, each the size of a baby's fist, set in oval gold settings around her neck made the guards fall back in amazement. Matched bracelets and armlets graced her wrists and arms. A cluster of gold chains met together between her breasts and then continued down to merge in to her girdle. She had slipped into the role of the pampered and spoilt consort as had Pushyamitra into that of a besotted and desperate man ensnared completely by her.

They had gone over their roles and characters innumerable times. They would have to function like a single entity to avoid exposure. Narsingh Dev was an intelligent opponent, almost insurmountable; any slip on their part would not only jeopardize Magadha's interests but could also mean death for them as spies from a neighbouring kingdom. They were walking on a sword edge and had only themselves to depend on.

'Remember, Misrakesi, there is no scope for any mistakes. We have decided on our story; do not change any of the details because you can be sure we will be questioned separately. When we are demanding entry and for a few days after that, follow my lead because you don't know the place and the people. Then dealing with Queen Shailanandini is up to you. We may not even get a chance to talk privately again, so be brave. And may the Lord Vaijayanta be with us!' Pushyamitra gave Misrakesi's hand a last squeeze and then spurred his horse to arrive at the gate in a whirl of dust. Misrakesi followed just a little behind.

The guards at the gate were thrown into confusion by the sight of what seemed to them to be a royal personage arriving without an entourage, just what seemed to them a divine apsara on a horse behind him, and demanding peremptory admittance. On being asked his name, his business and whether he had a permit, he merely barked that his business was with Narsingh Dev and nobody else. The name of the king's highest minister added an element of awe to the confusion. Neither Pushyamitra nor Misrakesi dismounted, the latter eyeing the soldiers with a supercilious and patently impatient air.

After some discussion and conferring amongst the soldiers, the Samaharta was called who addressed Pushyamitra respectfully, 'Arya, I would request you to state your name and business before we let you in. It would be completely against our rules and norms to let in a stranger otherwise. It will be my pleasure to send a message to Maha Amatya Narsingh Dev once I know who I have the honour of addressing.'

Pushyamitra appeared to relent at this graceful speech and announced grandly, 'You may send a message to him that Pushyamitra Sunga, the chief of the Nagarik Suraksha Vibhag of the illustrious city of Pataliputra in Magadha, has come to seek an audience with him.'

The Samaharta's jaw dropped. A high official from the enemy kingdom of Magadha demanding an audience with Narsingh Dev! Should he let him in or make him wait outside? It was sundown and the gates would soon close; if he left them outside and they went away he could get into all kinds of trouble. It would perhaps be better to let them in and keep them under close guard while he sent for urgent instructions from the Maha Amatya.

So they were led in by a group of soldiers into the city while the gates shut behind them. They dismounted and were led into a sparsely furnished tent which seemed to be a kind of waiting area. Misrakesi poked her head out and gave the soldiers leading their horses away an admonitory command to be careful with her possessions. A messenger was dispatched to Narsingh Dev, and

Pushyamitra and Misrakesi were left to wait. Pushyamitra had been respectfully asked to hand over his sword and he had refused indignantly, saying it was an insult.

'Stand back. My foolish fellows, do you think I have come to Kaikeya to start a single-handed sword fight with the entire army? But you cannot divest a soldier of his sword.'

Since they were not completely sure of the status of this Magadhan, they did stand back and spent their time gawking at Misrakesi who had arranged herself in a corner of the tent in an attitude of conscious beauty. She arranged and re-arranged her uttariya, smoothed her hair, examined her jewels and cast disparaging glances around the tent sighing impatiently.

As time passed her impatience increased and she finally spoke petulantly to Pushyamitra, 'Arya, how long do we have to wait here? I cannot sit in such a place. You had promised that...'

Before she could finish her sentence Pushyamitra went and took her hand and said in placatory tones, 'Just a while, Devi, while the Maha Amatya calls us. Please be a little patient.' He called to one of the wide-eyed soldiers, 'Hey you! Is this how you treat guests in Kaikeya? Can you not see that the lady is delicate and exhausted and cannot tolerate these rough surroundings? Tell your Samaharta to hurry up.'

The soldier who had been staring fascinated at Misrakesi's delicate form, dripping jewels and fluttering gestures jumped and scurried off to the Samaharta. This worthy gentleman was pacing up and down in the same worry. Night was falling and something would have to be done soon if the messenger did not come back. There was a guest house for royals and high personages but he could not take them there without authorization.

Fortunately for him, the problem was solved before it could become more acute. A messenger from the Maha Amatya galloped up on a frothing horse and conveyed his orders; the two Magadhans were to be asked to stay at the nearby guesthouse and Pushyamitra was to present himself to Narsingh Dev the next morning.

Things were going according to their plans. So far so good.

The guest palace was sumptuous and was furnished not adequately but luxuriously. As soon as they were alone Pushyamitra wrapped Misrakesi in a passionate kiss and whispered against her lips, 'Be alert. They must be watching us. You have done well. Do you think you can be a little more unreasonable so that we can journey to the royal palace?'

In answer Misrakesi pushed him away and flounced to the bed. 'That is enough, Arya. I am tired. And I know I will not be able to sleep on this coarse bedspread. The carpet hurts my feet and this chamber is really small and airless.'

Pushyamitra went up and said in an apologetic tone, 'I know this is not what you are used to, Priye, but make do with this tonight, please. After all I am here to make you comfortable.'

Misrakesi hunched a shoulder and said resignedly, 'As you say. I hope it is only for today and you are going to fulfill your promises. I have undertaken this long and difficult journey only because...'

'Yes, yes, my dear,' said Pushyamitra hastily, 'Can I help you become more comfortable, loosen your clothes, keep away your uttariya?'

Misrakesi tossed her head and said, 'Always thinking of only one thing, aren't you? Anyway you can start by helping me take off my jewellery. What are all the women here, atavikas? Don't they have dasis or oils or baths or any civilized comforts?'

Pushyamitra took his time helping her to take off and keep aside her numerous necklaces, rings, earrings, keyuras and kakshyabandha. Her uttariya was also removed and she stood forth in the full glory of her curvaceous body. Pushyamitra did not have to simulate the tremor of desire in his hands as he slowly untied her kanchuki. He slowly unhooked her complicated hair clasp and her hair spread against his hands in perfumed confusion.

As proof of the suspicion that they were being spied upon, in trooped a bunch of dasis with unguents, oil, and water for a bath. Pushyamitra was satisfied and let her go for a long and difficult (for the dasis) bath.

He had to hide his smile at times at the original and unreasonable objections and complaints Misrakesi came up with. She had thrown herself heart and soul into her new role, maybe she was enjoying it too, needling him on numerous occasions!

It was finally over, he had also freshened up and they sat down for a much-needed meal which, needless to say, did not find favour with Misrakesi. She criticized everything in languid and superior tones but, if anyone had kept track, consumed an inordinate amount of the food she was professing to find below her palate.

They were left alone at last, free to sleep in their bed. Misrakesi tossed and turned like a boat in the middle of the Ganges till Pushyamitra held her close and pinned her arms and legs down.

'Enough Misrakesi. I know you are pretending to be uncomfortable but if you keep doing this we will not be able to sleep a wink. And we need our wits about us tomorrow. Go to sleep.'

'But I am not pretending, Pushyamitra,' whispered Misrakesi. 'I simply cannot go to sleep and I cannot understand how you can. We are surrounded by enemies who may decide to put us to death tomorrow. And you are talking of sleep!'

Pushyamitra smiled wryly in the darkness. He had been in many dangerous situations, kill or be killed situations, but never such a hopeless one as this, alone against a kingdom. But that was what this mission was all about. The stakes were high and so were the risks.

'If they decide to kill us tomorrow there is absolutely nothing we can do about it. So let us ignore that possibility and concentrate on what we have to do if we are still alive. We have gone over it many times, so the only option now is sleep.'

'I can't.'

'You can. Empty your mind of all thoughts and concentrate. Use your meditation techniques. Sleep will follow naturally.'

Misrakesi woke up the next day to find herself in a bed after a long, long time and securely encircled in Pushyamitra arms, she smiled lazily and stretched. And then froze, her situation came back to her and she could see a number of eyes fixed on her with the dasis smiling politely. She collapsed back on the bed to find Pushyamitra looking at her with a warning in his eyes. She could not let her guard slip for even a moment.

This morning was the all-important meeting with Narsingh Dev. Pushyamitra debated whether he should ask for an audience with the king or an opportunity to address the Mantri Parishad and decided to put forward both these demands. He also decided that both he and Misrakesi should meet the Maha Amatya although she had not been mentioned by name in the message. The 'reason' for his flight from Magadha should be very evident.

Messengers from Narsingh Dev arrived almost before they were ready. It was not clear from the escort and its demeanour whether they were guests or prisoners. Misrakesi had taken it for granted that she was an honoured guest and sailed out looking alluring and unassailable. She beckoned to a couple of dasis to accompany her. One of the soldiers made as if to interfere but fell back before her affronted glance and the dasis' eager readiness.

Their horses had not been returned to them and the entire group set off on foot, albeit in grand style with chattradhars holding umbrellas over their heads and Misrakesi instructing the dasis to sweep the path before her. Since the previous night she had been filling up their ears with how powerful and important a personage Pushyamitra was and how she was used to a life of cosseting and luxury. She informed them that she came from a family of successful dancing girls, cleverly inserting Sukesi's name so that it would be disseminated. She did not tire of saying that she considered it below her dignity to live in the guest palace, given the style in which she was accustomed to be kept by her admirers.

Kaikeya had a history of hoary antiquity, being the home of one of the original Vedic tribes of the Purus, with one of its princesses of yore being the wicked stepmother of Lord Rama, the hero of the epic Ramayana; but Magadha was the rising star. It had the nouveau riche. The tales of the fabulously wealthy Setthis of this kingdom had taken root along with the dissemination of the Sakya Muni's cult up the Uttarapath since it was the merchant class which had most ardently embraced the creed of the Sakyan Prince Gautama. Their fame and the stories surrounding them had grown with the new cult. The dasis were ready to believe anything and had immediately begun to multiply the tales she told them.

Pushyamitra was quiet; Misrakesi was doing very well and he was going to have to put up the performance of his life before Narsingh Dev. Seemingly inconsequential but carefully calculated chatter mixed with complaints about Kaikeya's roads beguiled the way to the palace. It was not at all like Pataliputra or even Ujjaini, being a small hill town with few broad roads. Most of the roads were uneven and narrow, snaking up and down as per the gradient of the mountain. Some of the houses were grand, perched on the mountain side, but to the Magadhans the town looked like a very poor cousin of their capital.

The palace was nothing like the Sugaang Praasaad but an almost plain and functional wooden building of size. A guild head of Pataliputra would have been scornful of it. The Kaikeyans obviously did not believe in ostentation. Misrakesi was unimpressed. It had an indefinable air of silence, loss, and emptiness. Not surprisingly, the shadowy presence of the old and dying king hung over it; three sons dead and no one to take their place.

Once in the palace, they were led immediately into the Sabha Griha, the massive throne room with all but one of the minister's chairs empty. Up rose Narsingh Dev from the chair next to the throne. He was a man of about the same age as the acharya but there the resemblance ended. He was restless and intelligent with a still handsome face and virile body, he had aged exceptionally well. His eyes told of intellectual capacity and perception. One look at him and Misrakesi counted herself out of any effort to impress or woo him. He would see through her immediately.

They were being examined as carefully by him, but his expression did not change and there was no clue as to what he was thinking. Pushyamitra was also revising his plans; this man would be more difficult to deal with than he had calculated. The best they could hope for, would be to neutralize him or use his enemies to incapacitate him, he would never be defeated.

While the antagonists sized each other up mentally, gracious greetings were being exchanged. Nothing could have exceeded the affability of the Maha Amatya. He asked after their health and journey and even especially after his old friend the acharya. Once the preliminary courtesies had been exchanged, his tone became serious and he said, 'This is not a place where we can sit and confer informally. Come to my council room. And your... ummm...'

'My wife,' said Pushyamitra aggressively. A quick message passed between him and Misrakesi and she looked down coyly at the floor and blushed.

'Your wife?' said Narsingh Dev raising his eyebrows, 'but I was given to understand that...'

Before he could complete his sentence Pushyamitra cut in, 'We were married in the forest according to Gandharva rites.'

'Ah, the forest! You must also tell me, my dear Arya Pushyamitra how you survived the forests and have arrived here as if the vast forests of the Uttarapatha did not exist, for you and your delicate companion.'

'Surely not, Maha Amatya,' replied Pushyamitra with a glittering smile, 'you do not expect me to give out all my secrets and contacts with the atavikas and the villagers to you, do you?'

While the Maha Amatya and Pushyamitra were engaged in introductory sparring, in came a dasi, a messenger from Maharani Shailanandini. News of the arrival of Pushyamitra and Misrakesi from Magadha had spread like wildfire and the news that Sukesi's sister was actually in the palace had prompted the maharani to send for her immediately.

A fleeting expression of displeasure crossed Narsingh Dev's face before he clamped down on it and gave Misrakesi permission to leave. He had certainly not expected this and it was very undesirable from his point of view to allow these Magadhans any royal access. He could not, in spite of his all powerful status, countermand a direct message from the king's daughter and a maharani of Takshshila even though he wanted to. He had to swallow his objections and watch her go. The first part of the acharya's plan seemed to be working.

He turned to Pushyamitra, 'Now, Arya Pushyamitra. What brings the powerful chief of the Nagarik Suraksha Vibhag, the brother of the senapati of the fearsome army of Magadha, to Kaikeya?

'The ex-chief, Maha Amatya,' said Pushyamitra grimly. 'I will not insult your intelligence by expecting you to not know that I have fled from persecution and injustice in my motherland. I will be completely honest with you...'

Narsingh Dev's expression was openly sarcastic now and he said, 'Yes, that is always a good idea.'

They had been walking to a nearby chamber furnished with asanas and Narsingh Dev invited Pushyamitra to sit down with a sweeping gesture.

The two men sat down and Pushyamitra continued, 'I had to leave Pataliputra in ignominy, fleeing in the middle of the night because personal and degrading calumny against me was taken seriously by the royal authority. My brother was forced to sign the warrant of arrest against me on pain of being eased out himself.' His voice was bitter as he looked at the brilliant carpet from Herat which lay glowing on the floor.

There was a short silence, 'I believe this was a part of a concrete plan by the current administration. I have no future in Magadha because I was a Nanda dynasty loyalist. My brother's future is also in doubt.'

Narsingh Dev had been listening carefully. He intervened, 'Surely that is not correct. Many of the key posts in the kingdom including that of Amatya Katyayan, your brother, not to say yourself, and a host of other functionaries have been given to former Nanda loyalists.'

'Maha Amatya, I had faith in the impartiality of the Mauryan administration which is why I joined it after much introspection and heartburn. But that was then... things have changed now.'

'What do you mean?' asked Narsingh Dev.

'In the early days after Samrat Chandragupta had taken over the throne of Magadha he needed us, the Nanda loyalists who pulled the strings of power. He needed us to win over the citizens of Magadha, to strengthen the bases of Maurya power. Remember they had taken over in a sudden swoop which merely exiled Dhana Nanda and made him abdicate in favour of Chandragupta. Now we are not needed any more because the acharya's hold on Magadha rivals that of the Nandas. The samrat's marriage with Princess Dharini, ensured Nanda support. Donations to the followers of Shraman Mahavira and the Sakya Muni have ensured the support of the rich and powerful setthis. The powerful opinion makers in the acharya varga have always been his allies.'

Pushyamitra's voice took on an ironic timbre, 'And now the acharya is reforming the administration. This is another name for filling it with his own people.' He paused and then added more in sorrow than in anger, 'Where is the place for me?'

'And what about the honourable Agnimitra Sunga? What does he think?' Narsingh Dev leaned forward.

Pushyamitra looked at him for a fraction and then looked away, 'I may not speak for him now but the future is another matter.'

'Of course.' Narsingh Dev leant back with a satisfied look. 'So Arya Pushyamitra, what brings you here, to our kingdom? What do you want from us?'

'The protection of Kaikeya. I am a royal employee by birth, inclination and experience. I want to serve this kingdom in whichever capacity you feel befits my capabilities and status since my own kingdom has no place for me,' said Pushyamitra with what he hoped was a ring of conviction in his voice, looking the Maha Amatya straight in the eyes.

'Indeed! And why should we in Kaikeya offer you a place in the palace which has to be won even by Kaikeyans themselves after much effort and only if they possess extraordinary skills?'

Pushyamitra said smoothly, 'I do not think you will find me wanting in any skills you may want to test. However, I have something else which is invaluable to you at the moment, unsurpassed information on the Magadhan State and army. I know its innermost secrets, its strengths and more importantly, its weaknesses.'

'What makes you think we are interested in the information you have?'

'Maha Amatya, I have paid you the compliment of not underestimating your knowledge of Magadha. Do not underestimate mine of Kaikeya. Why do you think I have braved the dangers of the Uttarapath and travelled so far and so long to come here? Today there is only one kingdom in Jambudweepa that can take on the might of Magadha and that is Kaikeya. The Mauryan Empire will rise or forever sleep as it engages with Kaikeya.'

He paused and slid in casually, 'You are well aware of this fact I would say, Maha Amatya. After all, the entire effort to send in counterfeit coins and destabilize the economy of Magadha was not without thought, was it?'

Narsingh Dev gave no sign of comprehending what Pushyamitra was saying and the latter went on, 'You, Maha Amatya, are ideally poised to take on Magadha. Its power over the whole of Jambudweepa is growing at a phenomenal rate. Samrat Chandragupta is only in his fifth regnal year and already the jamun is within his grasp. The west has been won and provincial capitals are in the process of stabilizing in Ujjain and Suvamnagari under Pushyagupta. Only Kalinga holds out to some extent in the east, although it was part of the Nanda dominions. Reports of the expedition to the south say that they have run over all the civilized parts till the southern plateau. There is nothing but primal forest after that in the south. This leaves only the northern and Gandharan kingdoms since the central kingdoms have already accepted him as their suzerain. His ambition is to be another Bharata and it is only the Purus who can stop him and pluck the jamun from his grasp.'

Narsingh Dev looked at him consideringly after this long speech. He nodded his head and said, 'You seem to have a good understanding of the vision of my friend Vishnu. This one empire over Prithvi, the whole of the known world, is what he sees as his goal. Vishwa Vijaya for the boy he has picked to be Chakravartin. But we shall see. Narsingh Dev is not yet dead.' He said broodingly, his thoughts perhaps on the contrast with his broken and dying king.

He focused his snapping eyes on Pushyamitra, 'Tell me the specifics. What is it that you can inform me about?'

'Forgive me, Maha Amatya, I would also have to receive a few guarantees before I could agree to reveal any specifics. An opportunity to put my proposal before the Mantri Parishad and Maharaj Paurava perhaps?'

Narsingh Dev nodded; he had expected no less. This matter would take some time to resolve and wide consultation - not always his strong point - but it could well be necessary.

He said, rising, 'You will have to give me... us, some time to think and organize matters. I will inform you when you may appear before the Mantri Parishad. In the meanwhile think of yourselves as our esteemed guests and enjoy our beautiful city.'

'Perhaps,' suggested Pushyamitra in a slightly apologetic tone, 'you could make arrangements for us to move to a different palace. You see my wife...' he trailed off without completing the sentence.

Narsingh Dev turned away to hide a scornful smile. When it came to women even the most intelligent men were besotted fools. He had heard of the tantrums thrown by Misrakesi and congratulated himself yet again that he had never been in the power of any woman.

'Yes yes, it shall be done. You shall be housed more in keeping with your wife's wishes. After all, it is the wish of Kaikeya Raj that all guests are comfortable and happy.'

He turned around as a young man entered and greeted him deferentially. 'Ah, Suchak! Arya Pushyamitra, this is one of my assistants, who will show you around the city and take care of all your needs. Ask him for anything, do not hesitate. It is farewell for now.'

Pushyamitra bent his head slightly and joined his hands in a pranaam before letting Suchak lead him away. He was not told of Misrakesi's whereabouts and he stopped himself from asking. She would probably be in the royal women's apartments. It was up to her to play her part well.

Misrakesi had accompanied the maharani's dasi and the guards, very much dignified as a beautiful nartaki, and assumed the most supercilious expression she could manage. Her mind was working furiously as to the character she should assume and the role she should play. The pampered nartaki would not do. Maybe she should try to be a simple girl misled by a much more powerful and sophisticated man and persuaded to run away against her own inclinations.

They had reached an ascetically furnished apartment with none of the opulence associated with royalty. It had a strange and austere beauty all its own, especially with the open windows framing the valley, river, and the mountains beyond. There was a small garden grove outside with a shrine to the divine couple Shiva and Uma. There was a deep silence and peace pervaded the apartment with the faint chirping of birds from afar.

A silhouette at one of the windows turned and Misrakesi found herself face to face with Maharani Shailanandini. Their eyes met and Misrakesi was no longer the Magadhan spy out to dupe Kaikeya, she was only Sukesi's younger sister who had no troubles in the world and was secure in her loving embrace.

'Come here, my dear, and let me look at you,' said a low melodious voice. 'So you are my dearest sakhi Sukesi's sister!' She took Misrakesi's chin in her hand and raised up her face. 'Yes, you do have a look like hers. Although perhaps no one could be as beautiful as her,' and she smiled.

Misrakesi was spellbound. The maharani was not a young woman, she would be nearing the end of the fourth decade of her life but she was reputed to be the most beautiful princess of Jambudweepa. There were lines perhaps on her face now and a depth of sorrow in those lotus-eyes, but a different beauty shone forth from within. There was an aura of serenity and power surrounding her; she was not an ordinary princess. Her high-souled and noble spirit lent her a mystical and mesmerizing attraction.

Misrakesi silently allowed herself to be drawn down onto an asana next to the maharani. She felt it was Sukesi who was talking to her and welcoming her. All her plans about her role and character were forgotten and she was simply Misrakesi from Ujjain, a dancing girl who had come to Magadha to avenge her sister and seek her fortune.

She was gently questioned about Sukesi with empathy, her sorrow was also felt by the maharani who was quiet for a while and then said, 'I loved her like a sister, perhaps more. I have no sister of my own now, though I did once, long ago. I had made up my mind that Sukesi would be an ornament in Kaikeya or whichever kingdom my destiny took me to. It was not to be. Now, I have been given another chance by bhagya which has brought you here. You are now under my protection.'

Misrakesi felt again the same dissonance that always attacked her. She had come here to deceive and defeat this woman, and what she was getting in return was unconditional affection.

'But tell me about yourself, Little Sister. You don't mind me calling you that, do you? From now on, think of me in Sukesi's place.'

Misrakesi composed herself and cautioned herself against getting carried away by sentiment; her sister was a weak point of hers, but this fact should not lead to any mistakes. Her life story, such as it was, was unfolded to the maharani. From her training in Ujjain and the decision to avenge Sukesi's death to the successful storming of Magadha's dancing halls, her meeting with Pushyamitra, their ruin and decision to run away from Magadha. She included her suspicion that the acharya was behind Sukesi's death.

When she came to the end she said falteringly, 'Maharaniji, I cannot excuse myself for running away from Magadha but I am helpless in the hands of my husband. His wish is my command, I am like clay to his potter and he shapes me as he wills,' giving the impression of an innocent led astray by a sophisticate.

The maharani sighed, 'Yes, you are young yet. Never mind, forget the past. We will build both of you a new future in Kaikeya or Takshshila, as you wish. Now let us talk of more cheerful matters and let the dasis get you some food and wine. Forgive me for not joining you but I eat only once a day.'

Misrakesi wondered at this: eating once a day was for ascetics and shramans, not for royal ladies some of whom made eating a life's work. They indulged all their senses instead of disciplining them. She was to learn that this maharani was different. She was an ascetic queen. Misrakesi familiarized herself with the women's quarters and unobtrusively but efficiently scouted for future allies. She had already won the first battle but would need to consolidate her position.

~

Pushyamitra was spending some very profitable time with Suchak who took him around the city. He was a young man with a serious manner but adept at putting guests at ease; and in that process drawing out useful information from them, thought Pushyamitra, very much on his guard. It was a silent tussle between them as to who could extract more information from the other while giving out the least.

The Yavana influence after the occupation was very much visible here. Aramaic and Greek were as much heard in the market place as Sanskrit, Prakrit, or Kharoshti. People and goods from beyond the mountains from Kandahar to Herat to Ecbatana were much in evidence as were Yavana clothes and styles. It was a trade crossroads; pepper, textiles, metals, ivory, silk, and even animals such as the elephant and the rhinoceros were being bought and sold.

Suchak was forced to introduce a few people and places to Pushyamitra since he was new to the city. The places were easily introduced but people very sparingly so. His casual but searching questions were easily parried by Pushyamitra. Although he did not expect to meet any important people he thought it would be a good idea to discuss them.

'Arya Bhattarak is the senapati, isn't he? I have heard that he is the second most important man in the kingdom, after the Maha Amatya of course,' he asked.

Suchak was giving nothing away, 'Yes, he is certainly the senapati. As for importance, we are all servants of the most mighty and honorable Kaikeya Raj.'

'I believe he had three sons and all of them perished in the battle against Alakshendra?'

Suchak's expression was shuttered and he replied solemnly, 'Yes, it is true, Arya Pushyamitra. That was the biggest tragedy to befall the Purus and indeed this beautiful and prosperous Gandhara Pradesh. In our kingdom we do not like to talk about that time. It brought only death, destruction, and devastation. Entire tribes and villages were wiped out and our royal family...' he fell silent.

Pushyamitra's sympathy and interest were aroused. As a citizen of the powerful kingdom of Magadha, Alakshendra's meteoric streak through the Land of the Seven Rivers had left him untouched; it was a distant drum roll. For people here, it had been a ruinous time. The power of the Yavanas had been broken by the unceasing war waged by Chandragupta and his army of guerillas, but they were still a significant force. In fact, all the kings in the area were nominally appointed Satraps of Alakshendra and Eudemos, the only surviving Yavana satrap, was still a player in the area's politics. He would have to be dealt with, before Samrat Chandragupta could establish himself as suzerain of the area.

Suchak did not encourage him to ask any more questions and they soon traced their way back to the palace. It was time to take stock of Misrakesi.

Pushyamitra had decided on the spur of the moment that Misrakesi and he should pose as husband and wife because he had a shrewd suspicion that Narsingh Dev would try to separate them and that would have seriously weakened them. He indicated that he had had enough for the day and would like to go back and rest, and also ask after his wife's welfare. From the smirk on Suchak's face, he gathered that his reputation as the hapless husband of a beautiful and fascinating shrew had preceded him.

Luxurious quarters within the royal palace near Maharani Shailanandini's chambers had been prepared for them and he went in to find Misrakesi engaged in the completion of an elaborate toilet with scores of dasis in attendance. The king's daughter's kind glance was enough to make her an honoured guest in the palace.

The dasis made as if to withdraw but Misrakesi sharply commanded them to finish their work, 'How will I look beautiful for Aryaputra otherwise?' she said with a languorous glance at him. Only he understood the sarcasm behind using the formal appellation for a husband, 'Aryaputra', for him.

'Lavanika, Niharika, Karmanika, go and attend to him and make him comfortable.'

Pushyamitra relaxed with a soothing sandalwood massage and then a bath. He let the dasis minister to him, smiling inwardly. Misrakesi had certainly made herself comfortable and was ordering everyone around as if she had been born here. Soothed, shaved, cleaned, and clad in fresh clothes, he went and joined Misrakesi in the groves outside.

'You are now talking,' said Misrakesi in mock arrogant tones, 'to the younger sister of the daughter of Kaikeya Raj.'

'Misrakesi, I am proud of you. How do you manage all these kinship relations? Is it skill or luck? Mrinalini helped you save the samrat's life and the maharani may yet help to get the throne for him.' They were walking close together and conversing in low tones, ever vigilant about being spied upon.

Misrakesi laughed at his rueful tone and said, 'It must be that chief-of-the-Suraksha-Parishad manner of yours that puts people at a distance.'

His glance was thoughtful as he pulled her close to him. It was getting dark and they could be seen only as two faintly emerging shadows against the rushing waters of the Vitasta.

Shailanandini, Kamasundari and Others

And he should win over the seducible in the enemy's territories by means of conciliation and gifts and those not seducible by means of dissension and force, pointing out to them the defects of the enemy.

Arthashastra 1.14.8

The days passed and the two visitors settled down in the Paurava king's palace thanks to the blessings of the maharani. They could have deemed themselves honoured guests if it had not been for the hooded eyes of Narsingh Dev, the telltale presence of soldiers around them and the ever-present vigilance of their dasas and dasis.

In spite of their luxurious, not to say hedonistic existence, the political mission they had come to fulfill was languishing. The old king lay gravely ill, neither improving nor deteriorating. A galaxy of vaidyas was assisting the Raj Vaidya[58] but they were not able to make any headway. All royal decisions were conveyed either by Narsingh Dev or the maharani. The kingdom was poised in an uneasy silence.

Pushyamitra had neither been allowed an audience with the king nor an opportunity to address the Mantri Parishad. His reminders were met with smiling assurances but no action. He imposed patience on himself and looked around for alternative ways to meet the powerful members of the Inner Council that advised the king.

Apart from Narsingh Dev and Senapati Bhattaraka there were two others, the Purohita[59] and the Kul Guru[60] of the Purus. They were almost completely inaccessible to him as they moved in a private sphere where he had no entry; maybe Misrakesi would be able to meet them through the maharani. He had to focus on the senapati.

Their only positive achievement was the growing closeness between the maharani and Misrakesi. The maharani was not a formal member of the Inner Council but she had her father's ear. He depended upon her calm and sensible advice on all occasions. Her place in the court was informal but immensely powerful, especially as she was his only surviving child.

Misrakesi spent all her time with the maharani who led a very austere life. Her days were spent in prayer, meditation and discussions with learned pundits and acharyas. Influenced by the teachings of Shraman Mahavir and the Sakya Muni, she had given up the flesh of animals and all intoxicants.

She kept Misrakesi very close to her; it was as if she felt responsible for her. 'Now that Sukesi is no longer there, it is I who will care for you and protect you. Sukesi often talked to me about her hopes and dreams for you, you meant the world to her. I will make all her dreams come true,' she was fond of saying.

Often her face would then fall into lines of worry, 'Just let my father recover and take his rightful place again. There will be time enough for all these things. You will be the court dancer and we will look for an important position for your husband, too.'

Misrakesi had fallen under her spell and would spend the entire day, sometimes even the nights in the royal apartments. She was working towards generating an implicit trust in the maharani. The acharya's parting words were very much on her mind.

Gradually, the maharani also opened up. She would tell Misrakesi about her own happy carefree life as the adored only princess of the Kaikeyas, the days when princes from far and wide sent proposals of marriage for her and she was the most feted kumari in Jambudweepa. And then had come, like an avalanche devastating all in its way, Alakshendra and his army. The land had erupted in bloodshed and tragedy.

Her blue eyes would become dark with sorrow, unshed pools of tears, 'Do you know what I am, Misrakesi, I am part of the spoils of war,' she said sadly once.

Misrakesi's face reflected her curiosity.

'You wouldn't know what was happening here. Avanti was very far from the blood soaked story unfolding here,' the maharani paused and said reflectively, 'One man's lust for conquest and quest for ephemeral glory on this earth led to thousands being killed. Entire villages and tribes were decimated; the roll call of those tribes is heartbreaking; the Malavs, Kshudrakas, the Ashtaks... Do you know that an entire village of Brahmins in Mousikanos was slaughtered for opposing Alakshendra? Soldiers in Massaga who had surrendered in return for their lives being spared were treacherously slaughtered.'

Misrakesi was listening intently. As a citizen of faraway Avanti, she had only heard faint echoes of these events. She knew that the acharya and Samrat Chandragupta had been the ones to mobilize the people of the north and they had cut their fighting teeth in pushing back the Yavanas. The Yavanas were still a presence but a marginalized one. Alakshendra's conquests had been divided up between his generals and their internal warring left them with no resources to devote to winning back the Gandhara Pradesh. The city of Boukephala established by him on the banks of the Vitasta[61] and other cities like Nikaia where the battle with the Paurava king had taken place were the only testimonies of his meteoric path through the region. The Indian potentates Kaikeya Raj and Ambhi were now the defacto satraps and Eudemos an increasingly sidelined and frustrated lone Yavana satrap. Phillipus had been appointed by Alakshendra but had been murdered a little before the death of Alakshendra himself of a fever.

The maharani continued in a soft and abstracted voice staring unseeingly at the wintry landscape outside, 'Ambhi Raj was one of the princes who had sent emissaries for my hand in marriage but he was not favoured by my father and the Maha Amatya Narsingh Dev; Takshshila had always been subordinate to Kaikeya. He found his opportunity in welcoming and paying tribute to Alakshendra. Having acknowledged him as his suzerain, Ambhi Raj gained the satrapy of the area; he accepted his motherland as a gift from the Yavana,' her voice was hot with remembered indignation.

'And then,' her voice dropped to a whisper, 'Alakshendra's armies were on our borders. I well remember the day. His armies were on the other side of the Vitasta waiting for a chance to cross and engage with us. My father and brothers dressed for battle, fighting to keep the Yavana out of Jambudweepa. We had fifty thousand soldiers, three thousand horses, a thousand chariots, and a hundred and thirty elephants. Valiant fighters led by my father and brothers rode into battle to save their motherland. To their everlasting shame, none of the Gandharan kings came to his aid, except for the King of Kashmir, Abhisara.' Her eyes softened and her voice took on an indefinable note which made Misrakesi sit up.

'He was our only ally, the only one to send his armies to help us. Alas, his soldiers were too late. The river goddess herself was against us. Vitasta was in flood with the rains; the stormy night helped Alakshendra to cross with a feint and break upon our amassed army at dawn. The battle lasted the whole day... and at the end of the day the mighty Purus were humbled. My brothers were dead and my father a prisoner.' Her voice wavered but she controlled it. 'Our chariots were useless against the twenty foot-long lances, the sarissaas, of the Yavanas. They wore bronze armour, we fought with leather cuirasses. Our superiority with the long bow was of no avail. Our wounded elephants ran amok injuring our own soldiers.'

She paused, drew a jagged breath and said, 'It would have been best if both my father and I had also perished on that battlefield. It would have been a swift and honourable death instead of this long wasting away.'

When Misrakesi made a movement of protest she held up her hand and continued. 'Alakshendra was a magnanimous victor; he spared my father's life, exacted tribute from him and made him the

Yavana satrap of his own land. And I… I was forced to become the queen of Ambhi Raj as part of the terms forced on the defeated. Such are the fortunes of war.'

There was a long silence. Misrakesi could not help but sympathise with the tragedy of this most beautiful of princesses. The weak Ambhi was no match for this spirited and lovely woman, but she had been trapped into this forced political marriage. She thought of the Nanda princess, Dharini although she seemed to have settled down happily enough with Chandragupta. Sometimes fate was brutal to royal princesses. Commoners like her were better off. They did not have to bow to larger requirements of king and kingdom and could please themselves.

The maharani was lost in unpleasant thoughts of her own. She said, 'Alakshendra lost his appetite for war after that. Also in part because of the stories they were told about the might of Magadha's army. Inspite of all his efforts, his soldiers refused to fight and he was forced to turn back after hastily appointing satraps.

'It was after I had been part of Ambhi Raj's entourage of queens for sometime, swallowing my rage and humiliation with every breath, that I met a brilliant young acharya from the Takshshila Gurukul who was campaigning tirelessly to expel the Yavanas from this land.

'He was my Guru and saviour. I learnt to reconcile with my situation and to make a new life out of the ruins of my old.'

Misrakesi pressed the maharani's hands sympathetically and the former smiled sadly and said, 'I also decided to remain an aajivan brahmacharini.[62] Ambhi Raj may have forced me into marriage but he would never possess me. And he never had the courage to challenge this decision of mine. I will never, ever be a mother.' This was said low.

Misrakesi was shocked. A woman's societal standing was decided by her offspring, sons more than daughters. For a woman in grihasta ashram[63] to give up on having children was to willfully deprive herself of a pivot in her life. Her life would be without meaning and fulfillment. A wife's, indeed a queen's first duty was to have children. And here was someone deliberately depriving herself of that privilege.

Shailanandini smiled again at the shock on Misrakesi's face and gently withdrew her hand patting Misrakesi's instead.

'Never mind, my dear, all that is over. We have different problems and are living in different times now. I am going to visit my father and you should not neglect your husband.' She was sent off with a kindly smile.

Misrakesi made her way back to her chambers in a cautiously optimistic frame of mind. The maharani was certainly opening up and making her a confidant; she was on her way to doing what she had come to do.

She found a moody Pushyamitra standing on the terrace watching the tumbling waters of the Vitasta with his arms crossed and lips compressed. Misrakesi was surprised to see him there and said so as she went up and twined herself around him in a passionate kiss.

Pushyamitra's response was absent-minded, 'I don't think I am getting anywhere,' he announced in a flat voice. 'What about you?'

They were talking in low tones audible only to each other while appearing lovingly entwined to the dasas and dasis who were keeping them under observation.

Pushyamitra was frowning as he mechanically stroked Misrakesi's bare arms. 'Suchak is wasting my time. I am beginning to think that Narsingh Dev has no intention of letting me meet anyone. How do I infiltrate the Mantri Parishad and create dissension in it?'

'I am progressing. I am also making friends with the royal women and spend a lot of time chatting with them. Which is why I have a small tip which may help you.' Misrakesi smiled and reached up to gently nip his ear whispering, 'Kamasundari! The queen of all the male hearts of Kaikeya. Rumour has it that the Senapati Bhattaraka also languishes at her feet. Visiting her may be profitable as well as entertaining. A few tips for me from the Gandharan beauties perhaps?'

Pushyamitra's eyes narrowed and he turned around to look at her intently. She nodded. 'It is worth a try.'

There was a new purpose in Pushyamitra's stride the next day. He endured a day full of meaningless conversation and aimless wandering in the city. As evening approached he casually directed his steps towards the establishment of the famous ganika Kamasundari; Misrakesi had given him the directions. As they neared it he said to Suchak, 'I hear that nearby is the house of Kaikeya's queen of hearts, Kamasundari? How would it be if a pardesi from Magadha went in to sample the delights offered by her?'

Suchak was clearly unhappy and tried to say that it was not worth the time but Pushyamitra was not to be moved from his target. He jovially overruled all objections and went in to the dancing house.

The dancing house was like any other high-class establishment in Magadha. They were greeted at the door by two nubile, diaphanously-clad young women who greeted them with flowers and perfume. Suchak seemed to be well known and Pushyamitra's dress, demeanour and haughty face denoted a man of rank. They were seated ceremoniously on soft and multi-hued asanas meant for honoured guests and served with delicate but intoxicating flower wine. The atmosphere was far removed from the mundane and it would not have been surprising if the divine Apsara Urvashi herself were to put in an appearance.

Kamasundari was in the middle of a dance performance. The dance ended and there was enthusiastic applause. A small fortune in gold coins and gems found its way to the dancer's feet from where it was magically cleared up by her assistants. Her sleepy and inviting eyes swept in gratitude around the assembly and found a new guest; and that too with Suchak, Narsingh Dev's personal assistant from the palace. She dropped her eyes to the floor in an enchanting show of gratitude and soon made her way gracefully to Suchak.

She greeted him with great affection, mock-scolding him for coming after such a long interval. A bewitching smile was directed at Pushyamitra, 'Will you not make your honoured guest known to me? Rarely have I seen a man with his presence and attributes grace my humble establishment.'

She let her eyes slip admiringly from the reclining Pushyamitra's face to his broad chest, bull-like shoulders and muscled thighs. Pushyamitra smiled back and replied in kind with his bold glance appreciating this Gandharan beauty. Her skin was like marble, her hair was done up in Yavana style ringlets, and her face was an oval of perfection with sapphire-blue eyes and a sharp but delicate nose. The bursting fullness of her breasts was imperfectly contained by an artfully tied kanchuki, her narrow waist and full hips emphasized by a mekhala, and delicate feet outlined in red peeped from beneath her Ghaghra. He said nothing, waiting for Suchak to react.

Suchak was clearly unwilling but was as clearly left with no option but to reply to this direct command phrased as a request. 'This is Arya Pushyamitra Sunga, an honoured guest from Magadha,' was his succinct reply. The sleepiness in Kamasundari's eyes became more pronounced as she sat by Pushyamitra and proffered compliments and gratitude for having deigned to visit her. Soon, however, patrons from other parts of the room called to her and she rose with smiling regret promising to be back.

'My compliments to the women of your city, Bandhu. Are they all as delicious a morsel as this one?' said Pushyamitra to Suchak as she left.

Suchak pressed his lips together as he answered, 'She is beautiful indeed but you would be in grave danger of choking to death if you ever tried to swallow this morsel. So take my advice and let us leave. The lady is as dangerous and tough as a vajra ayudh.'

'Leave! Now?! When the night and the game are just beginning! Not on your life, Suchak. What are you? Man or monk? I have not enjoyed myself so much for months. I think the lady fancies me and I fancy waiting and watching for developments. I might get lucky. What do you think? In the meantime there is food and drink and other beautiful women. Have fun!'

And Pushyamitra called loudly for more wine and roasted venison. He scattered gold around to such effect that he had the other dancers and attendants vying to serve him. One of the lowliest of them employed to clean up after the clients had her uttariya covering her face so that only her eyes showed. Those eyes sharpened when they saw Pushyamitra, he glanced casually at her but showed no reaction and she soon went away.

Kamasundari had excused herself and gone into her inner apartments for a while. There was a man half lying on her bed surrounded by laughing women, everyone enjoying themselves. He was short and powerfully built and when he sat up on Kamasundari's entry it could be seen that he had a handsome face and an imperious nose. It was none other than the man Pushyamitra most wanted to meet, Senapati Bhattaraka.

He said lazily, 'What, finished already for the day, heart's dearest? Then come and make me happy.'

Kamasundari went and sat next to him and said urgently, 'Arya, I have something to tell you...' the rest was lost as she lowered her voice to a whisper.

In spite of a restless Suchak, Pushyamitra had settled down and was prepared to sit the night through in case his luck should turn. After some time spent flirting with a number of willing nartakis, he saw Kamasundari enter with another man and also saw Suchak's face fall dramatically; he understood that his luck had indeed turned.

It was the deepest part of the night and Misrakesi was in bed when she heard Pushyamitra's steps come in. He told the dasis to keep out and entered. It was a Pushyamitra she had never seen before. She sat up and watched with interest as he almost staggered in and sat heavily on the bed. With slow uncertain movements he removed his black silk uttariya and tried to open his headband, bajubands and other jewellery. As he fumbled, a surprised giggle escaped Misrakesi and she went to help him. His wrists were entwined with ketaki flowers, his eyes were bloodshot and he smelled equally of the fragrance of ketaki and of some exotic wine.

'Misrakesi,' he said softly and Misrakesi thought in wonder, *He is drunk!* There was a slur in his voice which he could not control.

She slowly took off all his jewellery and pushed him back till he was lying on the cushions. As her hands loosened his kayabandh and then set it aside he whispered again, his eyes half closed, 'Misrakesi, Misrakesi, dearest.'

She took her time running her hands lightly all over his body before she pulled herself to lie flat on top of him her elbows planted on both sides of his face so that he was completely enclosed within the boundaries of her body and her open hair.

'And where have you been, my lord, to return drunk to your *wife's* bed?'

'In heaven, perhaps?'

'Ah, I see. Heaven defined as the place where the celestial Apsara Kamasundari dwells, am I right?'

She nuzzled the side of his neck tenderly but said in a stern voice, 'Smelling of a different woman's perfume, too! Is this any way of coming to me, making a khandita naayika of me?'

'Forgive me.' His hands went up to touch her cheek and wander through her hair caressing the long soft strands as they fell in wild profusion over her body and his. 'It was a matter of upholding the honour of the men from Magadha. I could not say no to the women asking me to satisfy them especially when one of them was as potent as the wine I drank.'

'Women in the plural?! I assume you did not let the honour of Magadha down. But what about the one currently in your bed?' asked Misrakesi. She was looking into his eyes inflamed like a red lotus. This drunken Pushyamitra with his guard down, each expression in his vulnerable eyes reflecting her own, excited her unbearably and her senses were swimming with desire. At this moment in time, this man seemed to be hers and hers alone; they were together in a world adrift their gazes locked.

'What about her?'

'In the first place, I hate ketaki flowers,' she untwined them from his wrist and removed them from his neck.

'I know my atimukta. There is a creeper outside my window at home which makes me think of you every night.'

Misrakesi inched up, 'Pushyamitra,' her voice was a wisp of smoke in the air, 'It is my misfortune that you have satisfied so many women today, but I am destined to burn in desire all night.'

In answer he slipped his fingers through her hair and turning her over pressed her against the bed. Both her hands were caught in one of his and imprisoned above her head, his red eyes never wavering from her. He entered her like a piercing arrow and she let out a small scream which brought one of the night dasis running into see what the matter was.

The two of them were oblivious and never saw her retreating with a smile.

'Pushyamitra...' it was a sob of supplication or desire or both. Misrakesi was pushed against the bed, held immobile by his hand and loved till she could stand his strength no longer. She begged for mercy with hoarse little sentences but still he went on till she found herself in a whirling universe where pain, desire, and fulfillment were the same. Tremors racked her body and screams were stifled in her throat. They held each other close then, tight, till their tremors subsided and they came floating gently back to earth to find a safe haven.

'Satisfied or still burning?' the voice emerging from where Pushyamitra had his head buried against her was still slurred but arrogant and triumphant.

'Did I challenge your masculine pride then?' asked Misrakesi, lazily mischievous.

'No, you asked me for something. How could I not give it to you?'

'So you will make love to me whenever I so desire?'

'Hmm.'

'And, if I extend your promise, you will always give me what I want?'

'Yes.'

'Wonderful.' Misrakesi settled down to sleep with her arms around him and her head pillowed on his shoulder. 'That is indeed a useful promise to extract from such a powerful man. I will hold you to it, so do not forget.' Her voice was soft; she was in a daze of pleasure, her entire body relaxed.

'Forget?' He gave a small smile and shook his head.

The next morning the presence of the ubiquitous dasis listening to each word was an irritant since there was an urgent need for Pushyamitra to brief Misrakesi on the events of the earlier night.

They had obviously been well-informed by the night dasi and their glances and giggles as they looked at his back did succeed in embarrassing Misrakesi although he himself was unflappable.

She had an idea she had been saving for just such an occasion. 'Why don't we take a swim together in the Mandakini lake?'

'A swim in this weather?' Pushyamitra was puzzled by the suggestion though he had also been trying to think of a place where they could get solitude. But this would be a form of pure torture given the cold weather and icy waters of the local rivers and streams.

'The taal is fed by a hot water spring which comes from inside the ground. There are many stories surrounding it, but all you need to know is that we will be comfortably warm and it will probably be good for your old bones, it is supposed to have healing and magic properties.'

'My old bones, is it? I thought I had put that doubt to rest last night. Some more effort on my part seems to be indicated.'

One of the dasis stifled a giggle and Misrakesi lifted her eyes heavenward, exasperated. It was like living in a public house, this palace!

There was an ornamental grove surrounding the taal and the pond itself had been artificially made into an extensive water body which was, at this hour of the morning, empty, although it was usually quite popular with the local elite.

Some of the dasis were enthusiastic about entering the water and cavorting with Pushyamitra, but Misrakesi curtly told them all to stay on the bank and the two of them were finally quite alone.

'So you have acquired the reputation of being not only a shrew, but a jealous one too,' said Pushyamitra teasingly.

'That is the problem with us "Senior" wives! We cannot tolerate anyone else though I do not yet have a junior wife to contend with. Who knows, given your female following you may yet oblige me!'

They had swum out into the middle of the taal and were now floating on their backs. The water was pleasantly warm and the sun was shining. An idyllic morning but there was work to discuss.

'Pushyamitra, I know you are fascinating and irresistible, especially when you are drunk but what is the secret of your astonishing success with Kamasundari? From the little I gathered, you were made more than just welcome. And believe me, I know the tricks of the ganikas, this is not one of them. Sleeping with anyone on their first visit, without any payment, is unusual.'

'Last night was the opening I was looking for. Before I go into the details, let me tell you an interesting nugget, your ghost is here.'

'What! Chandramukhi?' Misrakesi turned over with a splash. 'What is she doing here?'

'Working in Kamasundari's establishment as a dasi. She must have found a lead to her husband. I do not know if she is going to interfere with what we are doing. I think not. She has her own revenge to complete. But we may be able to use her help. Let us swim to the opposite bank and then talk.'

Neck deep in the warm water they leaned side by side against the banks of the lake.

'The Mantri Parishad seems to be divided into two here. The senapati is a sworn enemy of Narsingh Dev and leads his own faction. He had heard of my arrival and was furious at not being allowed to meet me. He thinks that Narsingh Dev is going to try and use me as a secret weapon. He can do nothing against Narsingh Dev because he is the only one who has access to the king except for the Raj Purohit and Kul Guru who are apolitical persons and your maharani, of course. All royal orders are conveyed through Narsingh Dev. The situation is also very tense because of the question of the succession. The opposing faction thinks that Narsingh Dev is plotting to put his own puppet on the throne.'

Misrakesi digested this information in silence. She had heard the maharani discuss matters with some of her advisors which pertained to the affairs of the state, so she was also obviously an important political player. The senapati's frustration must have been increased by being left out altogether. It was perhaps not a wise move by Narsingh Dev, but he did have a dictatorial and unilateral temperament.

'As far as Kamasundari is concerned, she is a crucial member of the senapati's faction, one of his major allies and advisors. She is a powerful woman in Kaikeya and she maintains the balance amongst the various hot heads, from what I have gathered. This group wants to somehow use me to tilt the balance in their favour. They think I bring the vast power of the Magadhan army with me which will give them an advantage they do not have at the moment. So Kamasundari was deputed by Bhattaraka to tie me to her with chains of flowers. And believe me, she is good at it. I am a man with years of experience in using women for this very purpose and I know their tricks inside out but she made an impact on me. She is lethally attractive with an almost hypnotic power. And a sophisticate to her toes.' Pushyamitra was matter of fact, but Misrakesi could hear the undertones. What a woman she must be, to make such a strong impression on a cynic like the chief of the Nagarik Suraksha Parishad.

She had an urge to warn him to be wary but thought better of it. He could take care of himself, he also had to take care of Magadha's interests and that would always keep him vigilant.

They were swimming slowly now side by side both absorbed in the new information.

'I met Bhattaraka yesterday and he has invited me to a bhoj at one of his wives' houses, the senior wife, I believe. It will certainly be a political gathering and I will make the best of it. A path seems to be opening up now. We have now to wait for the activation of our network here. It is too dangerous for me to make a move, so we will just have to wait for Siddharthak, although it is getting late now. We should have had word by now. We will need help if we manage to go to the next phase of the plan.'

Misrakesi nodded. They decided to go back and follow their usual routines. As Misrakesi prepared to swim back Pushyamitra held her hand and stopped her, 'Misrakesi.'

She stood there with him stretching out his arm and holding her hand, 'What?'

His expression was unreadable. She walked up close and said, 'Don't worry; she will not eat you up.'

'And if she does? Will you rescue me?'

'Only if you want to be rescued,' she was smiling faintly.

'I am worried about you. In the next few days I am not going to be there with you. I have to spend time with Bhattarak and his cronies and in Kamasundari's clutches. Will you be very careful and take good care of yourself? You will be alone in the palace and you cannot even send a message to me if I am out somewhere, so will you promise to be really careful? Keep your dagger with you always and stay as close to the maharani as possible.' His tone was urgent.

'I can take care of myself, Pushyamitra. If I fail, the maharani is there; so you do not need worry. In any case, both of us have to do our work regardless of the risks.'

'I anticipate an attack on you but there is little we can do to stop it. If at all Narsingh Dev is suspicious of us he will concentrate on you as perhaps easier to break.'

'Pushyamitra, Pushyamitra, stop worrying. Nothing is going to happen to me or you. And he may not find it so easy to break me; I am tougher than I look.' I hope, she thought, sending up a prayer to Goddess Shree.

'Come here.' He untied the ochre bead he always wore on his forearm and, putting his arms around her, tied the bead around her neck.

'What are you doing? What is this for?' said Misrakesi, bemused. She had never seen him take this off and indeed he must not have opened it for years as there was a white mark around his forearm.

'This is my good luck charm. I found it twenty years ago while fighting for my life and it has never ever let me down. It will take care of you when I am not there.' And he gently kissed her throat against which the ochre bead lay.

But she went back more worried and depressed than she had been at any time since they had come to Kaikeya. His worrying had affected her. They followed their usual routine, with Misrakesi going off to the maharani's quarters and Pushyamitra spending another meaningless day with Suchak. He had deliberately not informed him of the bhoj he had been invited to since he was certain that efforts would be made to stop him from going. Maybe he would be left alone? But that was not to be; Suchak stuck to him like flies to honey.

As darkness fell there was a surprise in store. A beautifully decorated horse with a contingent of soldiers came up to the palace where Pushyamitra was staying and greeted him respectfully. He presented the senapati's compliments and said that he had come to escort him to the bhoj.

Suchak was caught off guard. He could not openly say that he did not have Narsingh Dev's permission to let Pushyamitra go, honoured guests did not need permission. He could not accompany him uninvited and did not want to risk a confrontation, given the company of soldiers. He could only watch helplessly as Pushyamitra bade him a smiling farewell and promised to meet him the next morning.

As expected, the bhoj was a lavish affair but was more political than social. Of the twenty-one members of the Mantri Parishad, half or more were present. As he went around meeting them and talking to them, Pushyamitra was soaking up information and impressions to be analyzed later. Some of them seemed to be implacably opposed to Narsingh Dev's hegemony while others were more neutral. The senapati and his faction would be easy to handle, it was the non-aligned group which would need the finesse.

But Pushyamitra did not let any of his calculations show in his actions or expressions. He was the ideal guest, meeting everyone with the same professions of happiness and taking care to meet as many of them as possible. He was the one they had all come to meet.

He spoke of his desire to serve Kaikeya and hinted at the secrets he held and was ready to trade. His brother, the senapati, was spoken of in hushed voices. He subtly painted, in glowing colours, the picture of a prosperous kingdom waiting to be plucked, with Pushyamitra and his brother willing to change sides.

He could see Bhattaraka's eyes shining with avarice and excitement. It was not so easy to carry along some of the older mantris on this flow. They had practical objections and questions to ask, which Pushyamitra answered skilfully, talking much and divulging little.

Bhattaraka was impatient with this. He was young and ready to fight, he dreamt of a big victory which would make his mark on Kaikeya. He had taken over from his father, Narsingh Dev's contemporary, and had yet to make his own name in leading the army. He was impatient to dispense with past defeats and give Kaikeyans a new chapter of victory to extol. He had quite a few young hot headed mantris with him who began to dream of a major victory for the Purus.

Pushyamitra had not expected to win over the majority at once. His work would demand subtlety and patience. Having been introduced to so many important personages of the state was the opening; he needed to meet them again and again and talk them over to his side. This was what he proceeded to do.

It was not to be expected that Narsingh Dev would let all this happen without any resistance. He was not so powerful that he could stop the senapati or the mantris from meeting Pushyamitra once the initial introduction had been made, and that was why he had been so assiduous in keeping Pushyamitra under his guard so to speak. He decided to warn Pushyamitra that he was still the most powerful man in Kaikeya and meeting with the others would not advance his cause.

Pushyamitra was summoned for a meeting where Suchak was also present. He looked supremely uncomfortable at Pushyamitra's interrogative glance like a brahmachari caught telling tales to the Guru. Pushyamitra then turned his gaze to Narsingh Dev and waited for him to speak.

'So, Arya Pushyamitra! How is Kaikeya treating you? I trust the royal palace is taking care of you and young Suchak here? You must tell us if we fall short and you have to accept the hospitality of others,' he started off.

'Are you referring to my visits to some of the mantris who I have met and grown to like? I did not know that there would be any problems with that. After all if I am to live and work here I have to get to know the others. And I think if I wish to spend my leisure time in a dancing house it is quite my own private affair,' this was said with a cutting glance at Suchak who flushed.

Narsingh Dev was thrown off balance at this direct approach; but recovered immediately and said smilingly, 'No, no, of course there is no problem. A man needs friends after all and some entertainment, especially if his wife is busy elsewhere.'

Pushyamitra looked offended at this reference to Misrakesi, but he knew full well that her growing intimacy with the maharani was being monitored by Narsingh Dev.

Narsingh Dev went on, 'And then again, it is time for you to put your proposition before the Mantri Parishad. I will fix a time and let you know.'

Pushyamitra nodded. Whether this was a serious offer or not did not make much difference to him now. He could not be any worse off and at best he would meet some of the mantris he had not yet met. The cracks which could be widened were already becoming visible to him. But he let anticipation show on his face and said forcefully, 'Maha Amatya, it is time for you to trust me and give me a formal role in serving Kaikeya. I have been here since the month of Karttika, and Phalguna[64] is now nearing its end. My brother is also awaiting my word. What word am I to send him when you have given me none?'

Narsingh Dev said grimly, 'You will be notified as soon as a meeting of the Mantri Parishad is called. Something has to be done about you. You cannot leave Kaikeya now, that is certain; you know too much about us,' the tone was almost threatening and Suchak looked apprehensive. He did not want a tragic fate for these Magadhans, especially Misrakesi who he admired intensely from afar.

Pushyamitra merely raised his eyebrows and said, 'Where is the question of leaving? I have tied my fate to Kaikeya and my only wish is to serve it.'

The audience was over.

Pushyamitra was to meet Bhattaraka at Kamasundari's dancing house as usual. The outer rooms, meant for the general public, no longer befitted his stature. He was a friend of the senapati and her current favourite lover. She had slept with him on the first day to ensure his later visits and now she had begun to look forward to these sessions. Pushyamitra rarely put himself out to be attractive to any woman, but his relationship with Misrakesi seemed to have given him a natural edge apart from the fact that he was trying harder than he ever had to keep Kamasundari's interest. Kamasundari had heard that he had taken a reigning ganika from Magadha as a wife and had fled to Kaikeya because of her. She shrugged her shoulders mentally: it was in the nature of men to tire of their wives, which was why ganikas had always been and would always be successful, in spite of all the wives in the world. Pushyamitra was now an intimate of their circle and spent his evenings and nights in drinking, dicing and dalliance, furthering his friendship with this clique.

There was a strange man present there tonight, Pushyamitra had never met him but he looked familiar. But of course! His mind went back to an underground chamber in Magadha a few months ago; this was Shreedhan, Chandramukhi's murderous husband. She was on the right trail and had followed him to Gandhara, pursuing her agenda of revenge.

He seemed to be tolerated in Bhattaraka's circle but was not really an insider. Pushyamitra made it a point to befriend him. He was the one who had taken up months of the Nagarik Suraksha Parishad's time with the distribution of the counterfeit coins. Pushyamitra wanted to know more about him and keep him under observation. There was a good chance that Chandramukhi and he would collide and maybe that could be made use of for Magadha's purposes.

Siddharthak had not yet activated the goodhpurush network of Kaikeya. It was not possible for Pushyamitra himself to make a move as he was under the surveillance of the administration, although he had some contacts to be used in case of an emergency. They needed someone inside the establishment for the next phase of their plan to be put into operation.

While waiting with increasing impatience for any word from Siddharthak, Pushyamitra was making good progress in sowing confusion and dissension amongst the mighty and powerful in Kaikeya. He was now to be seen daily at various social and political occasions in the city. He was making confidants of these people and subtly conveying that they were being underestimated and ignored by the current administration. He would cast Narsingh Dev or the senapati as the villain depending on who he was talking to, adding casually that things were different in Magadha. The overweening ambition of both these important players was always mentioned and the Mantri reminded that the king was dying and a palace coup could easily be imminent, men in high places had high ambitions, didn't they?

Pushyamitra was more and more everyone's friend but they were gradually less each other's friends. Each of them was told that they were fit for higher honours and soon believed it, feeling resentful at being overlooked. The topic of the succession was an obsession but there was no consensus on it. Narsingh Dev's choice was still a mystery, certainly not Ambhi with whom he had a longstanding enmity. Maybe it was Malayketu, the king's dissolute nephew, who could be made a puppet ruler? Pushyamitra encouraged this fear and this gave rise to an even greater discontent as they saw Narsingh Dev becoming more powerful than ever under a new ruler.

In all his peregrinations, Pushyamitra had not really been able to shake off Suchak completely. He would accompany him wherever possible and hang around nearby where not possible. He would always accompany him to Kamasundari's dancing hall even though he would normally have to sit outside in the public area. He was also a serious young man with no taste for wine, women, or song and these sessions were a strain on him, but he wasn't giving up. Pushyamitra was reasonably sure, however, that the content of his conversations was not finding its way to Suchak which was why his desperation was increasing.

The young man was, however, extremely struck by Misrakesi and would obliquely question Pushyamitra about her, much to the latter's amusement. He had often teased Misrakesi about her easy conquest, but there were almost no occasions when Suchak could actually meet her. He came out from Kamasundari's establishment one night to find him grimly stuck to his post in spite of the obvious weariness of his female companion. On a whim, he invited Suchak to come back with him to the palace. Suchak flushed with pleasure and agreed at once.

Pushyamitra sat down with Suchak in his outer reception room and looked at him smilingly, 'Shall we have some wine and something to eat?'

Dasis were already appearing with wine and food and after some time, with them also came Misrakesi, curious to know who Pushyamitra was entertaining and why.

Suchak was struck with admiration. Misrakesi sat down. Dealing with infatuated men was what she specialized in. Pushyamitra noticed that she was not really looking her best, the glow from her face was missing and she looked strained. The long months in an enemy palace were taking their toll; keeping up appearances was not easy. However, her admirer was obviously unaffected by such small details, Misrakesi was at her most gracious and informal and he was halfway in love with her before he knew it.

He was in no mood to end the interaction and Pushyamitra had to get up and indicate that it was time for them to retire. Suchak sprang up and in his confusion stepped on Misrakesi's uttariya which was bordered with small golden bells. Some of the bells were torn off and scattered in a jingle of confusion across the floor. The dasis ran to retrieve them, so did Suchak while Misrakesi stood with a patient smile on her face. Suchak picked up a few and gave them to Misrakesi with stammered excuses and a downcast face making good his escape. Misrakesi watched him go – something was not quite right.

She walked back slowly to the room where they slept and sat down on the bed. Absently she opened her closed palms and then stared transfixed. Between the small glittering bells also lay a plain gold ring. She had seen it before she thought as she quietly closed her palms again and asked the dasis to prepare the room for the night and leave them alone.

Pushyamitra walked in after seeing Suchak off and she went up to him and joined her lips to his in a deep kiss. He moulded her body to his and removed his lips only to issue a sharp command to the dasis to take themselves off. There were a few giggles at this, Pushyamitra had come to Misrakesi's bed in the night after a long time and many of the dasis sympathized with her on losing her husband to Kamasundari. They were happy to help in enticing her husband back and retired in a hurry.

'Out with it, Aryapatni, what is the secret of this sudden gush of affection?' he murmured against her lips. The familiar scent of Atimukta filled up his senses, her body fitted his with a rightness that felt like an anchor and suddenly he couldn't care less about their mission and its worries, just about holding her and loving her.

In response she delinked her hands from behind his shoulders and slid the ring onto one of his fingers. His eyes came alight as he saw it, he did not have to examine it to see the four snarling lions engraved on one side – he knew it was Siddharthak's ring.

'Well, well who would have thought it of Suchak? He is our contact here! What a clever boy he is! Now we can move forward.'

'To keep the ring safe, I think it is best that you wear it around your neck on a chain.' He pushed away her uttariya and teased out a long thin golden chain that she was wearing. She stood passively as he passed the ring into the chain and slipped it inside her kanchuki. His bead was lying against her throat gleaming against her skin as it never had against his.

His hands were cold against her and she shivered involuntarily.

Pushyamitra was looking at her with narrowed eyes, 'What is the matter with you, Misrakesi? There is a depression where your stomach used to be and I can feel your hip bones jutting out. I can almost span your waist with my hands,' and he held her by the waist to prove his point. 'You are looking ill.'

Misrakesi looked down at herself. It was true although she had not noticed it. Her curves were turning into angles.

Pushyamitra was looking unhappy and displeased. He picked her up and sat on the bed. 'Don't do this Misrakesi. It must be because of that maharani of yours with her ascetic lifestyle but you are not a queen who can afford these whims. If we had to run away tonight you would not even last a few hours. I am getting some food for you which you must eat immediately.'

Misrakesi made a gesture to stop him. She was on his lap, leaning against his chest with her head on his shoulders and tracing his collarbone. She had missed him. If he thought that the reason for her faded looks was the maharani she was not about to enlighten him, she would die before she told him that it was his absence which was doing this to her; that she missed him, that images of him with Kamasundari would not let her sleep or eat and that her calm and sensible exterior hid a very different reality.

She tightened her grip on his shoulders as a storm of emotions overwhelmed her. 'Just hold me now.'

'There is nothing left to hold,' Pushyamitra grumbled even as he complied. Misrakesi rubbed her lips against his shoulder where there was a faint mark from a passionate bite, hers, or was it Kamasundari's? Pushyamitra had tilted her head back so that he could kiss the lovely slim line of her throat. Although her eyes were closed she felt herself thrumming violently with something which was a volatile mixture of anger and desire.

'Don't go to sleep on me, please. I want you, I need you just now,' Pushyamitra mouthed on her creamy skin.

She opened her eyes which were bright with desire and a peculiar light he could not quite understand, and gave a throaty little laugh, 'Sleep! Not on your life!'

Her hand snaked into his hair and pulled it till his eyes smarted.

Pushyamitra frowned as he arched his head away. Misrakesi deliberately raked his back with her nails and sank her teeth into his bottom lip to draw blood. She slashed at his chest and pushed him down, his lower lip caught between her teeth. She was astride him now, sitting on him with a force that pushed his breath from his body.

'Oof!' Pushyamitra pulled her down on him as he fell. Her mouth was at his neck, not to love but to hurt.

Pushyamitra felt his temper rise. What was Misrakesi up to? He sat up and pulled her away from his body, pinning her hands together and twisting her hair around one wrist to stop her from biting him.

'What is the matter with you?' his voice started on a heated note but tapered off as he looked at her and the picture she was making imprinted itself in his eyes. He felt himself quicken; her lips were parted, teeth clenched, chest heaving agitatedly with an unnamed emotion and eyes flaming at him, her legs had clamped themselves around his hips like a vise. They had both lost their clothes somewhere along the way.

'Don't even try anything.' He growled threateningly deep in his throat as his hands moved to squeeze her waist cruelly, 'I can tear you apart with my bare hands.'

'Do it then,' she challenged him in a fierce whisper, 'Let us see who can tear the other apart.'

His hands were already at her waist and he detached her legs in a single decided sweep then roughly joined her body to his. Her arms flailed and she struggled to break his grip pushing at his shoulders and kicking her legs but he was too strong for her. Even as he thrust himself in and out of her forcefully, he, in turn brought his mouth down and bit her hard while twisting her arms behind her back with one hand.

As his teeth met mercilessly on her skin and her arms were ruthlessly twisted, the unwilling moans of pleasure being dragged out of Misrakesi changed into a cry of pain and tears started from her eyes.

'Oh, what have I done? Don't cry Priye, please, I am sorry.' Pushyamitra was distraught, all his anger vanishing in a stream of remorse.

He kissed her while Misrakesi held her breath, waiting for the pain to subside. He cradled her in his arms and muttered endearments, pressing small kisses on her while she sobbed her heart out, not too sure what she was crying about.

'Forgive me, my dearest, please. I ought to be whipped for doing this. I am a fool and a villain to use you so. Your body is my own precious flower, to be loved and protected. Can you ever forgive me?'

Misrakesi heard his voice through her own tears, and the tumultuous beating of his heart against which her face was pressed. Were these the words she had actually wanted to hear? Why had she provoked him so?

He laid her on the bed and caressed her, his touch was like rain on the parched earth and her over-stimulated body quietened down while he went on soothing it. Misrakesi was carried along from crest to crest, her world moved planes, she reached fulfillment again and again, moaning and heaving as she lay on the bed, hands crossed across her stomach.

She lay there quietly, spent in the aftermath of intense satisfaction. She felt herself being picked up and wrapped in a soft wool blanket. Pushyamitra came out and sat down outside on a couch holding her securely in his arms.

'Misrakesi,' he asked, 'what happened?'

She shifted and sat down next to him, their shoulders touching but not quite.

'Nothing, nothing at all; just a mood. I should say sorry,' she looked down at her fingers, 'I was angry.'

Pushyamitra shook his head, 'Yes, but why?'

He waited expectantly for an answer but Misrakesi continued to examine her fingers and polish her nails.

'Look at me.'

Their eyes met without any pretences and Pushyamitra got up with an exclamation of impatience, coming back to kneel in front of the couch.

'You *know* why...' his fists were clenched and lips set in a grim line, 'and you were the one who...'

Misrakesi interrupted him before he could continue, 'I am cold. I will wear some clothes and come.' She slipped off the couch and went in, leaving him to pace restlessly up and down.

He had never been in such a situation before and had never troubled himself to think about how his sleeping with one woman would affect another; he was torn between irritation and a new understanding. Did Kamasundari not often melt into the warm honey of Misrakesi in his arms when he closed his eyes?

Misrakesi was taking her time tying her antariya and throwing on an uttariya chastising herself all the while. Far from never telling Pushyamitra of her own reactions here she was, behaving perilously out of character. It was against all that she had been taught. This was just an assignment, she reminded herself, and she was working with a man who was her chief, the rest was incidental. She remembered that she was a ganika and went out with a smile.

She went and sat next to him where he was sitting pre-occupied, her fingers brushed over his back where angry red marks had already appeared and his neck where there were still small spots of dried blood. A cooling and healing aloe vera preparation was skilfully massaged onto his neck and back. She was an expert masseuse second to none; Pushyamitra lay on his stomach and was treated to one of the most relaxing and invigorating massages he had ever had.

'There you are then; this should be fine in a day or two. Will you forgive me and forget that this ever happened?'

He got up and shook his head moodily, 'No, I cannot forget it. I cannot forget that I lost my temper and hurt you. It was unpardonable.' He removed her uttariya to stroke her arms contritely.

He sat her down on the couch and in turn smoothed balm onto her.

'At least I have learnt enough to never challenge you again. I don't think I can win,' said Misrakesi smiling, trying to lighten the situation.

'Do you think so? I thought you had won. I certainly seem to be rapidly losing.' He was frowning as he gathered her into the wool blanket and sat hugging her close.

They were quiet, in some kind of temporary accord again and their thoughts moved on to their work. Both of them knew that their personal issues were of no import before the challenging task in front of them.

Their weapons were slowly coming to hand, now they had to be unleashed. They were entering a crucial phase of their covert war and it would be necessary to plan their steps with great care.

Dhritrashtra's Court

O Govinda... O destroyer of all afflictions
O Janardan rescue me who am sinking in the Kaurava ocean
O thou great yogin, thou soul of the universe
Thou creator of all things, O Govinda
Save me who am distressed.

Draupadi's cheer-haran lament from the Sabha Parva, Mahabharata

Pushyamitra awoke with a start; Misrakesi was gone, but only as far as the terrace. She was leaning against the wooden balustrade looking out at the river. He went up to stand behind her and hold her in his arms. He rested his chin on her head and said, 'So what conclusion have you come to?'

'It is time to take decisive action,' she said turning large and serious eyes to his. 'Although I cannot like it.'

'Misrakesi,' his voice was stern as he turned her around to face him. 'I thought we had completed the discussion on this. We really do not have a better alternative with a chance of succeeding. This is what has been decided and you will not help by raising doubts within yourself now. Again, remember, the decision is not yours to make.'

'Pushyamitra, how can you do it? Drink, dice and act as his friend one day, and the next...'

'Oh, with no trouble at all,' said Pushyamitra with a cold smile. 'In the current circumstances I do not have to do the killing personally but I would do it without a qualm, that is my job. If I may remind you, so is it yours, and these hesitations and doubts do you no good.'

She was silent, acknowledging the truth of what he was saying but not really convinced. 'Would you kill me as easily if need be?'

He shrugged his shoulders impatiently and said, 'Where is the question of killing you? Have you forgotten that we are both fighting for the same motherland? Steady yourself Misrakesi and concentrate on the work at hand. This is not the time for misplaced scruples.'

She turned away and nodded, saying, 'I know, but I cannot kill.'

'Find out about the maharani's next trip to any vihara or pilgrimage place and keep me informed. When are you going to give her the acharya's message?'

'The time is not ripe now. I will wait.'

They had a meal together where Pushyamitra insisted on his orders being followed so that Misrakesi ate a full meal washed down with a pot of milk after many days. When he was bent on feeding her with figs and grapes she protested, 'I admit I have not been eating for some time but I cannot eat for one week in one day. I promise to be careful. Spare me for now,' and she raised her hands in surrender.

'Well, as long as you remember. You must get back your strength as quickly as possible. You are not here to be a sanyasini, you know.'

They prepared to go off to their posts again. Pushyamitra's face was also showing signs of strain and Misrakesi held him close for a moment. 'We will win through, won't we?' she whispered softly.

'Yes.' He replied grimly, 'but be very careful. I sense from the atmosphere in the palace that we are the objects of grave suspicion and it is only the maharani and perhaps the senapati who are acting as a restraining factor or we would be in prison. In spite of their giggling and laughing the dasis are vigilant and suspicious. The ring is like a live ember, guard it with your life, it may mean your life.'

Misrakesi's shringar was of a perfunctory nature that day and she refused assistance from the dasis as far as possible. The ring nestled securely between her breasts under her kanchuki and she wanted to leave it there.

The maharani greeted her affectionately and asked after her torn uttariya.

Nothing, absolutely nothing in this palace was secret, thought Misrakesi vexed. Outwardly she laughed merrily and replied, 'The boy is young yet, maharaniji, enough to be taken in even by my poor youth and beauty. The bells can easily be stitched on again. In fact, I think they have been recovered and the uttariya is being repaired.' She had left the few bells she had had in her palms ostentatiously scattered around the bed.

Eager to change the topic she asked after the king's health. The maharani's face fell and she sighed sorrowfully, 'I have been praying and fasting for my father's recovery. His condition is not worsening but not showing the improvement it should.'

'Is it possible to go to a pilgrimage and offer special prayers? The Maaheshwar Sthan near my native Ujjain and of course Urubela Teerth near Magadha are very powerful places,' suggested Misrakesi disingenuously.

'Yes, there is the vihara of Sage Ananda. I have been thinking of going there. It is slightly far and I did not want to leave my father alone overnight but now perhaps it is time I went. I am willing to do anything that may help.'

'The hermitage of Sage Ananda. I know about it. Akshay once told me.' It was a slip and she realized it at once but maintained a serene face and went on, 'He is my adopted brother and has travelled extensively in this area. That is how I know some things about this area.'

The maharani was preoccupied with her father's health and considering plans for going to the vihara. It was taken for granted that Misrakesi would accompany her, subject to her husband's permission. The talk veered to details and Misrakesi breathed an internal sigh of relief. She did not notice the arrested look on one of the dasi's faces. The day passed as usual and Misrakesi went back to her own quarters at night, with an unexpressed hope that Pushyamitra would also come back today.

He did not come back, however, and she lay sleepless and alone in her bed. She was not able to sleep properly and drifted in and out of an uneasy doze.

Pushyamitra was gambling desultorily with the senapati, Shreedhan, and a few others. There was wine at his elbow and he was trying his best to be the life of the party. Kamasundari was still finishing her performance in the public hall or perhaps she was involved with a client. She had not put in an appearance yet.

The senapati put Pushyamitra's dullness at her door and said rallyingly, 'Be careful, my friend, I hope you are not in danger of losing your heart to her. She will break your heart in two and toss it back. Enjoy her, but keep her at a distance. You seem to be too struck.'

Pushyamitra acknowledged the advice with raised eyebrows, 'I hope I am too experienced for that. But I must admit that your Kamasundari is...'

The sentence remained unfinished as the woman in question herself walked in, bringing in her own aura and concentrating attention on herself effortlessly. Pushyamitra got up and stretched,

'Devi, my apologies. It is late and I am off to seek my own bed.'

'How can you leave just as I have come in? That will be unfair to me.' The voice was soft, intimate, only for him. She held his hand and pulled him close, murmuring, 'One cup of wine from my hands, and one kiss for me.' A cup of wine appeared in her hands as if by itself and she took a sip, offering the cup to Pushyamitra after that. He allowed himself to be persuaded by her.

Very soon, they had retired to her private room where she went through her nightly massage, inviting Pushyamitra to join her, exposing her perfect body to his appreciative and increasingly aroused gaze. The night passed and he did not return to the palace as he had decided to.

Misrakesi awoke before the morning light to the steady tramp of a contingent of soldiers. They stopped outside her apartment and she strained her ears to listen without moving. There was a whispered consultation with Lavanika, the dasi for the night, and then the door was rudely thrown open and her chamber was full of soldiers holding unsheathed swords.

Misrakesi sat up with her chadar clutched to her chin and snapped, 'What is this? Who are you and how dare you enter my sleeping chamber like this?'

The captain replied gruffly, 'We have been sent by the Maha Amatya Narsingh Dev to enforce your immediate attendance in the Sabha Griha where he is waiting to question you on a very serious matter relating to the security of the kingdom.'

Misrakesi understood, this was the consequence of what she had thought was a small slip. She spoke, however, in a calm dignified voice, 'Is this the way women are treated in the land of the Purus where once Pururavas gave his life for Urvashi? Leave my chamber now and tell your Maha Amatya I will come to his Sabha Griha in the morning, properly dressed and at a seemly hour with my husband. Go now.'

Her mind was working furiously. She was certainly going to be dragged to the Sabha Griha, by force if necessary, and she would have to inform the maharani in some way if she was to save herself. Lavanika was the only one who could take her message to the maharani, but she was looking carefully expressionless and refusing to meet Misrakesi's eyes.

The captain had his orders and was not to be moved. He repeated roughly, 'I am to enforce your immediate attendance under all circumstances.'

Misrakesi looked around desperately, she was wearing just a mulmul cloth around her hips. Was she going to meet a fate worse than Draupadi and be dragged to the Sabha Griha like this?

Lavanika was frowning now, uncomfortable with the situation. The captain and his soldiers walked up closer to the bed and he made a movement as if to advance upon Misrakesi. At this Lavanika's face suddenly changed and she burst out, 'Have you no shame, you, Captain. Is this the way to behave with a guest of maharani Shailanandini? Are you another Dusshasan to make a Draupadi of her? Stand back.'

The mention of the maharani gave a stop to the captain who hesitated. Misrakesi seized her advantage and snapped out in a furious voice, 'Wait outside. Since your Maha Amatya is unaware of the respect owed to women and guests in this kingdom, I shall get dressed and come with you alone even at this hour of the night. Out with you.'

After an uncertain moment and put on the defensive by the maharani's name as well as the accusing looks of the two women the captain said, 'I am waiting outside, but only for a few moments; I shall come in and drag you out after that.'

Misrakesi left the bed and dressed herself rapidly, conscious of the incriminating ring next to her skin. Then she said to Lavanika, 'I am going to the Sabha Griha. I do not know what the matter is and what they have planned for me. Why was I not being allowed to get dressed? You are the only one between me and dishonour. See if you can inform the maharani about what is happening. Otherwise I am in the hands of Lord Krishna.'

Misrakesi's mind was cold and sharp as the permanent snows of Mount Kailas and she called upon the Goddess Shree to give her strength. She had herself well under control in spite of the waves of panic rising up inside. She could not let Magadha down. And she prayed that Lavanika would inform the maharani.

She was surrounded by sword-wielding soldiers; two of them tried to catch hold of her by the shoulders but were repelled by her fiery glance. They had obviously been ordered to intimidate and subdue her, but she would not let herself be beaten down. She had won one victory in dressing herself properly and would preempt the captain again.

'Let us go. What are we waiting for?' She ordered in cold tones, interrupting the captain's barked out commands and walking off ahead of all the soldiers, looking more like a warrior queen than a prisoner.

As she moved across the palace towards the Sabha Griha, Pushyamitra stirred and opened his eyes beside Kamasundari on her bed. Maybe it was time to go back, he thought stretching and yawning. He thought of Misrakesi's drawn face of the previous night, his eyes staring into the darkness and decided to get up.

The Sabha Griha was lined with more soldiers. Sitting on his usual chair beside the empty throne was a menacing Narsingh Dev. Along with him were three or four more older mantris and some junior palace officials including Suchak who was looking straight ahead with a seemingly vindictive light shining from his eyes.

Misrakesi walked up straight to Narsingh Dev, ignoring the rest of the assembly. She put her hands together in a humble pranaam, 'Greetings, Maha Amatya. I, Misrakesi, citizen of Magadha and a guest of Maharani Shailanandini in Kaikeya, have come here in answer to your untimely summons. To what do I owe this honour in the middle of the night? I would have come even without the contingent of soldiers, your command would have been enough. Here I am, a woman alone, without the protection of her husband, in front of venerable high officers of Kaikeya and enough soldiers to quell an uprising, let alone a delicate, solitary woman. What is your will?'

This speech was delivered in an affronted but dignified tone and many of the men there looked shamefaced. The charges against her as described by Narsingh Dev were extremely serious and had persuaded them to be part of this assembly but... were they true? She was young enough to be their daughter, obviously defenceless but with a proud and innocent bearing.

Narsingh Dev transfixed her with his eagle eyes, 'You are accused of conspiring against the Kingdom of Kaikeya.'

'False. Not once but a thousand times. On what evidence do you base this accusation?' was the confident reply.

'Do you deny that you and your husband belong to Magadha, an enemy of Kaikeya?'

'Far from denying it, I stated it when I entered this Sabha Griha. My husband Pushyamitra Sunga of Magadha has his differences with the administration and we have come here to ask for the protection of Kaikeya. Do you deny that you have given us no opportunity to place the information we wish to trade before the Mantri Parishad?' shot back Misrakesi.

The mantris looked thoughtful and Narsingh Dev confounded at this counter-charge; but he pressed on, 'Do you deny that in league with Akshay, the senapati of Magadha's armies you are conspiring to overthrow this kingdom?'

This startled Misrakesi, but she calmly replied, 'I certainly do. The senapati of Magadha's army is Arya Agnimitra Sunga, my husband's elder brother who is in Magadha and has sent us as emissaries to discuss terms for his turning over to Kaikeya.'

There was a collective gasp from the other mantris and they turned burning eyes to Narsingh Dev. A very important piece of state information had been kept from them.

'Mantrigana, do not be taken in by this woman, she is as dangerous as a nagin,' thundered Narsingh Dev, trying to wrest the initiative back from Misrakesi. He gestured to two soldiers who stepped forward, one to twist her arms behind her back and the other to hold his sword blade at her throat. Misrakesi could have been carved from stone.

'Who is Akshay?'

'My brother, who has nothing to do with any army but is an acharya in Ujjain.'

'You are lying. Akshay was a student of the Takshshila Gurukul with Chandragupta, a student of Vishnugupta. You do not have any family.'

'And yet, Maha Amatya, there may be men in this world who look upon a dancing girl as a sister,' was the scornful answer.

Narsingh Dev frustration and anger were rising. In response to his signals the pressure on Misrakesi's neck had increased and she could hardly speak, her voice was emerging as a croak. One of the mantris stood up as if to put an end to the situation but Narsingh Dev ordered, 'Search her.'

Misrakesi knew she was lost.

Pushyamitra rode up to the palace entrance and gave his horse to a waiting dasa. The guards at the door looked at him and looked away. One of them made as if to speak but another stopped him with a glance. Pushyamitra was instantly suspicious and his hand went to his sword hilt. As he moved towards their quarters Lavanika came running up; she spoke and his heart lurched, fists balling up as he raced towards the Sabha Griha.

Misrakesi was standing alone in the middle of the Sabha Griha. Her uttariya was wrenched off and thrown to the ground. The soldier searching her put his hands to her throat, Pushyamitra's bead came to his hand and he stopped for a moment, intrigued, before pulling at the thin chain holding the ring.

That was Misrakesi's redemption. In that instant a voice rang out across the Sabha Griha, 'Stop. Immediately....' The voice was shaking with fury and the soldier sprang away from Misrakesi as if she was a burning fire. It was the maharani.

She swept up to Narsingh Dev's chair and he stood up with his hands coming together to greet her.

'How dare you, Narsingh Dev!' hissed the maharani and even Narsingh Dev looked shaken and took a step back.

'All the soldiers here have my permission to retire immediately,' commanded the maharani and the room was empty in moments.

'How dare you Narsingh Dev? You have gone too far this time and the king shall hear of it. What is this? Dhritrashtra's court convened in the middle of the night? A room full of mantris and soldiers against a defenceless woman. My father is old and ill but not blind yet and the Purus have never dishonoured a woman as you have done today. I have lost a lifetime of respect for you today.'

Narsingh Dev tried to speak and the other mantris hung their heads. No evidence had emerged of any complicity with Kaikeya's enemies and it did seem as if the entire assembly had been a farce to dishonour the wife of a Magadhan royal official and a guest of the maharani.

Misrakesi had been coughing and trying to recover her breath. The sword had cut the side of her neck and there was a thin line of dripping blood. Reaction set in and she swayed putting a hand to her forehead.

There was a murmur and commotion outside the Sabha Griha and Pushyamitra came in like an avenging God. He ignored everyone and went up to Misrakesi. He picked up her uttariya and put it around her shoulders with compressed lips and in silence. Then he picked her up in his arms and turned to face Narsingh Dev.

He looked like an incarnation of the Lord Skanda,[65] fury emanating from his eyes and hitting the Sabha Griha like a physical blow. His words were like a shower of arrows.

'I formally rescind all proposals made to the Kaikeya Kingdom. I refuse your hospitality and shall not stay here for even a moment more. The insult offered to my wife and to my honour is intolerable and I swear upon my ancestors that I shall avenge it. From this instant Kaikeya is my implacable enemy now and forever.'

And he started to walk out of the Sabha Griha. His way was barred by the maharani whose hands were folded and tears were running down her face. 'Stop, Arya Pushyamitra. Do not curse this unfortunate Kaikeya any more, I beg of you. How the Purus have fallen, to see this terrible farce enacted in the Sabha Griha where once the proud Paurava was the arbiter of honour in this world. Forgive us, I offer the abject apologies of my father, the king who lies ill and unaware of this travesty. Give us a chance to wash off this stigma, I beg you,' and she bent her head in front of Pushyamitra.

'Maharaniji, please do not bend in front of me, your subject,' said Pushyamitra genuinely shocked. Her tears served to cool down his fury and he returned to a realization of his situation, he had to stay in Kaikeya to complete the mission.

'Then you will forgive us and stay?' asked the maharani anxiously, 'I will not be able to bear it if you take my little sister away and leave us in disgrace. Let me make it up to her and to you.'

'Your wish is my command,' he said tersely as he looked down at the swooning Misrakesi.

'Bring her to my apartment. I will send for the Vaidyaraj at once. As for you Narsingh Dev, you shall hear more of this.' She stalked out followed by Pushyamitra with Misrakesi in his arms.

Narsingh Dev could only grind his teeth in frustration and anger. He would never know how close he had been to victory. The mantris were left to make their way back thoughtfully, pondering on their own roles and the correctness or otherwise of what had happened. The soldiers were standing at attention outside.

Misrakesi was laid down tenderly on the maharani's bed. She opened her eyes to look into Pushyamitra's intense ones who asked, 'Are you all right?'

She tried to clear her throat and say something, she put her hand to the side of her neck and it came away red with blood. The maharani uttered an exclamation of distress and Pushyamitra's eyes went blind with rage. He stood up with his hand to his sword hilt, ready to kill the soldiers who had marked Misrakesi.

'Don't, please.' Her voice was a whisper and she tried to hold his arm. He shook it away and looked at her with remote eyes.

'Maharaniji, please take care of her for some time. I shall be back very soon.' After decimating the contingent of soldiers which had dared to dishonour Misrakesi.

'Lie still, my dear. Let him do what he has to. It is his duty. Let the Vaidyaraj attend to you.' The maharani gently pushed her back to the bed when she would have risen. It was not the fault of the soldiers, they had merely been following orders.

Her wound was cleaned and anointed with a healing paste. She was given a reviving cordial to drink. The maharani herself sat beside her, chafing her hands and looking at her anxiously. The palace and the ranivas were in an uproar. Morning came without any of the routine being followed.

'Misrakesi , how can I ever look you in the face again? That this should have happened while you were under my protection! Will you ever be able to forgive me?'

Misrakesi gave a wan smile and pressed the maharani's hands. It was still difficult for her to speak.

'I have given instructions for you to be guarded by soldiers from my personal household. All the dasas and dasis will also be from my establishment. No one will be able to harm you now. You just need to rest and recover.'

The sun was high up in the sky when Pushyamitra came back. He was unrecognizable; he had fought with and single-handedly killed the captain and all the soldiers of the contingent which had dragged Misrakesi to the assembly. The soldier who had marked Misrakesi's throat had come in for a particularly brutal death. Misrakesi could not repress a shudder as she looked at him.

Her apartment had been cleared up and there were no signs of forced entry or her hurried exit. She was lying on her own bed. The intrusive staff had been replaced and they were alone in their inside quarters.

Pushyamitra sat at her side. He asked her in a controlled voice, 'What happened?'

This was a Pushyamitra she knew only too well, the chief of the Nagarik Suraksha Vibhag, her supervisor, asking for a report.

She told him all that had happened during the day and night including her mention of Akshay. His face darkened when he heard that, 'That was a mistake, Misrakesi, which I do not expect from you. And that too, after I had repeatedly warned you to be careful.' He was back to being the authoritative chief.

Misrakesi was still shaken and far more scared than she would admit even to herself. As usual, all her guilt fled at being faulted and she snapped back, 'I am well aware of that Arya Pushyamitra, I can only offer you my abject apologies. Perhaps you would like to remove me from this assignment?'

'Do not be childish, Misrakesi.'

Misrakesi went on, in the grip of anger, 'I did get myself into trouble but extricated myself without your expert intervention, thank you very much.'

Pushyamitra's face went white and he stood up with a jerk, he had been in Kamasundari's bed while Misrakesi was being dragged, mauled and humiliated. She was right; he had not been of any use.

Misrakesi saw the look but was too worked up to stop.

'Since I have had to pay for my mistake most terribly and will probably carry this scar to my dying day you can be certain that I will be as careful as I can possibly be. But unfortunately, I am unlike you, a mere maanav prone to mistakes and not a Deva. Now if you will excuse me I have had a very crowded and long night and would lie to rest for a while.' She turned her back to him and closed her eyes.

He paced up and down, lashed by guilt and a useless rage at the events. If only he had not stopped at Kamasundari's bidding, if only he had come back earlier and been at Misrakesi's side she would not have had to go through all this alone. He would have taken the blows instead of her. He had failed her and she was going to have a scar to remember that for life. Not prone to errors indeed, his had been the error to leave her alone and unprotected. He had done nothing to save her either, it was the maharani who had come as Lord Krishna himself.

But why had she been so careless? He was furious with her and even more with himself, in such a terrible turmoil that killing all those soldiers had been a lucky vent for his feelings. She did not approve of that either.

In one corner of the vast bed Misrakesi lay curled up into a ball, there was an empty space between her and Pushyamitra. She was angry with herself for being at fault and with him for his fault-finding. And her mind was going into what could have happened to her which was making her feel small and frightened. How could she have made a slip like that? If the soldier searching her had not stopped for a moment at Pushyamitra's bead they would have been exposed, months of work by so many would have gone down the drain and the two of them... Her imagination baulked at the rest. She decided to distract herself, but how?

The wound at the side of her neck was throbbing painfully and her arms and shoulders were sore from the night's manhandling. Never had she felt less like getting up and facing the world, but there was work to do and she would have to get up. It was better than imagining the worst.

She called for a dasi to help her and tried to go through the motions of her daily bath and shringar, but gave up halfway through, slumping dispiritedly on to an asana. Pushyamitra sat and pretended not to watch her with brooding eyes. Misrakesi wished he would go away and leave her alone instead of watching her with his tiger's eyes. She needed time to recover.

There was an interruption. The maharani had sent a fresh salve prepared by the Vaidya raj for application on the cut; it would minimize the scar too. There was also a message that Misrakesi should spend the day resting and that the maharani would visit her in the evening. Misrakesi gave the dasi a faint smile and sent back a grateful message. Then she looked around for some help with the application. Before she could call a dasi, Pushyamitra had taken the pot of salve from her and made her sit on a low stool.

'Be still.' He said when she would have resisted. The cut was washed with water boiled with Neem leaves brought in by a dasi and anointed with the salve. Pushyamitra examined the cut carefully, it was superficial and by no means dangerous but painful and annoying, and no woman, least of all Misrakesi, should have a sword cut on her body.

Misrakesi looked at herself in the full-length polished silver mirror in front of her and a sudden realization hit her. This was the end. The end of her life as a ganika; the first requirement of a ganika was complete physical perfection. No flaws were allowed to mar the beauty of a ganika's body and face and she had now sacrificed that perfection that had been hers since birth. The scar at her throat, even if a faint one would disqualify her from the community of ganikas. What would become of her?

She could see Pushyamitra watching her in the mirror and she quickly composed herself. There would be time enough to mourn her lost career if and when they emerged from this danger.

'Misrakesi, Misrakesi...' He whispered, 'It will go away, there will not be a mark on your body. Give it some time.' She nodded without looking at him and made to get up.

But he continued to stroke her aching head and soothe her aching shoulders and arms till she relaxed against his supportive body. Perhaps his hands and her body understood each other.

There was another interruption. A dasi came in to announce that Senapati Bhattaraka had come to enquire after Arya Pushyamitra's wife. The two of them exchanged a look. Events had started to unfold and this was a chance to take advantage of what had happened, if they could. Pushyamitra gave her shoulders a squeeze and went out. Misrakesi decided to rest for some more time before going to the maharani's quarters.

There were many visitors and numerous expressions of support throughout the day. The story had spread like wildfire through the palace and in the city and Narsingh Dev's prestige had taken a knock. The maharani's tirade against him was being repeated endlessly. Suchak had been careful to spread a word-by-word account.

The Mantri Parishad was tied up in knots discussing what Misrakesi had revealed about Pushyamitra's proposal and why Narsingh Dev had not informed them of it. This was a bad miscalculation on his part, and had sown doubts about his motives. Was he hoping to use the confidential information for his own benefit? And why had he targeted an innocent and defenceless young woman in this brutal manner. Was it true that he had been smitten by her beauty and angered by her refusal of his love proposal? There were as many stories as there were mouths.

Misrakesi had kept herself to her own apartment. By the afternoon, she had developed a fever and slight inflammation of the cut which worried the vaidya and he had dosed her with stronger medicine. She had sent her apologies to the maharani who had come hurrying to see her, and then was advised urgently to rest.

Pushyamitra came back as evening fell to find Misrakesi feverish and restless, walking in the little garden below the rooms. It was a flat projection of the mountain and commanded an unparalleled view of the Vitasta hurling herself over the rocks. A small pavilion had been made for enjoying the view and Misrakesi was pacing around this in spite of the instructions of the Vaidyaraj and the entreaties of the dasis. He went out to call her in.

'I do not want to go in. The walls are running in on me and I am feeling choked. I want some air.'

'All right, but at least sit down on the steps for a while.'

She sat down on the steps leading down to the river and Pushyamitra put his heavy woollen uttariya around her shoulders.

He sat down at her feet and looked up at her with a peculiar light shining deep in his eyes.

'Pushyamitra, tell me what has been happening. I have not met anyone except the maharani. The dasis are all new and keep a deferential distance. Which is of course a major relief and we can talk freely now.'

'The entire city is abuzz with this incident. Narsingh Dev's prestige has taken a knock from which I will see that it never recovers. There is massive speculation as to the reason for his actions. Your little slip has paved the way for our position to be strengthened as innocent and unfairly targeted. We can use it as a breakthrough and use our plan to discredit him completely.'

'I can still not understand why he did this? He must have hoped to throw me completely off balance and break down under questioning.'

'Yes, his instincts do not trust us but he has no evidence against us. This was an attempt to get that evidence. Instead of which, because you held out and, from what I can gather, turned the tables neatly on him, it is now his motives which are being questioned. Dropping our proposal into the Sabha Griha was a good idea.' He had taken her delicate and soft feet into his lap and was caressing them, his hands going up to her ankles and calves, his expression concentrated.

He looked up and laughed, 'Narsingh Dev does not deign to defend himself. Suchak is doing that for him, and in the process spreading canards each worse than the last under the pretext of denying them. He is a really talented boy. I will have to see about putting him in an appropriate place once we win through.'

She was leaning against a wall and her small feet were lost in Pushyamitra's big hands. His fingers were stroking and squeezing the pressure points on the soles of her feet warming her and relaxing her body but Misrakesi was always uncomfortable when Pushyamitra touched her feet, although he seemed to love it.

'Don't touch my feet,' she said.

His grip tightened and he asked, 'Why? This will help to ease your pain and fever.'

'I do not know, it just does not seem right.'

'I can touch your feet, you know, I can even kiss them.' And he touched his lips to her toes.

'Do you know it was probably your bead which saved me, and us? If that soldier had not been distracted for those crucial moments he would have found the ring before the maharani's entry and then even she would not have been able to do anything for us.' Misrakesi said after a while, placing a hand on the bent head before her.

'It has never let me down. And it will never let you down either, even if I do sometimes.' This was spoken sorrowfully and Misrakesi slipped down to raise his head.

'I am sorry I spoke to you like that in the morning. I was wrong, you were doing what you were supposed to do and how were you to know what was happening here? You are not Sanjaya, are you?'

His face was hard and glance glittering, 'I will never forgive myself even if you do. I was about to come back early but stopped when Kamasundari insisted. All this happened to you because of that delay.'

'I am not your responsibility but your partner.'

'You are mine to protect and I failed.'

Misrakesi was silent for a while, her head on his shoulder. Then she said, 'Think of how it is helping. In the end it was a good thing that this happened, wasn't it?'

'We would have thought of something else. You should not have had to sacrifice yourself. Come, I will take you inside now.'

They stood up to go in and he took her face in both his hands and tilted it up, 'I will make it up to you, I swear. I shall destroy that man yet.' And Misrakesi recognized the peculiar light in his eyes to be one of revenge.

'He shall end his days in ignominy and isolation. And this Kaikeya, too, shall be destroyed.'

'Sssh, Pushyamitra.' Misrakesi looked around nervously.

'I may have agreed to stop here but I have taken a vow which you will see fulfilled.'

'Don't, please do not talk like this, and don't make any promises. There is no need. I will recover. And we have a long fight before us which is just beginning. I have to recover as soon as possible.'

Pushyamitra enfolded her tightly in his arms and said softly against her hair, 'The battle has begun in earnest now, but just wait till we finish off these Kaikeyans.'

The Secret Weapon

As a bird is captured by a bait in the form of a bird, enemies should be destroyed by creating trust and offering a bait.

Arthashastra

~

Misrakesi bent her considerable will power to recovering as fast as possible, and in a few days, was allowed to move around in the palace and then, even outside. A date had been fixed for the visit to the vihara of Sage Ananda. Misrakesi agreed that she was not very well but professed a wish to visit the hermitage to calm herself after the ordeal and the maharani could not refuse her request. Special arrangements were made for her comfort.

It had become imperative for Pushyamitra to consult Suchak, especially since the date for the visit to the vihara had been decided. The meeting would have to be organized by Suchak since he was the one who had the resources.

Pushyamitra had stopped going out at night for a few days after the incident in spite of being chided by Misrakesi.

'I am only human, no matter what you may always have thought of me. And I cannot leave you alone, sick and weak.'

'But I am very well protected. All the dasis are from the maharani's entourage and fiercely loyal to her, and therefore to me. The palace security has also been taken away from Narsingh Dev and handed over to the senapati. Our apartments are guarded by the maharani's personal guards. Who can do anything to me now?'

'Don't argue, just rest.'

Pushyamitra was also satisfied that events were moving in the direction that he wanted. He could let them alone for a few days. The maharani had obviously spoken to the king about Narsingh Dev. Although Narsingh Dev appeared unperturbed, his power and influence with the king were on the wane. The maharani became all powerful and as a consequence the senapati was also called by the king on a few occasions and all decisions were no longer taken by Narsingh Dev. Taking the palace security away from him was a big blow to him but he did not show any emotion. As another consequence, the vigilance and spying on Misrakesi and Pushyamitra had also ceased and they had much more leeway in carrying out their plan.

As Misrakesi gained in strength, Pushyamitra decided to resume his normal routine and his visits to Kamasundari and see what was going on in that circle.

She met him with many professions of sympathy and support and was loud in her condemnation of Narsingh Dev.'He has become an autocrat and lost all his sense of values in his ambition to be the king maker, even king. It is high time he was removed from his position as Maha Amatya.' And someone from their group installed was the subtext.

There was a mood of jubilation in their circle, their arch enemy had been brought down, the senapati's star was on the rise. It was in a large measure due to their decision to support Pushyamitra and use him against Narsingh Dev; the strategy had worked.

Pushyamitra nodded his head and agreed forcefully. 'You can count on my support.'

'And that of your brother perhaps?' asked the senapati.

'Senapati, I have been waiting for some signal from Kaikeya to send word to my brother, but I have received none. What should I tell him?'

The senapati nodded thoughtfully. We are working on a plan to oust Narsingh Dev. I give you my word that we will arrive at some arrangement with you and your brother. Give me some time to firm up my plans.'

Pushyamitra was well content to wait. He had his own plans to firm up. As they were leaving together that night there was a tinkling sound of anklets and they turned to find a veiled female figure following them. She was young and comely and her veil ended just above her breasts, leaving her undoubted charms on display. She stopped as the two men turned and gave a tinkling laugh pointing at Pushyamitra. She beckoned to him and started off towards a dark veethi to the side.

'I think she is one of the women who works in Kamasundari's establishment and she has obviously taken a fancy to you,' said the senapati guffawing. 'Go on try your luck.' He was very fond of sexual adventures and in favour of sampling as many women as possible.

'Well, no harm in trying. Go on then and I will describe my encounter to you tomorrow.'

'Enjoy yourself, my friend.' The senapati was spending the night with one of his wives whose sexual appetite was as varied and voracious as his.

Slightly against his better judgement, Pushyamitra followed the girl down the veethi, keeping a distance from her. He had taken his sword out and was alert, shooting glances all around in case this was an attempt by Narsingh Dev to have him killed.

'Hurry up, it is not very far and there are people waiting for us,' hissed a familiar harsh and impatient voice completely at variance with the inviting body and Pushyamitra relaxed, it was Chandramukhi.

The veethi disappeared down an incline into the shadows and they entered a small house at the back of Kamasundari's dancing house. Chandramukhi shut the door and locked it as soon as they had entered. It was an ordinary enough house, but the two people sitting in the inner room were anything but ordinary. At the sight of the older man rising up at Suchak's side, his handsome face looking wryly amused; Pushyamitra's eyebrows drew together but he moved forward and the two men embraced.

'Siddharthak! What are you doing here? Have you lost your mind? We are in an enemy kingdom, not Magadha.'

'Relax. We are safe, in the house of this "dasi".' Siddharthak laughed and gestured towards Chandramukhi who had come in and was leaning against the wall with her uttariya back around her shoulders.

'Safe! If the three of us are found together it is the end of all of us. But now that we are here it is best that we confer and put everything in place.'

'Pushyamitra, is Misrakesi all right? Has she recovered? Suchak here told me that she had received a sword wound?' Siddharthak was full of concern.

'Yes, she is much better and ready to play her role.'

'She has really proved her mettle, anyone could have broken down in that situation but she turned the tables on Narsingh Dev. She is much tougher and smarter than I thought.'

'You have often underestimated her but yes, she did manage to escape by a whisker this time,' said Pushyamitra dismissively. He did not want to discuss Misrakesi's escape, it still gave him a cold shiver down his spine. 'Now let us get going, Suchak...'

Siddharthak, who understood Pushyamitra much more than the latter was comfortable with, gave him a speculative look but was silent. He also noted the absence of the bead and the thin white line on Pushyamitra's forearm.

It was much later that three shadows detached themselves from the small house and made their way back separately to their respective abodes.

Pushyamitra had a lot to think about. Siddharthak had brought him up to date on the movements from the Mauryan side. Akshay's army was waiting outside the borders of Kaikeya. The samrat had left from Magadha with the main army and was expected in Kaikeya in the near future. Events would have to be brought to a head before that.

There was worrying news, however, about movements in the Greek camp. Eudemos was the powerful Yavana satrap who had been given the command of the fort at Pushkalavati in the name of Peithon, the Yavana General in whose share Alakshendra's Indian territories west of the Indus had fallen. Pushkalavati was a major Gandharan stronghold a few days fast march from Kaikeya.

It seemed that he was making a bid to emerge as the leader of the scattered Yavana and Makdoonian soldiers and common people to establish Yavana rule again. It was doubtful if he had enough resources to achieve this but he could definitely make a difference to the game as it was being played out. Pushyamitra had sent advice to Akshay to try and hold off the Greeks, involve them in minor skirmishes and delay their arrival while he continued his moves in the city.

~

It was the day for the visit to the hermitage of Sage Ananda. The maharani accompanied by Misrakesi and a large group of royal women set out for the few hours long journey. They were to stay for a day and leave after praying for the health of the old king.

The hermitage was a peaceful and calm expanse of trees and rock-cut caves which served both as quarters for the bhikshus as also a place where pilgrims could stay. The entire royal party was settled in a part of the dharamshala.

The caves were decorated with beautiful paintings depicting events from the life of the Sakya Muni and Misrakesi could have spent forever looking at them. But she had work to do.

As the maharani sought the sage's personal blessings for her father, Misrakesi sat nervously under a tree and awaited developments. She had surrounded herself with dasis to provide witnesses to what was going to happen. She did not have to wait very long.

Groups of pilgrims were sitting around under the trees. At some distance, the bhikshus and bhikshunis were feeding the people who had come to seek the ashram's protection, the old, poor, indigent, sick and abandoned, a few struck by the diseases of the mind.

A woman wrapped in a white uttariya suddenly sprang up from this group and started running towards Misrakesi. Two bhikshunis restrained her but she struggled and screamed. The more they tried to calm her the more she struggled. Misrakesi was watching with some sympathy and she sent a dasi to find out what the problem was. The dasi came back with a surprised look on her face.

'She wants to meet you, Devi! The girl is an abandoned widow found wandering in the nearby forests. It seems she is from Magadha and someone told her today that a great lady from Magadha was here in this vihara. She has been begging to be allowed to meet you. She does not seem to be quite right in her senses, poor thing.'

'She is in distress,' said Misrakesi worriedly, 'How can I ignore her? Request the bhikshunis to bring her here and I will see if I can help.'

The dasi went off and two bhikshunis soon approached holding the woman between them. As they neared, the woman suddenly broke free and flung herself at Misrakesi's feet, sobbing loudly. She held Misrakesi's feet and would not let go. Misrakesi waved away the agitated bhikshunis and carefully raised the weeping figure.

'Hey Devi Uma, she is but a child!' She was, indeed, not more than sixteen and even in her coarse white dress the tear-streaked face was startlingly beautiful with dark, lotus eyes, moulded rosy lips and intoxicating youth breaking out from her every pore.

'Who is she?' asked Misrakesi

The bhikshunis shook their heads. 'She was found wandering in the forest and brought here by a passing traveller a few days ago. She does not seem to possess all her wits but keeps talking of Magadha. What fate left her alone in the forest we do not know,' said one of them sorrowfully.

The young girl had meanwhile curled herself into a ball and lay still clutching at Misrakesi's feet.

'I will take responsibility for this child,' said Misrakesi moved by the sight of the helpless woman. 'Wait here, my dear.' She patted the girl's head and disengaged her feet. 'Let me take permission from the maharani to take her back to the palace. She is very generous and will not refuse me.'

The maharani in her current mood would have tried to get the moon for Misrakesi had she expressed a desire for it; helping an abandoned woman was something her charitable soul delighted in.

She gave her immediate and gracious permission and the young girl was included in the royal party.

Misrakesi kept her close; she would not speak much but calmed down and was all smiles as soon as she understood that she was to stay with the lady from Magadha. The return journey was accomplished after two days. Anamika, for this was the name given to her by Misrakesi, travelled in Misrakesi's own ox-cart and reached the palace safely.

The sun had gone down by the time they reached the palace and Misrakesi ordered that the girl would sleep in her quarters. She was young and half-witted and would not be able to manage in the dasis' quarters.

Anamika was quiet and did not give anyone any trouble. She would sit staring at nothing or would make flower garlands and play with terracotta toys. She would also disappear into the trees outside the palace and she had even built herself a rudimentary shelter where she would sit singing songs to herself. In a very few, days she had ceased to be a novelty and was taken very much for granted as a protégé of Misrakesi's.

Pushyamitra took very good care to stay out of her way. Both of them were tense and on tenterhooks when in their apartments. Certain unusual items were slowly delivered to Misrakesi and passed on to Anamika. She was also fond of very strong and coarse prasanna which she would drink by the kudumba.[66] Strange crooning noises and weird songs could be heard faintly from her rude hut.

One day, Misrakesi expressed a wish for atimukta flowers from a vatika near the main temple of the city. A huge basket of these was delivered by Suchak's personal dasa. Misrakesi chose Anamika to spread them out for drying after which she would make the atimukta and chandan paste which was part of her identity.

No one but the two of them were witnesses to the small reed basket which was tightly clamped down at the bottom of the larger basket, and tied securely with strips of bamboo. Anamika picked it up from its hiding place and bore it away to her hut. It was left to the other dasis to spread the flowers in the sun and clear up after her, which they did, muttering under their breaths.

They were now ready.

It was winter and cold in the Gandhara Pradesh. As Pushyamitra and the senapati were preparing to leave one night from a convivial party at Shreedhan's house the former said casually, 'Just the night for snuggling up with a beautiful young woman to make you forget the cold.'

'Yes, indeed,' replied the senapati laughing and stretching, 'Do you have anyone specific in mind?'

'Well, now that you say so, there is someone... my wife's new dasi. What a girl. She is a shodashibala but knows enough tricks to keep you awake all night.'

'How do you know? Have you...? Of course, you would have.'

'You too can, if you wish. Shall I send her to you with a trusted dasa tonight?'

'No, no. My senior wife is at home and she is a very jealous woman. She will scratch the girl's eyes out, and mine, too.'

'Why don't you stay back here?'

Shreedhan acquiesced eagerly. He, too, was anxious to see this dasi, maybe he would also get a chance with her.

The senapati brightened up, the girl promised to be extraordinary and Pushyamitra took his leave promising to send the dasi immediately.

'Yes, she is indeed something out of the ordinary,' murmured Pushyamitra to himself as he walked back as fast as possible to the palace.

As he neared the palace, a shadow attached itself to him and waited outside in the darkness behind the pillars in a secluded corner of the palace walls.

He went in to his apartment and called softly, 'Misrakesi, bring her out, it is time.'

Anamika appeared, gorgeous in expensive silks and glittering jewels, her shringar fit for a queen. Her lips were red as if with blood and she ran her fingers restlessly over them. Her eyes were intoxicated, the pupils shrunk to small points. She was carrying a small reed basket in her hands and swaying slightly.

She swayed towards Pushyamitra and Misrakesi instinctively came and stood in front of him holding him back with her hands. Anamika smiled scornfully and walked on ahead.

'Come this way. Suchak is waiting for you and will take you to the senapati, you know what to do. It is all up to you now.' He led her out to a concealed doorway where Suchak was waiting, keeping a deliberate distance between them.

Suchak took over in an instant and they disappeared into the darkness.

Pushyamitra came back and sat down on the bed, his hands balled into fists. 'It is all up to her now. She is the best we have. But we can only wait now.' Misrakesi looked at him, eyes wide with a kind of terror.

Wait they did, hour after hour, saying little, faces drawn and worried, pacing up and down, sitting down, getting up, till dawn threatened to appear and still Anamika had not returned.

It was almost morning when Suchak came back followed by not one but two figures. He bundled them in through the secret doorway and whispered, 'It did not go exactly as planned but it is well enough. Chandramukhi will explain the rest. I am off.'

Chandramukhi! Misrakesi and Pushyamitra looked at each other, astonished and not a little apprehensive.

Anamika was in a stupor, not able to stand without support and swaying to and fro.

'We will have to help her change and put her back in her hut,' whispered Misrakesi but a superstitious fear made her hang back. She could not bring herself to touch Anamika.

'Come on, Misrakesi,' said Chandramukhi in her old sarcastic manner, 'She is not dangerous now. The poison has been spent and the cobra released.'

As Misrakesi froze, Chandramukhi said casually, 'Yes, I know. I know that she is a Vish Kanya and you have used her to kill the senapati. He is dead and so is Shreedhan but not by my hand, unfortunately. Let us put Anamika back in her place and then I will tell you what happened.'

It was quick work, between Chandramukhi and Misrakesi, Anamika was soon asleep in her widows' dress. Then Chandramukhi told them what had happened.

'You know I was on Shreedhan's trail,' she said, looking at Pushyamitra who nodded. 'Tonight was the night I had decided to finish him off. When I entered his house, I found that he was alone with Anamika and was bent on forcing himself on her before the senapati came in.'

Her face flamed in remembered anger, 'I, I... was going to kill him but she did that before me. She kissed him and he fell down, foaming at the mouth, dead within moments. She robbed me of my revenge but he is dead and I hope he has gone to the Kumbhipaknarak[67] he deserves.'

She resumed after a short silence, 'There we were. Shreedhan dead, the senapati alive and probably going to enter at any moment. He would have discovered your plan and that would have been the end of everything. I thought quickly and decided that Shreedhan's body would have to be hidden and Anamika would have to take another dose of the poison for the senapati.'

Even the stoic Chandramukhi shuddered and her voice took on a horrified tenor, 'I have seen many strange and revolting sights in this world but I hope never to see such a one again, a cobra biting a vish kanya on the tongue. Her speaking to the cobra and the dance with it froze my blood. I hid myself and the senapati entered. It was all over in a minute. He lay dead on the floor. Anamika was dazed, probably by the double dose of poison. I bundled her out of the window and screamed, being careful to show my face so that your poisonous young dasi is not suspected. We found Suchak waiting at a distance and he helped me bring her here.'

Pushyamitra and Misrakesi listened to her in stunned silence. Their plan could have fallen apart, but it had been salvaged by Chandramukhi. They were in her debt.

Misrakesi was the first to speak. She embraced Chandramukhi and said, 'Chandramukhi, how can we express our gratitude? You have been our saviour.'

Pushyamitra came up and took her by the shoulder saying seriously, 'Magadha owes you a debt of gratitude. And you will not find me wanting in repaying that debt.'

Chandramukhi gave him a considering look and said, 'I will remember that at the appropriate time, Chief. I am off now and the two of you had better be on guard.'

It was morning now. Both of them went in and pretended to sleep. They were woken up very soon by an agitated dasi who broke the news to them; Senapati Bhattaraka was dead under some very mysterious circumstances and rumour was rife... had Narsingh Dev had him killed? To clear his way to the throne? Who knew the answer? Certainly not the scared and shaken city of Kaikeya.

The End of the Purus

Sowing, at the outset, a tiny seed of the plot,
He (Kautilya) plans for its further elaboration;
When the seed germinates, its eventual fruition,
Hidden and mysterious, is gradually revealed.

Vishakhadatta's Mudra Rakshasa

There was a numbed feeling in Kaikeya that day. The young and valiant senapati struck down in his prime!

The army was plunged into turmoil. Jayasena, the up-senapati was hastily appointed as the new senapati. He was trying his best to control the situation and restore a semblance of normalcy but it was becoming increasingly clear that he was unequal to the task. There were many hotheads in the Mantri Parishad and the army which wanted revenge. Although there was no real evidence that Narsingh Dev was responsible, the whisper campaign against him had taken on the semblance of reality and he had already been pronounced guilty by the populace. He would not deign to explain himself against such an absurd charge and was getting the worst of the benefit of the doubt.

Kaikeya Raj had taken a turn for the worse on being told the news of the senapati's murder. He had turned his face away when Narsingh Dev had come to meet him. He would only tolerate the Raj Vaidya and the Purohita near him apart from his daughter of course. Narsingh Dev, for the first time in his long and successful career, found himself isolated.

It was a bitter blow for him, who had devoted his entire life to the service of the king and his kingdom. That his own king and people should abandon him out of distrust cut him to the heart. He knew that he had done nothing to warrant this suspicion and the fact that it was being accepted as the truth meant that there was a conspiracy behind it. He had been deserted even by his own people and did not know where to start proving his innocence. He was certain that the campaign of vilification against him was being orchestrated by Misrakesi and Pushyamitra probably with the help of the embedded Magadhan spies in his kingdom but he had no evidence against them and was helpless in the face of his rapidly diminishing credibility with king and commoner alike.

The matter of the succession became even more urgent, with it becoming clear to the Mantri Parishad that the kingdom was on the verge of imploding. The strong hand needed to keep it together was missing. The entire populace was awash with rumours about the state of health of the king and the future of the kingdom, each more worrying and dreadful than the last. Siddharthak's network of Magadhan spies in Kaikeya was successfully engaged in destabilizing Kaikeya. His faux sadhus, jatils and ascetics went around making dire predictions; groups of singers, dancers, actors and jesters mingled with the common people in the outlying villages of the kingdom and spread contradictory news which they purported to bring from the capital city.

There was disquieting news, too, of a vast army making its way to Kaikeya up the Uttarapath. Some said the army was Mauryan, some said it was Greek, but all were united in their dread of what its intentions were.

Chandragupta's name was cleverly inserted into the discourse. He was a familiar and loved figure in the area from the time he had studied in the Takshshila Gurukul and waged a guerilla war against the Greeks. Acharya Chanakya was a revered figure. The initial core of the army they had gathered had been recruited from these very areas and there were many who were personally loyal to him and the acharya. Gradually a diffuse wish grew strong that a courageous and powerful king like him should have been there to take up the reins of the kingdom.

In the midst of all these events orchestrated and precipitated by them, Pushyamitra and Misrakesi sat as quietly as a spider sits in the middle of a web woven by it. Pushyamitra was now seen in a new light. From a person who had come to seek the favours of Kaikeya, he had turned into a person who many were looking wistfully at as a saviour, a messenger from the powerful kingdom of Magadha. It was almost time for him to reveal himself as an emissary of the Magadh Samrat. First, however, they decided that Misrakesi would carry the acharya's message to the maharani.

A few days after the senapati's death a man had come asking for an audience with the great lady from Magadha. He fell at Misrakesi's feet and thanked her for looking after his young sister who had been separated from him in the forests near Sage Ananda's hermitage. He met Anamika with great joy and even she ran and fell at his feet sobbing.

'Do I have your permission to take my sister with me, Devi Misrakesi? I can never thank you enough for taking care of her when she was left alone without protection,' said Prahast, the man who was claiming to be Anamika's brother. She was standing with smiles wreathing her face, holding his hand in complete trust.

Misrakesi turned to one of the senior ladies of the ranivas, 'What do you think? She seems to know him and he says that he is her brother. They even have a look of each other. I think I can safely let her go with him.'

The lady nodded and agreed. In any case, the fate of a crazy dasi was nobody's priority. So Misrakesi let Anamika go with many gifts for both the brother and sister, and heaved a secret sigh of relief.

The maharani was a deeply worried woman. Her sorrow at the slow but sure loss of her father was overlaid with a dread of the future. She now had it in her hands to get her husband appointed as the successor of her father but an unknown hesitation checked her steps, calling to her to heed her actions. Would that weak and dissolute prince prove an able monarch and see to the wellbeing of the people she loved? Did he have the strength, resolution and character to take forward the legacy of the Purus? What about her duty to him as his wife?

She would wrestle alone with these questions, sitting in her Shrine grove and praying for an answer. She was sitting there with her eyes closed one afternoon when Misrakesi approached softly and sat down beside her. When the maharani opened her eyes she saw the sun glinting on a Hemasutra,[68] a very familiar and dearly beloved Hemasutra which she had last seen many years ago. She shaded her eyes and looked at it silently as Misrakesi offered it to her with both hands.

'So, it has come… the acharya's call to me.' She looked deep into Misrakesi's eyes with an inscrutable expression, 'And you are his messenger. Why am I not surprised?'

She was lost in thought for a while, her fingers tracing the precious stones set in the centre of the Hemasutra.

'I had given this to the acharya ten years ago, as the newest queen of Takshshila. It was my contribution to the acharya and the young Chandragupta's efforts to push out the Yavanas. This was when my husband was a satrap of the Yavanas and drunk with their power. It was part of my stridhan and my conscience permitted me to contribute this to the idea of a motherland, a Jambudweepa united against invaders. Chandragupta and his group of friends were not even snataks then, just a few young men fiercely committed to their motherland.'

Misrakesi was listening, fascinated. The maharani had known the current rulers of Magadha in the days of their humble origins.

'I know why the acharya has sent this to me now. To remind me of our endless discussions on what Jambudweepa meant and whether it had any chance of coming to existence over and above loyalties of clan, tribe and kingdom. He was a passionate optimist and I was highly influenced by him.'

'Look at him now,' she resumed. 'He is bringing into existence that which was just a dream. The days of divided loyalties have to end and he is asking for my contribution to that shared dream.

Chandragupta, the acharya… and a safe, prosperous Jambudweepa where all Kaikeyans can also live in peace and prosperity. Is this possible?' She was talking to herself now.

The maharani looked up, 'Go now, Misrakesi and leave me alone to think. I need solitude.'

Misrakesi walked away, all her eloquent arguments stifled unsaid. It was up to Shailanandini and her inner voice now. But Misrakesi had great faith in the influence of the acharya.

Pushyamitra then commenced meetings with the members of the Mantri Parishad. He revealed himself as an emissary of Samrat Chandragupta and far from being denounced he was clutched at as a saviour. Kaikeya had been broken from within and was being slowly surmounted from without. Pushyamitra placed a proposal before them, the anointing of Chandragupta as Kaikeya Raj's successor and all mantris to be retained in their positions if they so wished; the larger world of the Magadhan Rajtantra would also thus be open to them.

While the mantris debated this proposal the maharani went with heavy steps to her father's chamber where the ruins of a once gigantic and fearsome leader of men lay dying. She held his hands between hers and they talked of many things, the past and the future, their shattered dreams and her dead brothers. His dark night was drawing to a close, to whom would he entrust the new morning? Shailanandini's soft voice and the king's laboured and rasping replies went on for hours well in to the night, till the Raj Vaidya was alarmed and asked her to desist. But in the last burst of a dying flame the king waved him away and sat up with a semblance of his old energy. He had a great deal to think about and decide.

The following day brought some unwelcome news. Eudemos, the only remaining Yavana satrap, had asked for an audience with Kaikeya Raj in the name of Peithon, the Yavana who had been made the nominal ruler of the territories of Alakshendra that lay to the west of the Indus.

Pushyamitra had discussed him in his secret meeting with Siddharthak and knew that he had a small army of 120 elephants as well as some cavalry and infantry, much of which had been poached from the Kaikeyan army through intimidation and bribery. The lack of a firm hand on the ship of state was costing the Kaikeyans dear. He had been granted audience by the king who had suddenly and mysteriously regained his lost energy and had thrown himself into the business of governing. The Raj Vaidya was deeply worried and privately thought that this was a sign of the very end but he was unable to convince the king to rest.

Suchak had come to inform Pushyamitra of this and the two of them were thinking of the implications.

'When is the audience?' asked Pushyamitra.

'Today. In fact, after the lamps are lit. Eudemos is not going to be there but he has sent a small group of representatives. Why has he done so at this juncture? I have also received reports that Eudemos himself is at half a day's march or even less, from the city. Why does he not come himself and what can he have to say to Kaikeya Raj that is so important?'

Pushyamitra nodded, frowning. 'Peithon is busy fighting with the other generals of Alakshendra for his share of the spoils. I do not think he has any time or resources to devote to this area. This is just a ploy to get inside the palace and that too after dark. But to what end?'

Suchak was silent and Pushyamitra himself provided the answer: 'Does he plan to assassinate the king? And then move in with the waiting army?'

As Suchak looked shocked, Pushyamitra got up and started pacing worriedly, 'We have to do something to protect the king, if no one else will do so.'

'But what can we do? We are not going to be allowed in there.'

'The maharani will be there. Misrakesi can contrive to be there with her permission. Where is the nearest place you can take me to the king's chamber, so that both of us can be available in case we are needed?'

Suchak thought and said, 'There is an unused audience chamber a little way from the king's chamber. We can hide there.'

Pushyamitra whirled around, his face tense, 'The security of this palace has become very lax. There is no one to take care of the royal family. Narsingh Dev does not care to take it up again after being removed and the current senapati has his hands full dealing with the turmoil in the army, anything can happen in the hiatus. Suchak, send one of your men to Akshay to start marching towards the city as fast as possible. I want the Magadhan Army to be here. The time for being secretive is over. I am going to talk to Misrakesi so that she accompanies the maharani to the king's chamber during the audience.'

Misrakesi and Pushyamitra conferred together and off she went to meet the maharani and put in her request. But there was a shock in store for her. The maharani was abstracted and thoughtful and completely refused to let Misrakesi accompany her. 'What will you do there, my sister? You can meet my father, if you really want to, after the audience. You have no place there during the audience.'

Short of telling her that she suspected foul play, Misrakesi could do nothing. And even saying that could have had no effect on the maharani; she would not necessarily believe in the danger. Pushyamitra was looking at many events in conjunction with each other while she was inside the palace and preoccupied with different matters. So what were they to do?

'Well, then do your best. Be as close to the king's chamber as possible and inform me of the number of Yavanas who come in and what weapons they have. We will then decide if we need to take any action.'

'What else can we do? Can we get any help? Suchak?' asked Misrakesi.

He looked uncomfortable and then finally said, 'I should not really be telling you this but there are a few soldiers who are personally loyal to me. I can call on them in an emergency.'

'This is an emergency,' said Pushyamitra forcefully, 'You may think that I am over-reacting but believe me, I am a veteran of takeovers and assassinations and this smells of one.'

Darkness was falling and it was almost time for the Yavanas to arrive. Misrakesi left for the ranivas. Suchak paused only to send an urgent messenger to Akshay and one of his men to the palace entrance to report as soon as the Yavanas were granted entry. Then Pushyamitra and he left to wait in the audience chamber, hoping against hope that nothing untoward would happen.

Misrakesi watched the maharani leave for her father's chamber with a kindly smile for her. She was quite willing that Misrakesi wait for her to come back although she looked a little puzzled at the solicitude being shown.

Time crawled by; Misrakesi was on edge, wandering around the queen's chamber, and Pushyamitra paced up and down the audience chamber. The Yavanas were very late in arriving. When they did there was more cause for concern. There were ten of them, heavily armed, young giants who managed, by intimidating and confusing the captain on guard, to enter the palace with their arms. In normal times to seek an audience with the king bearing arms would not have been permitted under any circumstances, but these were not normal times; the entire edifice of the Kaikeyan state seemed to be crumbling.

As soon as Pushyamitra heard this he knew that some action was imperative. Even if they would not go so far as to kill Kaikeya Raj, who knew what else they could demand through intimidation.

'I am willing to take a risk, Suchak, and force my way in to the king's chamber without permission.'

Suchak looked worried, 'You could be imprisoned for this; it is treason.'

'I told you I am willing to take a risk. Besides, the times are not normal. If outsiders can enter the palace with arms what is the mere entering of the king's chamber worth? Let us go.'

In the king's chamber the situation was fraught. As soon as the maharani realized that the foreigners had entered her father's chamber without giving up their arms, she suspected trouble and quickly sent a dasi to call her captain of the guards. In the meanwhile, the formalities were observed. The Yavanas greeted the king, even if not respectfully, as well as the maharani and Narsingh Dev, who was also present. The Raj Vaidya was also there, making an aushadhi for the king's nightly dose. The visitors looked around and boldly walked up closer to the king on the massive bed.

'Stand back, Yavana warrior,' said the maharani sharply. 'My father is ill. Whatever you wish to say shall be conveyed to him by me. He cannot withstand normal conversation in his present state.'

The leader of the Yavanas fell back but only by a negligible distance.

'Well, what is the message from the Yavana General, Peithon? We are waiting to hear it.'

'This!' And he drew his sword striking at the dying king and plunging his sword into his chest. The next instant he was pulled back and his head flew off to the floor. The chamber was full of fighting men. Pushyamitra and Suchak had arrived. They had had no time to bring in Suchak's loyal soldiers.

'Father!' It was a despairing cry torn from her throat as Shailanandini rushed to her father's side with no regard for her own safety. Her cry was the first thing Misrakesi heard as she came hurrying in with the captain from Takshshila.

She rushed to the maharani's side, ignoring the melee of fighting men. One of the Yavanas lunged at the maharani as she bent over her father, only to meet his own death as Misrakesi's poisoned dagger sank into his neck. Pushyamitra, Suchak and the captain were fighting for their lives as Narsingh Dev and the Raj Vaidya stood rooted to the spot, deep in shock.

The maharani was oblivious to the fighting men and, with an ashen face and stricken eyes, was staunching the flow of blood seeping out from her father's chest. Her hands were steady as she called out to Misrakesi, 'Call the Raj Vaidya here quickly, tell him to do something.'

The old king was beyond any help. He was weak and had been struck in the heart. What was important now was to save the maharani. It was clear that after the king the Yavanas' next target was his daughter. Misrakesi tried to pull the maharani away but she would not move. In desperation she picked up the sword of the fallen Yavana and stood over the maharani in protection.

Two of the Yavanas were dead but that still left Pushyamitra, Suchak and the captain outnumbered by more than double. The killers were pushing the three men towards the bed where the king's life blood was oozing out and his daughter was desperately trying to staunch it.

There was no time to call anyone in for help. By the time anyone would be able to come, the fight would be over. Pushyamitra had to bring all his sword skills into play; handling three men at the same time. One of them was dispatched by a thrust into the heart and the sword arm of the other was cut off but the third brought his sword down with both hands to hit a blow which would slice across Pushyamitra's throat. Misrakesi was right behind the Yavana, and disregarding all rules of fair play, drove her sword into his back with all her strength. The fatal blow was softened and fell over Pushyamitra's shoulder grazing him harmlessly.

The captain from Takshshila was a renowned fighter and the life of his maharani was at stake, he was fighting like a man possessed and very soon between him and Pushyamitra the remaining Yavana killers lay dead on the floor.

The maharani lay sobbing at her father's bedside. A faint voice said, 'Shailanandini, my dear daughter,' and she looked up with sudden hope.

'Daughter, do not grieve for me. It is long past time that I went to join my forefathers. Remember me as I was, not as I go. And come here, I am entrusting my royal ring and seal to you to be given to my successor.'

His voice gathered a faint strength, 'I call on all of you to be my witnesses. Come here, Narsingh Dev, Raj Vaidya and all of you who are here. You are Pushyamitra, the envoy of the Mauryans? Come near me.'

They gathered around his bed as darkness fell over this last of the Purus. 'As Lord Mahadeva is my witness, I pass on my kingdom to the samrat of Magadha, Chandragupta, and may the gods be merciful to him and help him to be a great king, the protector and father of my people.' His voice was strong and assured; the last words he would say before it was silenced forever.

The quiet sobs of his daughter were all that marked his passing.

'There is no time to waste. The news of the king's death must not get out till the Mauryan army arrives. Misrakesi, take the maharani to the ranivas and guard her with your life, with the help of the Takshshilan forces. The maharani must call a meeting of the Sabha Parishad where we shall break the news of the king's passing and the anointment of his successor.' Pushyamitra was urgent. He had to shoulder the responsibility for the transition of power.

Misrakesi tried to raise the maharani and then said, 'It is useless Pushyamitra. We cannot move her from here. Leave us here with the captain and his contingent for protection. You can send Suchak to guide Akshay here. I think you should also stay here till our army arrives and we can secure the palace.'

'All right, Suchak, make your way out and bring Akshay here with all the dispatch possible. The city and the palace should be surrounded by the army. Akshay knows what to do, he has his instructions. Come back here with him and we will then call the Sabha Parishad. The next few hours are crucial.'

Suchak left immediately. Pushyamitra spoke again, 'Captain, since I am here for the security of your maharani, I would like you to throw a cordon around this chamber. No one, not a dasi, not anyone, must come in. And no one from here will go out. The maharani will emerge only for the Sabha Parishad meeting where I will accept the royal seal and ring on behalf of Samrat Chandragupta.'

The captain looked to his maharani for orders. She raised her head and said simply, 'Follow his orders as you would follow mine,' and went back to her sad contemplation of her father's dead face, holding his lifeless hand in hers.

The captain left the room, his blood spattered clothes and body shocking and horrifying the dasas outside. He refused to say a word and only followed Pushyamitra's orders grimly and efficiently.

The king's chamber was as still as a fresco on the wall. The Raj Vaidya had come near the king's bed and stood with bowed head, tears coursing down his face. Narsingh Dev, who had been standing on the sidelines through the fight and the death of the king, could have been carved from wood. Kaikeya was slipping through his fingers and he could do nothing about it. The king was dead and so was an era.

Misrakesi left the stricken maharani at her father's bedside and came over to stand next to Pushyamitra near the massive closed wooden door.

He was looking at her with a strange, almost shocked look in his eyes as if he were seeing her for the first time in his life, 'You killed two men to save my life.'

Misrakesi squeezed his hand and said, carefully clearing her throat and trying to sound normal, 'I have never killed anyone before.' Her knees were shaking and she was feeling sick but this was not the time to give in to emotions.

The next few hours were the most dangerous. If something was to happen before the arrival of the Mauryan army, Pushyamitra would be able to do nothing. The king may have appointed Samrat Chandragupta as his successor, but brute power could always snatch away the kingdom, and the Kaikeya army would be easily able to overpower the few in the palace who were the witnesses of the old king's wishes.

There was a commotion outside and the captain came in, his face flaming, 'The Raj Purohit refuses to stay outside. He says that he has never ever been barred from the king's presence and does not propose to start now.'

'Let him come in,' said the maharani quietly. 'My father died without Tulsi and Gangajal in his mouth. Maybe he can suggest expiation.'

Pushyamitra nodded and the Raj Purohit came rushing in livid with anger, only to stop in mid-stride at the scene of carnage and the king lying dead on the royal bed.

Pushyamitra's forethought and correct anticipation of events turned out to be of great help. Suchak was able to meet the Mauryan army almost outside the city. Akshay moved quickly and decisively. The bulk of the army was dispatched with his most trusted lieutenants to cordon the city. The advancing Yavanas under Eudemos would have to contend with them.

He himself, with a selected battalion, thundered off to the royal palace to cast the mantle of Mauryan protection over the royal family and the palace.

There was no question about the entry of Akshay into the palace. The Magadhan army was a formidable fighting machine and struck dread into the city as the horses swooped into it in the thick of night. The inhabitants sat up in their beds and wondered what disaster had now befallen them.

Akshay went straight in and met Pushyamitra with a brief embrace before sitting down with him to confer on what to do next. Now that security was assured and the palace and city under their control, the Sabha Parishad could be called to witness the public dissemination of the old king's announcement made on his death bed.

Messengers were dispatched to the members of the Sabha Parishad and very soon a group of sleepy and bewildered men in various stages of hurried dress were gathered in the Sabha Griha; all apprehensive.

The maharani came in, supported by Misrakesi and flanked by Akshay in full armor and a blood-spattered Pushyamitra. Narsingh Dev and the Raj Vaidya as well as the Raj Purohit followed them. Suchak was behind all of them.

The members of the Sabha Parishad were struck dumb with terror when they saw the maharani with bloodied hands, carrying the ring and seal before her. They knew Pushyamitra, but who was this armoured stranger? And why was he in the Sabha Parishad. The senapati stood up only to be motioned down by the maharani.

The Sabha Parishad heard the announcement in a stunned silence. There was no room for dissent. Most of the members had already been won over and the rest had to contend with the threatening presence of Akshay and the army which could be heard outside and which had already been seen by them as they came in. The king's will was conveyed to them by the grief-stricken maharani; it was endorsed by the Raj Vaidya and even by an expressionless Narsingh Dev.

Pushyamitra accepted the ring and seal on behalf of the samrat and formally took over the administration of the palace and the city till the arrival of Chandragupta himself. He informed them that the samrat was already on his way and would arrive in a few days time. The Sabha was dispersed, only to be reconvened after the Rajtilak of the samrat. All its functions and duties were taken over by Pushyamitra and Akshay. The latter was to separately confer with the current senapati and Pushyamitra with Narsingh Dev, regarding administrative matters. All of the Sabha Parishad members were to hold themselves ready to offer any help, as and when needed.

With the consent of the maharani, Misrakesi was handed over the charge of the ranivas and its security, the Takshshilan soldiers as well as more divisions from the Mauryan army were detailed for the security of the palace and the remaining royal family. The treasury was also inside the palace and no chances would be taken with its security.

The coup was not completely bloodless. There was news of the Yavana army engaging with the Mauryans and Akshay left in a hurry. It became apparent that the Yavanas had been working to a well-defined plan in assassinating the king; their army was ready to move in. Part of their plan had worked and Eudemos was going ahead with his attempt to subjugate the city. He was leading his men and had not contended with the cordon thrown around the city. There was a brutal fight to the finish and Akshay left nothing to chance. It was only because Eudemos had retired behind his soldiers when the going became tough that he was able to escape with his life and a few men, to return to Peithon. It would be a long time before the Yavanas would be bold enough to try their luck in Chandragupta's regions again.

The city of Kaikeya was on edge. The army was restive but not breaking out as yet mainly because all the men who could act as flash points were under an undeclared house arrest under the pretext of urgent discussions and negotiations. Till the arrival of reinforcements, the balance of power was a delicate one. The fact that Chandragupta had been declared as his successor by the dead

Puru Raj had served to quieten resistance temporarily, intelligent manoeuvring would have to do the rest.

The royal cremation was done as per time-honoured rituals. Malayketu, Kaikeya Raj's nephew and only surviving male relative, had, on consideration, been allowed to come in to give Agni to his pyre. Even after the thirteenth day ceremonies, the maharani remained withdrawn into her own quarters, silent and uncommunicative.

Misrakesi's changed status made the women in the ranivas look at her with a mixture of awe and resentment. It was now clear that she had been playing a role for the past few months and was actually an agent of Magadha. Although no one actually dared say anything to her directly, it could be seen on their faces. But at the same time they were also eager to win her favour. The ranivas was being broken up and the women would be given resources as per their standing and allowed to reside in a place of their choosing. Misrakesi was interviewing all the women on behalf of the new administration, and worked to prepare proposals to be put before the new command. Many of the women were therefore going to be dependent on what Misrakesi thought of them.

Pushyamitra and Misrakesi barely met each other. They were frantically busy with their respective responsibilities. Misrakesi had unilaterally decided to move into the maharani's quarters to stay with her. Although Misrakesi's real mission was now out in the open, the maharani did not mention that in any manner either. She was sorrowful, quiet and withdrawn, communicating only when necessary.

Chandragupta and his army were now making good time in reaching the city and were in daily communication with Pushyamitra, making his task that much easier as he received directions on thorny issues. He was instructed to make the city ready for the new king's Rajtilak. The samrat would enter the city directly, be anointed as king and then go out in a royal procession to meet the people. It was Pushyamitra's first duty to organize these flawlessly.

The day of the Rajtilak drew near but there was a surprise in store the night before. Without any warning, a tall, magnetic young man accompanied by a group of warriors drew up in front of the palace. The guards came up to stop him but fell back in awe when they saw his face. He went in alone, up to the ranivas. He entered and went straight to the maharani's shrine where she was praying.

'Maharaniji!!'

Shailanandini turned; *Who was this man and how had he come in?*

The simply dressed young man with an aura of invincibility and royalty around him looked familiar, she had met him before. Could he be...? Yes, he was.

He touched her feet and she raised him up,'Samrat Chandragupta!'

'No, your younger brother, my dear elder sister!'

No one had called her by this name for years since the death of all her brothers including her younger brother. Tears fell unchecked from her eyes. There was no one to witness this emotional meeting but the samrat wiped away the tears and also the last of the conflict in Shailanandini's mind; she had done well, she was right. He would carry on the traditions of the Purus; he was her brother, found again after years.

A small spare man entered, casting a long shadow in the flickering lamps and the maharani fell at his feet; he raised her up and smiled with deep wisdom and understanding into her eyes; yes, she had done well indeed.

Samrat Chandragupta

He is the ruler who is the protector of the orphaned, refuge of the refugees, guide to the afflicted, protector of the frightened, the support of the unsteady, the friend, the relative, the master, the benefactor, the teacher, father, mother, brother to all.

Chanakya Rajnitishastra

The city of Pataliputra was dressed like a bride. It was no ordinary occasion; it was the Rajtilak of Chandragupta as the Chakravartin samrat of Jambudweepa. The victorious king was returning after the annexation of Kaikeya and also the other neighbouring kingdoms of Gandhara. Akshay had been appointed the viceroy of what had essentially become the northern province of the empire. The empire now had four provincial capitals, Ujjain in the heart of the land, Suvamnagari in the south, and Tosali in the east, apart from Takshshila in the north. Pataliputra, of course remained the main capital of his empire.

Chandragupta's procession was to enter the city gates and then move slowly through the streets to the royal palace where he would be anointed the Chakravartin by the Rajpurohit. He had become the undisputed suzerain of Prithvi and the special ceremony to mark this was being held in Pataliputra. The procession had, after much thought, not been given the colour of a military entry. Rather than a king at the head of his army it would be a king entering a city of his loved people.

The most important members of the court were to be part of the procession; only the acharya was missing. He never formed a part of the ostentatious royal occasions; his part was very much in the background. He had already entered the city unobtrusively and had been closeted with Maha Amatya Katyayan for most of the night being briefed on events during his absence.

The Praja had made an all pervasive and immense effort to decorate the city, and even their own homes. The streets had been swept and white sand from the shores of the Ganga River had been scattered on the streets. Triumphal arches had been set up at important places festooned with flowers and leaves and waving with flags. Flowers of five colours, the purple Akunda, the cream Champa, the scarlet Bandhook, the yellow Kovidara and the white Sepahalika were glowing in every corner. At the important crossroads, plantain trees and jars brimming with fruits both fresh and dry were placed for the citizens to enjoy. Swings had been put up for the enjoyment of the people, and singers and dancers were putting up performances in the margs and veethis.

The people were dressed in their best clothes and out in the streets waiting for the procession. There was a festive and happy atmosphere which was being closely orchestrated by the Magadh goodhpurush network. Siddharthak was hard at work. Chandragupta had come back as an all-conquering hero and Magadha was proud of him. This feeling was encouraged to its maximum extent. There were periodic tumultuous outpourings of admiration and love for the samrat. Royal sponsored sutas were singing poems in praise of the Mauryan Samrat. Drums and mridangams were being beaten across the city and auspicious instruments were being played.

The procession was to begin just before dawn and would reach the palace as the first rays of the sun were striking the earth symbolizing the start of a new era and a new kingship. The royal guards were on the alert in the melee of people with perfumed garlands, flowers, parasols lamps, and flags.

There was a stirring amongst the waiting populace, the procession seemed to be approaching. Far ahead, groups of dasis clad in finery with silver vessels in their hands were sprinkling Kewra perfumed water on the path. Others with silver Dhoopdanis were spreading gentle clouds of perfume in the air which gradually reached the citizens and swirled around them creating a heavenly almost divine ambience. The signal for the arrival of the royal procession on the north-south Rajmarga at the end of which stood the palace was given by a group of men beating the drums and the mridangam and ringing huge bells.

Far away, atop one of the high terraces of the palace decorated for the occasion, Misrakesi watched the procession approach. She was one of the honoured guests invited by the administration to watch the procession with the royal family, a mark of favour indeed; but then she was very much in the good books of the Mauryas, as were the other three – Pushyamitra, Akshay and Siddharthak. It was their efforts in carrying out the plan decided by the Acharya Chanakya that had seen the annexation of the Gandharan kingdoms. In fact, Pushyamitra had been asked to take part in the procession and was out there with the senapati. Misrakesi, too, had been asked but had conveyed her unwillingness to form part of the king's entourage of courtesans; she was too conscious of the scar at her neck and did not want that her participation should cast even the remotest shadow of inauspiciousness on the sacred and joyous occasion. Siddharthak was, of course, too busy orchestrating the spy network in the city to be part of the guests or the procession.

Misrakesi was dressed in simple but elegant ivory and gold today. Each piece of jewellery was a masterpiece and she managed to look like a cool white Kunda beauty amongst the exhibition of coloured silks and stones by the women present. She was feeling out of place, she was a royal employee and this was the first time she was present as a guest so she was very much a picture of dignity, smiling and talking to everyone with the appropriate degree of respect. Only her eyes betrayed her inner feelings.

She could now see Shrunottara riding a white caparisoned horse and holding up the peacock flag of the Mauryas. Two women followed her, one with the four lions snarling on the flag and the other with a Garud-dhwaj flying high. A little distance after them came a row of bejewelled elephants, all of them laden with filigree-patterned, gold and silver ornaments which covered almost their entire massive bodies, and then came 11 four-horse chariots. Pairs of matched oxen which were of a special racing breed and could run as fast as horses were stomping and snorting, spooked by the crowd but under the control of their handlers.

The people were amazed as these picturesque animals and people went by. But what was to come was even more amazing.

Misrakesi watched with unseeing eyes, an automatic smile on her lips but her mind on her last days in Kaikeya.

The acharya and the samrat had arrived and taken over the load from their shoulders, the strain of handling the security and the administration of a recently annexed kingdom had almost crushed the four of them.

Misrakesi and Pushyamitra had met that night by chance in their erstwhile quarters as Misrakesi had come to cross-check her clothes and jewellery. They had not met for days and were both exhausted.

'Come Misrakesi, let us sit for a while in the pavilion, I have not even seen you since... I don't know when.'

Someone had put a swing in the pavilion now that spring was in the air, and they sat down as it swung up and down gently.

'It's over, Misrakesi. We won.' Pushyamitra had given a sigh of satisfaction and put his arm around her. His face, which he liked to control, showed his triumph.

Misrakesi had been not been able to reflect the triumph.

'Yes, we won, but someone lost.' The maharani's sorrowful and dejected face swam before her eyes. How could she be happy when the maharani was so sad?

Pushyamitra had shaken his head impatiently, he would never be able to understand Misrakesi's mixed feelings. War, whether open or covert, was war, and so was victory. He had changed the subject.

'What are your plans now?'

'Why? Is that the chief of the Nagarik Suraksha Parishad asking?' She had looked up at him with an inscrutable glance.

'No.'

She had been sunk in her own reflections and looked up only to say, 'Go back to Pataliputra, I suppose, and pick up my life in Apsara Sabha. If I can.' And her hand had gone involuntarily to the scar at her neck which she kept hidden by a tightly wrapped uttariya all the time, very little of her body could be seen after the wound.

Pushyamitra had removed the uttariya and kissed her neck till her eyes darkened and she grasped a handful of his hair to stop him.

'Dearest, you are no less beautiful for this scratch. Let me show it to you if you don't believe me.' His throaty whisper had made her hair stand on end and she had surrendered herself to him amid the leaves rustling in the spring breeze next to the swift current of the Vitasta.

But she had been upset and shaken out of her equilibrium; she loved him wildly one minute and asked for reassurance the next. He was perturbed; he did not have the words to reassure her.

She decided to leave for Pataliputra almost immediately.

'What is the hurry? Wait for a few days and we will go together.'

She shook her head obstinately, 'No, I have to go. I have to think. I have to be alone.'

Pushyamitra had let her go without any further comment.

She had taken an emotional leave from the maharani who was joining Sage Ananda's vihara as a bhikshuni and endowing it with all her worldly goods. The Mauryan administration was also being very generous to the vihara.

She had not been able to ask for her forgiveness but the maharani had said, 'Go in peace and be happy, little sister.' She had put her hand on her head and said, 'Leave this life of deceit, my dear, if you can.' That was all. She had come back to Pataliputra with an escort provided by Akshay who was wistful as she left.

Misrakesi came back with a start to the present. There were exclamations at the sight far below.

Scores of dasas and dasis wearing lavish clothes were walking by holding golden wine and water jars studded with a variety of gems; vaidurya, emeralds, rubies; the list was endless. There were also, massive bronze plates piled with uncut gems, zari and kimkhwab cloth of gold and beautifully fashioned jewellery.

Then came the really strange and exotic animals from across the land, some caught by the royal hunters and others gifted to the king by vassals: black buffaloes, tame lions, tigers and cheetahs, yaks, camels, varieties of gibbering monkeys and apes, fierce hunting dogs, deer, antelopes, rhinoceros, and other forest animals.

And the birds... tree branches were held aloft by the dasas and beautiful, melodious exotic birds sat on them. The melodious Kirat and the stunning multicoloured Kateru had the place of pride, but there were many more of all sizes, shapes and colours. There were even some ox-carts laden with large-leaved tree branches amongst which birds flew around and sang. They were all trained and tame, their handlers exhibiting consummate skill.

Then there was the samrat. In spite of herself Misrakesi was transfixed. On a pure milk white stallion surrounded by his army of women bodyguards, he was like Indra surrounded by apsaras. The most beautiful ganikas from Magadha and all the other capitals attended to his Chhattra and Chamar and walked behind the golden Rajsinghasan and Palki', the royal throne and palanquin, being carried along with the procession. Some of them had jars filled with gold and silver coins which were being showered on a stunned populace.

Today, the Rajlakshmi coveted by all kings truly seemed to be Chandragupta's adornment, he was majestic, tall as a Sal tree, brawny chest scored by the twanging of ceaseless bows in war, his bull like neck and long strong arms gave his magnificent frame the look of a mighty tusker roaming the forests. His broad chest was bare, covered only by multiple strands of jewels. The gems and jewellery seemed but incidental, the thin, almost transparent red mulmul antariya he wore, embroidered with gold wire vines and leaves gathered attraction from him rather than enhanced his appearance. Yet, the easy charm and magnetism on the handsome face struck the people and no one who saw the sight ever forgot it, even in the midst of all the wonders to marvel at. The jayjaykaar reached a crescendo.

Another group of bodyguards came behind him, armed soldiers and then the avian experts who were walking with the samrat's favourite birds on tree branches, parrots which had been taught to speak and whose ceaseless chatter rose above the din. They flew around the branches and chattered, never going too far and looking like a moving yellow, green, and red cloud.

The royal court followed behind, each with their own small procession, the Raj Purohit, Kul Guru, Maha Amatya, Senapati and then the Mantri Parishad members. Misrakesi felt a tremor going through her... there was Pushyamitra; splendidly dressed and looking serious, riding next to his brother, looking neither to the right nor to the left in the thick of the cheering populace. A selected few of the richest Setthis had also been allowed to be part of the procession and they brought up the rear.

She had not seen him since she had left Kaikeya. She had come back to a heroine's welcome, Mrinalini had wept, and Manjari had hugged her as if she would never let go. She had exclaimed at Som, who had shot up into a strapping young lad towering over her. They had taken good care of Apsara Sabha and it was prospering. Misrakesi just had to fit back into her old groove. She was feted and made much of; there was a stream of important visitors as it was clear that she was going to be, if not already so, an important player in Pataliputra politics.

She had slowly picked up the slack strings of her old life but she knew that it was only for the sake of appearances. She was a ganika only in name now; she had stopped performing and did not even go down for the nightly gatherings. But if not a ganika, what or who was she? That had been her identity since she could remember and she knew of no life outside of it. The scar on the side of her neck had faded and could hardly be seen, but it had imprinted itself on her consciousness and raised doubts she wrestled with every day. She would have to decide soon. After all, Apsara Sabha was not owned by her, it was a state institution and she would have to earn her keep, to say nothing of her strict duty to the state to function as a ganika.

After their assignment was over, she and Pushyamitra were back to being chief and subordinate, but did she want something else, something which was not possible? Siddharthak's words came back to haunt her. She had given herself body and soul to one man, forgetting her dharma as a ganika. She would have to pay the price for that now.

Pushyamitra came back to Pataliputra, but she did not meet him. Whether because he was too busy or for any other reason he did not come to meet her and she did not go to him either.

She was gripped by a strange lassitude; she put up a cheerful and animated face for all her visitors but was sometimes hard put to even summon up the energy to get out of bed. Mrinalini and Manjari knew very well what was happening but she simply refused to discuss anything with them.

The procession had now reached the palace and Misrakesi was forced to pay attention. There was a row of twenty-four decorated and bejewelled elephants arrayed at the entrance to give the samrat a military salute. At a signal from the head mahout, they raised up their trunks in the air and roared before bending on their two front feet to do obeisance to the samrat. Chandragupta was well pleased and smiled his approval before dismounting to be welcomed with a tilak and aarti by his chief queen, Pattrajmahishi Maharani Dharini, and led in for the Chakravartin abhishek performed by the Raj Purohit.

As the ceremony was being performed the city was still in the grip of festive fever. There were horse races with the rich gambling on the outcome, racing bulls yoked with a fast horse in between also raced furiously, egged on by their backers. Elsewhere, wild elephants and horned animals fought to the finish for the entertainment of the populace. There were smaller cock and bater fights. Street plays had been organized as well as singing dancing and free flowing madira. The trees had been festooned with swings and men, women, children as well as amorous couples were taking full advantage of this. This day would be remembered for generations. A Yavana visitor from Gandhara was recording his impressions which would reverberate down the centuries.

The abhishek was over. A special session of the royal court was in progress where Pushyamitra, Misrakesi and Siddharthak had also been summoned. The administration was being restructured and expanded, and there were many new appointments and changes. The new elite of the Mauryan administration were being put into place. Rewards for loyalty and good work were being announced and the three of them would receive their share.

Pushyamitra, Misrakesi and Siddharthak were amongst the few honoured by the samrat himself. All three of them were granted land near Vesali, off the Uttarapath, to the tune of twenty villages in the Nisrishti announcements, transferring certain rights from the crown to individuals. The purpose of the grant was the development of agriculture.

Pushyamitra was beside Misrakesi looking expressionless as usual, remote and formal. She could hardly believe he was the man she had lived with for so many months, the tenderest of lovers, the most caring of companions, with whom she often had the feeling of being at one.

The Nisrishti announcements went on and Misrakesi was also granted Apsara Sabha in perpetuity, the property also to be enjoyed by her heirs. She was now not only a land owner in her own right but also a rich woman. Her material problems seemed to be over.

The list was over and then began the list of amounts waived by the state in recognition of stellar services, the list of Parihar announcements. She was called up and Sharangarava, who was reading out the list, went on, 'For Devi Misrakesi, the amount of twenty-four thousand Karshapans in lieu of her release from the state duties of a ganika, henceforth she is a free woman, to lead her life as she wills.'

Her hands had been folded and her head bent but at this announcement she went white and then red and the throne room floor rose up and swayed before her. She raised shocked eyes and looked up at Sharangarava disbelievingly, as her identity had been cruelly snatched from her in one fell swoop, what was she to do now?

Exerting all her will power she slowly walked back and out of the court and leaned against the wall in one of the small rooms leading out. The list went on but the floor refused to stop swaying, her senses were swimming and she missed the public announcements of royal appointments, the Sarvatrag. A new post was being created in the Mantri Parishad; the spy network for the entire empire was being placed under this Amatyaapsarp or the Mantri for the goodhpurush network and activities. The appointee was none other than the erstwhile chief of the Nagarik Suraksha Parishad, Pushyamitra Sunga, the youngest minister to ever be appointed into the Mantri Parishad.

The senapati's face flamed with pride and pleasure as Pushyamitra, whose eyes had followed Misrakesi outside, stepped forward to accept the appointment in all humility. Siddharthak was appointed the chief of the Nagarik Suraksha Vibhag in his stead.

Misrakesi put a hand to her forehead; waves of nausea rose up and threatened to engulf her as she looked around for help. The palace was usually teeming with dasis for every purpose but she could not find anyone when she needed help the most.

And then like a blessing, that most loved of all voices came to her ears, 'Sit down Misrakesi, I am here now.' Pushyamitra made her sit and gently stroked her back as she coughed and tried to throw up but nothing emerged from her empty stomach. He had summoned the missing dasis.

One of them arrived with Kewra water and a soft cloth. She rinsed her mouth and Pushyamitra washed her face and gently dried it, motioning the dasi away. He held her quietly in his arms till her stomach settled down and her breathing returned to normal. There was another dasi waiting with a drink but she could not bring herself to swallow anything.

'I am sorry,' a thick voice emerged and a miserable face was turned up, 'I do not know what happened. It must be something I ate.'

Pushyamitra shook his head and smiled with a look that squeezed her heart painfully, 'No, it is not something you have eaten. I doubt that you have eaten anything at all. That, dearest is my son making his presence felt.'

She kept her eyes on the pigeon's egg vaidurya on his chest, but said nothing.

'Marry me and give me my son, our son, who will be as courageous and lion-hearted as his mother.'

'You know very well that I cannot marry you or anyone, I am a ganika…' the answer emerged before she could stop herself. Her voice faltered.

'Not any longer, are you?'

His hands were possessive as they spanned her waist, 'You and my son belong only to me.'

'Then why did you not come to me all this while?'

'Why did you run away?'

'I was confused.'

'And now?'

Misrakesi did not know what to say.

'I wanted to give you time to think, as much time as you wanted. I knew I wanted you at my side for all time when you killed to save my life, but I was willing to wait for you to make up your mind. I knew you would come to me. But my son is not as patient as I am.'

Misrakesi stood up, 'I am not going to marry you because I am with your child. I can...'

'You are going to marry me because you want to,' his voice was steady, 'our son would have happened later, he has happened sooner.'

'A coincidence?' Misrakesi's eyes narrowed as she thought of the mysterious disappearance of her supply of fennel seeds, which she normally ate first thing every morning, during her days in Kaikeya. She had been too preoccupied to replenish them and the result was there for her to see.

The beginnings of a smile appeared on Pushyamitra's lips as he looked innocent and said, 'The ways of the gods are not for us to understand,' and drew her into his embrace, again into that lost magic circle.

'Misrakesi,' the entreaty in his voice had her tightening her hold on his uttariya, crushing the fine silk as she fought to make sense of her chaotic mind.

'But is there place for me in your life? What happens if I come between you and your duty to Magadha again?' Her voice was accusing.

Pushyamitra looked resigned and shook his head, 'You will never let me live that down, will you. Never trust me? For the record, that is why I want us to be tied by the vivaha-bandhan. I have spent my life in the pursuit of Dharma and Artha. Now we will attain the goals of Dharma, Artha, Kama and Moksha[69] together.' His voice was low and determined with the promise of the future in it and his hands held her shoulders in a bruising grip.

At this inopportune moment Siddharthak sauntered in and sat down. Misrakesi pulled her hands away from Pushyamitra's uttariya and moved away from his hold.

'So Bandhu, she is being obstinate and difficult as usual, is she? Thinks she can do this all by herself?' he said, looking pointedly at her stomach.

Misrakesi looked aghast and instinctively drew her uttariya around herself. 'Is nothing private in this city?' she said crossly.

'I very much doubt it,' was the casual answer, 'and the arrival of the heir to the house of the Sungas? Most certainly not. Which brings me to why I have come here. Pushyamitra, I am the bearer of a message from the acharya, he has summoned both of you to his office together. I also believe that the samrat has expressed a wish to bless the couple during the marriage ceremonies and the senapati wants this to happen immediately so that the baby is born in the Sunga palace where you were born.'

It was Pushyamitra's turn to look aghast, 'Wait a minute, who said anything about marriage ceremonies. We are going to pledge ourselves with a Gandharva vivaha and three witnesses. I am not going to set myself up for the entertainment of family and friends and turn it into a Basantotsav.'

Siddharthak shrugged, 'I wouldn't bet on it. You are not going to be able to convince anyone, but you can try.'

He walked up to Misrakesi and pulled her gently to her feet, looking at her and shaking his head, smiling. 'I told you that this man was very powerful and determined and would take you away from your dharma as a ganika. You are not even a ganika now.'

He kissed her forehead in blessing and placing his right hand on her head, said, 'Be happy. Saubhagyavati bhava.'

Misrakesi – who felt that she was being borne away on an inexorable current not of her making – suddenly relaxed. This was what she wanted, so why was she worried and doubtful. The problems would take care of themselves.

'By the way, Misrakesi, you will have to ask Siddharthak for his permission to get married,' said Pushyamitra who had been standing and watching this scene with a satisfied look on his face.

'Really? Pray why should I do that?' said Misrakesi frowning.

Pushyamitra – who was well aware of the undercurrent of rivalry between the two of them – laughed and said, 'Because he is your new chief.'

'My new chief! Then what about...'

'You were otherwise engaged, or you would not have missed the Sarvatrag. Bandhu Pushyamitra is now a mantri, the new Amatyaapsarp, in charge of the entire spy network of the empire, the youngest mantri ever to be appointed to the Parishad. You are going to have a brilliant and successful husband.'

'Pushyamitra!'

He nodded and a boyish and happy look of triumph spread through his features. She kissed him and he swung her up in the air before suddenly realizing her condition and putting her down.

'And as for you,' said Misrakesi advancing upon Siddharthak and giving him a congratulatory hug too, 'You can accept my immediate resignation.'

Siddharthak looked taken aback; he had been banking on re-starting the covert activities of the Apsara Sabha.

'Resign! Why?'

The maharani's parting words had made a deep impression on Misrakesi and she had been thinking of resigning from the spy network. This was as good an opportunity as any with the change of guard; and Apsara Sabha was now hers to make decisions about.

Siddharthak shook his head as they walked down the corridor, 'I cannot accept this. I will talk to you about this later. You must make haste, the acharya is waiting.' He was off with a nod and a wave.

Misrakesi was thoughtful as they walked down the corridor; she had agreed to the unthinkable – marriage! Was she wrong? Surely not, if the samrat and the acharya were giving her their blessings? There was no bigger temporal authority than the samrat. If it had been against Dharma, the acharya would never have agreed; after all she was not the first ganika to buy her freedom and marry, although, she was probably the most famous one to do so. She sighed and Pushyamitra tightened his hold on her hand.

'No second thoughts, please.'

She would have liked to sit quietly with Pushyamitra for a while but this was not the time and place. It was the palace and they were going to meet the acharya.

An unpleasant thought crossed her mind, 'Pushyamitra, of the four of us, Akshay has been made the viceroy of the northern regions, you a mantri and Siddharthak the chief. What about me? Why has the administration ignored me? Do they think that giving me the freedom I did not even ask for is enough? The work I have done has not been recognized at all. What is my professional future? I do not wish to work as a secret agent any more, and so at the moment, I seem to be nothing at all.'

'Misrakesi, none of these appointments would have been suitable for you. As for what you are or can be, that is limited only by your efforts or imagination, a poet, a dancer, a Guru, a scribe? You have so many skills; you can paint your own vision of what you want to do with your life. You have every resource you want; it is up to you to use it as you will.'

'Maybe you are right. You are certainly very encouraging.'

They had reached the acharya's room and Misrakesi had a curiously disoriented feeling; this was where she had started this journey five years ago. She had come here determined to kill the acharya, it seemed unbelievable now. Her life had changed beyond recognition.

The acharya was standing near one of the open windows, spare and stern as ever. But his face changed when he saw the two of them, his eyes softened as both of them bent to touch his feet and take his blessings.

'Putri, Akhand Saubhagyavati Bhava!'

And she was transported straight back to the gates of Pataliputra where the all-knowing acharya had given her this same blessing that was traditionally given to married women, when she had been leaving for Kaikeya with Pushyamitra beside her. She had been very upset then but today was a different matter. At this blessing and approval from the acharya a flush of happiness spread across her face and she remained bent before him till he raised her up with a fatherly pat on the head.

'Putravatibhava![70] Now sit down both of you. I have an important proposition for Misrakesi.' He looked around and said, 'Ah, there you are, Sharangarava, just in time.'

Sharangarava sat down at the spartan wooden desk which was just like the acharya's. He cultivated a look which was as similar to the acharya as possible and had also decided to be a lifelong brahmachari.

'A suggestion from the samrat which was most timely and suitable for me and my scribe here. Devi Misrakesi, I am happy to offer you the position of an assistant scribe to work with me in the taking down and dissemination of all royal orders throughout the kingdom. You will work in close co-operation with the Prashastra, or the Communications Minister, who has to disseminate royal orders through the empire. Are you ready to shoulder this responsibility? It will of course mean that you will have to give up your position in the Stree Varangana Sena and will no longer be a part of the spy network. What do you say?' His eyes were twinkling because this was a formality, very well did he know what the answer would be.

Misrakesi felt a thrill go through her. She had not been ignored after all. This could be as important a position potentially as the others; she would be in the centre of decision making and the first to know of the decisions after they were made. And she was excellent as a scribe; it was one of her special skills painstakingly brought to perfection in Ujjain. Accept, of course, she would!

'I have one small request, Acharya.' She looked at Pushyamitra who nodded slightly in agreement.

She went to stand in front of him with folded hands, 'I have no father, no family, no one who can perform my kanya-daan.' Her voice wavered but she went on, 'Will you, Acharya Chanakya, be as my father and perform the vivaha rituals for Pushyamitra and me?'

No one had seen tears in Acharya Chanakya's eyes and no one ever would, but the three people present there came very close to it.

He placed his hand on her head and said in his firm voice, 'Yes, my daughter, it shall be as you wish.'

And so it was that three days after this, Misrakesi and Pushyamitra took the saptapadi[71] around the sacred fire with Acharya Chanakya officiating and the samrat and the senapati as their witnesses.

Misrakesi's new life had begun.

Epilogue

Chandragupta Maurya went from strength to strength as did the Sunga family. In a few years time the Mauryan hold was firmly established in the subcontinent and it was time to try conclusions with the most illustrious General of Alakshendra, Seleucus, who made an attempt to wrest back erstwhile Yavana territories. He was easily worsted by the First Maurya and a treaty concluded which extended Mauryan territories up to Herat, Kandahar, Makran, and Kabul.

Acharya Chanakya further expanded the reach of the bureaucracy and our old friends Misrakesi and Pushyamitra prospered in the set up. Misrakesi became an unofficial troubleshooter for Acharya Chanakya and also, sometimes for her husband and Siddharthak.

The close contacts and exchanges with the Yavanas after the treaty with Seleucus led also to the exchange of ambassadors. Megasthenes was an honoured guest in Pataliputra and often a visitor to Misrakesi and Pushyamitra's home. They were blessed with twin children, a son and a daughter, and their lives continue to be even fuller and more complicated than before.

Notes

1 Assembly Hall of Ministers
2 Council of Ministers
3 Parchment of cloth or leaf used for writing
4 Twenty-stringed pearl necklace with a ruby gemstone centre
5 Elaborate pendant earrings, seven stringed necklace, hip girdle
6 Way of fashioning jewellery with gems inlaid on strips of gold
7 The Rig-Veda, Yajur-Veda, Sama-Veda, related subjects; Philosophy; Science of Government
8 Lower body cloth pulled up between the legs to form trouser like garment
9 Unstitched upper body garment
10 Celestial being
11 Fifteen days and nights of the waxing moon
12 Auspicious moment
13 An ancient cross and circle game played with cowrie shells and dice
14 Sacrificial offering to the yagna
15 Royal Highway

16 One of the four aims of human life, the pursuit of pleasure and sensual desire

17 See pages xii-xiii for a plan of the city of Pataliputra

18 A kind of expensive silk cloth

19 Flat necklace generally made of beaten gold

20 Dancing houses and theatres

21 Evil spirits

22 Benevolent spirit

23 An old language spoken in the Andhra area about the 5th century BCE

24 Familiar as the Kathasaritsagar or the Singhasan Battisi and Vetaal Pachisi

25 Tussar silk

26 All high quality liquors

27 Wine

28 The measure of liquor akin to a peg

29 Gold beaten into paper thin sheets for covering edible items

30 Abode of the gods where souls go after death

31 A terrace supported by 4 columns with the heads of crocodiles carved atop each

32 Herbs and spices

33 A good quality liquor

34 Exclusive wine from the Gandhara Pradesh

35 Rhythm marked by a percussion instrument

36 See page viii for a map of Mauryan India

37 Rivers Chenab and Ravi

38 River Jhelum

39 King of Kings

40 Spring

41 God of Love

42 Another name for Basantotsav emphasising its erotic aspect

43 Lord of Victory, Indra

44 Mint Master

45 Followers of a tantric sect

46 Very small denomination coins

47 Gaya in Bihar where Buddha found his enlightenment

48 Clinics

49 Goddess of Love, the Consort of Kamadeva

50 Forest dwellers thought to be amongst the original inhabitants of Jambudweepa

51 A simple skirt gathered up at the waist

52 The basic knot with which the lower garment was tied

53 Carinated clay pot with a long neck

54 A round-wheeled water lift

55 Special drink made for travel so as to last for six months

56 The story of the epic Mahabharata

57 Spies embedded undercover in the kingdom of Kaikeya

58 Royal physician

59 Royal priest

60 Royal family preceptor

61 Jhelum river

62 A woman who has taken a vow of celibacy

63 The third, householder phase, of the four phases of life as set down in the Griha Sutras

64 Autumn and Winter

65 Son of Lord Shiva and the most valiant fighter amongst the gods

66 Strong liquor and its measure

67 The worst degree of hell

68 A gold neck chain with precious stones in the middle

69 The four goals of human existence, righteousness, power, pleasure and

liberation from the cycle of birth and death

70 May you be the mother of sons

71 Seven steps which symbolize and complete the Vedic marriage

Misrakesi is at the cusp of the life of her dreams with the man she loves. But is her future quite so simple? The Mauryan empire is looking at new frontiers to conquer and the Urnabhih must go in advance… to the hotly contested north west; Kandhahar, Herat, where Alexander's General Seleucus has by no means given up his desire to control the erstwhile Greek dominions. Pushyamitra and his spies have to be in the vanguard of this.

And what about Pataliputra? Can she deal with being the scribe of Acharya Chanakya? Can her personal life survive the onslaught of politics and Pushyamitra's past? Even in the fortress that is the house of the Sungas, can she save herself and her unborn child? Who are the enemies behind the attacks on her life?

Join Misrakesi as she walks on the perilous path of her future entwined with that of the Peacock Flag… in the second book.

Coming soon